Y0-AUY-992

Lord of Chaos

The Beginning of the Dark Ages

Howard H. Howard

Llumina
Press

Published by: Rue Antibes Corporation
746 Cable Beach Lane
North Palm Beach, FL 33410

Copyright Rue Antibes Corporation, 2011
All rights reserved

© 2011 Rue Antibes Corporation, Subsidiary of
Horvath, Jarnut & Brun Spa, Milano, Italia
USA E-Mail: hjbruns@yahoo.com

All rights reserved. No part of this publication may be reproduced or transmitted in any form or by any means electronic or mechanical, including photocopy, recording, or any information storage and retrieval system, without permission in writing from both the copyright owner and the publisher.

Requests for permission to make copies of any part of this work should be mailed to Permissions Department, Llumina Press, 7101 W. Commercial Blvd., Ste. 4E, Tamarac, FL 33319.

ISBN: 978-1-60594-592-7 (PB)
       978-1-60594-593-4 (EB)

Printed in the United States of America by Llumina Press

Library of Congress Control Number: 2010911429

Main Characters

Lucius Domitilla—young man from Assisi in the Umbrian Valley of Italy

Bruné (pronounced Bru-Nay), a.k.a. Bruné-Hilda—daughter of Gunther

Gunther (deceased)—chieftain of the Brandin Clan of the Burgundian nation

Freya-Gund—queen of Burgundia and a sorceress

Galla Placidia—sister to Emperor Honorius, daughter of Theodosius the Great, wife of the Gothic King Athaulf

Minor Characters

Adiutor—Master General Constantius's personal messenger

Araxius—provost of the Sacred Cubicle

Athaulf—King of the Goths

Baha—captain of the *Evening Star* (a Rhine River barge)

Barnabas Frugi (deceased)—traitor to Rome and uncle to Lucius Domitilla

Battaric—chieftain of the Siling Vandals at Baetica, Spain

Batyr—son of Tyr (god of the Siling Vandals); Lucius pretends to be him

Binah—astral shaman of the Kabbalah

Bittar—senior elder of the Goths

Blind beggar, a.k.a. Alfadur (All-Father)—street mercenary of Rome

Bucellarii—Galla Placidia's personal guard

Brute—son of Bruné

Constantius—Master General of the Western Empire

Corina—widow in Massilia who seduces Lucius

Crazy Chloe—woman of mystery in Assisi a.k.a. Cintasio

Cybelina—Barnabas's mistress in Rome

Deitzer—leper

Elpida—old servant to Galla Placidia

Euplutius—imperial agent (*agentes en rebus*)

Euric—slave/companion to Barnabas and Cybelina

Eutropius (deceased)—a eunuch and hoarder of gems in Constantinople

Evervulf—assassinated King Athaulf of the Goths

Flaccus, Mrs.—wife of murdered Jovius Flaccus (former blacksmith of Assisi)

Flavius Abinnaeus—*primus pilus* (senior centurion) from Salona on the Dalmatian coast

Frugi—barber in Assisi

Glyceric the dwarf—Burgundian fop, word-man, and person of great wisdom

Hemond—Burgundian commander of the guard and second in command of the militia

Irontooth—(see Wulfus)

Jovinus—usurper of authority of Rome and Ravenna and magistrate of Mainz region

Lazarus—bishop of Assisi

Mahaki—mysterious estate manager from Ancona, among many other things

Marcus—glassmaker of Assisi

Medusa—street beggar of Rome and associate of the blind beggar

Metropolitan, a.k.a. Charisius—bishop and metropolitan of Tuscia-Umbra Province

Paco—stonemason of Assisi

Papylas—sea captain who transported Lucius to Rome and Freya-Gund to Massilia

Patricius, M. Succat (St. Patrick)—nursed Lucius back to health at dungeon in Valance

Peg-Leg—street beggar in Rome and associate of blind beggar

Ponti Lepius Filipi (deceased)—powerful elder statesman of Umbria and the "last real Roman"

Poppaea—slave of Rusticus family of Assisi, betrothed to Paco

Propius—count of the Privy Purse

Rufus—shepherd guide at Ravenna

Rusadir—captain of *Malaca Moon* (a Spanish cargo vessel)

Sara—Galla Placidia's handmaiden

Sarus (deceased)—pretender to Gothic throne, killed by Athaulf

Scarface—Lucius's goat, trained as a watchdog by Adefonsic the innkeeper

Scholares—imperial guardsmen

Serena (deceased)—wife of the executed Master General Stilicho
Sigrun—wife of Battaric, the Vandal chieftain
Singerich—cousin to Athaulf, half brother to Stairnon (King Alaric's widow)
Symmachus, Aurelius Anicius—cousin to Fabius Memmius Symmachus
Symmachus, Fabius Memmius—son of Quintus Aurelius Symmachus
Tauriac—Singerich hires him to accompany Irontooth to kill Lucius
Tonantius—blacksmith at the hamlet on the Doubs River south of Besancon
Tungus—male wolfhound owned by the astral shaman Binah
Tyr—god of the Siling Vandals
Valam—Flaccus's slave
Vesuvius—street beggar of Rome and associate of the blind beggar
Wallia—Gothic king after Athaulf and Singerich
Wulfus, a.k.a. Irontooth—captures Lucius and takes him to Narbo; Singerich sends him to kill Lucius

CITIES & MUNICIPALITIES   LEGIONS

Then	Now	
Then	**Now**	
Antipolis	Antibes	III (Third) Theodosius at Ravenna
Aquae Sextiae	Aix-en-Provence	VI (Sixth) Diocletian at Arles
Bagnois en Foret	same	XXVII Augustus recently of Briton
Gades	Cadiz (Spain)	XIV Constantine fought at
Forum Julii	Frejus	Frigidus R. now disbanded
Massilia	Marseilles	
Monaecus	Monaco	
Narbo	Narbonne	
Nicaea	Nice	
Point Croisus	Point Croisette (Cannes)	
Tolosa	Toulouse	
Llva	Elba	

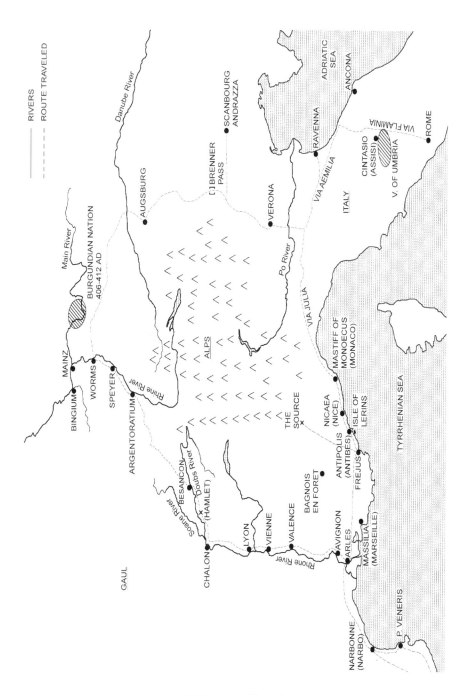

Map of Gaul

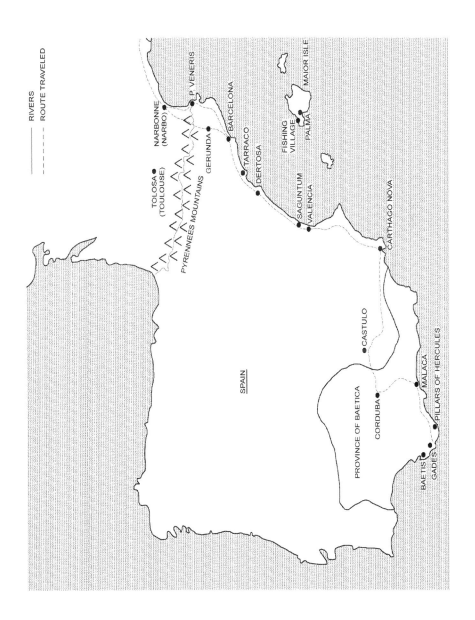

Map of Spain

PREFACE

Nothing can twist the brain more than those earth-shattering events of the early fifth century—the last years of civility before the Dark Ages. Wow! What a sentence. And, you might ask, what do the words mean? What happened? Who were the villains, and equally important, how can a thousand plus years of civilization get turned upside down so easily? Yes, a tidal wave of change washed across the world brought on by . . . well, let's not get ahead of the story.

You know what happened in the years 1492 and 1776, and if a "Brit," the year 1066 (Hastings), yet so little is known of the year that led to five hundred years of social and economic regression—the Dark Ages. I spent ten years investigating, turning over the rocks of history that, surprisingly, suddenly became mountains. For years I trudged the countryside of Europe before putting the first word to paper. Now I have three books, one published last year, this work you hold in your hand is the second, and the third book, which is actually the forerunner, sits in my personal library waiting to be published as a "retro". Don't fret. Each book stands alone and need not be read in succession.

All this began in the year 410 A.D. with the sacking of the greatest city in the world—a place of eminence, distinction, and renown. This dastardly deed, this crime not only against Rome but against all of humanity, was done by barbarians who were, in fact, not barbarian at all. Yes, there are times when the hard facts of geologists refute the impressions left by ancient historians. This is one of those times. But I digress. Where was I? Oh yes, the Dark Ages.

The unpublished book deals with the event itself—the sack of Rome—primarily the four-month buildup by the invaders in the Umbrian Valley, a short hundred miles north of Rome. This accounting is entitled *The Stones of Lucic*.

Book II of the trilogy, *Fortune's Odyssey*, was published last year and deals with the aftermath. Like when a dam bursts, life downstream is never the same for a long, long time. Book III, the one you hold in your hand, focuses on the intrigue and adventure of a final attempt to save the Western Empire by a "young troublemaker" in concert with one of the great women of history, an aristocrat of superior pedigree kidnapped during the sack and then elevated to the most exalted position any woman attained to that point in history. Her journey alone is worth the reading.

Despite what we think of their "dastardly deeds", the bards sang heroically of their feats as the "barbarians," an appellation not only prejudicial but misleading, moved to the forefront of the world stage—and remain there to this day. Their successes and defeats were put to paper centuries later and passed down to us in such works as *Beowulf*, *The Nibelungenlied*, and *The Volsung Saga*, among other lays, Eddas, and skalds.

The events I have recorded here are seen through the eyes of a Tom Sawyer–type character; several daring and colorful warlords; the beautiful daughter of a barbarian chieftain; an enchantingly evil sorceress, probably the most contemptuous woman to walk the face of the earth; and, as I said above, one of the preeminent women of history, the daughter of Theodosius the Great. Of course, where would a story be without a host of fools, friends, and villainous characters who color the pages with their unpredictable vulgarity, excitement, and sexual escapades?

The year is 414 A.D. by the modern calendar, a time when the empire remained in shock from the sacking of Rome four years earlier. The West was still gasping for air. The tale begins at Worms, a small walled city on the Rhine River 25 miles south of Mainz (see map). Of little note, but of *enormous historical significance,* Worms was the hub of the NEW Germanic kingdom of Burgundia, the first of several barbarian kingdoms founded within the borders of a disintegrating empire. Yet this little kingdom somehow effected Roman domination, a domination that began well over a thousand years before.

Unfortunately, this new kingdom already began to suffer the treachery of power and was facing a second coronation within a year. Things were not going well in the kingdom. The historical records recorded by scribes (monks) centuries later show a contentious, superstitious yet heroic people weaving enchanting adventures onto the tapestry of history—adventures that endured the mists of time by being sung at campfires and banquets for centuries before being put to paper. Yet, one adventure—this one—stands above them all. That quest, and its aftermath, is our story.

The treasure hoard stolen from Rome—maybe the greatest treasure ever amassed—created more trouble for the *thieves* than its worth, but in the end . . . well, again, I'm getting ahead of the anecdotal content contained in this bawdy accounting of history.

By the way, other *NOTE WORTHIES* to walk the earth during these changing times are: St. Augustine, the bishop of Hippo; St. Jerome, who translated the Bible from Greek into Vulgate Latin; M. Succat Patricius (a.k.a. St. Patrick); St. Ambrose, bishop of Milan and the first to invoke church authority over an emperor; Attila the Hun who became obsessed with the treasure stolen from Rome; John Chrysostom; Cyril the Patriarch of Alexandria; Alaric, king of the Visigoths; and my favorite, the exalted one, Galla Placidia, whose life experiences and pedigree eclipse all women throughout history. Far too little of her magnificent life is accounted for by historians.

I hope you enjoyed the reading as much as I enjoyed the writing. HHH

For more information Google: >hhhdarkages.com<

READER/CONSULTANTS

Ron Chabot
Ann Culberson
Sandy Gozzo
Lisa Palmieri
Jan Ross

The year is 410 AD. The story begins in the valley of Umbria a hundred miles north of Rome. Having suffered a glancing blow from the siege on Rome, Lucius and Bruné go north to a safer, quieter place. She has been raped, and he lost all he knew and loved.

CHAPTER 1

In a walled city along the Rhine River, five men sat around a wooden table. They were nervous. All held a prominent position within the local hierarchy except for one—the captain of the *Evening Star*. The unimposing house in which they met was, at the moment, the focal point of the new kingdom of Burgundia. It held the answer to a mystery that had since the coronation turned the kingdom upside down. Stone-faced, the five had yet to say a word. They prayed only that the queen's tirade would end.

By modern calculations it was the fourteenth year of the fifth century; for those in the room, the year was of no consequence, only the here and now mattered. They wanted only for the accusations to end, the enigma solved, and most of all, the woman to stop ranting. Unfortunately, it was only the beginning of what would go on and on until the heavy-handed wife of the king got the answers she wanted. Freya-Gund, the newly crowned queen, stopped in front of the fireplace, held up the chiseled head of a demon and continued to spew her venom. Her face turned red, a vein pulsed in her neck as she spoke.

"See this!" she hissed. "See what I hold here! This effigy goes missing from the cemetery months ago, and miraculously ends up *here*!" She stared menacingly at those around the table. Frightened, one of the men grabbed the edge of the table with both hands to steady himself.

"What does that tell you, any of you?" she demanded, beginning to pace again, her statuesque carriage belying a gruff nature. The queen was a handsome woman: tall and lithe with strong arms, a full head of hair, olive complexion, and sated lips that circled a twisted mouth. Without question she was more ruthless than any man in the room—some might question her veracity because of past indiscretions but none dare say it to her face.

Impatient for an answer, she said, "Let me tell you what finding this symbol of evil in this house reveals in just two words—Lucius Domitilla. Yes, you heard me, Lucius Domitilla. That curly-haired imp has been a thorn in my side for two and a half years. First, he destroys this effigy that guarded a crypt under my protection and then brings its ugly head here. The question is *why*. Why would anyone disturb the death gods by creeping through a cemetery at night to deface one particular crypt? One I personally selected in which to hide a treasure. A treasure, I remind you, I pursued all the way from Constantinople before I finally found its hiding place outside Rome. Coincidence is it? Coincidence he chose that one crypt to deface? Is that what you all think? Eh?"

None dared answer or return her glare. They knew the queen could cast a spell with the point of a finger; at least that was what she wanted the world around her to believe.

"I think not!" she shouted, answering her own question. "He knew. Yes, Lucius somehow found out what I hid in that crypt. But how? The lid to the sarcophagus took four men to lift."

"Who are now dead I assume," responded one, finally breaking the death grip he held on the table.

"Of course they're dead! Dead men don't talk. Do you think I would let someone—anyone—walk around with such a secret? Well?" She paused, but no one dare answer. "Now, sirs, how did Lucius manage that lid I ask, or the iron gate? Only one person could resolve such an elaborate riddle. And that one person is none other than the imp himself!"

Two shifted anxiously. This tirade was unexpected; not what they first thought when Freya-Gund demanded they hasten here in the middle of the night. Bruné, the dead king's daughter had gone missing. Sure, she was a threat to succession, everyone understood that. So the former king's daughter was kept prisoner in this house in the weeks leading up to the coronation to prevent her from interfering with Freya-Gund's crowning. But gone missing along with a treasure? That was news.

Except for the captain, those around the table this night were leaders: two councilmen of the city of Worms, Hemond the commander of the guard, Glyceric the word-man of the Burgundian Nation plus Captain Baha of the *Evening Star*. Up until now, the queen kept it secret that the missing treasure existed much less where it was hidden. She also kept to herself that the richest treasure trove in the Roman Empire had been taken during the sack of Rome and transported here. She was the only one alive who knew where it was hidden—or so she thought.

Only after the coronation festivities did the theft come to light. Captain Baha was found to be complicit, tracked down on the river near Mainz, arrested and dragged back to Worms. After a beating, he admitted everything: two mysterious passengers who boarded his barge the night of the coronation carrying a baby and a large, heavily wrapped package—a package the size of a grown man. His admissions eventually led here, to the house where Bruné had been held prisoner. In the dark corner next to the fireplace, a small entrance to a secret room was found which solved more of the puzzle. That secret place led to a tunnel under the city wall. To a devious mind like Freya-Gund's, it was not difficult to piece it all together: the raid on her crypt, the escape through the tunnel, and the deceptive escape aboard the river barge. Piece by piece it fell together like a beaver building a dam.

"Lucius was here!" she bellowed. "His scent is everywhere: in the loft, in that secret hiding place, in the tunnel, and outside the walls in that house wagon. That tunnel is how they came and went undetected while my guards sat outside the front door."

The others disagreed, none more vigorously than Hemond, the respected head of the Burgundian militia. Hemond was a big man like all Burgundians but old. No longer the warrior he once was, his main weapon now was appeasement. "Impossible," he said respectfully. Even though he, like the others, loathed the queen, he honored her newly acquired status. "I was here visiting with the princess Bruné on two occasions," he said. "The guards were outside day and night making certain she went nowhere and received no visitors unless approved by you personally, madam, as instructed. Lucius never returned to this house. He is dead, madam. I assure you he was killed in that ambush south of Speyer eight months ago."

"You're an old fool, Hemond. His body was never found. That little blonde bitch Bruné, the one we thought was holed up inside this house, tricked you as she did everyone else with that innocent little smile. Lucius Domitilla lives, I tell you; lives to steal my treasure, lives on to harass me."

Turning to Captain Baha, a short, thick man with no neck, she roared, "And you, you imbecile, you say the woman carried a baby aboard your barge, eh?" She paced back and forth, adjusted the whip that curled up her left arm. "Did the baby cry? No. Did the baby walk?" She poked him with the whip handle that protruded from her left hand. "Of course not. That bastard child is over two years old, you goat-legged ape. You don't swaddle a boy that size. That bundle you thought a baby was no more than a sham to fool you. What you glimpsed, you never fully grasped, did you?"

Still bleeding from the flogging, Captain Baha twitched, too afraid to say anything that would inflame the queen.

"As for that woman in the cloak—the pretender," she said, grabbing the captain by his already torn shirt, "did she say anything that night, anything at all?"

The captain flinched.

"Of course not. You are not a deep thinker, are you, captain? Did she reveal any part of her body? A leg, maybe an arm? Anything at all to indicate she was no more than a sun-drenched field worker and not the dead king's fair-skinned daughter? Did she do anything at all but sit on the prow all bundled up as you floated down river, acting out the part she played, holding tight to that bundle that supposedly contained a real baby?"

Baha tried to pull free. The man looked terrified. Like the others, he knew the queen's reputation. But, after tasting her whip and seeing that look in her eye, he now knew far more. She was a sorceress with an indefatigable strength of will.

"That was not Bruné, you idiot. She could never keep her mouth shut that long. She spends hours before a looking glass admiring her reflection."Freya-Gund pushed the captain away and whirled in a circle, hair flying. "Did the dogs Bis and Brug board the barge, or that smelly goat they call Scarface?"

"The goat has not been seen, madam. May I remind you, he disappeared along with Lucius eight months ago," said Hemond.

"Yes, I forgot. I hope the hogs got him." Leaning closer to the table, she whispered, "Forget the goat. Are the dogs roaming the city or the countryside? No. Did the guards hear them barking in the days before I gave the order to break down this door? Eh? Of course they didn't. The hounds were long gone along with the real Bruné and the real baby," she said, kicking the table before rising to her full height, her voice swelling to a threatening timbre. "While all of you were busy consorting with the other drunken sots at the coronation, they fooled my guards and snuck out through that secret tunnel with that ghost Lucius, the one none of you believes to be alive—a ghost who hid in the loft of this house for who knows how long after his return from the dead."

Hemond started to speak but Freya-Gund held up a hand.

"Now tell me, who puts himself at risk stealing a treasure of that magnitude—a treasure I remind you that was hidden inside a sealed crypt—then lets that same treasure slip out of his grasp and fall from the captain's barge and into the river. No one is that shrewd one day and so inept the next. This was all part of a clever plan to fool me."

All but Captain Baha nodded. He was in too much pain.

"We wasted two days dredging the river for a package the size of a man that, when we finally found it, held nothing but a hollowed-out log weighted with rocks so it would sink to the bottom of the Rhine. Furthermore, their slave Chuppa, who supposedly ran off with Bruné and the baby, was never cunning enough to think up such a ploy. There is only one so clever—Lucius Domitilla. The imp is alive I tell you. Like Attis, he returns from the dead to destroy my world. But unlike Attis, he still has his manhood in tact. I'll see to that when I catch him." With those words she let out a shriek and then slung the serpent head across the room. It hit the rock wall and exploded into a hundred pieces. Was this an act or was she losing control of her emotions for one of the few times in her nefarious life?

"Are you certain, madam?" asked Glyceric the dwarf, the highly respected word-man of the clan. "Are you sure the robbery did not take place weeks or months ago?"

"Think me dimwitted, you feckless little freak?" she screeched, nostrils flaring. "I check on the treasure every few days. The gate on the crypt had eight wax seals. If anyone tampered with it, I would know. Preoccupied with *my* coronation, the—"

"The king's coronation, madam, not yours," corrected Hemond, who, in addition to the militia, commanded the king's guard and was strict on protocol since attaining that position. The sacking of Rome and their successful escape over the Alps gave all Burgundians a new sense of structure.

"Yes, of course, my lord Hemond," she said sarcastically, "my *husband's* coronation. You've become quite the nobleman, haven't you, since acquiring status. And, lest we forget, all that new wealth— or should we say, plunder. Remember, in the eyes of the Roman aristocracy, you remain an illiterate barbarian thief."

Hemond cleared his throat.

"Back to my problem," spit the queen. "The timing was perfect for larceny of any sort if one was so inclined, was it not? This ass," pointing her perfectly shaped nose at the captain, "this ass who calls himself a *captain*, admitted his barge left the night of the coronation, not the night before as scheduled. How convenient. After a little coaxing with my whip, he confessed to being paid to delay his departure for one day by Bruné's slave Chuppa. Then he sailed with Chuppa and that bundled-up female and her baby to Mainz, taking along a large parcel shaped like the one hidden in my crypt. That little deception intended, of course, to throw me off—the ploy of a brash trickster, a charlatan, a pretender of unparalleled panache. And who does that description fit, eh? Anyone? A trickster, a charlatan, and a pretender? Who, I ask? Well, let me tell you again who— Lucius Domitilla!"

That got a slight smile out of all those around the table but the captain. They all knew Lucius to be that and more.

"If the decoy went north to Mainz, then the real Bruné went south with Lucius, the baby, the two dogs, and my precious treasure."

"Why south?" asked Glyceric the dwarf. "Why not east. The mountain passes will open soon. If Lucius is alive and stole your precious treasure, he would take the most familiar route, would he not?"

"Precisely. And if he's alive who is to say he is not even more familiar with the southern route. Is it not possible that he may have been driven south those many months ago by the usurper's army, which, I remind you, filled both sides of the Rhine River with thousands of warriors as they marched south to meet their end at Valance?"

Glyceric the dwarf shook his head.

Freya-Gund ignored him. "Whether you think me right or otherwise, my guards and I shall race south. The horses are being readied as we speak." Suddenly the left side of her lip formed a wicked arch—an involuntary response of a huntress about to track an easy kill. "If I am to catch them, which I promise you I will, I must do so before they reach the confluence of the Soane and the Rhone rivers."

"Oh?" groused Glyceric the dwarf. "Why may I ask?"

"A flooded Rhone, says this fool of a captain here, will sweep them into the land of the Goths in a matter of days. The Goths will not give up the treasure once they realize its value. And the emperor's sister certainly knows its real worth, if anyone does."

"And how would she know that, madam?" asked Glyceric the dwarf.

"Because the treasure originally came from the palace in Constantinople where she grew up."

"And what exactly is it?" pressed Glyceric, having shown little interest in the mysterious package up until now, though he had always suspected Freya-Gund carried something special in that black wagon when retreating from the sacking of Rome.

"Oh, have I neglected to tell you," she said with a wry smile. "It's the infamous Statue of Fortune—the treasure of all treasures. Its value is said to be worth half of Constantinople. There is nothing like it anywhere in the world."

"And why, madam, would Lucius, if alive as you believe, take this statue to the Goths if it is as valuable as you claim?"

"Not to the Goths, you fool, to *her*—to Galla Placidia. He once saved her life and now feels this cherished princess, this daughter of Theodosius the Great, is indebted to him sufficiently to grant him protection."

A smile swept Glyceric's face. "I believe Ponti Lepius saved the princess back in Umbria, madam. Lucius played a small role in her survival, which, incidentally, nearly got the poor young woman killed. She loathes Lucius with all her being. She would be the last person he'd run to—if, as you suggest, he is alive."

Lucius Domitilla had little trouble crossing the river as the current was light. He carried Scarface the goat across and the two donkeys lumbered through behind him. On the run from Worms for well over a month now, he was tired, sore, and wet. Resting on the bank, he tried to estimate how long it would be before he reached Narbo and safety. Maybe three days, he decided, five at the most. Once there, he promised himself he would sleep for a week.

Lucius was a fine-looking lad of average height and build with black hair, sharp blue eyes, and a full beard that he grew when imprisoned in the dungeons of Valance. He found that it not only made him look older but also served as a disguise. Even Bruné-Hilda did not recognize him when he first returned to Worms after an eight-month absence. The beard not only afforded a new appearance but implied the new life he faced without her. For Bruné-Hilda, his love, was now dead just like everyone else who mattered: his parents; his mentor, Ponti Lepius Filipi; Jingo, his friend since boyhood; Ignatius, the great hero of the Vallone; and Gunther, the first king of Burgundia. All that kept him going now was the chase. Unfortunately, he was the hunted. His last hope—his only hope—was reaching the princess of Rome, Galla Placidia, before the fiendish sorceress caught up with him. How she unraveled his ingenious plan still befuddled him.

As he prepared to make camp that evening, both donkeys became nervous and Scarface the goat sniffed the air. An animal creeping, maybe a falling timber, he thought, yet a peculiar feeling swept over him, a sort of dread. Was it her? Then reason took hold. Had he not outsmarted the sorceress at the hamlet and again

at the river? He was now too deep in the forest and too far from
everything civilized to worry, so Lucius ignored the warnings and
went about his chores. First he relieved the smaller donkey of the
items it carried, his belongings, water, and food, before attempting
to remove the heavily wrapped package that contained the treasure
from the crypt. It lay on the larger donkey's back like it grew there.
In the shape of an Egyptian mummy, the weight of it equaled that of
a grown man—meaning it was too heavy for him to lift.

After floating the Doubs, Soane, and Rhone rivers for the past
two weeks, he was put ashore just north of Arles, where he purchased
the donkeys. There, a savvy over-the-roader taught him a rather
clever method of loading and unloading the heavy burden from the
donkey's back. Every evening he got better at it. Placing the donkey
under a tree, he looped a rope over a low limb, attached it to one of
the eight thick cords that bound the package, and then lifted one end
half a measure. Repeating this with the other end, he was able to free
the animal of its burden with little effort. Leaving the package hang
in the tree until morning, he would then reverse the process.

Partway through the unloading this evening, the donkey stirred
and the goat's ears flattened. Something was indeed out there.
Lucius hitched the rope and stopped what he was doing. Reaching
for his boot knife, he prepared for trouble. A person or persons, not
an animal, was watching from the dense undergrowth. The smell
was definitely human. A bead of sweat appeared on Lucius's upper
lip. Was this the moment he'd been dreading since sneaking away
from Worms? Yet somehow he was thankful, even gratified. Being
hunted gnawed at his innards like a squirrel on a nut. He braced for
an attack.

A voice from the shadows said, "Put that knife away and tether
the goat!"

The words were in a familiar dialect but with an eastern twang.
Unable to decide what to do, Lucius froze.

"I varn you for the last time—put that knife away and tie up the
goat!"

The V inflection gave him hope. No one in Freya-Gund's private
militia spoke that way. Obediently, he put the knife back in his
boot and tethered the goat. Two men came out from the trees but

kept their distance, probably making sure the tether held. With no inclination to run, Lucius calmed Scarface, who was scratching the earth preparing, as trained, to do battle. At first glance the two were not loathsome-looking men; but after a closer look, he was not so sure.

"Who are you? And *v*hy are you here?" asked the spokesman moving a step closer. He raised a hand and several more men appeared from the other side of the clearing. The leader, the one who spoke, had a large iron tooth, tattoos on both forearms, and wore a torque around his neck. For certain, these men were not the mercenaries that had been chasing him for the last four hundred miles. Just the same, Lucius did not relax; he felt vulnerable ever since that day on the Doubs River when Freya-Gund's men inadvertently set the fire that killed his love Bruné.

"My name is unimportant," answered Lucius, making every effort to mask his fear. "I come from the Rhine River country via the Rhone."

"*V*e care little from *v*here you come. Move a*v*ay from the donkey. Put this around the goat and secure him to that tree." He tossed Lucius a rope, adding, "*V*hat have you there?" pointing to the oversized bundle, one end still tied to the donkey's pack rack, the other end to the tree limb.

"A present," Lucius said, doing as instructed.

"Present? Present for whom?"

"First tell me who you are? And why you accosted me in the middle of the forest?" Lucius demanded as though in charge of this affair. It was false bravado, of course. "Do my goat and I frighten you and your men?"

"You're a bold rascal you are. Have you a legion hidden out there?"

"Not a legion, Irontooth, but a force as fearsome. A sorceress chases after me accompanied by a hundred warriors. They want to steal this present before it reaches its new owner. Now, sir, unless you want your head on a pike, tell me who you are and from where you come."

"*V*e're simple bandits from here and there," Irontooth said, then began laughing. He was trying to hide what Lucius knew he felt—fear of a trap. Lucius measured this fear by the way the bandit twisted his wrist with the thumb and forefinger of his other hand. It was telltale, an inherited Germanic trait when wary. He also noticed that the bandit's confidence evaporated.

"Your bluster does not vork here in our forest," the bandit continued. Then he turned to one of his men and nodded. The man disappeared in the direction from which Lucius had come, no doubt to see if a larger force approached. "Now," Irontooth said turning back to Lucius, "let's have a look at vhat's lashed to that donkey. It appears heavy. The load's killing the animal."

Lucius shot up a hand. "Stop!" he commanded. "If you are who I think you are, then the lady will have your heads."

"Oh? And who exactly are ve? And who might this lady be?"

"Your words and clothes give you up, you wrong-headed mole. You're a Germani. And the lady I refer to is the princess. This," he said, pointing to his cargo, "is for Galla Placidia."

"You're in the forest, traveling a back trail alone, to bring a present to the princess," the bandit said, his nostrils flaring. "Ha. Ha. That, Your Lordship, is better than any ve've heard this season—a present for the princess." The bandit paused for a response but got none. "Okay then, untie the fucking thing or I vill snap your neck like a twig. Vhich is it?"

The bandit was serious enough, and from the size of his arms he could do it. Still, Lucius did not back down. He could smell the apprehension on the bandit. "You have it all wrong, friend," he said, trying his best to maintain a cool composure. "I lose her present, you and your comrades will hang. That should not be too complicated for even you to understand."

This time the bandit did not respond.

Gaining confidence, Lucius stepped up to the donkey and put a hand on the bundle, daring them to take it. "This is a special gift for a special occasion."

"You are a bit late. The vedding is four months past."

Lucius blinked. *Wedding? What wedding? Did she get married? If so, to whom?* Concealing his surprise, he quickly regained himself. "No present is too late, my wrong-headed friend. Of course it's for the wedding."

"Let's have a look," said Irontooth. "Although bold, you're not convincing."

Lucius blocked the donkey with his body. "I warn you," he said, lowering his voice to a threatening whisper. "You touch one cord on her present and I promise, *your* head will roll, not mine."

"Hang. Cut off my head. *V*hich is it?" the bandit said and began laughing again. His actions betrayed his swagger though. He took a half step back. "I ask for the last time, *v*hy are you really here?" His voice was high, but his bravado was all but gone.

With Irontooth's deportment ruptured, Lucius stepped into the breach. "I'm a friend of Alaric," a name only a true Goth would recognize. It was the final test.

"Alaric is dead. *V*e buried him three seasons ago. Athaulf is king now and made that Roman princess *v*e captured at Rome our queen."

Lucius felt a great weight lift from his shoulders. These men were actually Goths, not a roving band of deadly Vandals. "I know that," he said, using a friendlier tone. "Alaric's death makes me no less a friend now, does it? It was I who had the privilege of returning the tail of Ferox to your former king."

"Ferox?"

"His beloved horse. The tail was cut off at the Vallone by my kin. My brother is the Butcher of the Vallone." It was a small yet necessary lie. He needed to maintain control of this still perilous situation. Goths or no Goths, these men were dangerous. Just then the one sent scouting returned and shook his head. Lucius had no followers nor were there any mercenaries nearby.

Irontooth scratched his scruffy beard confused. "So you're kin to the Butcher."

"Indeed I am. And if you are of true Gothic blood, you've heard songs sung about the Vallone at your campfires."

"*V*e're East Goths—Ostrogoths you Romans say—and *v*e did not march into the ambush at the Vallone as did our brethren the Visigoths. Having avoided that trap, yes, *v*e know of the Butcher's mighty feats. Athaulf leads us now, not Alaric. Alaric belonged to the *V*est Goths who ran off like children *v*hen the Huns crossed the Marmara Sea. *V*hen he died—"

"Athaulf rules all of you, does he not?" interrupted Lucius. "I am as familiar as you with the history. And he holds the princess for ransom even though they wed."

Irontooth said nothing for a time, but then he offered this telling remark, "The emperor's sister is not looked upon as a captive for ransom. She is now one of us."

"Hmm, is that so. My king will be pleased to hear that. I once saved the princess's life, you know," he said, never missing an opportunity to pound his chest or take credit for deeds not his. "Because of this service," Lucius added, "she now prays I am delivered to her safely as surely as this donkey has four legs, two ears, and a set of—"

"Ah yes, your past service to the lady, *sire*," Irontooth said and bowed.

"You mock me now, but not for long, I promise you. My king also desires my safe return after I deliver this generous gift in his name."

"And who is your king, sire?"

"Didn't I mention him? He is Gunther the Burgundian," Lucius said, guessing that the news of his murder had not yet traveled this far south. "The hero responsible for the gates of Rome being thrown open for all you Goths to enter. Now take me to Galla Placidia. If you cause me and my animals no harm, I promise you will not hang for this inconvenience."

The bandit stared at Lucius for the longest time, and then he glanced over to his men. One kicked at the dirt, the others looked away, probably unsure of what to think.

"*Ve vill* do as asked," said the bandit. "And if all this proves untrue, I swear on the hammer of Thor you *vill* lose more than *vhat's* on that poor donkey's back."

They wend their way through the forest toward Narbo, the wagon surrounded by outriders, the donkeys and goat trailing behind. Two men rode inside the wagon stabilizing the precious bundle while Lucius sat in the driver's box next to Irontooth. Neither spoke. They made good time. After crossing a narrow stream, they gained a grassy rise and there it was—Narbo. The low walls dominated the landscape, and not in a pleasing manner. Weathered, gray and in need of repair, Lucius assumed they were damaged by the Vandals on their way to Spain years before the Goths arrived. These walls would never withstand another siege.

His eyes wandered beyond the walls to the grassy marshes that ran southeast to the sea. Hamlets dotted the higher landscape to his right. When the Goths gathered in the Umbrian Valley before their march on Rome, not counting allies, they were no more than fifty thousand warriors with that many dependents camped to the north in wagonburgs. Gauging from the cooking fires and buildings, there were at least that many here with, according to Irontooth, half again that many spread out along the foothills of the Pyrenees all the way to Tolosa. Lucius was impressed. Obviously many of Germani blood enslaved by Rome came away with the Goths after the sacking.

After entering the city, Lucius was taken to a small room near the palace—the palace being the former curia of Narbo—and made reasonably comfortable. An attendant came with food.

"Who are you?" the attendant asked after setting the provisions before him. "And from whom does this gift come?"

"Tell the princess only this: I am a favored apprentice of a man she admires most in this world—Ponti Lepius Filipi of Umbria. Should I write that out?"

The attendant shook her head.

"Good. Remind the princess she is alive today because of me, although she preferred death to deliverance at the time—or so she said. Say it as I just did, if you will. The words shall bring a smile to your mistress' face."

It did not take long before a small, olive-skinned young woman appeared at the door dressed quite unremarkably. She took one look at Lucius and ordered the guards to drag him off to the dungeon.

"Wait!" ordered Lucius as cocky as ever. He was not the least bit phased by her reaction. "This beard is new! And I have grown taller and thicker since you saw me last," he said, trying to push away the guards without much success. "Besides, madam," he yelled halfway out the door, "There are events only I would know if I am truly who I say I am."

"Such as?" she asked, halting his removal yet maintaining a certain air of aristocratic aloofness. Lucius knew otherwise. That expression belied her false indifference groomed in the palaces wherever the aristocracy reigned, a mannerism he dealt with during their first encounter back in Umbria.

"Bursting through the baker's house and over his garden wall for one," he began smugly, removing one of the guard's hands from his arm. "You scraped your leg, didn't you? Have you the scar on your left knee? I wager you do."

"The right," she blurted, caught herself, and then resumed that insolent stance—hand on hip, head thrown back.

"The garlic sausage roll that made you puke, the dank barn you could not wait to be rid of. Do you still suffer that malady?"

"What malady?"

"Closeness."

She looked on absently.

"Those two boys we rescued from the bully, Ponti's grand library of forty thousand books that took your breath away, and the long ride beyond the Topino to the wine barge on the Nar where I delivered you to the boatmen who carried you safely to Rome. And how can one ever forget that wonderful man, Jolly John, who brought you to our rock where Jingo and I sold honey cakes and sweet water to travelers. You arrived disguised as a groom."

"And you and your red-headed friend treated me like a scamp," she scoffed, "thinking me less than dirt." Turning to her attendant she ordered, "Shave and bathe the cretin—though a provincial, he need not look like a shipwrecked Phoenician. Arrange for fresh clothes and burn those he wears. He smells like a three-day-old night pot. When presentable, bring him to my apartments."

Lucius entered Galla Placidia's apartments followed by two slaves carrying the wrapped bundle. He looked strikingly different. So much so, his entrance caused the princess to slap her face with both hands. "Great Jupiter, it really is you! Call the guards!" she bellowed, causing the pigeons to scatter on the windowsill. "This one's a menace. No, the guards cannot cope with the likes of him, summon the militia and prepare the gallows. The ghost of Caligula has invaded our kingdom."

Her attendants did not know what to do. Motioning for everyone to leave, Galla broke into a wide grin. "He is who he claims to be—which does not portend well for my sanity or our kingdom. No wait, Sara. Better still, bring me a poisoned apple."

"For him, madam?"

"No, for me." And they all laughed heartily. For Lucius, it was the first time in a long, long while.

Lucius grabbed the attendant named Sara by the arm as she left. "Inform the one with the iron tooth that he will no longer be needed."

"Who?"

"The bandit with the tattoos here and here," he said, pointing to his own forearms. "He is by the fountain no doubt weaving a hangman's noose. Say the princess loathes but loves me. Then add: I'll speak well of him if he takes good care of my goat and the two donkeys."

"Did not Virgil warn against Greeks bearing gifts?" interrupted Galla in her customary tart manner. Although mannered, she could be feisty.

"I'm not Greek, madam, nor am I a provincial. I'm as Roman as you," he said with a smile.

"To the point now, what do you really want of me, Lucius? You are far from home and come dressed like a beggar, sporting an unbrushed beard and obviously running from something."

"As are you, Galla."

"I repeat, Lucius, what do you want?"

"I've been running from that answer half my life it seems. Now I believe I actually know what I want."

"And what, pray tell, does that mean?"

"Since half my municipality was destroyed, I started running from everyone and everything, not toward anything." Giving his own words more thought, words that somehow appeared on his lips, he added, "All I wanted at first was vengeance for what happened in Umbria. What I received in exchange was heartache when the only loved one I had left in this world died in a fire back on the Doubs."

"What is the Doubs?"

"A river, madam. A river that connects with the Soane, which flows into the Rhone."

"I have enough heartaches of my own. Sorry, but I cannot share yours. You know I was kidnapped, trotted half the world. First to the straits of Massina where disaster struck the Goths, then back north to Frejus, then Arles and then here where I live among strange people. Again, what is it you want of me, Lucius?"

"To save Rome, rebuild Capricorne, and change the course of events," he said absently. "But what does it matter what I want." Lucius moved to the tightly wrapped package lying on the large, heavy-legged table. "It is what I bring that matters now. What's inside this well-traveled bundle," he said putting a hand to it, "will in and of itself change the future for you, me, and our countless dreams, whatever they may be."

"Dreams? Who in this changing world has dreams!" she rudely interrupted. "I have been held against my will for years, Lucius."

"Then this bundle may answer all your prayers, if not your dreams."

"And what could possibly do that?"

"Frankly, I don't really know. Let's see—together." Lucius took a deep breath. He had not laid eyes on what lay beneath the neatly wrapped bundle since departing Worms. And he was not sure he wanted to know for fear it was less than expected. "Have the guards cut the cording and then order them to leave. No one should see what's hidden here but the two of us."

Lucius spoke with such conviction that the words put Galla under the same spell that he'd been under since Freya-Gund rode into Scanborg-Andrazza alongside the mysterious wagon that held the bundle. All he knew was that she had stolen it from a magnificent villa in a summer refuge for the wealthy. That summer refuge was named Tibur, and it lay in the hills west of Rome. "Strange isn't it," he muttered as he watched the guards cut the cords, "how curiosity is more pleasing than the reality. I'm terrified."

The princess, also excited, could not take her eyes off the bundle. Somehow she understood that this was more than another of Lucius's exaggerations. When the guards left, Lucius pushed a couch in front of the door, pulled the draperies, and then used a lighted candle to ignite several more. The room changed. It took on a different aura— that of a cave or a mysterious hideout. Breathing hard, together they slowly undid the bundle growing increasingly eager with each layer of wrapping. Soon it lay there fully exposed for the first time since leaving Tibur nearly three years ago. Lucius followed the princess's reaction carefully, his eyes darting back and forth between her face and what they had unwrapped. At first she seemed unsure what it was. With enormous effort they tilted it upright.

"Umph!" The thing weighed more than the average man. Galla, eyes wide and mouth agape, stepped back, took a long look at the upright object and then let out a scream that had the guards banging on the door. She shooed them away. "I'm all right! I'm fine!" she yelled. "Be off!"

"Great Jupiter, Lucius," she whispered trying to calm herself. "This is that infamous statue from Constantinople," she said, wiping the perspiration from her brow. "Where did you . . . Jesus, Mary, and Joseph! Lucius, do you know what this is, what you've brought me!?" grabbing him by the shoulders. "Well, do you!?" shaking him violently.

With difficulty, he pried her hands away, stepped away and shrugged.

What they gaped at was a full-length figure of a woman, maybe five feet tall. The likeness was that of a priestess with almond-shaped eyes and a down-turned mouth. She wore a series of descending jeweled necklaces, the longest dropping below her breasts, tiered emerald earrings, and a jeweled headband adorned with eight large rubies and covered with a finely sculpted palla. The workmanship was exquisite. Her feet were bare and one hand held what appeared to be a conical seashell; the other hand was missing. From the position of the arm with the missing hand, it looked as if it had held a significant object—maybe a trident. The most unusual features, however, were the statue's distended stomach and buttocks. The entire figure had been painted over, most likely to disguise what it actually was. One crack revealed at least six layers of paint. Defaced by the paint, the statue was not an impressive looking piece. In fact, like so many works of Eastern art he had viewed in Ponti's villa, Lucius thought it hideous.

Looking as if she might faint, Galla shook herself, picked up a knife, steadied herself on the edge of the table, and then began chipping at the paint. "Look here," she said, elbowing Lucius. "This section is pure gold." She tapped the belly with the butt of the knife. "The cavity's full, listen." She repeated the tapping. "That's good! Very, very good indeed."

"Full, you say?" Lucius asked, running his hand across the statue's distended stomach. "Full of what?" He suspected, but he wanted her to say it.

"Gems, Lucius, Eutropius's magnificent hoard." Then she examined the statue's back. "No one's tampered here, have they?"

"How would I know," he said, shaking his head. "I took it the very day I left Worms and have been on the run since."

She tried to shake the statue but it was far too heavy. "It's filled with generation upon generation of greed. Plunder, Lucius, plunder from senseless pillaging of places like Armenia, Parthia, Carthage, Cilicia, Mesopotamia, and Phoenicia dating back beyond Pompey. Have you any idea . . . ?" Unable to finish, Galla seemed overwhelmed by the notion.

"I had a suspicion," he admitted.

"Wh . . . Why, Lucius, why?"

"Why was I suspicious?"

"No. Why bring it to me?" she asked, still fighting her emotions. "Why me, Lucius? Why here? Why now?" Pulling him close, she kissed him on the cheek. "There is only one person on earth who, although dressed like a shipwrecked voyager, could bring me the greatest treasure on earth on the back of a broken-down donkey."

Lucius went over to the window and sat down on a cushioned bench, wondering how best to react to this unexpected exuberance. After a time, he said, "I came here to . . . to buy your freedom, madam, and to save Rome from becoming Gothia."

"Gothia? Now where did you come up with that? Furthermore, pray . . . how exactly do you plan to save Rome?" rubbing her hands over the distended stomach, unable to take her eyes off the statue. "Even you have limits."

"By buying those who would elevate you to the throne for a start. Ponti Lepius obsessed over the dark cloud from the North that would one day cover us all, not to mention a dying aristocracy and a disinterested emperor. He saw you as the last thread with the past.

With your brother the emperor childless, and some say dull-witted, you are Rome's only hope. Daughter to an emperor, granddaughter to another, sister to two more, and kin to that child sitting on the throne in Constantinople. In a thousand years of imperialism, no one has more claims to Imperium than you. And if you're not thinking of yourself, think of your offspring, my lady."

Galla Placidia scooted her backside up onto the table and put an arm around the statue, looked at it for a time, and then gave it a hug. "Go on, Lucius," she said, "you seem to have thought this through."

"No. No I haven't really. Everyone is aware your brother hides behind the walls of Ravenna unable to govern while the empire around him crumbles. True?"

"True," she agreed, though stiffening. *Was the princess taking this personally?*

"The Rhine and Danube Rivers are now roadways instead of borders. Is that not a fact?"

Galla nodded. "It hurts to admit it, but yes."

He continued, "Rome got sacked in four days, Spain falls to the Vandals without a struggle, and the Franks march at will throughout Belgica. With Briton abdicated, Africa will surely be next. And with the African breadbasket gone, how will Rome feed the restless? The slaves will revolt! The glory days spoken so eloquently of by Cicero now lay fallow in failure and overindulgence."

"Athaulf already says Africa is next," she confessed.

"There you have it. Romans not only need inspiration, they need leadership."

"Need I remind you, Lucius, that adoration and allegiance are far different passions."

"No they're not, Galla. They're entwined like earth and sky."

"Athaulf is my husband, Lucius. I married a heathen king!"

"Good. That makes you a Germani queen as well as a Roman princess. Who better to save the empire than one who can unite both worlds."

"Save the empire," she mouthed massaging the back of her neck, "is that what you want?" She slipped off the table and circled the Statue of Fortune. Without warning, Galla grabbed Lucius by his arms. "Save the empire?" and shook him as hard as she could.

"Is that why you came here, to save the empire? Save the fucking empire for whom!"

Much happened during the following months. Lucius changed during this time—those who came to know him in Narbo might say he matured. Also, rumors had it he was much too close to the queen. True or not, the time arrived for him to move on, to put into play the plot he and Galla Placidia conceived using the great wealth found in Fortune's belly.

About to board a ship for Rome, he carried credentials, two letters, and a cache of jewels sewn into the hem of his heavy cloak. The jewels, a small portion of those found in the belly of the Statue of Fortune, were intended to plant a seed that would one day put Galla Placidia in the chair of Caesar. A seat occupied by such authoritarians as Octavian, Hadrian, the philosopher Marcus Aurelius, and Galla's father, Theodosius the Great. Galla instructed Lucius to meet secretly with certain senators with whom, in those terrible days before the sack, she'd allied with in arming the slaves in a last-ditch effort to save the city. It did not work, of course, but the process elevated her status in the eyes of many. Not put to paper for obvious reasons, the senators' names were emblazoned in his memory.

"Be vague, speak privately, seek only advice, and promise nothing," were her first instructions. "Speak of the statue, not how you obtained it," came next. "Say its belly is full of the past, they will understand. And then say whatever else your lucid tongue deems necessary, short of getting yourself strangled for tyranny."

She further instructed Lucius to go from Rome to Ravenna to confer with the like-minded who lurked in the shadows of the throne, particularly Araxius, the provost of the Sacred Cubicle, and Propius, the count of the Privy Purse—both confidants of hers. "However," she warned, "although trustworthy, these two are in constant fear for their lives and keep a ship at the ready just in case. Never totally put your faith in anyone."

Yes, she said things but none more important than this: How all bureaucrats exuded a "cut and run" loyalty except one man. And that one man might hold the ultimate key to everything. That man, Galla informed him, was Constantius the master-general, celebrated for crushing the usurpers Constantine II and Jovinus and for keeping the heel of his boot on other would-be traitors over the years. To him and to him only, Lucius was to propose a more intimate alliance that only a fool would not consider. That alliance, however delicate, had but one obstacle: Galla's husband, the Gothic king. On the other hand, Galla believed Athaulf would not live much longer. Since wounded at Massilia, the vultures circled; and if his wounds did not do him in, a coup d'état would. "It's a matter of time," she whispered in his ear on the docks of Narbo along with other salacious pleasantries. The first time such words had been exchanged was in her private chamber months ago, doors locked, curtains pulled.

Yes, as the gossip suggested, they had grown close; how close, only the Great Mother knew. Pressing harder against him, she murmured, "God has a plan, Lucius, and sent you to me to fulfill it." Slipping a note into the sinus of his cloak, she added, "Read this only after you sail, my dearest. It shall inspire your mission."

As the ship left the harbor of Narbo and began to make its way along the coast of Gaul, Lucius sat in the hold nestled against Scarface as they had so often done on nights during their odyssey. He explained to the goat how they now faced the greatest challenge of all since leaving the Umbrian Valley. Because of the many gifts nature bestowed, Lucius had progressed from provincial rube to a daring backroom lover of a barbarian queen who also was a Roman princess. By circumstance, the Statue of Fortune gave him the power to grasp things beyond his reach, and she, Galla, had the lineage to make him believe he could actually achieve the aspirations to which they both aspired. His hasty suggestion at their first reunion grew into a quest: resurrect the empire's corpse, invigorate the loyalists, and release her from captivity for the glory of Rome. As a result of this ill thought out outburst that day, Lucius was afloat in narcissism.

Now that his beloved Bruné-Hilda was dead, Lucius's only connection to the past was Scarface the goat. The suddenness of this rise to power made him dizzy. To reverse everything wrong in the world was in his grasp. Yes, him, *a little shit* from Umbria as the innkeeper often called him was about to make his mark on the landed aristocracy of Rome. Could this be his destiny, although he never believed in destiny? Was he to eclipse the accomplishments of his childhood heroes Ponti, Gunther, and the Butcher? Embarrassed by such absurdity, he tried to shrug it off but could not. It buzzed like a bothersome bee.

The wind blew and the sea boiled, yet neither could touch him in the hold on this day, so full of himself was he. Was his life of impunity preordained? Was he soaring on a different wind than others? So many tried but none succeeded in blocking his way. He always danced free. Why? Was it divine intervention or just good fortune? Just as the shroud of Medea protected the mythical Jason in his search for the Golden Fleece, so too would his beloved Bruné-Hilda shield him. Yes, her spirit would bewitch all who challenged him so long as he remained faithful to her memory—a trust at which the fickle Jason failed.

The thought of Jason's quest reminded him of something. He reached into the sinus of his cloak and pulled out the note Galla had given him on the dock. The message was simple, to the point, and unsigned. It read: "I carry your child."

Stunned, he went dumb. *I carry your child.* He read it one more time to be sure, and then a third and fourth time before crushing the note into a ball and tossing it toward the bulkhead. Scarface ambled over, picked up the crumpled paper, and then carried it back to Lucius. He pushed the goat away, jumped to his feet, and charged up the ladder. When the salt air hit him, he screamed as loud as he could. But the snapping of the sails and the clanging of the rigging stifled the sound. The seamen went about their work as though he did not exist. Maybe this was all a dream. Looking through the ropes toward the horizon, Lucius searched the sky for a sign from Bruné-Hilda, a sign that was always there when he needed it. This time there was nothing but clouds—dark, heavy clouds. It started to rain.

Orders rang out from the captain. The deckhands collapsed the mainsail for the come about and the boat exploded in a new direction. The prow now plowed through a heavier sea. Lucius let the rain pelt his face. The pain was good. He needed pain. He needed cleansing. Maybe it would wash away this bitter taste of betrayal. For the first time in his life he felt genuine guilt. Would his beloved Bruné forgive him for what he had done? After all, neither he nor

Galla could help themselves. She was lonely and so was he; both starving in so many ways. It just happened the first time; but not the second or the third.

"Oh, Bruné, how I have betrayed you!" He shouted and then slumped against the railing crying.

After the fire of burning guilt lessened, his thoughts shifted to his friend Patricius and the isle of Lerins, that great haven of forgiveness, that monastery in the sea. A place where a person could pull himself from the fires of hell and find himself again. Yes, his good friend Patricius had told him that; explained how one might be able to reconnect with the spirits of the past before going forward. Was it not on the isle of Lerins where his companion in the dungeons of Valance, the goodly Patricius, was reborn? Had that very island not been his and Bruné's original destination before Freya-Gund caught up with them that terrible morning at the Doubs River hamlet? His thoughts flew back to that horrible time: the surprise attack, the fire, his escape. Yes, the isle of Lerins would heal his guilt, strengthen his spirit.

Of course the captain knew of Lerins. "A group of islands just off the coast of Gaul between Frejus and Antipolis," he said. "I once sought refuge there during a storm. It's a wonderful place. We normally give it plenty of room, though, because of the shoals."

It took five days in an unfavorable wind to reach Lerins. They dropped anchor off the leeward side of the main island. Lucius waited impatiently for the small craft to put down. Difficult as it was in that roiling sea, it was not long before Lucius was put ashore by the oarsmen and moving on foot toward a large group of weathered buildings that ignored the outside world by facing inward.

He was directed to the vineyards to petition the only one who could approve his brief stay. As Patricius foretold, Lucius's identity or where he came from were not at issue, only that he bore no letter of recommendation or invitation from the headmaster. That obstacle was defeated by a generous donation. Unfortunately, his arrival coincided with the busiest time of a winemaker's year. Patricius's mentor Honoratus was no longer in charge having been lured to the mainland for "an even greater calling." Since the ship was under Lucius's charge, thanks to Galla, he had full authority to extend its stay as long as he desired. Accordingly, the ship was rowed to safe harbor and the crew sequestered on a separate island. Lucius took refuge on the main island, where he was housed in an empty room above a wine-aging cellar.

No one on the island spoke much. When they did, it was obvious they knew little of the outside world. The new headmaster would not arrive for another month. On the third day of his stay, Lucius had a brief conversation with a barefoot monk toting a basket of grapes. His interest was piqued when the monk mentioned something regarding one of the dependents housed on a separate island. A strange young woman, he said, had arrived unescorted a month or so earlier. She stayed to herself, spoke Latin with a heavy accent, and, although always protected by an oversized palla, was said to be fair-skinned with strange hair hidden under a floppy-eared scullery maid's cap.

Each day following the daily service, which he attended more out of curiosity than devotion, Lucius would walk the shoreline and observe the monks and apprentices working in the vineyards. Dressed in stained sackcloth, they seemed content if not overtly happy. He could also see during these walks that other island, the one where the dependents resided. It lay a mile closer to the mainland. He was curious about it, no more. Men were allowed there one day a week and then only for the daylight hours.

At the first opportunity, he climbed aboard a shuttle barge, grabbed an oar to hasten the trip, and then stepped out onto this island of screaming children, busy women, and widely separated huts—more than forty, maybe a hundred—that were scattered about this low, treeless pile of rock and sand. "It's better on the side nearer the mainland," his oar mate whispered on seeing the disappointment on his face. All day Lucius walked the desolate island looking for the young, fair-skinned woman with strange hair hidden under a scullery cap.

With visiting time nearly exhausted, he finally spotted her cupping water from a rain barrel. Her movements were hauntingly familiar although she moved with a limp. It could be her, yet he hesitated. He'd been fooled so many times before on the *vici* and the roads around Narbo. *Don't frighten her! It could be anybody!* a voice whispered inside his head. He obeyed the voice and only watched. She was covered head to toe in a palla that had seen better days. Watching from behind a bush, he saw her hook the cup to the side of the jug, hoist it to her shoulder, and begin to limp the other way. He followed. She walked into a stable and disappeared. He waited. When she did not reemerge, he entered. It was dark and empty except for a sore infested old donkey. *Hmm. Strange. Where had she gone?* Then he noticed a curtain in the back moving slightly in the breeze. He walked to it, coughed to announce his presence, and then entered.

On the far side of the little room stood a female silhouetted in the only window. The light was such that he could not see her face or much else.

"Bruné?"

"Who are . . . ," she began, pulling the palla up to hide one side of her face.

"Bruné-Hilda?" he asked, saying the name that only he used.

"My gawd!" she said and began to cry. "Lucius?"

His entire world changed in that one, white-hot instant. Bruné-Hilda was alive, although he sensed something was wrong—desperately wrong. She withdrew farther inside the palla and turned to the wall. He closed the distance between them, put both hands on her shoulders, and slowly, gently pressed himself against her back. She seemed to shrink. Her entire body quivered. No words passed between them, just touching and breathing. They remained like this for what seemed an eternity—touching and breathing, touching and breathing. A thousand words raced through his mind, but none appropriate. No words could possibly express what he felt in this moment of this bittersweet reunion.

"I knew you would come," she whispered at last, "even though a part of me prayed you would not."

He squeezed her, saying nothing.

"I am not who I once was, Lucius, inside or out."

He pressed his lips against the back of her head. It did not matter who or what she was now. Only that he loved her so much, he had given her all he had to give from the first day they met.

"Lucius, please. Pull the drape across the window. I cannot permit you to . . ."

He would not let her finish. He understood. Moving to the window, he pulled the drapes. The room went from dim to dark. She moved to the other side of the room and sat behind a small table. The hood of the palla slipped from her head and fell lazily over her shoulders. Bruné picked up something from the table and pulled it on. He could not make it out, but assumed it was the floppy-eared scullery maid's cap she'd been wearing at the rain barrel. After carefully tying it under her chin, she handed him two flint stones and pointed. He stepped closer to the votive altar and lit a single candle. It threw off just enough light for him to see while allowing her to remain in shadow. What he saw was a pathetic figure of a young woman on the far side of a three-legged table wearing a strange cap that covered both sides of her face.

Moving to the table, Lucius reached for her right hand. She withdrew it, giving him her left instead. He raised Bruné to her feet, walked her over to the small bed in the corner, laid her down, and then stretched out beside her. He held her close, letting all that happened dissolve into the warmth of their embrace.

When darkness fell, Lucius knew that he had missed the shuttle to the main island. But it did not matter. Whatever trouble that would bring paled to the suffering the two of them had shared the past few years. Leaving the rubble of his once beautiful municipality behind, reuniting with the Brandin Clan at Scanborg-Andrazza after their attack on Rome, the journey over the Alps with a thousand wagonloads of treasure, the founding of the kingdom of Burgundia at Worms, the Hun's arrow, imprisonment at Valance, her father's murder, the theft of the statue, the attack at the hamlet on the Doubs River, and the escape from the sorceress had all led here. He had gotten through it all in one piece; she had not. Circumstance had dealt Bruné an ugly blow—but at least she was still alive.

His beautiful barbarian princess, his fiery Bruné-Hilda, was all he wanted, all he ever needed. He would eat when she ate, obey her every instruction, speak on those topics exclusively hers, and show passion when she was passionate. He loved who she was, not how she might look now. What happened to them was not fated, it was circumstance, nothing more—believing in the fates was for the ignorant. Lucius recalled Ponti Lepius's words: "The gods help those who help themselves." Those words became his lifelong mantra.

Two weeks passed before Lucius reboarded the ship and pushed out to sea. His departure was unsettling because Bruné would not come with him. She insisted on staying despite his entreaties. She was alive, but the incident at the hamlet on the Doubs River changed her, not only in body, but in spirit. She lost everything: a child, the faithful hound her father cherished, the unforgettable face and smooth white skin, and the beautiful hair that became her signature. Lucius felt her shaking every night when reliving that morning on the Doubs.

Unable to suppress it any longer, he too began to relive that terrible morning, saw it happen from where he hid in the nearby well. When the roof collapsed on Bruné, Lucius's world collapsed too. Nothing mattered after that. For a time, he lived in a mindless daze of the netherworld, his actions mechanical. Now he realized that what he saw from his hiding place was not the whole story. Believing the worst, unaware of the miracle happening under the ashes of the Tonantius cottage, he ran off. And Bruné refused to reveal any more about the mystery of her supposed death that morning other than to say she survived.

"One day I will tell you," she promised him. "For now, it's too awful to experience again. The screams, the dying, and the unbearable heat are all too much to put into words." She mechanically repeated those words when pressed during their time together before his departure.

Now, as he stood on the stern of the ship departing the isle of Lerins, he looked out over the ship's swirling wake. A coastal bird swooped down, snatched something out of the water, and flew off. Bruné-Hilda was once as resourceful as that bird. He thought of her all covered up, her cap pulled down and tied tightly to hide her face, and how she limped about the island barely able to do her chores with only the one good hand. How easy it was for that bird when all its parts worked. For Bruné, life was . . . he paused to search for the right words. But there were none. No words could articulate what he felt about Bruné's life now. His thoughts flew back to one particular day, the seventh day they were together on the island.

He stood transfixed that day as she pulled the drapes and lit the single candle on the votive altar. When she asked him to kneel, he obeyed. She retreated to the far side of the room behind a three-legged table and stared at him for what seemed like hours. Then, slowly, she began to remove her palla, then her cap. Laying one atop the other on the stool, she turned to the wall and let her tunic drop. She was completely naked except for a small undergarment tied at the hip. Lucius did not know what to say or think.

She turned around slowly and remained in the shadows for a time. It looked to him like she was steeling her nerve. Overcoming that reluctance, she picked up one of the garments from the stool and held it in front of her like a shield. He heard her take several deep breaths and then watched as she shuffled out from behind the stool and into the halo of light cast by that single votive candle.

But what he remembered most was the silence. How he remained that way with his arms folded looking straight into her eyes. In that light, he was unable to see their color, only the deep, dark sockets that encased them, but he sensed they were wet with tears. Slowly, Bruné let slip the garment that shielded her body. It fell at her feet. Then she nodded to him, begging him to look down, look at more than just her eyes. He did not want to. But she nodded more forcefully. He could do nothing but obey. Taking all of her in, he cringed and covered his face; then Lucius began to cry like he had never cried before. She reached down with her hand, a claw now, and patted his head.

That all happened seven days ago.

As he looked out from the stern of the ship, that scene kept repeating over and over in his mind's eye—and the tears returned.

During their time together at Lerins, Lucius insisted Bruné move out of the stable and into a small house he bought for her. Located on the north side of the isle, the pretty side and the one closest to the mainland, the house had a garden, a tree, and a picket fence of untrimmed wood. He also arranged for a woman to care for her needs until she was fully recovered and left Scarface the goat behind to guard her.

As for the chest of gold coins her father had given her before he died, she'd used some to rebuild the Tonantius house before leaving the Doubs River and to pay two Vesontii river men to guide her to Arles where she boarded a supply ship for Lerins. She retained the rest of the gold coins for the future—a sum that could sustain her for a long time. Bis the hound, sister to Brug, had also survived the attack at the hamlet but was kept elsewhere on the island until Bruné was able to care for the faithful pet.

During their time together, Lucius told Bruné about his own narrow escape, about how he found the twin dugouts downstream from the hamlet with the Statue of Fortune safely hidden under the animal fodder, and about how he floated down the Doubs, Soane, and Rhone rivers half delirious from the experience. And then, after Freya-Gund and her mercenaries had caught up with him at Avignon, he decided to forget going to Lerins and seek sanctuary with Galla Placidia. It was in Narbo where he unwrapped the mysterious package for the first time. Finally, and with that "certain look in his eyes"—at least that was what Bruné said in her recounting of it—he explained in detail his quest to ransom the princess and save Rome.

After seeing that look in his eyes, Bruné insisted he not abandon his quest, although it sounded, well, "absurd" was the word she used. Besides, she needed more time: time to think, time to heal, and there was no better place, she said, than the solitude of Lerins where no one cared who you were or where you came from.

So he left her there to heal and think, promising to return. Now he stood aboard the ship watching that island of solitude disappear over the horizon. Although Bruné no longer looked the same, he loved her more. Not out of pity but because of who she was: an indomitable spirit, a candle that refused to be snuffed, a lonely fig buried by a desert storm. Yes, that young woman's essence generated his undying devotion, not her appearance.

But deep down he somehow suspected he would never see her again.

He was alone now. Oh god was he alone. Lonelier than when he believed Bruné dead. His life had been one big circle of running: from Umbria, to Scanborg, then Worms, the hamlet, Narbo, Lerins, and now he was heading back east toward Umbria. But unlike the wake trailing the ship, the experiences in his past did not melt into the sea. They left a scar, a big permanent scar.

Scar!

"Oh good gawd!" he cried aloud. Scarface! The goat was not down in the hold faithfully awaiting his footsteps. The two had been companions for years, from Umbria to Scanborg-Andrazza, across the Alps, and down the rivers of Germania and Gaul. The most traveled goat in history was no longer by his side. Just as with his parents and his mentor Ponti, he would never see Bruné or Scarface again. He was sailing into a vortex of his own making. Was saving Rome worth sacrificing what little true companionship he had left in this world?

CHAPTER 2

The harbor laid portside. Because of the trailing wind, they made good time getting to Antipolis. Sails reefed, oars in, the ship plowed through the harbor chop. The captain found a spot well away from the docks, gave the signal, and the anchor splashed into the water. "Comin' in at this hour is not to my likin'," he said. "Most harbors along this coast have shifting bottoms."

Lucius shrugged. The harbor looked tidy enough to him. But then, he had never been aboard a ship that ran aground.

The captain went ashore with two crewmen and four empty amphorae, jars he would use to barter for the supplies unavailable at Lerins. Lucius's remained aboard awash in guilt. If he went ashore, he feared he might rush back to Bruné-Hilda by land.

The next morning, the captain announced that they would depart at midday. The wind and weather looked favorable enough to make the crossing rather than hug the coast. The crew cheered, it would save three days. Much to his dismay, Lucius discovered soon enough what the word "crossing" meant to these seamen. They would take a southeasterly direction into open water and head directly for the tip of Corsica, a large island in the middle of the Tyrrhenian Sea. Most of that distance would be run by night, leaving them to arrive off the coast around dawn. Giving the dangerous shoals protecting the tip of Corsica plenty of room, they would bypass the island and arrive at a port on Llva around midday, dusk at the latest if the winds slackened.

Lucius had no idea how dark it could get at sea or how frightening it was to sail into nothingness without a coastline to guide the ship.

When he nervously inquired about the absent coastline, the captain understood his angst and took him to the sternpost. "See that star?" he asked.

Lucius nodded.

"It be our shoreline for the first few turns of the glass. Soon another will rise to take its place, then a third."

Lucius could see the bowsprit pointing directly at the star.

"Next month that alignment will shift this much," the captain said, extending his hands at arms length, "and so on and so on."

"Amazing," said Lucius, beginning to relax a little. "So you seamen can actually steer by the stars."

"And the moon and sun. The trick is to know where they are in relation to where you be goin'. Each season they shift. More exactly, each month. My father was a captain and a celestial, ah, let's see now—what was the word he used? Authority, yes, authority. He was a celestial authority as was his father and his before him. My grandfather taught me to use the sky before I were twelve. Also, I have this," he said, pulling up an old skin on a scroll. "My grandfather's. A map of the stars for every month of the year."

"What of the Adriatic, the Aegean, and the Black seas? Can you sail those?"

"No. I know these waters and this sky, as did my ancestors. This chart is for Narbo to Napoli and back—and the isles in between. No ship have I lost to the sea, nor one on a shoal. Scraped the bottom a few times I have. But what captain worth his salt hasn't?"

Despite these reassurances, Lucius remained up all night searching the dark. The thought of being out of sight of land made him uneasy. When the sun finally rose, he saw, to his delight, the tall mountains of Corsica off the starboard bow as predicted. The captain joined him on the prow.

"See that thumb of land?" he said. "It juts out—see? Runs for miles north of the mainland. Wild it is, this part of Corsica—wild and sparse. Never set a foot on that shore and don't plan to. A few did, but not by choice. They run aground, fooled by the sea gods, and never been seen again. When Poseidon plays his tricks, you laugh and then outsmart the bastard. But when wickedness and evil shows up, you go the other way."

Lucius laughed, but the captain was dead serious.

Passing far to the north of the Corsica thumb, Lucius wondered what kind of people would want to live in a forlorn place like that. Soon enough the thumb was out of sight and, not long after, out of mind.

By midday they approached the coast of the island called Llva, which sat forty miles to the east. They docked at Portus Argous where the captain went ashore to barter for as much grain as he could get. He had seven hundred and eighty empty amphorae in the ship's hold. They were high-quality, conical-shaped storage jars from Narbo, and he traded forty-seven of them for enough grain to fill a hundred amphorae. With the Goths unable to grow enough crops to feed their people, they were running dangerously low on food. According to the captain, his original mission, before agreeing to deliver Lucius safely to Rome, was to obtain as much grain as possible. Since Narbo produced the finest amphorae in the province of Narbonensis, it was the only currency they had to trade with besides what they looted from Rome. And because it was forbidden to trade with the Goths, the captain carried the flag of Baleares Major, an isle off the coast of Spain.

Moving from port to port, they worked their way south along the Italian coast. On the final day at sea, Lucius's anxiety built. Rome lay not far ahead. "Captain, you spoke highly of your kin the other day. I do not mean to pry, but I was wondering"—he paused more for emphasis than courtesy—"I assume he continues in this adventurous profession at sea? I refer to your father, of course. I further assume your grandfather is a bit too old now."

"You made assumptions that belie the facts," said the captain. "I did not speak highly of either, my young friend, only respectfully. I valued their knowledge of the sea. They were retired when I was maybe nineteen or twenty."

"Is that a fact, huh? And you said 'were' retired? Not willingly retired, then."

"No, not willingly. Executed they were, my boy. Hanged."

Surprised, Lucius grabbed the captain by the arm. "Both? Your father and grandfather? Good Jupiter! For what?"

"Pirating. All my kin were Baleares pirates, including my two uncles. I'm the first to sail these waters without robbing every ship in distress."

To Lucius's dismay and before the captain could tell him more about his sordid ancestral past, a crewman shouted, "Portus! Portus!" which sparked a flurry of action. Sails were reefed, oars lowered, and the captain took his customary position next to the helmsman. All was made ready to enter the harbor. Excitement was in the air as the ship dug into the chopping seas surrounding the port. Clearing the final spit that protected the mouth of Portus, Lucius got his first view of the busiest harbor in the empire. And an amazing sight it was!

In addition to those pressing against the docks that lined the port on three sides, ships of all sizes and shapes moved about the harbor: Byzantines with triangular sails; cumbersome square riggers; a long, double-oared slaver like the one Lucius's uncle, Barnabas, was on; a string of flat-bottom barges similar to those that floated the Topino in Umbria; a few fishing boats; and countless cargo ships like the one beneath his feet. Pulling at their anchors in the middle of all this sat two galley warships with long, metal-tipped bow-rams. He had never before seen an actual warship, only a painting in Ponti's *tablinum*. This was exciting stuff. Some of the vessels were heading out, colors flying, sails half-furled, and oars pulling hard at the water; others were coming in with sails down and oars cautiously working the choppy waters of the port. Still others just sat, waiting for a space to dock. In all the ports they had visited since leaving Narbo, none had had such confusion. Yet it was somehow made manageable by some unwritten code of the sea. All the incoming and outgoing ships had lanes. None of the helmsmen appeared to be the least bit flustered. And many of the oarsmen just leaned on their oars looking bored by it all. In fact, the longer Lucius stared at this apparent muddle, the more he realized the bedlam was in fact manageable.

Quickly sizing up the situation, the captain called the ship to windward, whistled for the sails to go up, and ordered the ship to Ostia. The helmsman looked hard to see if the captain was serious. "Ostia is silted, sir," he said.

"We can manage. Turn south I say!" A crewman retrieved something from the aft box. It was a knotted line and weight. With it he prepared to "sound-the-bottom" when they reached Ostia.

The captain called Lucius to the helm. "Ostia be but a few miles south of here. I need dock space to unload my amphorae. Portus is overflowing. It happens. Take that worried look off your face, Lucius. We'll manage."

Ostia had only two ships at the dock, a dock that had once held up to sixty ships from the looks of it. The crewmen tied up at the end of the first pier, lessening the chances of running aground. Although the warehouses that ringed the docks appeared empty, the two- and three-story apartment buildings called *insulae* were interspersed with food bars and a large, oddly, active marketplace. One large building—so said the helmsman—held a public bath, gymnasium, and the largest public latrine in the empire. That the harbor was little used was apparently of little consequence to the dwellers of this coastal city whose livelihood, obviously, no longer depended on commercial shipping.

After they docked and the ship was secured, Lucius shouted his farewells to the crew before pulling the captain aside. "I desperately need a word, sir; needed to ask this of you since our last talk."

"What?"

"It's about the island you lived on."

"Baleares Major."

"Yes. Baleares Major. A good friend's father was a Balerusian pirate," Lucius said. "Although this friend of mine spoke little of him, I do know his father ended his thieving ways on the isle of Panteria. Is Panteria near here? If so, how can I get there? I would like to see the place where this friend was born, and maybe visit his mother if she still lives."

Preoccupied with overseeing his men, the captain had only been half-listening to Lucius. But when he heard the word "Panteria," he stopped what he was doing and turned his full attention to Lucius. "Panteria, you say? Hmm. What an interesting question. That's the place where the old wives of the aristocracy are exiled—usually on false charges. These wealthy men want younger women you see. Good to be wealthy and powerful, isn't it?"

"So my friend told me. He was reared on that forsaken place and joined the legion at fifteen just to get away."

The captain's interest was piqued even more. "What's your friend's name?"

"Quadratilla. My friend—he's dead now—was called Ignatius. Ignatius Quadratilla."

"Huh." The captain bit his lower lip and mulled over a thought, his expression changing several times before he responded. "Ye know, Lucius, I shouldn't be telling ye this, but my family name—my cognomen if you will—is Quadratilla. And me father's older brother, a squat, ugly rogue of a man he was too, got himself caught pirating and sentenced to dat isle you mentioned. Ugly is what saved 'is surly ass from the garrote. Dat's the last we heard of the sot. Dat place is forbidden to the likes of us or anyone normal."

Lucius noticed that the captain's speech pattern had suddenly changed now that he was reflecting on his past. The man had for some reason suddenly remade himself.

The captain continued with his cautionary advice, "Ye can't ever visit the island. Although dose women are prisoners, deir only crime was getting old—but dey know things. The overseers of the place, whoever they be, choose really ugly criminals like me uncle to do deir daily bidding I'm told, just to torment those poor, sorry souls all da more."

"My friend had the face of a horse," Lucius offered with a laugh. "His knuckles dragged and he had no neck. But he did have a tender heart and a pleasant smile."

"What happened to your friend, this Ignatius fellow, no doubt my uncle's son?"

"He was killed. Then hung like a butchered hog outside the gates of my city. He remains the most decorated hero of our time, you know."

"Hero? Never heard dat—I mean that," he added quickly, catching himself for the first time. "What did he do to earn that name?"

"Cut a man in two at Lake Como. Split the poor bastard from nape to nuts. That's where he got the name 'the Butcher.' It was at the Vallone where he earned his real fame, however, when he slew the Gothic king's entire guard. After that, he was known as 'the Butcher of the Vallone.'"

The captain slapped his knee. "Unthinkable that, if true. My uncle's son, the Butcher of the Vallone. But all that's too good to be . . . probably just a myth."

Lucius jumped to the dock and reached back for his two sacks of belongings. "True or not, Captain, you might consider using it. I *surely* have. Being kin to the likes of him can be useful at times. It earns respect, opens a lot of doors, puts fear in the fearless. Now sir, before I bid you farewell, tell me, what will you do next?"

"Trade off some more of my jars for grain. If I fill five hundred amphorae with anything but water, it will make for a profitable trip. Galla Placidia paid me well to bring you here. The underfed back at Narbo will pay even more to fill their empty bellies once the cold sets in. Now then, my young adventurer, I say to you farewell. Hopefully we'll meet again one day. However, the next time you leave me waiting for two weeks on some crusty island, I'll kick that bony ass of yours over the side," he said, and laughed good-naturedly.

During one of those heartfelt days when Lucius was caring for Bruné at Lerins, a drama began to unfold back at Narbo. Singerich, half brother to the former queen Stairnon and cousin to the present Gothic King Athaulf, slipped quietly out of bed. He walked to the window of his cramped apartment next to the makeshift palace and threw open the heavy drapes. Pleased, he looked at Sara who remained sound asleep. Pleased he was not so much with the raucous night of sex with Galla Placidia's servant girl but with what she so indelicately let slip—her mistress fornicated with Lucius when the king was away. *That tidbit might one day buy me the throne,* he thought. Although Galla Placidia would favor Wallia to succeed her husband the king, her favor could be changed with what he now knew. Not only adept at blackmail, he was well practiced in the art of palace intrigue. After all, as head of the palace guard, he spent two years in Constantinople avoiding the pitfalls of court life while wet-nursing the infantile emperor of the East. Yes, he was very well practiced in the art of intrigue.

Not long ago, when he was certain that Athaulf had bought a seat at Odin's table after being unhorsed before the walls of Massilia, Singerich had begun to plot. But no, the lucky bastard survived the wound. Now he was off again, banging at the walls of Tolosa while his wife was banging Lucius. Would the king ever learn? Without the Burgundians' skillful connivances, the Goths would forever knock on doors that would never open, on walls that would never fall. "We Goths depend too much on the brute and not enough on the guile," his father often said following yet another failed siege in Greece. "But with Gunther the Burgundian—"

Sara sighed, interrupting his reverie.

"Good morning, pretty one," he said, forcing a smile. "Sleep well?"

Singerich moved to the table and poured two cups of wine. Then he sat down on the edge of the bed and handed her one, saying, "Now, little princess, tell me, what else is happening in the life of your mistress?"

❖

After Sara departed, Singerich sent for Wulfus, his iron-toothed informant. If Wulfus thought this meeting was going to be just another inquiry into the stale gossip of Narbo, he was wrong. His life was about to change forever.

When he shuffled in, Singerich offered him a chair. Never before had he asked him to sit. That should have been his first indicator, but Wulfus was thick. Singerich got right to the point. "I recall you've had some contact with this young Umbrian fellow called Lucius, more recently of the new kingdom of Burgundia, yes?"

"Contact? Huh. Damn near killed that sharp-tongued, blue-eyed shit. If Galla hadn't intervened, I *v*ould have. The bastard made me his goatherder *v*hile everyone else treated him like an Eastern satrap."

"What if I give you that chance?" asked Singerich.

"Too late. He's been gone for days, maybe *v*eeks."

"Gone! Without my knowing? How!"

"The story *v*as that he *v*as in the hills hunting *v*ith that goat. But I eventually discovered that he sailed off instead, on one of those supply ships, along *v*ith that wretched goat. Damn, but that goat's a mean son-of-a-bitch. Those two—"

"What else have you heard?"

"Just that. His leaving vas abrupt and the deception not one bit thin, like some secret undertaking."

"For whom?"

"For Galla, I assume. Maybe to ransom her, maybe to buy food. Our lockers are a mite empty and vinter's comin', and Ravenna's blocked all shipments, they say."

"Yes, yes. I know about that. Go on."

"Or," Wulfus began and laughed, "or maybe the twit goes to Rome to acquire a better vedding present. I understand that the damnedest looking statue anyone's laid eyes on came out of that package ve carried here for him. Or so Galla's guards say."

"Enough about the statue. Listen carefully, you fool," Singerich said, lowering his tone. "I want you to go after him. Leave as soon as possible; pick someone to accompany you. Not just anyone, mind you, choose someone familiar with that part of the world; someone with a well-tested mean streak and certainly not a self-righteous Christian or sanctimonious Jew. When you catch up with him, I want you to kill the bastard and bring his head back to me."

"Vhy?"

"Why the head?"

"No. Vhy kill him? His mouth is big, but it ain't hurt a soul."

Singerich rubbed his chin and walked to the window and looked out. "There are reasons I cannot divulge, my faithful friend, except for this. His actions are counter to the interests of Gothia."

"Gothia?"

"Yes, Gothia. The Gothic Empire. Now go quickly and find an assassin."

After Wulfus departed, Singerich poured a cup of wine and walked to the bed. Looking down at it, he reflected on everything Sara had told him the night before except for Lucius's quiet departure. Then it struck him. Sara suspected Galla might be pregnant. It was an off-hand comment that he dismissed as nonsense. But could it be true? Her husband had been recovering from the wound he'd received at Massilia before rushing off to attack the walls of Tolosa. If pregnant, could the child belong to Lucius? Ransoming Galla was one thing, but ransoming a pregnant queen with an heir in her belly was a horse of a different color. Confounded by all this, Singerich walked back to the window and looked out. His eyes roamed the square until they fell on the perfectly shaped phallus Athaulf pilfered from Rome. It had replaced a statue in the middle of the square. Was that phallus now speaking to him, warning him? If so, what was it saying? He wondered how much of a head start Lucius actually had.

Lucius traveled the short distance to Portus from Ostia on the back of a hay wagon. From there, his plan was to catch one of the many transports to Rome. Hungry, he saw a man under a tree having a snack. "Sir, is that a garlic sausage roll? If so, where might I buy one?" When the man looked up he appeared familiar. Then Lucius noticed a desert scarf lying in his lap. "We have met before, have we not?" he asked without hesitation. "At the Cintessimo Bridge in Umbria, I recall. My horse shied and knocked you into a ditch."

The man got to his feet, shielded his eyes from the sun, and gave Lucius a good look. "I don't think so," he said.

"You gave me a thong with a stone attached, the fall bloodied your knee. My companion and I drove you to Nucera-Umbra where you took the road to Ancona. I remember the entire episode quite clearly."

Acting as if Lucius was about to rob him, the little man gathered his things, put on his desert head wrap, and walked away.

"Why do you run, sir? Do I frighten you?"

The man stopped. He stood with his back to Lucius thinking. Then he turned around slowly. "You were with that beautiful blonde girl—the chieftain's daughter, I believe—driving an oversized house wagon pulled by two oxen and trailing three horses and a goat. I remember it quite clearly as well. You have grown considerably since then. Oh yes, one more thing. I swore if I ever fell under your shadow again I would kill myself."

Lucius laughed. "I have that effect on people at times. The chieftain you refer to became a king, you know. His daughter, that beautiful blonde girl, a princess, and me—"

"A troublemaker!" he interjected with a big smile on his face. "I know only that you were one big thorn in everyone's ass."

"Yes, that might describe me," Lucius said, maintaining his poise, "if you were Adefonsic, the traitorous innkeeper; Calla

Lanilla, the slave trader who profited in human flesh; or Lazarus, the bishop who espouses the virtue of poverty while wearing silk robes and red slippers from Jerusalem. Then again, others might say I do no more than frustrate evildoers. Into which group do you fall, sir?"

The sun set behind them as Lucius and the little man with the desert head wrap approached Rome in the back of a two-wheeled cart with another traveler and the driver. The cost was a pittance. While Lucius had his sausage roll back in Portus, the little man went on to finish his business in Portus and Ostia. The day passed quickly after their chance meeting under the tree.

The little man called himself Mahaki and was an agent for five estates on the Adriatic coast. He was awaiting two more grain ships that would arrive sometime later in the week. One ended up arriving that morning. At Lucius's suggestion, they returned to Ostia where the estate agent agreed with Captain Quadratilla to trade his grain for the captain's amphorae. Lighter in weight and stronger than most, the Narbonensis amphorae were good currency. The captain was pleased, and Mahaki was so grateful that he agreed to travel to Rome with Lucius.

"Where will you stay?" Mahaki asked on the way to Rome.

"I have no place. Maybe I'll let a room above some barbershop. I have found barbershops to be the soul of every municipality I've been to. Maybe it is so here."

"Bah! When in Rome, I stay at the Hostia Inn just beyond the Salarian Gate, a bit closer to the Nomentana Gate. It is outside the walls, so the air is healthier, and its close enough to any place you might choose to visit."

"The Salarian Gate, you say. Where the . . . ?"

"Yes, the 'Traitor's Gate'—the one let open to the invaders from the North, the gate the entire Gothic horde rode through to do their dirty work. I should think you would approve being close to treachery," kidded Mahaki with a smile.

Lucius laughed. He enjoyed the little man despite the strange headdress.

It was just getting dark when Lucius and Mahaki walked into the inn. Just before they entered, Mahaki pulled the trailing scarf from his head wrap across his face, pointed Lucius toward a man at the corner table, and then disappeared up a narrow flight of stairs. The man at the table turned out to be the innkeeper. He ushered Lucius to a third-floor back room where Lucius paid him a week's rental in advance before the man left the room. Then Lucius threw his belongings on the other bed and fell fast asleep. Living aboard ship all this time had weakened his legs and arms but not his spirit.

By the time the sun rose the next morning, Lucius was already standing before the Salarian Gate, the now famous "Traitor's Gate," the place through which the Brandin Clan of the Burgundian nation had led the barbarous sacking of the greatest city in the world. The walls rose half again as high as those of his home city of Assisi, and twice that of Worms. Their construction was brick, which surprised him since the base of Assisi's walls were large tufa blocks laid by the Etruscans and fieldstone laid by succeeding generations of Latins and Romans.

The archway over the gate loomed above the entrance and was guarded by two massive towers. Three large alcoves—or were they windows?—broke the monotony. As far as he could see in either direction, the wall was interrupted by parapets every hundred paces. It presented an impregnable barrier. No wonder the invaders resorted to subterfuge. Without Gunther's and Freya-Gund's ruse, the uncivilized hordes from the north would still be knocking on the gates of Rome.

As Lucius stood in awe admiring this great wonder of the world, the area suddenly came alive. Vendors began to set up their wares, a wagon pulled up loaded with geese, a man with a pushcart appeared from nowhere, and a blind beggar poked along with a walking stick. The beggar retrieved a reed mat from a crevice and sat by the entrance. Lucius recalled Glyceric the dwarf's tale of the attack on Rome and how he'd said there was a trench—a moat of sorts—guarding the gate when the Brandins rode up that stormy night of the assault. Lucius remembered the retelling clearly. Where was the moat now? It must have been a temporary defense, of course. He looked to the top of the tower where, according to Glyceric, Freya-Gund had stood that dark, stormy night posing as a

Valkyrie war goddess, surrounded by torches dipped in tar, waving the invaders into the city. His uncle Barnabas, along with Freya-Gund and another mysterious "woman of means," had been part of the grand conspiracy to throw open the gates. Their treachery had brought the greatest city the world had ever seen to its knees, a blow so devastating that it threatened to unbalance the earth forever. But he never found out who this mysterious woman of means was. And it made him wonder.

Lucius took a deep breath and began to slowly walk toward the gate. For him, this was a momentous moment. With Etruscan blood pulsing in his veins and having been well schooled in the ways of the barbarian hordes these past years, he carried on his back not only the full weight of the past but the promise of tomorrow. The city of Rome had been here, it seemed, forever. But nothing was forever— Ponti Lepius had taught him that. And now, eleven hundred and sixty-nine years after Romulus founded Rome, Lucius was about to take his first step into the greatest and grandest accomplishment of man—the City of Lights and Enlightenment. And he would do it through the same gate that Gunther the Burgundian led the Gothic hordes. With a different brand of cunning, Lucius presented a new challenge to the city and to the aristocracy that controlled it. Both were about to be invaded by a young man with a mission, a mission to save the city from itself. But those who might suffer most from the consequences of his quest did not visualize, realize, or, most importantly, fear his invasion. Had they suspected the outcome, they may well have re-dug the moat, slammed the gate, and manned the parapets.

As he entered, Lucius dropped a coin into the blind beggar's cup.

"Go in peace," said the blind man, brushing his hand against Lucius's robe.

"And with you," said Lucius, pausing. "Your cup, though empty, overflows with gratitude."

"As does your generosity. A blind man has a good ear. I can distinguish gold from copper, kind sir," he said.

"From your pronunciations, I detect an upper rather than lower upbringing, if you don't mind my saying so, my good fellow. You are more than a humble street beggar I wager. But I must be off now. I have much to see and far more to do."

"Ah, a philosopher, I see. Return for a visit, young man. I too can sense the inner man. By your voice, your urgency, and the feel of your cloth, I can tell you are young, ambitious, and on an uncommon errand. Except for the midday meal, I am here all day, every day. I may be of assistance to your cause. You are from Umbria, yes? Which means you have Etruscan blood pulsing in your veins? Have you come to reclaim the city by chance?"

That stopped Lucius cold. *How could the man know that?* "I am from everywhere, sir, Umbria being but one place I've lived. How did you know?"

"Having sat here through Honorius's triumphal procession, Innocent's election to the papacy, Serena's execution, and the Gothic invasion, I have seen it all—though blind," said the beggar.

"What made you say Umbria, when Italy has so many cultural regions?"

"You Umbrians are discourteous to your vowels, except for the letter *O*, which you worship at the altar of exaggeration. Plus, you roll your *R*'s."

Lucius was dumbfounded.

"To a trained ear," continued the beggar, "no man is a stranger for long."

With that, Lucius bid farewell and promised to return. What the beggar had said piqued his interest. He had many questions for a man who had *seen* so much. Lucius walked through the entrance and into the city thinking about the beggar. But the man was soon forgotten a few blocks down the Vicus Salaria when he realized why Mahaki wanted to house himself outside the walls. The sun had not yet risen and already people were crawling over one another. Shops were open. People were pushing through crowds and doorways. Carts flew by, their iron wheels echoing off the buildings. But those sounds could not drown out the hawkers—the merchants advertising their wares, the cult followers preaching, and the mothers shouting after the school children from the high windows. The place was a menagerie of rudeness and offensive smells.

He reached the Via Lata where a measure of sanity reigned and turned right toward the Palatine and the Forum Romanum, the two centers of power in Rome: the former housing the aristocracy, the latter the bureaucracy. Soon enough he stood on Palatine Hill looking down on the Forum. Good god Jupiter! The place was in ruins. The barbarians, he was told by a bystander, had destroyed many of the buildings. Only the honorary monument to Augustus and the memoriam to Titus, plus two he could not identify, remained standing. Nothing had been repaired in the four years since the sack. The site was now, tragically, a quarry. He watched two men cart away stones from the Basilica that Julius Caesar had built. Its destruction had caused the people to backlash, although he did remember Glyceric the dwarf saying that Gunther attempted to stop the rampage during the sack, but arrived too late.

Next to the Basilica Julia ruins stood the gray, moss-covered remnants of the Temple of Castor and Pollux, which had served as the treasury of Rome since the days of Theodosius. Gunther looted tons of gold coins from it before the building had been brought down on the last day of the siege. A crime perpetrated by those who had found its vaults empty of swag. The site reminded Lucius of the temple back home, once the centerpiece of the municipality before the church atop the hill was built. That temple had been put upon by some of the great mischief makers of Umbria. It had been unceremoniously boarded up by Governor T. Aemilius Melissus, looted by Bishop Lazarus, and it had been the site where Freya-Gund's bloody bull massacre had taken place.

After a lengthy tour of the city, Lucius returned to the Salarian Gate eager to question the blind beggar. After exchanging a few pleasantries with the man, he got directly to the point that had brought him back. "Four years ago, after the barbarians' siege, a man was seen hanging by the neck from the gate. Can you tell me what you know of this?"

"Hmm. Interesting," the beggar said and reached for Lucius to pull him closer. "May I ask," he queried mysteriously, "why you inquire?" taking the material of Lucius's cloak between his fingers.

"Yes, of course, sir," Lucius said while pulling back. The beggar's fondling of his cloak made him feel strange. "He is—

or was—my uncle. His name, Barnabas Frugi, a graduate of the Academy of Engineering here in Rome. I believe he was much decorated for his academic excellence and, to his disgrace, a lover of matrons among the wealthy of Tibur. This led to his conviction for negligence and adultery, which in turn led to his castration. After his release from the prison ship, he became a drunkard and ensnarled—"

"Say no more," interrupted the beggar. "You have painted an adequate picture. Drop another coin and I will tell you all I know."

Lucius did.

"Quite a mystery it was, you know. Yes, yes, yes, quite a mystery." He cleared his throat. "Let me think now. So much has happened since. Those were challenging times, the invasion, the sudden withdrawal, some running north, others going south and then returning. The barbarians remained inside the walls only five nights and four days, you understand, looting and hooting and destroying. After they departed, the man you say was your uncle was found hanging by his neck right over there," pointing to the far side of the tower. "His body was removed with care by loving hands, I'm told—I could only hear the commotion, of course. I'm told they buried the poor soul not far from here at Alban Villa."

"Alban Villa, you say. Where is this villa located?" asked Lucius eagerly.

"I'll get to that. Be patient, there's more. The gossipmongers say every so often a mysterious woman visits his grave. They say no one knows who she is or why she comes. But she's always surrounded by attendants, protected from the curious and concealed from view by veils."

"On what day does this mystery woman appear?"

"Fourth or fifth day before the kalends, which could be soon. I have little reason to track the days exactly. One is like the other."

"Now tell me please, where is this Alban Villa located?"

"Not far. It sits on the grounds from which the barbarians launched their final assault that terrible, stormy night. Some believe there is a connection. They charged through this very gate, opened by conspirators, the moat bridged by a hundred sordid hands."

Lucius began to wonder who this beggar really was. He said, "Now sir, if it is not asking too much of a blind man, can you point me toward this villa?"

The beggar smiled. "That direction, a thousand paces more or less. You'll find the villa, the graveyard as well. Ask anyone along the way."

Lucius spent part of that day and the next walking the graveyard, waiting for the mysterious woman to appear. He even asked the groundskeeper and grave visitors about her, but to no avail. Had the blind beggar simply lied to gain another coin for his cup?

Discouraged, Lucius went back to his original mission. On the fourth day, as he was returning from another failed attempt to locate those Galla Placidia had instructed him to see, he stopped by the Alban Villa out of curiosity. And there she was. It had to be her. Covered head to toe in an elegant wool cloak and guarded by six attendants, she leaned against the side of a large, ornate crypt, her head bent in prayer. A crypt! Of course, a crypt! Lucius had not considered checking the row of expensive crypts. They were reserved only for the very wealthy, not a nut-less criminal who had disgraced himself by serving five years aboard a slave ship.

When he approached, one of the men blocked his way. "Sorry, please," the servant said politely, "this is a private observance. She will not be long."

"I too apologize," said Lucius. "But I must speak to the lady on an urgent matter. Is that the burial place of Barnabas Frugi? If yes, I request an audience with the lady."

Another servant joined the first and both delicately but firmly pushed Lucius back.

"Madam!" he shouted over the heads of the two servants. "Heya! Heya! You must listen to what I have to say!"

She turned.

"Barnabas Frugi was my uncle—my mother's brother. I am Lucius Domitilla."

The mysterious woman raised a hand and immediately the servants stopped pushing him. "Bring him here," she ordered and looked around to see if anyone was watching, then flipped back the veil covering her face. Although approaching middle age, the woman was stunningly beautiful. She had dark hair, round eyes, fair skin, and an elegant line to her nose and chin. She motioned for him to come closer.

"I am Lucius of Umbria," he said breathlessly as he approached her. "And I am guessing you are Cybelina."

She nodded in that graceful manner imbued in those born to the aristocracy. "I am she. And I know of you as well. Your uncle spoke often of you. He was proud of you, you know. Said you were set to accomplish great things."

"Thank you. If I knew more of you, I would surely return the compliment. If I may inquire, what exactly is going on here? Is my uncle in that crypt?"

She blinked at his directness. "This is no place to talk. Where are you staying? I will send someone. Then we can discuss all these things. When is it convenient?"

He told her.

Outside the east gate of Narbo in far-off Gaul, three men slipped through the evening shadows into a nearby stable. Assured they were alone, they settled down. Then the husky one spoke. "They call me Tauriac," he said, keeping his voice low.

"They do, do they," said Singerich. "And what do *you* call yourself?"

"I call myself fool. Only a fool would agree to resurrect an unrewarded career for a promise." Tauriac was not only muscular, he was surly. He also sported a ring in his left ear. Because he shaved his head, he looked like a Hun but wasn't.

"Rewards are earned, my friend," said Singerich, who called this meeting in the stable. "Obviously you are not of Gothic blood. This city could be dangerous for one of your breed. What brings you here to Narbo?"

"I followed one crazy man to the Rhine and another down the Rhone. The second one had, let's say, mixed loyalties."

"Ah, you refer to that usurper from Mainz who gambled and lost his war outside Valence."

"Yes, that one. Attached to the Alani auxiliaries, I came south with that pompous jackal and the rebellious XXVII legion from Briton led by General GaisoWarock Magnus. With a name like that, how could he lose? But he did. The plan was to take over Gaul until you Goths reversed your loyalties at the last moment and sided with the emperor's forces. Only a fool could miss seeing the outcome, so I switched sides—and not for the first time. I'm a mercenary by choice and far from home by chance."

That exchange set the tone for their meeting. The three—Singerich, discontented brother to the former queen, Wulfus the iron toothed one, and Tauriac the mercenary—moved deeper into the shadows of the stable. No good could come from a gathering of these three.

"Could you be more specific about your history," asked Singerich once they resettled. "Wulfus here speaks well of you, and I like your straight talk, but I must be certain. This is no fool's errand."

Tauriac retrieved a piece of straw from the stable floor and began picking his teeth. "I am of the Tauri people who reside in the mountains on the north shore of the Black Sea."

"The Bosporus," said Singerich.

"Yes, the Bosporus. My ancestors lived there for centuries defending their ways against the Romans, your Gothic ancestors, and then the Huns. As a boy I was captured and condemned to a Roman galley ship. Three years later, no longer a boy, I led a mutiny and took over the ship. Now a marauder of the seas, I ended that career running aground near the Avar outpost of Gamzat with a price on my head and a belly full of disappointment."

"How did you get to this part of the world?" asked Singerich. "You are a long, long way from home."

"They had a brash, young champion, these Avars of Gamzat. He was chosen to lead an expedition to avenge an injustice against a far-off place I'd never heard of. Being inexperienced and wild, I accepted the father's challenge to watch his son's, the brash champion's back. However, his brothers," and he started laughing, enjoying this part of the story, "paid me to kill the young upstart when this senseless expedition was over. I accepted their money and agreed to do both. The leader, Sassen, was despised by everyone—

including me, eventually. When their vengeance was sated and the church made from the stones from their once-proud city destroyed, Sassen was murdered."

"By you?" asked Singerich intrigued by the man's tale.

"No, by a woman, the most frightening female I've ever come across. Not only a sorceress and disciple of Ahriman, she was the one who threw open the gates of Rome. As a result, your former king put me in charge of the Avars and forced them all to join him on the siege of Rome. The Avars were only eight hundred strong, but they could shoot an arrow—in the back, of course."

Lost in thought, Singerich rubbed his chin. "Some of this I am aware of," he said. "We needed every man then. However, Wulfus did not mention it was you who led the Avars into Rome, which means it was you who caused the uprising at the Forum that nearly brought disaster to the entire venture."

"Then you should know all the history. I did not lead them into Rome. Believing the whole affair a waste of time and blood, I abandoned the role, which I had not sought nor wanted, and sold my services to an imperial agent, a Hun, after the capture of Ostia. He led me halfway around the world chasing after something that wasn't there. That is how I came across Lucius, who seems to have aroused everyone's animus. He is a slippery devil, you know. Now that I have answered your questions, sir, I have just one—what exactly do you want of me?"

Singerich paced back and forth thinking. He liked this man who obviously changes sides on a whim. "Are you steadfast?" he asked.

"Steadfast? Absolutely not. I am a heathen with principles—my own principles. A disciple of another's beliefs I am not."

"Good. I like that. I want you to accompany Wulfus on a mission to kill Lucius. The two of you must stop him before he reaches Ravenna."

"Why?" asked Tauriac.

"You need not know why. You need only to know how," said Singerich. "Wulfus tells me you knew Lucius, but not that well. That's good. I understand you are also familiar with the terrain and, most importantly, that killing is not foreign to you."

"How much for his head?"

"How much is enough?" asked Singerich.

"Enough to retire on. I'm getting old. I want Narbo to be my last stop."

Singerich laughed. "Of course you want that. Every warrior dreams of retiring, but few live long enough. Now then, how much for his head you want to know? Lucius is carrying enough gems to ransom an army. They are sewn into his cloak."

"And how would you know that?" asked Tauriac. "That young lad is as slippery as an oiled pig, I tell you."

"I know of the gems from the person who helped with the sewing."

Lucius stood in front of the Milliarium Aureum, the famous Golden Milestone, its gilded bronze exterior gleaming proudly in the sunlight. It was the only monument still maintained in the Forum.

"Huh," he grunted. "Gunther told me he stole it."

He stopped and looked around to see if anyone had seen him talking to himself. Yes, Gunther did tell him he stole the Milestone. Lucius had seen it lying in the wagon the day the Burgundians returned north following the sack. Yet here it stood. Obviously the one the Burgundian chieftain pilfered was a replica that had been displayed in anticipation of the siege. Besides, the one in the wagon was half this size. Whatever the story, it was here and here it belonged.

Lucius walked the sixty paces across the Forum and banged on the door of the Curia Julia for the fourth time. The big, square building where the Senate met looked empty. He had been told they would soon take up where they left off last spring. And he assumed that he would at least be able to catch the presiding magistrate at work preparing for the upcoming session. Obviously he assumed wrong.

The Senate was a mere shadow of its former self, relegated to governing the city and the surrounding area and making recommendations rather than rulings to Ravenna and the papacy— recommendations, Lucius was told, that were seldom followed. The power of the Senate now lay more in the wealth of its individual aristocrats than in its feeble attempts at collectivism. That notwithstanding, Galla Placidia had felt it important to "take their temperatures" as she'd put it. So Lucius had a list of people to see, all memorized of course. But if no one answered his knocking, how could he plead his case on behalf of Galla taking to the throne. He went to the back and side doors and knocked—nothing.

Returning from his fourth attempt to see one of the senators, Lucius left the city through the Salarian Gate. He stopped to thank the blind beggar for the information that had led him to the cemetery.

"I am about to depart for my noon meal," the beggar said. "Please, young sir, join me? There is something of great importance I must tell you. Come, please."

When the beggar, whom Lucius had only seen squatting against the wall, stood up, he became a bear. He was tall, strong, and a half a head taller than Lucius.

"Follow me," he commanded in a deeper voice than he used to garner his prey. The way he said it gave Lucius no choice.

The beggar disappeared through the gate into the city scoring the way with his stick, making just enough noise to announce his coming. Those accustomed to his presence moved out of his way. Turning a sharp corner, he dropped into an entrance and disappeared. When Lucius reached the same opening—no more than a seam between two buildings—an arm reached out and pulled him into the shadows.

"Stay close," the beggar ordered. He led Lucius down a flight of stairs, made two sharp turns, and then down a second flight of stairs. The deepening shadows slowly melted into absolute darkness. In the bowels of this mysterious building, the beggar found a door. Or was it a crack in the foundation? Lucius was not sure. They passed through the opening and descended more steps. The beggar, although obviously familiar with these surroundings, kept tapping his stick. They were now in a tunnel that zigzagged to the left and then the right and then the left again, all the while descending. From the brush of air against his skin, Lucius sensed they were passing openings he could not see in the pitch dark. At last the labyrinth of steps, tunnels, and breaches emptied into a chamber. And thanks to a tiny oil lamp on the distant wall he could see at last. *Amazing what just a little bit of—*

"Good gawd!" he screamed, recoiling from what he saw. Cut deep into the tufa walls that surrounded him were dozens of small memorials, and each held what appeared to be petrified bones piled beneath a human skull of a loved one long forgotten. This chamber contained maybe forty or fifty dovecotes that were embedded in the walls in neat rows, one just above the other, running all the way to the high ceiling. Well-worn lettering danced in the flickering light below each shrine identifying the deceased. Lucius shivered. This hole in the earth was a domicile of the departed. Instinctively, he pulled his cloak tighter to ward off whatever might fly out from one of these funerary recesses.

The beggar grunted, and then he moved on to yet another tunnel. By the time Lucius caught up, the light from the chamber had waned and he was again back in the world of the blind—absolute and unrelenting darkness.

After a time, he did not know how long or how many steps he had taken, the beggar stopped, turned, and whispered, "Silence. No matter what you feel, no matter what you perceive as danger, remain absolutely silent."

They soon came upon another hollowed-out cavity housing what looked to Lucius like some of the street people he'd seen lurking in the alleyways far above them. Some were consuming what appeared to be garbage; others were eating food probably stolen from the open market. In here there was more light than the prior chamber, although he soon wished otherwise. The cheerless bony faces, rags, and smells were disgusting. He searched each pathetic visage. Their sockets were as empty as the skulls in the dovecotes. The whole scene was eerie!

One man scooted closer to Lucius, his eyes darting beneath his scab-covered pate. The man's skin was pasty, his nails were bitten to a nub, and his extremities covered with putrefied sores. As Lucius passed, the poor soul jerked his head straight up, eyes rolling until they locked onto Lucius. The suddenness of his stare was haunting. Lucius tried not to look back, but he couldn't help himself. The effect was hypnotic. Then the man performed an act Lucius had never before seen another human do. This dispossessed soul stuck out his lizard-like tongue and swabbed his entire nose with it before slumping to one side in what appeared to be a stupor. Shuddering, Lucius moved on. He had taken no more than a few steps when something fell on his shoulder.

"Agh!" he yelled, swiping at it with his left hand. It felt cold and wet and had legs. "*Merda*," he whimpered and moved with renewed fervor, the blood pulsing faster through his veins.

The blind beggar only grunted his displeasure at Lucius's outburst. He'd seen nothing.

Then something landed on Lucius's head. "Great Jupiter, Juno, and Mars!" he shouted, dancing about trying to dislodge it.

"What? What?" said the beggar irritably. "Jupiter, Juno, and Mars have nothing to do with this place."

"Where in the love of the gods are you taking me?" Lucius asked, pulling on the beggar's robe like a child.

"Out of harm's way, my friend, out of harm's way. Now pull yourself together. We safely transited the Cult of the Dead. Now we may do the same with the Passage to Insanity, if"—lowering his voice to a whisper—"if you get control and quiet down. For if you don't . . ." He paused, chuckling with a slight touch of cynicism in his pitch. "If you don't, they might discover, hee hee hee, you're not one of them, and have you for dinner."

The beggar moved on, feeling his way along until he faded from sight once again. Lucius could hear the click, click of his stick against the uneven tufa floor. Just then, a hand reached out and groped his bare leg. The fingers felt sticky. He reached down and, with difficulty, pulled it away one finger at a time and rushed toward the spot where the blind beggar vanished. For one of the few times in his young life, Lucius felt completely helpless, like he'd suddenly found himself on a crumbling ledge atop a high cliff. But that was a recurring nightmare he had since a child; this was real.

Before entering yet another tunnel to nowhere, he shook himself. The click, click of the blind beggar's stick stopped, probably to make sure he was following, and then continued on. His head began pounding to the rhythm of the clicks. His breathing was labored, as though buried in a grave. A chill swept through his body. Lucius was on the verge of hysteria. Taking three deep breaths, he slapped his face repeatedly to regain control and then wrapped his cloak even tighter around his shoulders. Nothing helped. Then he remembered the fortune in gems sewn into his cloak and grabbed the hem to make sure they were still there. They were. Was all that he came to Rome for now at risk in this godforsaken, dank, unforgiving hellhole? He cursed for being so trusting and then resigned himself to the inevitable. With no way out, what else could he do? He had been led into this maze of death and near-death funereal confusion by a blind man. Whatever his purpose, the beggar was his only lifeline.

Suddenly the clicking halted. Lucius stopped and listened. What was that? A noise . . . like knuckles rapping on wood! The faintest hint of light crept across the floor of the tunnel. A door opened, and a blast of light shot out. There were voices, garbled, but rational; then the blind beggar vanished. Lucius moved quickly. As soon as he reached the spot, he was pulled through an opening and into blinding light. When his eyes adjusted, he found himself in a room with doors and people—three other people besides the beggar. The air tasted sweet. There was a fireplace and chairs, and mugs on a table.

Lucius watched as one of the three closed the small, rather thick, door behind him. The man dropped a metal crossbar into place sealing it tight. Then he carefully replaced a heavy cloth at the bottom of the door, no doubt to prevent any light from escaping into the tunnel, and released a heavy drape gathered on a large hook to the left of the door. Now no telltale light or sound could escape into the tunnel. This room, with its several doors and modest furniture, had to be an ingeniously designed secret hideout buried so deep beneath the entrails of Rome that no authority could possibly find it.

"Is this the Pretty Boy you spoke of?" asked one of the three. The man had only one leg and was half sitting on the table struggling to release a strap around his thigh. "There, that's better," he said, and a second leg swung down. He stomped his foot a few times to regain feeling in it.

"Indeed he is," answered the blind beggar untying the rag that bound his eyes. "His name is Lucius, though, not Pretty Boy. Lucius, meet Peg-Leg, my good and loyal friend. And yes," he said, addressing Lucius squarely, "as you can see, he can stand and walk with the best of men. Ha!" The beggar blinked a few times when the cloth fell away from his eyes. He rubbed the darkened sockets and looked right at Lucius. "As you've surmised by now, none of our, shall we say, *maladies* are real. Begging is our livelihood, deception our means."

Lucius watched as the woman with only one arm suddenly grew one. "Meet Medusa," the beggar said with a laugh. "That's her street name anyway. And him"—he pointed to the one with the hump—"his game is rickets. If you see him struggling along the main *vicus*, you'll understand just how good an actor he is. Bravura! Hey, remove the hump, will you please." Turning back to Lucius he explained, "He knows I can't eat while looking at that damnable thing. The kids on the street call him Vesuvius because of the hump. So there you have it. These are my street friends: Peg-Leg, Medusa, and Vesuvius."

"And what do they call you?" asked Lucius, having partially regained himself.

"My longtime friends here call me Alfadur—or All-Father to an educated Northlander."

Just then a stout woman came through the door cut into the far wall carrying a tray of bowls and a pitcher. She placed the items on the table and said, "Ah, I see we have a guest. I'll bring another bowl of food. It won't take long." She retreated through the door with the empty tray.

"Now then, young Lucius, as you can see, like you, the four of us are a gang of frauds keeping our bellies full pretending to be something we're not. And we have been getting by with it for a very long time."

"Why do you tell me this?" asked Lucius, hiding his apprehension while studying everything in the room. There was the door he'd come through, the metal bar now hidden by the heavy drape, and two lanterns that lit the room. There were also three other doors, including the one the woman had used; that one led to a kitchen no doubt, the other two probably to bedrooms. He assumed they all lived here. But what made the air so sweet? How did the other three and the cook get down here from the surface? There had to be a second way in.

"You wonder why I tell you these things," said the beggar. "Because, like us, you are also not what you pretend, my lad." The beggar sat down at the table. "Come closer. Let me have a look at that cloak. That first day we spoke of your uncle it was windy. The cloak brushed across me more than once. Did you notice what I did?"

Lucius gave a puzzled look.

"Of course you didn't. No one pays attention to the roving hands of a blind man. Blind men have heightened senses you know," he said and laughed. "You have something more than thread sewn into that garment, don't you? Gold coins maybe, some precious metals? Show us what you have hidden there."

In that white-hot instant of awareness, Lucius knew he was about to be robbed, or worse. While his wits rose commensurate with the threat, calm settled in. At once he knew what he had to do—and quickly. He threw out both hands to halt any advances on his person.

"First, let me *tell* you what's in this cloak, and then I'll show you," he said in a voice that belied his angst. "It holds the future of Rome. A whole new beginning for you, me, for all that is Roman." He pulled out his boot knife, grabbed the bottom of his cloak, and spread it over the table pretending to struggle with the seam. "Wait," he whispered. His voice was composed, his hand steady. They gathered closer. Whispering always had that effect on people. Made them feel drawn in. "I need more light so as not to ruin what's hidden in these seams. I must see clearly."

Peg-Leg retrieved the lantern from the wall and set it down in the middle of the table. Moving the food bowls aside, Lucius started to work on the hem again. Then he stopped. "Can you get the other lantern please?" he whispered. Peg-Leg did and Lucius set it down next to the first lantern. "Thank you. Now, everyone move to the far side of the table. If any of the gems spill, you can catch them before they roll off and find a crack in the floor."

He could see their eyes widen at the word "gems." When the four beggars were in place on the other side of the heavy table, he leaned over the two lanterns, closed his eyes and paused, pretending to mumble a prayer to some ancient god. He wanted his eyes to adjust to the dark that was about to envelop the entire room. Taking as deep a breath as he could, he blew with all his strength. Out went both lanterns. Without a word he upended the table, throwing the others back against the far wall. Then he leaped toward the door he came through, all while remaining composed. Any misstep now would be disastrous.

Although the room was black as pitch with the two lanterns out, the image of each item's place in the room remained clear in his head. In one motion he swept aside the drape that blocked the door, kicked the rag out of the way, and pulled open the door. But instead of running out, he pressed himself flat against the wall behind the open door and held his breath. Predictably, the four beggars ran blindly past him and out into the tunnel assuming that he had scurried off like a frightened rat.

When the last one cleared the doorway, Lucius slammed it shut, dropped the metal bar in place, and fingered his way along the wall before finding the door through which the rotund servant woman departed. There was a dying candle in the far corner of the next room giving off just enough light for him to see that the room was not a kitchen at all, nor was the woman anywhere to be seen. The food had come from someplace else. Good! He grabbed the candle, shielded it with his hand, and began looking for another way out. There! He went through a curtain, followed a short tunnel to a set of stairs, snuffed out the candle so as not to alert her, and ascended. Going up he noticed for the first time that he still held his knife. He slipped it into his boot and continued on up toward the light. Before long he was in the subterranean level of a very large building.

Two rows of staunch pillars, larger than any he'd thought possible, lined the room. *The building above must be enormous,* he thought. He heard someone and hid. It was the servant woman carrying a bowl of food and a mug. She walked past his pillar toward the entrance through which he had just come. Lucius remained quiet, heard the door close, and then a key enter a lock and turn. He retreated to where he had entered but could find no door. It was cleverly hidden in the wood paneling. *So that was their game.* Fortunately, she had carelessly left it ajar when she came up to get more food. Although his subterfuge won his release from the dungeon, Lucius did not have much time to complete his escape before his good fortune ran out. They would certainly be banging on the door to the hideaway below soon, if not now.

He discovered several openings before finding a set of steps. It did not take long before he was standing in the apse of a church—a very, very old church. Where that woman had gone to get food, he did not know nor did he care. Not before he scurried out the back and into the open air, did he fully realize how trusting of the blind beggard he was and how he must be more creative in hiding Fortune's gems.

Lucius knew exactly what to do. It did not take him long. He went to the nearest barbershop and inquired.

"You'll find everything known to man in the Subura district," said the barber. Following the barber's directions, Lucius found the large insula on Vicus Vespa, climbed the steps to a second-floor apartment, and knocked. A pleasant, rather chubby, middle-aged woman answered.

"You're a seamstress, madam?" he inquired.

She nodded.

"I need a vest cut and sewn at once, assuming your busy schedule permits, of course."

"It does not, I'm sorry," she answered. "My daughters and I have too much now."

Lucius was prepared. The barber had said she was the best in this part of the city, but busy. He dropped a coin in her hand. She looked at it, put it between her teeth, and bit down hard.

"Come in," she said with a smile. "My daughters will be home from *schola* soon. Between the three of us, we should be able to accommodate your needs, sir."

"Do you know what a cuirass is?" he asked.

"Of course, I've refit many for the older legionaries throughout the years. They grow quite fat with time, the old ones do."

"Can you make one out of quality cloth—not burlap, and nothing coarse or scratchy? Four pockets in the front and four in the back, each with a small opening that can be tied or laced shut."

"Slipped on or tied at the shoulders?" she asked.

"Slipped on over my head and tied at the sides," he said, knowing precisely what he wanted.

"Sketch the exact size of the pockets and locations. I'll get my string to measure your chest." Surprisingly, she handed him a scrap of paper and a stylus. Obviously this woman was one of the contradictions of an increasingly illiterate population. When done with all the necessities, she promised to have the vest completed by day's end. Lucius bid her farewell and descended the steps to the alleyway.

So long as he was here, Lucius decided to explore the nearby Subura slum. Much had been said and written about this place where every sin known to man was practiced in the contraband shops, smoking emporiums, and houses of prostitution. There was even an occasional cobbler, weaver, and dyer interspersed amongst these places of sin. This low-lying area situated between the Viminal and Esquiline hills was not only noisy but tasteless. He found a bench just off Vicus Longus and sat. Immediately his senses were overwhelmed by the sight of dilapidated buildings and the smell of garbage.

A woman limped by reminding him of Bruné-Hilda. The sight caused a wave of guilt to wash over him. What was he doing? Risking everything to save this? The place was a sewer. What level of arrogance did it take to even consider such a foolish idea? Observing all these useless people, it was no wonder Galla had screamed, "Save Rome for fucking whom?" when he'd put forth the scheme. He should be in Lerins caring for Bruné-Hilda and not here.

In the doorway across the way sat a poor woman nursing her newborn. Had he pushed the baby thing to the back of his mind? Galla Placidia, the queen of the Goths, was with child—his child. Gawd Zeus! What had he done? He was not accustomed to depression, but these reminders were not at all uplifting.

A woman on the second floor across the way suddenly threw open her shutters and unfurled a cloth banner upon which was written "Teller of the Future". His thoughts leaped from Bruné-Hilda and the pregnant queen to the sorceress Freya-Gund who used osier sticks to foretell events. She had used them effectively the first time they met. "Lucius is not worth the straw to pick a beggar's teeth," she had announced to those smelly barbarians who surrounded him in the tent when the black stick covered three whites.

Shaking his head at these terrible memories, he jumped up and ran. It did no good. "No one can outrun the 'hauntings'," Ponti Lepius Filipi had said so often. Now life was teaching him this lesson.

Back at Narbo, two queens of the nomadic Northerners met, though oddly enough, neither was of Northern blood. Although the doors and windows were open, the room was very hot despite summer being long past.

"Thank you for the audience, Your Highness," said Freya-Gund. "I appreciate the kindness you extended to my men. The camp is more than adequate. They are in need of a good rest."

"And you?" asked Galla Placidia.

"Me? I sleep in the saddle. Only my horse tires."

"How else may I serve you, madam? You've strayed far from your kingdom." Her words were hollow. Galla knew very well why she was here.

"To catch a thief, Your Highness. A certain person broke into a crypt near Worms and stole an object that belonged to me. I wish only to retrieve it so my people can enjoy its beauty. Then I mean to punish the imp for his, let's say, indiscretion."

"In addition to its beauty, it must be of great value for you to have traveled this far. I should warn you our king has become an unpredictable man since his wounding at the walls of Massilia. Surely you know his reputation from your experience in Rome. You risk losing your escorts and possibly your head by coming here. He was not pleased with, let's say, certain actions you took during the assault on my city." She paused for emphasis and then added, "Or so I am told."

Freya-Gund scoffed at that. "Your Athaulf would still be circling the walls of Rome waving his sword at the clouds if not for me. You know that. I know that. Gossip is an imprecise art practiced by the jealous, *Your Highness*," she said with a bow. "His coffers are full because of my actions."

"And those of the Burgundians," added Galla.

"Yes, of course. All that notwithstanding, I request your cooperation on behalf of my people, not myself."

"Hmm. Indeed, your people, of course." Galla rose from the couch and moved to the large tapestry over the fireplace that depicted the celebrated beheading of St. Valentine. "Is there anyone you do not attempt to manipulate, beguile, or seduce with words?"

Freya-Gund did not blink. "When saddled with a reputation, it rides forever."

"Quite true; and is it not also true that your former king's unexpected demise rides in that saddle as well?" asked Galla, not intimidated by this woman's immense repute, the one who allegedly threw open the gates of Rome to the invaders.

"I do what I must and get sorely accused of more. As a disciple of Ahriman, I am endowed with certain powers."

"Then use them wisely. You have only a few days, maybe a week, before my husband returns from Tolosa. He believes you betrayed the Goths in favor of others before the walls of Rome. He may choose to rectify that slight."

"We waste time. Let me be direct," Freya-Gund said sharply. "Where's my statue?"

Galla Placidia took pause. She had not expected an alien from afar, surrounded by those who might do her harm, to be so brazen. Freya-Gund acted like her minions just conquered the entire province of Narbonensis. So Galla altered her approach. "Come," she said, "let me show you something of interest," leading her into the next room. "Could this possibly be the only reason why you're here, or is there more?"

Sitting on a pedestal in the center of the room was the Statue of Fortune. The six layers of paint had been removed, and its original gilded luster gleamed in the sunlight that pierced the high window. It was the statue Freya-Gund had carried halfway around the empire: from Rome to Scanborg-Andrazza, then across the Alps to Worms, where it had been surreptitiously removed from where she'd hidden it. The statue was said to hold a belly full of precious gems, the finest the world had ever known. Gems that had passed through many greedy hands over the centuries; gems men fought and died for; gems women had given themselves to men just to wear.

Freya-Gund's breathing quickened, a vein on the side of her forehead swelled, her neck reddened. She had not laid eyes on the actual statue in four years—four long years ago when it was carefully wrapped and tied at the luxurious villa de Zenobia in Tibur the night of the raid. So much of her had gone into unraveling its mystery since the days when she was growing up in far-off Phrygia:

tracking it from Constantinople to Rome, locating the hiding place in Tibur in the hills outside Rome, plotting its recovery, and then secretly transporting it from one end of the empire to the other, only to have it stolen by that twit Lucius.

"Have you . . . has anyone . . . ?"

"Yes, Freya-Gund, I have," said Galla, fully understanding what the sorceress needed to know. "Let me show you." Galla moved to the back of the statue and opened a small square door above the extended buttocks. "See for yourself."

Freya-Gund reached into the small door and retrieved a handful of pebbles.

"It was all a hoax, Freya-Gund; all the talk over the years about a fortune being inside was just rumor. Eutropius' vast collection of gems was just an empty fable. Forty measures of stones, Freya-Gund, all that effort you put into gaining this statue was for a mere forty *librae* of worthless rock."

Freya-Gund's eyes went cold. "If anyone here in Narbo is trying to dupe me, I will cast a spell so wide the mountains will crumble, the seas rise, and the air turn to fire."

"Do not forget to salt our fields," interrupted a voice from the other room. Through the open door strutted Singerich.

"Do you ever think to announce yourself," snapped Galla Placidia. It was obvious she did not approve of the man despite his being the former queen's brother.

"Not when my lady's life may be in danger. Are you aware with whom you granted this audience? Thank Odin, one of your guards had the good sense to alert me."

Galla stepped in front of Freya-Gund and snapped, "Now that you're here, Singerich, why don't you tell us both how dangerous she is."

"Okay, I can play this game if you must. Her history is only partially known to me. But I do know she murdered the Avar chieftain and rolled his head down the center aisle of the warlords' summit before we marched on Rome. Now, how many women would dare be that bold?"

"Or that capable," interjected Galla.

"Before that, she lured a raging bull into a temple filled with innocent people. I saw the aftermath: Dozens gored to death, three times that many injured. She was also responsible—partially, I should add—for half Assisi being destroyed, which nearly cost us our most important ally."

"You refer to Gunther the Burgundian?"

"Yes, the Burgundian chieftain who eventually became their nations king. This woman here has left a bloody trail from Phrygia to half way around the world."

"I am aware," said Galla. "But afraid? I think not. She and I have much in common. Yes, so very much, like being put upon and misused by men such as you. Does not every living thing, human or otherwise, when put upon, strike back?"

Singerich, somewhat shocked by what he just heard, put two fingers to his mouth and let forth a loud whistle. In rushed four guards. Over Galla's protests, they dragged Freya-Gund away kicking and screaming.

Singerich entered the makeshift prison where Freya-Gund was being held and instructed the guards to leave. When alone, he untied her hands, pulled aside a heavy drape and guided her up a hidden flight of stairs to a private room where he offered her a cup and a chair. Pulling up another chair, he sat so close their knees touched. Speaking in a low voice, it was obvious he did not want to be overheard. "Sorry for the harsh treatment. It was necessary." He poured her a drink. "As for Galla Placidia, do not believe a word of what she said. She is not your friend or mine. The wench speaks with a forked tongue."

"Oh?" she said, gulping down the water. "I expected more of—"

"We chase after the same quarry," he interrupted. "I need your help. You do not yet know it, but you likewise need mine."

She belched and then took another long swig from the goblet. Leaning toward Singerich's face, she used a unsettling tone so characteristic of her, "And why do you think that?"

He flinched, pulled back, and got up, unable to match the intensity of those steel-gray eyes. "Why else would you be here?"

"Yes, why else," she said sarcastically. "Where is Lucius?"

"Off to Rome. And then I believe he goes to Ravenna, all in an effort to ransom Galla Placidia."

"Ransom Galla with *what*?" she asked.

"Gems, madam, gems. Hundreds of precious gems."

Jerking her head around, her gray eyes burned into his once again. "And you, for some reason, do not want that to happen."

"I share this information for a return," said Singerich, turning toward the window.

"When did the twit leave?" she asked.

"A week ago, maybe longer, I'm not exactly certain."

"How?"

"By ship."

"How long will it take for that ship to reach Rome?"

"Depends," he answered.

"On what?"

"Wind, currents, the courage of the captain. Most hop from port to port afraid of the open water," said Singerich.

Freya-Gund fell off into thought. When he started to speak, she put up a hand. "Quiet," she muttered. The woman was plotting. When she finally spoke, she offered only this: "I was hoping you'd bring me something to eat. It's been awhile—a long while. Remember, I am married to a King, the son of the former King Gunther, and accustomed to being tended to without begging."

Singerich smiled. He exited the room without saying a word; she could hear him hastening down the steps. She sprang to the door, closed it quietly, and then ran to the window. Reaching under her cape she quickly uncoiled the ever-present eight-strand cross-plaited bullwhip from around her left arm, having kept the butt hidden up her sleeve all this time. When Singerich returned, she was gone. He checked all the places she could hide. Nothing. Yelling at the guards on the first level if anyone had slipped out, but they saw no one. The only other way out was the window, a two-story drop. Then he noticed that one of the heavy window drapes was missing. Looking down, he saw how she did it. He ordered the guards to rush to where her men camped. If there, they were to bring her back—willingly or not.

"We are but seven, sir," pleaded one. "All our men are banging on the gates of Tolosa with the king. What if she refuses?"

"Don't permit a refusal," Singerich said furtively.

Less than an hour later the guards returned. "She's abandoned her men, sir," reported the one he appointed to lead them. "They can't believe she ran off like that."

"What do you mean 'ran off'?" asked Singerich.

"According to their word-man—I could only find one who speaks our tongue—she rushed into camp, changed, and raced off with six of their best riders pulling a string of horses. They headed east toward the Rhone River."

Singerich smiled. "So she has taken the bait. Now I have a retaliator chasing the fox as well. Lucius has no chance of surviving."

"What?" asked the guard.

"Nothing, just reflecting. Tell me, did you actually see them ride off?"

"Yes, from the top of a nearby hill. In the distance we could see them all galloping off as fast as those animals could go, the spares being pulled along. We clearly saw all seven."

If Singerich actually believed Freya-Gund had taken the bait and gone after Lucius, he was wrong, not unlike so many others who thought they had taken the measure of this crafty sorceress.

The following morning, a hunched back old woman with gnarled hands and long, stringy hair appeared at the main gate of Narbo. The gnarled hands were actually chicken bones, and the hair cut from a horse's tail. The filthy black cape and hood were fashioned from a shepherd's cape—a shepherd who no longer had need of a cape or walking crook. She sat near the entrance pretending to beg. But she was not begging. Freya-Gund was observing and plotting.

Forty measures of rock, she thought. Who did Galla think she was dealing with, some ignorant toady from Antioch? Who weighs rock? Who but a fool preserves proof that they have been duped? If you find rocks instead of gems, you throw them out. Ha! Forty measures. Who weighs fucking rock? You weigh gems. You count them. You separate them: the precious from the more precious from the even more precious. And why would he say Lucius took gems to Rome? Singerich didn't just let that slip. He wanted me to chase after the imp. Yeah! Only a fool would do that. Rocks, gems, rocks, gems—what kind of fool do they take me for? I know there were gems in the belly, lots of gems. How many can be sewn into a cloak? A couple handfuls at most. Whatever he took is nowhere near all of it; the bulk of that treasure is here. If I found the statue in Tibur, I can find the gems in Narbo.

A man passed by breaking her reveries by dropping a piece of bread into her lap. In a squeaky voice she thanked him for his kindness. Already she had become like the local castoffs—a pathetic non-person. Good.

CHAPTER 3

When Lucius returned to the Hostia Inn with the vest, a messenger was waiting for him. "My mistress requests your company for the midday meal," Said the messenger.

"When?" asked Lucius excitedly.

"On the morrow," he answered. He was young, dressed in a knee-length *paenula*, and exceedingly polite. "If you agree, Euric will guide you to her villa."

This was the breakthrough Lucius needed. Of course he'd meet her. Not only would he get answers about his uncle, Cybelina would surely have connections with the aristocracy. When the messenger departed, Lucius went out behind the inn to collect several handfuls of pebbles. Once up in his room, he removed his cloak and laid it on the bed, then he slit open each end of the hem and gently slid out eight tubular sleeves, each holding between twenty and thirty precious gems that he gently set aside. He picked up the identical tubular sleeves the seamstress had made and began filling them with pebbles. Then he slid them into the hem of his cloak and closed each end using a bone needle and thread supplied by the seamstress. Next, he folded each of the eight cloth sleeves containing the gems into neat square packets that he carefully slipped into the four pockets on the front of the vest and the four on the back. He massaged each bulge until they lay flat. Then he cut a strand of hemp into eight shorter lengths. Using the shorter lengths, he laced each pocket shut by threading the hemp pieces through the five holes cut into the flaps and top portions of each pocket; he knotted the ends of the hemp when he was through.

Slipping the vest over his bare chest, he laced each side until it fit snuggly against his body. Putting on his tunic, he made sure no part of the vest was exposed. "Perfect." No one could detect that he carried a fortune in gems. And what he carried was marginal compared to the one thousand and thirty larger gems he'd left at Narbo with Galla Placidia. The cloak with the pebbles in the hem would serve as a decoy if the beggars or any of their subterranean friends decided to pay him a visit. He now needed a companion, someone to watch his back. The little man Mahaki came to mind.

The assassins were on their way to Rome in search of Lucius. Three days earlier, Irontooth and Tauriac had crossed the Rhone River north of Arles. They had been forced upriver before finding a ferry that would cross with their four horses, and they were not too happy about that at all. It cost them an entire day—one day too many. Now, they were nearing Frejus on the Aurelian Way making excellent time. When they reached Frejus, their plan was to sell the horses and find a cargo ship that would take them as close to Rome as possible, as unseasonably heavy snow in the lower Alps had made it difficult if not impossible to travel the land route from Nicaea to Albiso—or so a wagoner told them after he himself was forced to turn back. Continuing by ship was their only alternative. They were going as fast as they could under the conditions.

Cybelina's villa lay outside the walls located on the road to Tibur named, not surprisingly, Via Tiburtina. Sitting back maybe a hundred paces, the villa was protected by a wall and a tall iron gate. The grounds were huge and the gardens beautiful, even this time of year. The main dwelling was every bit as large as Capricorne—Ponti Lepius's hilltop villa in Umbria.

She waited for Lucius at a stone table on the veranda overlooking a small pond. Four female servants dressed in identical long-sleeved *stolas* of reddish-violet stood in waiting. Five small terracotta furnaces surrounded the table making the air quite comfortable despite the late fall chill.

While being guided here, Lucius had gotten the impression Euric was more than a house slave, although the mark between his thumb and forefinger indicated otherwise. And when he joined them at the table sans invitation, Lucius was convinced. Euric gave his cloak to one of the attendants, washed his hands in a silver bowl held by another, and then sat directly across from Cybelina. They were all served a cup of watered wine and offered a selection of canapés.

"Euric knew your uncle before I did, Lucius," said Cybelina, noticing his curious look and then took a sip of her wine. "He was given as a slave to your uncle by my then future husband. They became friends and—"

"So that's who you are," interrupted Lucius, jumping up from his chair with the idea of giving Euric a warm embrace. But Euric saw it coming and grabbed Lucius by both forearms in the Germanic manner. "My uncle spoke of you often. You two did Tibur together."

"You mean they did every matron in Tibur together," said Cybelina, laughing. The lines around her eyes wrinkled, which did nothing to dampen her exquisite beauty. "Although this handsome thoroughbred still denies it to this day, I know the truth of their younger days together."

"It's so sad now that those days are over," said Euric. "I so miss the social gatherings, the impromptu, shall we say, entanglements of yesterday."

"Yesterday?" echoed Cybelina. "There's no such thing. The past doesn't exist, Euric. When you clap, there's sound, then nothing. So goes life. Bards die, meanings change, and memories fade."

Lucius thrived on conversations like this. He had missed having intellectual exchanges while living among the barbarians for the last four years. "When books are destroyed, what happens?" he asked.

"When books are destroyed, the words die," answered Cybelina. "The past—*poof*—is not only gone, it's forgotten. What is left is only the now."

"Wow! That's profound," said Lucius, slapping his forehead.

"Profound? Me? Ha! Your uncle was the philosopher, Lucius," said Cybelina. "Do you know what his brilliance was? He could speak every dialect of the conquered lands, recite poems from Sappho, and spew Martial's satires and Marsus's biting witticisms word for word. Barnabas could make snow in summer and blossoms in winter, remember the name of everyone he met, and make a woman tingle," she said, touching her breast.

"Your uncle was invited to every gathering during the season. Not only was he a clever wag, he could dance and sing to the shocking delight of the genteel." She paused a moment, gathering her thoughts. "Your uncle was the only man I ever loved. Then when the scaffolding collapsed on the north wall killing a senator's son at the same time my husband, Ibbas Alibas—an old and bitter man— found out about us, these two wounded aristocrats sought each other out and collaborated against your uncle. My husband did not act only because of me, mind you. No, he did it also because he himself was a jealous lover. He was infatuated with your uncle."

Lucius's eyes widened.

She smiled knowingly and said, "Yes, Lucius, your uncle had indiscretions with men as well as women. The summer season in Tibur accommodated all conceivable pleasures of the flesh. We lived in decadent times then, Lucius. When my husband and the senator, wounded by the loss of his son, insisted on retribution, society turned its back on your uncle. Nothing could have saved him then. He was condemned, sent to sea, and . . . well, you probably know the rest."

"Obviously not. What did the collapse have to do with any of it?"

"The work on the north wall was Barnabas's responsibility. He was an engineer, you recall, graduated with the highest honors from the academy. That was where my husband encountered your uncle and took him under his wing. Barnabas was given responsibility of the north wall repairs—a task he never took to or visited. It was his undoing."

"Who ordered the castration?"

"No one knows," said Euric. "An evil act of reprisal, it was. But we never found out."

"And why in the world did the three of you get involved with the gate episode—the Traitor's Gate?"

"It is hard to piece together. I speak of the gate when I say what we did brought the aristocracy and their high-brow *intelligentsia* to their knees, didn't we?" she asked, looking toward Euric for affirmation. "Revenge is such sweet nectar."

Euric rose, went to her side of the table, and took her hand. He must have seen the tears building in her eyes.

"We did what we did for what they did to Barnabas," said Euric, looking down at her. "And for what they did to us, the three of us. Sending him off on that slave ship ruined our lives as well."

She squeezed Euric's hand and let it drop, turning to Lucius. "You see, Lucius, our bitterness got out of hand," she explained. "It grew wings that manifested into hatred for everything in this city. And that horrid woman from Phrygia uncovered this hatred and used it against Rome. When she brought the idea to us, we thought it was a hoax from a disturbed mind. We never meant for it to go so far. So many great families were ruined, so many fled to Africa, Sardinia, Sicily, and Greece to never return. That entire episode created a desert where greatness once reigned. The city to this day has never recovered."

"And after the siege, who hung my uncle from the Salarian Gate?" asked Lucius matter-of-factly.

"We never found out. But the truth will emerge," said Cybelina, "it always does."

Lucius sat back, took a deep drink from his cup, and let out a sigh. "I actually know who, or I think I do. When I confirm it, I'll make sure you know."

"Good," was all she said. Surprisingly, Cybelina did not push the issue. The question now was why these two trusted him with information so dangerous to their persons. Were they being foolish or was he. The three continued talking late into the afternoon. And Euric continued to be very much a part of it.

When all was said that needed to be said about his uncle, and when he was satisfied that he'd heard all he needed to hear about the siege and its aftermath, the talk shifted to why he was in Rome. "I'm on a mission—a quest, if you will," he began, pulling out a letter from his cloak, handing it to Cybelina. "It's from Galla Placidia to certain senators of Rome introducing me as her spokesman. You can see from the seal that it is authentic."

"Go on," said Cybelina as she started to read it.

"Our goal—Galla's and mine—is to reverse all that her brother the emperor has done, or better said, not done. He hides behind the walls of Ravenna, has no heirs, and is easily influenced by the next person to walk through the door. This encourages every ambitious adventurer to take a chunk out of the West. Tyrants can smell weakness. And although Galla is a person of strength and pedigree, she recognizes that no woman has ever ruled. I am here to reverse that. But first she must be set free of the Goths."

"You mean ransomed," said Euric.

"Yes, ransomed."

"How?"

"I have the means. Please, ask no more. Just be assured it can be managed."

"Can we assume someone will use the treasure looted from the city to buy her freedom?" asked Cybelina.

"You might assume that, yes."

"How can we help?" she asked, leaning forward. "You do understand that some senators consider Galla Placidia to be an imperial snit, right? Not all, of course. Others think she was the only one with the mettle to make a stand when the Goths first knocked on the gates."

"She gave me the names of five men who may be like-minded. I'll write their names on that clay tablet sitting over there. Tell me the ones you can arrange for me to meet. Getting anywhere close to them has proven impossible."

"What specifically do you want of them?"

"We need their support if and when Honorius dies, or when another usurper from inside or outside Ravenna attempts to overthrow him. No more weak-kneed figureheads. The House of Theodosius must continue to rule." With that, he retrieved the clay tablet and wrote down several names. When he was finished, he handed the tablet to Cybelina.

She went down the list writing yes or no beside each name.

"Strange," she said, handing the tablet back to Lucius. "I happen to know that all five on this list are Hellenist, as am I. They secretly follow the ancient rites rather than submit to the state religion. This one," she said, pointing to the second name, "will be of little help. He is ill—maybe mad. But this one . . ." tapping the last name on the list, "....is an able man from a powerful family. He stays on his estate in Campania most of the time. I suggest you see his cousin, also a powerful senator but more inclined to the cerebral than action. He spends his days gathering letters his father wrote and editing them for posterity. You'll find him accessible with a willingness to listen once I recommend you."

Lucius nodded as she continued, "I will arrange for a meeting at once. He is indebted to me. Now then, there are others—not the landed aristocracy Galla sent you to see—but those who are addicted to power and wealth. The merchants of Rome hold great influence throughout the empire. The head of the Shipbuilders Guild, for example, helped me free your uncle from the slave ship when no one else could. His name is T. Rutilius Lucianus. Then there is M. Dasumis Maecianus, whose villa we used in Narni when plotting with that woman from Phrygia."

"You refer to Freya-Gund, of course."

"Yes, but I vowed never to say her name again. This Maecianus fellow leads the largest Funerary Guild in Rome. Some say no one dies without his permission. There are others. The point being, while the old ways are dying, an entire second layer of influence is willing to challenge the bureaucracy at Ravenna. All they need is leadership."

When darkness fell, the three went inside. Soon the drink took hold and they collapsed on the couches, falling asleep near the fire. The servants covered them and then snuffed the lanterns and candles. The grand villa fell silent. Lucius had not yet come to realize, probably because of the wine, that the gate leading to the power centers of Rome had swung open.

Irontooth was at the rail for the third time. He wiped the spittle off his mouth, turned to Tauriac, and shouted above the howling wind, "You sure this captain knows *v*hat he's doing?"

They had signed aboard a barnacle-laden freighter at Frejus as part of a six-boat flotilla. Just before dark, a sudden storm churned up the seas. Not long afterward they lost sight of the other ships. Then it got dark—very dark. The waves got higher, the wind shifted, and water began washing over the bow. It was the beginning of a very long night. The storm seemed to follow them. Toward morning another tempest hit with even greater force. The seas raged. One of the sails tore. Tauriac could hear the captain shouting, "Trim the bastards, you seadogs! Keep the prow pointed, damn you! Throw a line on the boom! Tighten that rigging!"

But nothing seemed to work. The ship was floundering. Whatever the captain did, the sea gods countered it. The storm was the master now. Then a wrenching jolt struck the starboard bow, a horrid scraping sounded along the keel unlike anything Tauriac had ever heard during his many years at sea. A second jolt followed. He held on knowing, one way or the other, that this could be the merciful end to a night of misery. The ship's bow rose sharply out of the water—then everything stopped. They were hard aground.

When the clouds parted, they could all see that the ship was stranded on the rocks of the thumb of Corsica. The captain signaled the skiff into the water with six of the strongest men aboard. Their orders were to attach a line to the stern and row the ship off. The rest of the crew, including Tauriac and Irontooth, used the long oars to push off. But the heavy ship would not budge; it was stuck fast.

Tauriac searched the craggy cliffs above and saw a wisp of smoke. It was enough. He knew what that smoke portended. Poking Irontooth, he whispered, "We've got to get off this thing. *Now.*"

"*Vhy?*"

"Our lives won't be worth spit if we don't."

They slipped below when the captain began shouting orders at the skiff crew. Gathering their things, they waited for the right moment. When it came, they jumped into the water and waded ashore. They could hear the captain's angry epithets as they disappeared into the woodlands that crowded the rocky shore. Tauriac had been at sea enough times to know what the captain apparently had not yet realized. He soon would. Not only was the ship finished, but danger lurked in those hills.

Before they could go far, they were jumped by two men and two grown boys. But the attackers were no match for the two hardened warriors. Killing one man, they disabled the other as the two boys ran off up the hill. Tauriac stepped over the wounded one, gave him an uncaring smile, and slit his throat.

They followed the boys up the hill, making sure they weren't seen. The trail led to a mountain hamlet. Hiding in the woods, they waited. Soon enough, as Tauriac predicted, the two boys led a mob of about eighteen armed men down the mountain and past the place where Tauriac and Irontooth hid, no doubt assuming they had run back to the safety of the ship. But the ship was the last place Tauriac wanted to be. When Irontooth started to get up, Tauriac held him down.

"Wait," he whispered. "There'll be more." Soon enough, four boys ran past carrying coils of rope with treble hooks. "I knew it," Tauriac mumbled, slapping Irontooth on the back. "Follow me."

They crept closer to the hamlet. The big house on the edge of the hill caught Tauriac's attention immediately. When they were certain only women and children remained in the hamlet, they inched closer. Hiding behind a stack of firewood, they watched until the women grew tired of gossiping and returned to their chores. Tauriac kept his eyes trained on the big house. When a woman and two girls emerged and headed for the barn, they crawled around back. Built on a hillside, the rear of the house was supported by six finely carved heavy timbers—the kind used to build ships. The window above them had a pane of thick, strange looking glass in it. They found a ladder under the house, put it up to the side, and climbed to and through one of the two shuttered windows hinged at the top by large, brass hinges. Once inside they found lanterns, nets, stacks of coiled rope with treble hooks attached with square knots, and a heavy table with holes in the legs so it could be bolted to the floor.

"These people are wreckers," said Tauriac. "See all this? They make a living off disasters like ours. That's why there're no lanterns or stakes marking them rocks. These kindly folks *want* ships to run aground. Look at this," he said, and he reached into a trunk and pulled out boots tied in pairs and a stack of neatly folded breeches. He found a pair of boots that matched his feet and set them aside. "Might as well take what we need." He laughed. "They surely did."

Tauriac looked out the window searching for something. "There!" he shouted, pointing. "See that platform. It's a lookout."

He put on one of the owner's cloaks and a floppy hat, just in case he was spotted by one of the women. Crossing the yard, he climbed the ladder to the top of the high platform. Immediately Tauriac spotted their ship on the rocks below, three-quarters to a mile away as the crow flies. The ship was under attack by the hamlet people. He looked south and spotted smoke from a town on the other side of the thumb, a distance of about twenty miles. He then turned his attention back to the fighting below to see how much time he and Irontooth had. Already one of the treble hooks had snared the rigging. Then another caught the railing, a third snagged the bowsprit, and another the stern. The ship was now firmly anchored to the rocks. Soon it would be finished. The crew aboard would meet the same fate as all the unlucky seamen before had. Those in the skiff rowed away as fast as they could, but the inevitable would soon catch up with them as well.

Tauriac returned to the house. "Those poor bastards are done for," he said. "Get your head out of that sea chest. It's time to leave."

But before they could, two girls followed by a woman came through the door, the woman carrying a bucket. One of the girls was blonde with blue eyes unlike the darker people of the hamlet. Tauriac immediately grabbed the woman and clamped a hand over her mouth spilling the bucket of milk onto the floor. Irontooth took hold of the blonde and put a knife to her throat. That hushed the girls up.

After tying the younger one to a post, Irontooth dragged the blonde behind the bedroom curtain, drove his knife into the wall above the bed, and began to have his way with her. Tauriac released the older woman, jumped through the curtain, grabbed Irontooth by the back of his belt and pulled him off. "You damn fool!" he shouted. "Losing a life while trying to take one is the price a thief pays. My people were wreckers. I know how they think. But abusing their women is a misdeed for which they will hunt you down to the end of the earth. Let's not inflame these sorry sots any more. They have a comfortable life doing what they do, why despoil it and ours by doing something stupid."

Irontooth pulled out a second knife, ready to challenge his comrade. "Don't be a fool," Tauriac said. "A man can buy a little *cubitus* anywhere. Now sheath that damn thing and let's get out of here."

They bound and gagged the three. Then they slipped away toward the distant village that Tauriac had spotted from the tower taking only those items that suited their needs.

Euric led Lucius through Rome to a meeting with Fabius Memmius Symmachus, one of the powerful men Galla Placidia had instructed him to see and, coincidently, a close acquaintance of Cybelina. He resided, of course, on the Palatine. On their way, they came across an insula that had collapsed days earlier. The smell from the rotting corpses fouled the air. The building once held twenty flats of poor people. Lucius's disgust with his first week in Rome escalated.

Upon entering the finely detailed villa, and once the customary introductions were complete, Lucius and his host Memmius Symmachus moved to the tablinum where they exchanged polite words until Lucius could no longer contain his frustration. "For days I have toured this sewer you refer to as the 'City of Light' and have witnessed an ugliness below what I thought humanly possible. Does not the prefect of the city see this as well?"

"See what?" asked his host, obviously taken back by this opening barrage.

"Your *primores*, the 'landed aristocracy' as they haughtily refer to themselves, obviously came into this world with one eye closed. Oh, I see my words stun you. I understand you feel insulted, but hear me out. The aristocracy of this city appears disinterested in helping their fellow men: not *one* sorry soul do they minister to, not *one* room do they heat, and not *one* pot do they fill. Don't get up!" Lucius ordered, throwing up his hand when Memmius started to bolt.

"I beg you to stay and listen." Lucius's outburst surprised even him. His experiences this week compromised any pretense of good manners. "The noble are anything but noble; in fact, from what I've seen, they are cruel, not only to their slaves, but to their agents, neighbors, and *coloni*. The upper class emote a superior air that says all things that exist, exist for their advantage, as if everything was created solely for their comfort. And the Subura—have you been there? It's a living hell. So much neglect. How do you permit such a place to continue?"

"And how is it in your Umbria?" asked Memmius smugly.

"Different. Better. Humane. Our 'landed aristocracy,' if you will, although I hate that designation, was led by a man who saw to it, as did others, that the wealth was shared—not equally mind you—but equitably."

"Pfff! Foolishness!"

"Foolishness, eh? All right. Then suffer, if you will, a few more of my vinegary observations. My father gave a partnership in our estate to a family that was indentured for a minor crime long forgotten. They lived in our house, and the father, now a freedman thanks to my father, became my father's keeper, his youngest my best friend. Of course Umbria has villainous sorts like every municipality: the slave trader, the innkeeper, the governor who took his own life once exposed as a practitioner of the forbidden Rite of the Bull. That, sir, is a tale you might enjoy. Even our bishop had to be dealt with for his outrageous arrogance."

"Okay, okay, I see."

"No, to a certain extent, I don't think you do. Your lips say it, but . . ." Lucius let it hang. "Before I was born, our entire valley was hit by a strange blight that ruined the olive trees. This generous man I referred to brought thousands of saplings in from the isle of Corfu and distributed them freely throughout the seven cities of the valley. He felt it his duty. He had scribes copy all the great works, not just for his pleasure, but to teach others. His library held forty thousand books and scrolls. There was never a day that he did not do a good deed for someone." Lucius leaned forward, closer to Memmius.

"And when the invaders entered our valley," he continued, "my mentor drove to their encampment and asked them: 'Why are you here?' Unafraid, he first berated and then befriended their chieftain. The result, you may wish to ask? Our valley was saved. Their friendship was founded on mutual respect, not fear. When a Gothic envoy pushed on to Rome, the Senate here laughed, belittled their demands for the gold promised them for keeping Dalmatia quiet— and then ordered the guards to throw rocks down on their heads. You know the rest. They returned here with sixty-five thousand strong. The point is that I see only boorish behavior here, not generosity. Handing out a small measure of bread to placate the classes is not generosity; it's an effort to keep the masses hushed so the primores feel safe in their villas, at the hot baths in Spoletium, in Tibur enjoying the cool air or the ocean-side breezes at Formiae. May I suggest you climb that hill over there—what do you call it?"

"Mount Anio."

"Yes, Mount Anio. Climb it and look down as surely as the gods look down on you. Fill your soul with what you see: the selfishness, the idleness, and, most importantly, the lack of awareness. One day these buildings will crumble and the people will leave. Then there will be nothing left. *Nothing!* No one to empty your night pot, till the soil, feed your mules, transcribe your indolent letters, or man your oars to help you escape the hell you created. Since the senatorial aristocracy is incapable of anything but leisure, the rubble will turn to dust, the land will lie fallow, the harbors will silt—already Ostia has—and your grain ships shall sink from worm rot. No Roman, no matter his heritage, no matter his appointment, has the right to do so much wrong."

As Lucius spoke, Memmius Symmachus' face slowly drained of blood, his hand curled, and his foot began to tap to a rhythm that most certainly beat inside his breast. While Memmius slumped inside his toga, Lucius rose and walked about. A heavy burden lifted from his soul.

Clearing his throat, Memmius feigned an attempt at propriety. "Can I invite you for the noon meal? My cousin Aurelius Anicius Symmachus is at one of the family estates in Campania . . . Apulia I believe. You absolutely must share your opinions with him when he returns."

"And when might that be?" asked Lucius.

"On the third day before the kalends; however, I warn you, he and I are not of the same temperament. He may be provoked sufficiently to strike you across the face."

"Duly warned," replied Lucius with a big smile. They moved along the colonnaded walkway to the atrium where two small tables had been set in front of the fireplace. Lucius removed his cloak as his host sat. "Now, sir, may I get to the purpose for which I requested this audience."

"Good," said Memmius. "I'm pleased your anger is sated."

"Thank you. I was not angry, just discouraged. Now then, I am here to seek your help and that of your cousin Anicius' in a most vital enterprise. I wish to save Rome from the abyss of which I just spoke."

"Save Rome is it." And he laughed politely. "You are here to save Rome." Memmius rose from his small, backless chair, walked to the fireplace, and poked it with an iron. He then motioned to one of the house slaves. "Teresa, come. Please bring this wizard-of-the-absurd a live chicken. Let's see if he can kill, pluck, and prepare it for our midday meal as an assessment of his powers. You see, he wants to save Rome."

Lucius thought about Memmius's reaction for a moment, and then laughed. "Now, sir," Lucius said holding on to the wide smile, "that wit you just demonstrated might be the basis of a fine friendship. I apologize for my audacity. Nevertheless, I assure you I am quite serious."

Four days later Lucius returned to Memmius's villa on the Palatine. They strolled about the peristyle garden talking about the warm winter day. A tall slender man passed through the atrium and approached them. "Ah, my favorite cousin," the man said in a deep, well-varnished voice, grasping the shorter Memmius by the shoulders. Lucius knew at once who dominated this relationship.

"May I present Lucius Domitilla of Umbria," said Memmius, struggling to break free of his cousin's grasp. "Please, Aurelius, enjoy the fresh air with us. It is a lovely day, isn't it?"

The tall man looked around the garden, spotted a couch under the overhang, and motioned for a servant to move it closer. When it was positioned just right, he reclined.

"Ah," said Lucius. "You prefer the old ways. I myself choose the new habits."

"Then the barbarians have gotten to you as they have to my cousin here. Now, my new friend, to business: My name is Aurelius Anicius Symmachus." He spoke with such upper-class nuance that Lucius knew he enjoyed reminding people he was a member of the most prominent patrician family in Rome.

"My mentor often mentioned to me the name Symmachus."

"I'm not surprised. And who might your mentor be?" asked Aurelius.

"Ponti Filipi," he answered, looking for an acknowledgement. Receiving none, he continued, "Ponti Lepius Filipi of the equally well-known Lepii family."

Receiving no more than a raised eyebrow, Lucius assumed Aurelius was playing with him, so he added, "When only a year or two older than I am now, my mentor was a member of the Methodus along with your uncle, Quintus Aurelius Symmachus."

Anicius sat straight up. "What, pray tell, do you know of the Methodus, my friend?" he asked, jumping to his feet and hastily closing all the doors leading to the atrium and the tablinum.

"Everything," said Lucius, aware he had struck a nerve. "How they put Julian on the throne. I know the whole scheme from beginning to end. How they—"

"Never mind the details," interrupted Memmius. "I have all my father's letters and diaries. There is not one reference to the Methodus."

"Of course not," said Lucius at once aware that this was his leverage. "Since Julian's short reign was such a disaster—or should I say 'unpopular with the Christians'—I quite imagine all letters and diaries dealing with the affair were burned long ago. All but one, that is. That one Ponti kept in a box in his tablinum. And it so happens that I found that letter after his death," he lied. "In the letter, Quintus Aurelius Symmachus, your famous ancestor, speaks honestly and openly of the Julian affair. And he specifically mentions how the Methodus paid dozens of centurions and two tribunes a pound of silver each to, let's say, *motivate* the legionaries to elevate Julian from Caesar to Augustus by proclamation fully aware that adding Augustus to his title would create a civil war. Yes, a civil war gentlemen, pitting the followers of the ancient rites against the official Christian church as well as the ordained ruler over East and West, Constantius."

"We are very familiar with the affair," said Aurelius. "Life is not measured by the breaths we take but, as Cicero said, these breathless moments in time. Now, sir, may we have this letter."

"Of course you may," said Lucius. "I have no cause to bring disgrace upon your house. Its disclosure would be like a ball of flaming tar hitting the House of Symmachus."

"Well . . . ?" Aurelius asked, holding out his hand.

"It's in Umbria. When traveling to Ravenna, I will rescue this document from its hiding place and burn it. There's no reason to have the good Symmachus name destroyed. Now, can we move on? I wish to discuss the purpose for which I came to Rome."

"Please," said Aurelius.

"Form, flavor, and cleverness are the lessons I learned from Ponti Lepius."

"Of the pen?" asked Memmius, his interest piqued.

"No," he laughed. "Of the tongue, my new friends, of the tongue—can't you tell? I, Lucius Domitilla of Umbria, wish to share a dream. That dream is to save the collapse of the Senatorial aristocracy by saving Rome. Rome has reverted to a city-state, a still powerful one of course, but within a collapsing empire. Ravenna has lost its ability to lead; the emperor only oversees. We need a leader, not an overseer."

"For every successful dream, a thousand die," said Aurelius.

"Indeed," said Lucius. "And for every failure, ten thousand lives are destroyed. How many usurpers can we endure? Isn't it time we put a stop to these adventurers? Galla Placidia sent me to you, gentlemen, to see if you are of like minds." Lucius pulled out the letter from Galla Placidia, the daughter of Theodosius the Great.

Back in Corsica, Tauriac and Irontooth arrived at the small town of Mariana—the place Tauriac spotted from the mountain hamlet. It was a disappointment; the harbor was not busy and the town had no means of sea transport. They were directed farther down the coast to Aleria. They wasted three days getting there. A vibrant place, it had everything, including a smoking emporium and a row of brothels. After a night at the emporium smoking hemp, it did not take long for them to find an ore barge in need of two oarsmen. It was bound for Tarqinii. Blessed with an easy crossing, they at last arrived on the coast of Italy. Although their hands and arms ached from rowing, it mattered little. Soon that little twit Lucius would be dead and they rich. They set out walking the fifty-eight miles to Rome on the Via Aurelia, one of the oldest roads in the empire. And from the condition, it looked it.

"These are men who once read the entrails of chickens for guidance," complained Lucius. "Now they propose a common sense approach to succession."

Lucius had just returned to Cybelina's villa from his third meeting with the Symmachus cousins, attended this time by five "like-minded" senators. Cybelina smiled like she knew more than she would allow herself to reveal. "Go on," she urged Lucius. "I'm interested in how you handled this."

"They claim that six years ago Galla stood silently by while Stilicho's widow was executed, and that she did even less when the son, Eucheris, was strangled. Did you know Serena was so admired?"

"Yes, of course I knew; a tragedy of the worst proportions. A simple appeal by Galla to her brother Honorius would have halted it all: Stilicho's beheading by Heraclian, then Serena's garroting, followed by Eucheris's strangling upended the entire community. Odd, isn't it? Most certainly she had her reasons. But I cannot possibly imagine what they were. Serena and Stilicho helped to raise Galla after her father died, you know."

"Further, none of the senators believe she was kidnapped by the Goths. They think she ran off. I was in Narbo with her and told them the truth—she was kidnapped. The first year was a living hell for Galla. She only improved her condition through guile. What I witnessed there was a heroine, not a traitor. Galla did not abandon Rome."

"What were their reactions to her marriage to the Gothic king?"

"They all see it as a disgrace," said Lucius. "One even said she should have killed herself before submitting to such humiliation."

"Everyone you met, all those on Galla's list, are Hellenist— followers of the ancient rites. Yet Galla herself is an ardent Christian. I find it hard to believe that she thought support would come from men such as these."

"Maybe one of these senators has higher ambitions. Had you thought of that?" he asked.

"That escaped me. But it would explain a lot."

"They didn't just oppose everything I said. They bitterly rejected my ideas, as if they were prompted or rehearsed. I argued, 'You need someone to believe in. Why not Galla? She has the pedigree.'"

"What was their answer?"

"'We already have someone we believe in.' So there you have it. They have someone. There was not one thread of loyalty in that room for Rome, the people, *or* the House of Theodosius. They think only of themselves. Every man in that room was potbellied and pale skinned, except for Aurelius Anicius Symmachus—not what I hoped to find. I became accustomed to living among the barbarians over the last four years. Those are real men, not refined lumps of lard."

"Now, now, now, you're overreacting. Let me arrange a meeting with a few others," she said, trying to buoy his spirits.

"Thank you, but no. No more effeminate aristocracy, please. I plan to go to Ravenna in a few days. My associate, Mahaki, is making the arrangements."

"Hmm."

"Cybelina, do you know that not one of those senators has any idea how much gold the invaders of this city got away with, especially the Burgundians?"

"Not to mention the Statue of Fortune," said Cybelina.

Lucius's jaw dropped unable to conceal his surprise.

"You didn't realize I knew about the statue, did you? Who do you think helped your uncle locate it? Old men in Tibur have a tendency to reveal too much in the heat of passion—especially wrinkly old men."

"Freya-Gund used my uncle, and he wasn't old. In the years following his release from the slave ship, he became the laughingstock of our municipality—a drunk who left his manhood hanging on a mandrel literally and figuratively. Then Freya-Gund brought him back to life. Whatever she asked, he did. You knew that, of course."

"I didn't at first," said Cybelina, "but I did after it was too late. Also, Lucius, that is not a very pleasant picture you paint of him. I loved your uncle very much."

"Sorry."

Four days earlier, Freya-Gund, still in disguise, sat against the wall of Narbo watching the triumphant king of the Goths lead his guard through the gates. They had been successful in their campaign against Tolosa. And yesterday, word that the queen was with child—in fact, very well along with child—began to circulate among the citizenry. Now, today, the news circulating the marketplace was that the king was moving his command to Barcelona, maybe within the month.

Up till now, Freya-Gund had not received so much as a trace of information about where the jewels were hidden. This convinced her that the only one who knew was the queen—which did not surprise her. The queen was not only smart but careful. An hour ago, though, she learned that Singerich's source of information was the queen's personal servant, a young woman named Sara. If Singerich could extract secrets from a peasant wench, so could she. *A sorceress has ways a man never thought possible*, she thought. It would not be the first time she used the lure of the animal to get what she wanted. The feat would require a new disguise, a warm bath, and some scented saffron. Freya-Gund fingered the metal pendant around her neck, thinking of the undulating body of a young, naked woman. A hint of saliva ran down the side of her well-formed chin.

While Lucius readied the two-wheeled gig for departure, the innkeeper rushed up. "I forgot," he blurted breathlessly, "a messenger came and begged for you not to leave until a man named Euric arrived. He said you would understand."

Lucius thanked him and continued strapping their belongings into the area behind the seat. Mahaki had arranged for the gig and the two horses—a spotted white and a roan. He had seen better horses, but Mahaki said they were sturdy enough. The little man had finished with his business for the season and was readying to return to Ancona when Lucius convinced him to travel north with him.

The loading complete, Lucius was retreating to the warmth of the inn when a carriage and wagon pulled up. The door opened and Euric stepped to the ground, followed by Cybelina. She shouted,

"You can't leave just yet." Then she motioned to one of her attendants who ran over with a tightly rolled bundle. "Here," she said. "It's a blanket of greased goat hair. Traveling in an open gig is much too chilly in winter. The blanket's warmth will keep you comfortable; the grease will keep you dry. You shall thank me when you return one day."

Lucius took the rolled bundle and handed it to Mahaki, who tossed it in the gig.

"Also," she said, "I have arranged for you to have this." She handed Lucius a pouch with an official seal on the outside. "It is authorization from the urban prefect to use the *cursus publicus.* Bribes were paid to obtain it; however, there are restrictions. You must avoid two of the inns. And beware, half the innkeepers along the way are thieves, the other half worse. I exaggerate, of course— but not by much. So, to further protect you on your journey, I want you to wear one of these." She gave him two rings of a different size. "See which one fits; little finger, left hand. *Always* the little finger, left hand—remember that. Go ahead, try them on."

Lucius looked puzzled.

"I will explain. First, see which one fits."

The first one was too large. The second fit perfectly. Lucius examined the ring more closely. It was made of dull iron, the large stone was black and in the shape of a hand. He raised an eyebrow. "Now what?"

"Show this to the innkeepers by doing this." She itched her left cheek with her left hand and then tugged on her left earlobe. "The message is in the ring. Anyone can steal a gesture. Be assured, Lucius, you shall be safe after you pull that ear. You need to know no more than that. Now then, my young friend, may the gods watch over you both on this long journey. Here." She slipped a leather pouch into his hand and withdrew into the carriage. The pouch was full of gold coins.

"Who was that?" asked Mahaki, watching the carriage and wagon continue on down the road.

"A loyal friend," he said dryly. "She goes to my uncle's grave to dream of yesterday, all the while professing there are no 'yesterdays.' Now, Mahaki, I have one errand to run before we depart. Go inside and keep warm if you like. I won't be long." With that, Lucius headed toward the Salarian Gate. The blind beggar was in his usual spot against the wall. Lucius had avoided the gate since their last encounter. Approaching the blind beggar as silently as he could, he dropped a handful of gold coins into his cup before the man knew he was there.

"What is this?" he asked, moving his head back and forth trying to locate the donor.

"It's me," said Lucius.

"Ah, my Umbrian friend. Where have you been hiding?"

"Around. I've been investigating you."

"Ah. And what have you found?"

"Much, and not all bad," said Lucius with a smile in his voice.

"Oh?"

"I have met the aristocracy on the Palatine and the poor in Subura and a few in between. With their help, I have woven a tapestry of your deeds."

"Is that a fact." It was not a question.

"For example, the Hostia innkeeper said you and your friends take the helpless and provide them warmth in winter so they do not freeze; and nurture the hungry so they do not starve. That was what I witnessed in the passageway beneath the city. Instead of a chamber of horrors, it is a cocoon for those who cannot do for themselves. That is why they call you Alfadur. Let me tell you, my good friend, your work is known from Subura to the Palatine and under the bridges across the Tiber. All-Father, you are a guardian in thief's clothing."

"That's a bit strong, don't you think. Our rewards come. We live in peace and eat well. Yes, we were going to transfer some of your good fortune to others, but only if you refused a voluntary donation. Now, young man, you be about your business and let me be about mine. Say nothing of this to anyone, and you will serve me well. Have a safe journey north."

"How did you . . . ?"

"Never mind how, but I do learn things. Just know this: my friends and I are here if you need help in your worthwhile endeavors."

❖

Back in Narbo, Freya-Gund found the opportunity to transform herself from a decrepit beggar woman to a seer. It was not difficult. An old woman who had once made her living reading the entrails of chickens had the costume, jewelry, and head wrap that Freya-Gund needed, plus a colorful tent in which to sit lined in gold fringe tassels. To further disguise herself, she wore a vulgar amulet on her forehead, colored her face, blackened her eyes, and braided her hair, twirling it atop her head.

She set up the tent near the open market a hundred paces left of the east gate. There she waited. Sara, Galla Placidia's handmaiden shopped at this market two days a week. At the first chance, Freya-Gund lured Galla's servant into her tent with the offer of a free reading. Using her persuasive powers, Freya-Gund quickly aroused the young woman's interest in the future—she was young and, most importantly, vulnerable. She whispered secrets Sara thought no one knew, unsettled her with lurid prospects, titillated her with forbidden subjects, and ingratiated her with soft lighting, scented fragrances, and sensual touching. By the third session, Sara begged to return; from top to bottom the girl was under Freya-Gund's influence. The next step would be to immerse Sara in the corporal world of Sappho. That would take place at the baths of Narbo. Though decrepit, the baths were available for a price, or, in Freya-Gund's case, a promise. With little coaxing, she obtained use of the bath when normally not in use—the middle of the night. This seduction was going to be easy, the salacious method irresistible.

Lucius woke up sweating. Something was wrong. He looked around the room, checked his vest. Nothing was wrong, everything was fine. What was it? Out of the fog of sleep, it all came back to him. The nightmare! The same one that haunted him since leaving Bruné-Hilda on that island, the dream where he watched helplessly as she walked to the beach, disrobed, turned to show off her scars, and then walked into the sea. Her words echoed in his head. "I can't live without you, Lucius! I can't live without you! I can't possibly live without you!" It ended with the sea swallowing her.

He shook himself and then looked over at the other bed where Mahaki was sound asleep. Taking a deep breath, Lucius got up, walked to the window, and pushed open one of the shutters. Still dark, the half-moon was just above the trees. This was their second night on the road to Ravenna. They had arrived at the posting station late, having had trouble with the left wheel. And when the stable master said they were locked down for the night and would not take in the horses, and the innkeeper wanted double for getting him out of bed, the iron ring Cybelina gave him worked wonders. Having no idea why, but the simple gesture of scratching his cheek with the ring finger and pulling his left ear suddenly made the impossible doable.

The first day out of Rome, because of their late start, they made it to Falerii. The second day, because of the wheel, they only made it here, to Narnia. Lucius retreated from the window and lay back down. When Mahaki woke, they ate and then were in the gig again heading north. At Narnia the "old" Via Flaminia separated from the "new."

"Strange, isn't it," said Lucius, snapping the reins more out of boredom than need, "that the so-called New Flaminia is hundreds of years old yet they still call it 'new.'"

"That's because the old one still exists—still used by the locals when dry."

"How do you know all that?" asked Lucius.

"Remember, I'm an estate manager. Knowing the roads is part of my profession. Getting product to customers is an iffy thing. We don't ship everything by water to Rome. There are hundreds of hamlets and municipalities within range of Ancona."

"I didn't know you worked in this region."

"Your memory is, at times, lacking, yet also frighteningly precise. Did you forget that you knocked me into a ditch at the Hundred Mile Bridge?" Mahaki asked with a smile.

"Of course. And I distinctly remember you saying, 'One day I will tell you the story behind the rock tied to that thong.' Remember? You gave it to me four years ago. I threw away the rock but still have the thong."

The comment put a pained expression on Mahaki's face. "And one day I shall tell you the story, Lucius. Today is not that day." With that, and nothing else to talk about, Lucius slumped back into boredom, occasionally snapping the whip to break the monotony.

The Via Flaminia ran straight as an arrow. A few of the six-foot mile markers still existed, although most had been stolen to serve a more immediate purpose. The roadway in this section was paved with large tufa blocks laid at angles atop a bed of broken stones and pebbles that were sealed with a cement-sand base. The tunnels and bridges were wide, the ditches deep enough to hold the runoff. Most of the curbstones, though, had long since been put to another use as well. Roadways were among Rome's greatest achievements, but their upkeep of late was a disgrace. At the seventy-eighth mile marker from Rome, they arrived at Spoletium.

"Isn't that a magnificent sight," said Lucius as they approached, nudging the half-asleep Mahaki. "Those walls held strong against Hannibal. Even the Goths gave them plenty of room fearful of the deadly darts thrown by the Ballista."

"Often its reputation is stronger than the weapon itself. The dart thrower is a highly inaccurate tool of war. What's that building?" asked Mahaki.

"A Christian Basilica, certainly the most beautiful in the region since the one atop Mt. Este was destroyed. Myth has it that cyclopes resided here long before the walls were built."

"I love myths," said Mahaki. "They tease the imagination."

"Indeed they do . . . particularly yours. Who are you really?" asked Lucius.

Mahaki harrumphed, slumped back without answering and closed his eyes.

They went as far as Forum Flaminii that day, situated on the edge of the Umbrian Valley. The horses were tired, as was Mahaki, so they stayed the night. Lucius hated the place. It brought back too many memories, so many of them bad. The man who'd kept the Forum "alive" as a cover for his smuggling activities—Junius Probus—was dead. With the loss of his controlling hand, the posting station was no longer well kept and the large market shed was now used for storage. Lucius recalled how the barbarian warlords used the shed to plot their final assault on Rome. The innkeeper complained that the life was sucked out of the Forum the summer of the barbarian occupation. He had no idea of Lucius's involvement in the affair, and Lucius decided to keep it that way.

Strangely, during their time there, Mahaki kept his headdress on and the lower half of his face covered by the trailing scarf. Lucius paid it no mind, but he should have inquired why the little man retreated into his little cocoon when around people. The next day, over Mahaki's objections, Lucius detoured down the Via Umbria toward the municipality of his birthplace.

On the road to Assisi, they passed the pink walls of Spello. Lucius told Mahaki of Bruné-Hilda's great feat there: how she beat the six champions of the valley during the spring festival. Her father had been so proud of his "little princess," a name he'd given her before she was one; and how that victory put him back into the giant Gunther's good graces.

Six miles beyond Spello they reached Assisi. The biggest surprise was that there was no surprise except for the walls. Assisi was almost exactly as he left it four years ago when he and Bruné-Hilda departed for the North Country. The gray scars from the mudslide were still visible, and the walls, once buried in mud, had fully emerged. Sitting out in the open before the walls was the smithy's house and barn; and the large boulder where Lucius and Jucundus once sold honey biscuits and spring water still remained, though it was now surrounded by scrub bushes. The road south to the other side of the valley appeared heavily tracked, which meant that Monbelluna was still using the water from the Sacred Springs of Assisi, and no structure had replaced the church atop Mt. Este. That, he had not expected. Surely the bishop would have rebuilt it by now.

"Brings back memories?" asked Mahaki.

"More than you know, my friend. All that happened here is seared into my memory." Standing up in the gig, he pointed. "Up there, to the right, see; beyond the wall, a third of the ways up. That's where I was born and lived until the night my world slid down the mountain. Above it, nearly to the top, stood Capricorne, Ponti Lepius Filipi's grand villa, the finest in all Umbria. The slide took it and everything this side of Boethius Frugi's barbershop. Everything up there"—he pointed again—"ended up down here on the valley floor. My parents remain buried somewhere out there with hundreds of good, caring citizens."

Lucius paused for a moment reflecting, and then continued, "By some miracle, the barbershop survived—you can see it from here now that the other buildings are gone. Statius Agaclytus's shop of lamps and wicks also remains. But everything there," he ran his finger on an angle, "down to there," pointing to the wall, "disappeared."

"How did you survive?" asked Mahaki.

"Me? Ha!" he said, sitting back down in the gig. "That's a long story. I was in the vault, the bishop's treasure vault, beneath the altar. Like a fool, I was trying to save him from the Avars while he was trying to protect what he stole from the temple and his faithful parishioners. I didn't know that at the time, you understand. When the church collapsed, I was trapped under it."

"How in the name of Jove did—"

"A tunnel, my friend, a tunnel some people dug centuries ago that had been long forgotten. It led to the stone quarry on the back side of Mt. Este. The force of the collapse revealed an opening beneath the bishop's treasure vault that led to the tunnel. I made my way out with six sacks of hidden reliquaries, chalices and religious trinkets and the knowledge that the goodly bishop was a thief. Eventually, I returned half to the faithful. The rest, those items he looted from the temple, I took with me to Scanborg and then across the Alps to Worms."

"When the bishop finds out you're back, then what?"

Lucius shrugged but did not answer.

"Don't call me madam, Sara, call me sister," Freya-Gund said as they entered the bathhouse on the south end of Narbo. It was empty as Freya-Gund wanted.

Sara looked Freya-Gund full in the face, any sign of servitude gone. "I'll call you *madam* if it pleases me, thank you."

Freya-Gund knew then that this young woman was no easy mark. She had cracked tougher ones, but they were men. Pulling from her bodice a metal pendant suspended on a leather thong, she asked, "Does this mean anything to you?"

Sara inspected it carefully. Then she answered disinterestedly, "No. Looks to me like a piece of bronze rubbish."

"Aren't you the sassy one. I thought you of Gothic blood," said Freya-Gund.

"Of course I am." She paused and then added sarcastically, "Well, partly. The other part"—she laughed—"the other part my mother wasn't too certain of. She shared her charms with so many."

"This piece of 'rubbish,' as you call it, is the Rune of Thurisaz, the Demon Rune. I thought you said—"

"I lied, madam. I'd say anything to get an evening away from the palace."

Freya-Gund took a deep breath. "Never mind," she mumbled and tucked the pendant back into her bodice. A rage began to build within her. She grabbed Sara's arm, ready to punish her insolence, and then stopped when her fingers touched the girl's soft, young flesh. A tingling washed over Freya-Gund's body. In that instant, she knew this encounter was going to be a singularly unique experience. She was not only materialistically attracted to the young servant girl but physically as well—irresistibly so. Could she be walking in the shadow of her younger self?

Passing beyond a second set of doors, they stopped. Freya-Gund gave the servant girl a tender hug, apologized for her brusqueness, and began massaging her shoulders and back. Sara responded with a sigh. The gentle rubbing seemed to please the girl, so Freya-Gund shifted to the more responsive side of her body. Saying nothing, she slowly walked her fingers across Sara's breasts and up to her lips. Gently, ever so gently, she pushed her finger past those tender, young lips and began to stroke Sara's tongue as one might a butterfly. That generated a different response, one more sensual. Sara was ready to be taken as had so many before her.

Moving to the pool's edge, Freya-Gund removed her stola and let drop her chemise. Then she tossed a handful of saffron into the pool and slipped into the warmth of its waters.

"Come, Sara," she whispered in an enticingly low voice. "It's so very soothing. Please join me."

Obediently, Sara stepped to the edge, unfastened her girdle, kicked off her sandals, and let drop the ankle-length tunic. She stood there for a second, showing off her young body. Compact, rolling, and magnificently agile it was. Her nipples firmed as she slipped into the water.

Freya-Gund was instantly there kissing and fondling, crazy with lust. Sara's response was equally unrestrained. She wrapped a leg around Freya-Gund's hip and pressed. Their tongues engaged, and Freya-Gund became lost in the moment. In that heated, enchanting flash, the seducer became the seduced. It would not do. To regain control, Freya-Gund reached up, grabbed the girl's hair, and yanked. With her other hand, she explored the outer reaches of Sara's femininity. Now it was Sara's turn to submit—actually, she seemed to like it rough. The deeper Freya-Gund probed, the more the girl's heart pounded, her grip tightened, and her hips thrust. Although consistent with other licentious encounters in Freya-Gund's life— and she had experienced many with both sexes—this one had already exceeded her expectations. Just when Sara was about to reach her peak, Freya-Gund forced herself to stop.

"Uh! Oo, oo . . ." Sara moaned, continuing to climb that unending hill of gratification. "What are—why did you . . . ?" She threw her other leg around Freya-Gund's hip. "Come on."

"The gems, Sara, where are the gems?" Freya-Gund whispered.

"More, come on, give me more!"

"Where!" she spat. "Where are the gems hidden!"

"Don't tease me, please, please. Finish, please, I'm nearly there," Sara begged, frantically kissing Freya-Gund over and over. "I beg you! Finish me!"

But Freya-Gund, having fully regained control, was not about to concede. She pulled back, and for reasons even she did not understand, she grabbed Sara's throat with both hands and pushed her under the water.

Letting up for a second, she screamed, "Where are they hidden, you bitch!" Getting no answer, she pushed Sara under again. After a time, she pulled her back up.

"Okay! Okay!" Sara said frantically grabbing at Freya-Gund's hair.

The headband flew off, and Freya-Gund's plaited hair cascaded down around her shoulders. The thick face paint she had used to disguise her features was now running down her neck and onto her chest. She was no longer the teller of the future. Instead of turning away to replace her headband and readjust her disguise, she unwisely took a step back to regroup.

Sara took a long look at her seductress, blinked twice, and then announced coolly, "I know you." She shouted coughing up more water. "I've made a shambles of your disguise, haven't I? You're not a seer at all, are you? You're that woman, that Burgundian woman my mistress detests."

She should not have said that.

Freya-Gund stiffened; she could not let her presence in Narbo be known. "Go on," she seethed through clenched teeth. "Tell me what else your mistress says of me." Freya-Gund was not really interested in what Galla Placidia or anyone else in Narbo thought of her. She just needed time to come up with a new plan, and quickly. This one was not working, her deception had been uncovered. The girl knew.

Sara immediately realized that she had said too much. Instead of melting before the great sorceress of the North, infuriated by the attempt to deceive her, Sara reacted the only way she knew how. The way she had always reacted whenever her mother's clients had tried to have their way with her. She kneed the taller woman in the stomach snapping her head forward, and then drove her forehead into her face. The vicious blow sent the sorceress back against the pool's edge, blood spurting from her nose, the taste of it sending Freya-Gund into a frenzied fury.

Unchecked rage was not like the cold, calculating goddess of Ahriman who conquered every affront with guile. Yes, she saw something familiar in this servant girl, something unsettling, something that caused her to act irrationally—she saw her younger self. Screaming like a madwoman, she grabbed Sara's hair and tried once more to push her under the water shouting, "Think you know who I am, do you?"

Sara's response was different than the last time. Waiting for the right moment, she struck back with a ferocity Freya-Gund had never before witnessed, striking her in the throat with the edge of her hand and kicking her in the chest with the heel of her foot. Before the sorceress could recover, Sara broke free, dove under the water and disappeared. Growling, Freya-Gund chased after her to the far side of the pool. *Nothing!* All her thrashing about served only to blur the water. The young woman could swim underwater like a fish.

Sara circled back to the near side, resurfaced, and pulled herself up onto the edge of the pool. Picking up her things, she shouted, "*Valedico,* madam," and ran off laughing, a trail of steam streaming from her naked body.

Freya-Gund stood there stunned. No one had ever humiliated her like this. Far too proud to be shamed by a common wench, she lowered herself until the water reached her chin, wiped the blood from her face, and began to plot. *Yes, Sara was very much like the younger me,* she thought. And that she could not, would not, let stand.

The next morning, Sara was found in an alleyway near the palace. It took some time to identify the mutilated body, but when it was, her murder created an uneasiness that spread through the marketplace where Sara had shopped two days a week. "Who would dare lay a finger on that refined young woman?" asked the butcher. The cheese merchant in the next stall had no answer, nor did anyone else.

Not long afterward, the hunched beggar woman was back in her spot at the east gate. The seer of events and the tent with the golden tassels that had been used to gain the young girl's confidence were never seen at the marketplace again.

CHAPTER 4

While Mahaki preferred to stay at the inn, Lucius spent the night at the Flaccus compound. The house, barn, and shop sat outside the walls of Assisi, two hundred paces west of the gate. Until his murder, Jovius Flaccus was the only smithy in Assisi. Now there were two. *Matrona* Flaccus, her two children, and the slave, Valam, worked hard, but without Jovius, they won few jobs. For the family, this multiplied his tragic loss. After hearing about their struggles over breakfast, Lucius wandered into the city hoping to walk off his despair. It did no good. Everything that happened that summer four years ago pierced his heart like a dagger: the Flaccus loss, his own family gone, Capricorne's demise, the torching of Monbelluna, Ignatius's hanging, the rape of Bruné-Hilda, and all the other tragedies that befell this world he loved, the only one he knew, because of one man's ambition. And that man was Bishop Lazarus. Lucius felt fresh hatred for the man flow through his body. All the tragedies, all the losses had been the consequences of greed and bias—the destroying of that small hamlet called Lucic simply for its blocks of marble. The sin of the Lucic massacre would never die so long as Bishop Lazarus walked the alleyways of Assisi pretending to be an earthly saint. The church atop the hill, built by the bishop from the ruins of Lucic was the instrument that brought down Lucius's world.

He wandered into his favorite shop. He was taller now, heavier, and had a squint line between his eyes that altered his appearance, but not so much as the length of his hair. As a result, not one person in the shop recognized him. Lucius stood there for a moment, waiting.

Frugi the barber asked, "May I be of service, sir?" to which Lucius was able to repeat his most favorite response, "No, I had my throat cut last week, thank you." That brought Frugi and the shop idlers up out of their chairs. Lucius was mauled by their welcomes.

"I'll be a three-legged monkey if it isn't my favorite troublemaker," roared Frugi. "The Lord of Mischief and Chaos is back from the underworld and none the worse for it. Guess Satan couldn't stand ya. We thought you dead, boy!"

"Darn near was a few times. But you know *merda* doesn't die, it just sits there and smells up the place."

"Yeah, yeah, yeah," said Frugi, slapping Lucius on the back. "You remember Paco, don't you?" he asked, laughing.

"Of course. He cut an epitaph into my parents' marker before I left. How are you, Paco? Did you marry Poppaea?"

"We'll talk about that later," Frugi said, cutting off whatever Paco was about to say. "Where have you been these past few years? And you've grown! Whoa. Just look at you." He grabbed Lucius by both arms. "And the hair! What a mess. You need a cut."

"You leave my hair alone," said Lucius, unable to get the smile off his face. "Where I've been will take some tellin', and the hair was part of it." He blinked an eye like he knew more than he could tell. The warmth in their welcomes felt good. He forgot how much he missed being the troublemaker with impunity, the young'un who got into everything.

"Over there is Adrianus, your old classmate at Capricorne. He married the Carpus girl, and next to him is the grandson of Jolly John Macedonicus. You remember Jolly John, I'm sure."

Lucius nodded to them both. "Of course I know John. I came across that old teamster up at the Brenner Pass four years ago and again outside Verona."

"And Marcus should be coming by. You recall Marcus?" asked Frugi.

"Sure. He's the glassmaker who spends more time here than making glass."

"That's not changed, nor has his father-in-law." They all laughed. His wife's father, who owned the business, thought Marcus was a slacker—and back then he was. Apparently he hadn't changed.

"Now, let's get to it," said Lucius with a smirk. "What's the latest?" He was well aware that any gossip worth spit passed through these doors.

Looking toward Paco for help, Frugi said, "Well, let's see, where to start?"

"Let me help," said Lucius, "how 'bout Madam Fromage, Adefonsic, the bishop, Crazy Chloe, and the old sausage maker, Tiro. Any of 'um is worthy of a good tale. Just the name Tiro makes me hungry for one of his garlic sausage rolls."

"Adefonsic the innkeeper would be as good as any," said Paco. "They found what was left of him up on Mount Subasio a week after you left here. From the broken bones and markings, some think the son-of-a-bitch got mauled by a goat. Wasn't he training goats to be watchdogs? Maybe one came back." They all laughed.

"Hmm," was all Lucius could manage. Adefonsic was the one who had turned his pet goat, Scarface, into a killer.

"Well, whatever he got, he deserved," said Paco. "I never met an ornerier snake."

Frugi picked up the telling: "Madam Fromage put on weight. She's not well, not well at all. Rusticus spends his days caring for her. As for Crazy Chloe, she should be out there on that rock selling her honey biscuits just as you and that red-haired boy used to do."

"I looked for her on the way up here, but she wasn't there," said Lucius.

"Try tomorrow. Sometimes her dough doesn't rise."

"Damn, if that doesn't happen to my friend here," said Frugi, slapping Paco on the back. They all joined in a good laugh—at Paco's expense of course.

"Let's get to your favorite," said the barber, intoning a more sober mood. "The fine bishop of this here municipality says you'll burn in hell, Lucius, if he has anything to say about it. I don't know what you did to that man, but whatever it was is seared into his memory like hot iron. And if you believe his sermons, he not only has the ear of the Big Guy in the sky, but the provincial governor as well."

"My, my, my," said Lucius, perking up. "The governor, you say. The bishop who always thwarted the governor's authority now befriends it? Huh! Does that holy man still put church law above everything else on earth?"

"When it suits his purpose, yes," said Adrianus from the back of the shop. "That man's a thief who'd walk a mile for a donation but nary a step to feed the hungry."

Lucius thought of the blind beggar back in Rome and all his goodly deeds. *What a contrast,* he thought. He wondered what the four of them were doing now, probably lunching down in the bowels of Rome.

"You should know," said Frugi, interrupting Lucius's reverie, "his church *still* lies in pieces out there across the valley floor. From Lucic that marble came, to Lucic those blocks returned. After surviving the slide tied to that damnable pine tree, his parishioners sanctified the man. He's now a walking saint. They use the old bathhouse as a church until he can raise enough support to build a new one."

"Ah-ha!" roared Lucius. "So that's his game. It's why he kisses both the governor's ass cheeks, I bet. He wants the governor to build him a new church."

"Of course," replied Frugi. "Why else?"

"Maybe this time the church won't be so grandiose," said Paco with his customary spark of cynicism. "That Mother of Satan's fanatical beliefs brought an end to that *heathen* village out in the middle of our valley."

"And the church he built from it brought about the ruination of our fine municipality," said Adrianus. "You know, Lucius, it has never been the same here."

"Amen to that," said Frugi.

"Amen," echoed the others sitting toward the back of the shop.

Lucius started to speak but a commotion outside interrupted them all. A commanding voice shouted, "EEE! Mark!" Before anyone could reach the door for a look, four legionaries burst into the shop followed by a centurion. Lucius could tell his rank by the feathery plume atop his helmet.

"Which of you is Lucius Domitilla?" asked the centurion in a forced intonation of authority.

"I am," said Lucius, stepping forward.

"I arrest you in the name of the governor of the province of Tuscia-Umbra."

"What!" roared Frugi, who never saw a uniform he respected.

"Impossible," echoed Paco. "He just returned. It's a mistake."

"No mistake, sir, I assure you," the centurion said, grabbing Lucius by the arm. "Come quietly or we'll be forced to take measures."

"May I see the complaint, officer," Lucius asked calmly. "By law, you must have a signed complaint to arrest a citizen of Rome."

The centurion looked flustered. Lucius knew the garrison at Spello was a token force of no more than eight legionaries and the centurion usually a retired officer overseeing rejects from the field army.

"That's up to the governor," the centurion said. "My orders are to take you into custody."

Lucius shrugged, put on his cloak, and turned to Frugi. "Would you send word to my traveling companion. He's at the inn, his name is Mahaki." Wrenching his arm free of the centurion, he inquired, "Where are you taking me?"

"Spello. It's the only lockup we have. Sorry, sir, but we are simply following a directive from the governor."

"Where is the governor?" he asked. "Spoletium?"

"No sir, he's here. We accompanied him. He confers with Bishop Lazarus."

Mahaki was not far behind when the small contingent passed through the gates of Spello six miles east of Assisi. From what he could see, they were not mistreating Lucius; that notwithstanding, it took the remainder of the day before he was allowed to enter the *praetorium* where Lucius was being held.

"What's this all about?" Mahaki asked upon entering the small cell.

Putting a finger to his lips, Lucius whispered, "They may be listening. Something's up, I'm just not sure what." He put his mouth to Mahaki's ear and spoke the next words slowly, "The *bishop* had me arrested."

Mahaki raised an eyebrow.

"If the governor is that much under the bishop's influence, it does not bode well for my future safety."

Mahaki raised the other eyebrow. "By 'bishop,' do you mean Lazarus?"

Lucius nodded. "He desperately wants back what I stole."

"You stole from the bishop," Mahaki repeated matter-of-factly. "What did you steal, may I ask?"

"Artifacts from the Temple of Castor and Pollux," said Lucius. He paused before adding, "Plus one other thing."

"I'm listening."

"The cup of Christ. Before I departed four years ago, I stole the cup of Christ. I returned the other Christian artifacts to his parishioners. Believe this, if you believe nothing else I say. Although fake, which it is, this cup opens doors. This magnificent forgery got me through more than one ugly situation. The public, particularly those in Gaul, are incredibly gullible when it comes to matters of faith. Here, let me show you what it looks like." Lucius drew the outline of the cup in the dirt floor of his cell. "It could not be of a simpler design or of a plainer construction, which speaks well for its legitimacy. Their Christ, you understand, was a simple man."

Mahaki paused. "You want me to find a plain cup of clay."

"Yes."

"And return it to the bishop in exchange for your release."

Lucius nodded.

"That's easy enough. What other items did you steal that he might want back?"

"Seven gold sacrificial plates, some jeweled chalices, three candelabra, two ornate torches, and a jeweled knife used to sacrifice lambs and chickens. All items used to practice the banned ancient rites, most very old, a few of little beauty, although all precious."

"Do you have all of it still? If so, where?" asked Mahaki.

"I gave it all away for one reason or another to get by. You must find one or two similar pieces. I'm certain he does not remember what they looked like."

"What did you—no, wait. I have a better question. Remind me, how did you get your hands on these artifacts?"

Lucius smiled. "Ah, right to the heart of it, eh? Well, do you remember I told you I was buried beneath the church when it collapsed? The artifacts were some of the things he stored in the vault in which I hid. The rest of the story is too long to repeat, but remember, I told you I returned half to his parishioners before I departed the valley—mainly the valuables the wealthy faithful had donated over the years. What he stole from the old temple I kept, plus the fake cup of Christ. When I departed Worms, I gave most of what I took to the local bishop."

Mahaki slumped back, his mind racing. He asked, "Do you think you'll be safe here for a few days? They won't try anything, will they?"

"I'll be fine. Their hearts are not in this, especially the centurion's. What else is going through that head of yours besides my release?"

"Unfinished business, my young friend. Just some unfinished business."

"Unfinished business, you say," Lucius repeated. "What kind of dealings would you have in my valley that are, as you say, 'unfinished'?"

"Need I remind you that you and that beautiful young lady knocked me loose while scurrying off from this valley four years ago? Well, lad, I was not just picking daisies along the roadway. Maybe someone here did me a wrong, did far more than accidentally knock me into a ditch because they did not know how to manage two oxen pulling an oversized wagon."

More familiar with the Umbrian Valley than he let on, Mahaki kept silent about the role he played during that hectic summer four years ago. There was no pretext to his silence. He just preferred to keep the lid on the hatred that had driven him to do what he did—a sinful response to a painful loathing that festered for twenty-three years. Now, without warning, the scab had once again been ripped off that painful loathing, and it hurt like hell. Evil never went away. It just lay dormant for a time and then reappeared unexpectedly. Why the faithful in this valley did not see the true character of their bishop remained a mystery to him.

That night Mahaki tossed and turned in his bed at the Icarus Horse Inn. After mulling over several ideas—for he was not a reckless man—Mahaki decided to put a stop to the bishop's wickedness once and for all. At the inn, he heard about men living amid the ruins of Lucic along the banks of a small stream called the Topino. Pulling down his desert headdress and throwing the head scarf across his face, in the gig he drove the five miles to a place he vowed never to return to, the place where his infant sons, Razan and Ruko, died horrible deaths. Not one living there amid the ruins of Lucic recognized him at first. But he knew them. They were the refugees from the assault on Rome. Castoffs who were unwilling or unable to make the long journey back to the Avar homeland beyond the Black Sea. There were only nine of them, and all living like hermits. Three had missing limbs, one was half blind, and the remainder had lesser problems. He needed only two to do what he planned.

It took three days to gather what he needed: three burlap sacks; an old candelabrum, purchased from the shop of wicks and lamps; two good-sized boulders, each too heavy for one man to lift; tools; rope and cord; a piece of eight-by-four-foot netting; and, the hardest to obtain, an old clay cup that resembled as closely as possible the outline Lucius had drawn. With the rope and netting, he would make a *tajuk*, a trap that his ancestors used to capture mountain lions that ravaged their flocks.

On the fourth day after Lucius's arrest, Mahaki sent word to the bishop's residence that the treasure Lucius stole, including the cup of Christ, could be reclaimed at Assisi's Overlook Piazza in exchange for Lucius's freedom. He also recommended that the bishop bring along enough men to carry off the collection. As Mahaki had assumed he would, the bishop replied with a request that the exchange take place at the darkest hour with no witnesses; and he warned that if anything went wrong, Lucius would suffer the "consequences." Of course Mahaki's assumptions were correct; they always were when he measured human nature. And the "consequences" the bishop threatened were of no concern for he was a meticulous planner.

The bishop came with three men and a pushcart, and true to form, ordered his men to wait in the main square while he made his way alone through the curia archway and out onto the Overlook Piazza.

It was just the two of them now. Mahaki met him halfway between the arch and the railing where the three burlap sacks sat. There was no moon, and the valley floor far beneath the Overlook was dark. The only light came from the single torch affixed to the curia, which formed the back wall of the Overlook Piazza. Normally there were two torches, but Mahaki had seen to it that there was only one this night.

The railing of the spacious Overlook rested on thirty-two four-foot-high pillars that were spaced six paces apart. The balustrade was affixed to each pillar by metal fittings. It was of sturdy maple, made smooth by decades of visitors leaning over it to enjoy the view. Under the top rail were vertical balusters equally spaced that connected to a bottom support. Mahaki and the two he had chosen among the refugees had placed the two large boulders atop the two pillars guarding the sacks of treasure. A candelabrum resembling one of those the bishop stole from the Temple of Castor and Pollux was on display with a simple cup, the one pretender to the cup of Christ. Mahaki knew the bishop would not appreciate a full display of all the treasure. For, even though the use of temples had been forbidden throughout the empire for thirty years, it was strictly prohibited to loot them. So the bishop would not find it unusual if Mahaki only displayed the two items. And Mahaki was depending on the cup of Christ giving him the distraction he needed. This was going to be Mahaki's finest hour.

"All is here, Your Eminence, I assure you," said Mahaki. "But first, I am instructed to read this message." He pulled out a small piece of paper. "Lucius writes this with the sincerity of a repentant sinner: 'I regret my errant ways,' he writes, 'and pray you forgive my transgressions. Here before you lies all I stole in an hour of selfish behavior.' It is signed 'Lucius Domitilla.'"

Bishop Lazarus, a tall, heavy man, wearing one of his elegant silk robes and the red shoes he imported from Jerusalem, shoes that had walked the path Christ had traveled to Golgotha where he was crucified, cleared his throat—and then roared. "You arrogant little bastard you! You have the audacity to address me, the bishop of this jurisdiction, with that cloth over your face."

"I apologize, Excellency. But understand that I have an affliction that would offend you sensibilities where you to view it."

"Affliction, bah! Furthermore, how can you even suggest that Lucius be spared my wrath just because he begs for forgiveness. He should pray that I do not order the governor to execute him at once. Stealing from a sanctuary of the Lord in and of itself condemns his soul to eternal damnation. For stealing from me, the appointed arbiter of the Lord, he should be slowly divided into four equal parts."

Mahaki bowed. "We should all practice the words we pray, Excellency."

"Before I call my attendants, please remove the cup and candelabrum. Hide them in one of those sacks so—"

"So your attendants will not see them. I completely understand, Excellency," Mahaki said, hiding a smile behind the desert head cloth. The bishop was so predictable, and oh so very arrogant. If Mahaki had any doubts about what he would do next, the bishop's pompous posture, self-serving words, and affected facial expressions, condemned him.

"Sir," Mahaki said in his modest tone that was so convincing, "I have performed the service for which I was paid. The artifacts are yours to do with as you wish." And he withdrew into the shadows, leaving the bishop alone with the three sacks, the candelabrum, and the cup. The trap was set.

Standing in the middle of the spacious piazza, his garments blowing in the breeze, Bishop Lazarus looked around. Seeing nothing, he moved quickly to where the cup sat in front of the three sacks. Excited over his triumph and eager to hide the cup and candelabrum from his attendants, he paid no attention to the rope on the ground or the two boulders sitting atop the pillars. And the single torch was too distant to illuminate much more than the area around it. When the bishop was five paces from the cup, he tripped over a rope, cursed it but gave it no further thought. The man was totally focused, as Mahaki knew he would be, on hiding his cherished plunder from his followers. No one should know he was a common thief. When he bent over to pick up the cup, a sound startled him. He straightened. The sound was that of a bird—a melodious warbler—a bird that normally did not sing at night. But what did a man who led a flock know of birds?

As he inspected the cup, two cords attached to the shims holding the boulders in place atop the railing supports were silently pulled free by two men crouched beyond the railing; two men who had been precariously balancing themselves on the edge of the precipice all this time, one ten paces to the east, the other the same distance to the west. Once free of the shims, both boulders shifted. Then they rolled off the pillars and bounded down the slope toward the valley floor. Firmly fastened to the boulders was the shorter of the two ropes that the bishop had absentmindedly tripped over. The rope jumped to life and sped toward the preoccupied bishop. It was immediately followed by a second rope, a slighter longer one. They separated, fully stretching the netting between them enough to snare the unsuspecting victim.

The bishop cocked his head at the hissing sound the ropes made as they slid past him on both sides. Swoosh! The netting caught him, launching his huge body up and over the railing and into the dark night. The initial contact of the upper rope knocked the wind out of his lungs preventing any sound from escaping his lips as he flew through the air, not that a terror-filled scream would have disappointed Mahaki. But, on the other hand, the silence during his long journey to the valley floor would add to the mystery of his sudden disappearance. That was the last anyone saw of the bishop until morning when his body was found smashed against the rocks far below.

The three attendants the bishop had brought with him concluded, when their patience was exhausted waiting for him in the main square, that the bishop had departed the Overlook by a different way—at the time they just had no idea how different. They shrugged and retrieved the three sacks that held nothing but brush. They also found a cheap candelabrum that had somehow gotten smashed against the railing. Predictably, the bishop did not surrounded himself with deep thinkers.

After watching them depart from the shadows, Mahaki and his two associates worked their way down the cliff by a side path, cut the ropes and netting free, collected the shards from the broken cup the bishop had been holding, and pushed one of the boulders farther down to avoid anyone deducing the truth of what happened this night. For all the faithful would know, the bishop had an unfortunate accident or maybe killed himself. Who knew? In either case, different camps would hold differing views. Some would say it was a just end to a duplicitous man. Others would say that the holy man's sermons changed their lives. And still others might say that the building of the church out of the bloody marble blocks from Lucic was, in the end, a curse. In any event, his faithful followers would eventually die off, but the gossip, particularly that emanating from the barbershop, would become lore of the most scandalous sort.

When word reached Spello that the bishop was dead, Lucius was immediately freed. After spending another night at the Flaccus compound, he headed toward the inn to collect Mahaki and to prepare for their departure to Ravenna. Approaching the big rock that sat along the roadway, Lucius spotted Crazy Chloe there selling her freshly baked honey cakes and sweet water. She crowed upon seeing him in the distance. "Prophetic isn't it that the man who survived the collapse of his church atop Mt. Este four long years ago had his life's thread cut at the bottom of the hill in its ruins. Could that be the handiwork of the *Fatae*, my dear boy?"

Closing the distance to the rock, Lucius replied, "Ponti would say yes to that and then add, 'The hand of justice again is proven just.'"

"Do you actually believe it was 'the hand of justice' that pushed him over the edge?" she asked. "Well do you? Come up here and sit with this decrepit old woman for a moment, Lucius, and tell me what you think. You are about to leave us again, aren't you?"

"I am," he answered, climbing up. He was the only one in Assisi who treated her with respect despite her unsightly appearance and mysterious ways. "What in your great wisdom do you predict for me this time, Chloe?"

"It's not me who has anything in store for thee; it's Nyx, the mother of the Fatae."

He gained the top of the rock by climbing up the back side just as he'd always done. The high rock served as a shield from the occasional troublemaker who traveled the Via Umbria. They sat there looking south toward Monbelluna for a time saying nothing. The air was clean and sweet. Up here was where he and his boyhood friend Jingo sat that spring morning when they first spotted the smoke from the cooking fires in Thor Pass. Those fires had foretold the first coming of the barbarian vanguard disguised as migrant farmers. From that cool spring morning on, the peacefulness of the valley was disturbed and eventually lost when the entire Gothic horde arrived months later.

"No need coming back here again, Lucius," she said, breaking the silence.

"Why, Chloe, why would you say such a thing? This is my home. Restoring the villa of Capricorne and everything it stood for might well be my destiny. Voices long dead call to me and say, 'Recreate, resurrect, and restore.' I hear them every night in my sleep."

"What was can never be again. That world is dead, Lucius. Do you still have the bishop's staff I gave you four years ago?"

"No. It served me well, thank you, but perished in a fire at a hamlet along with my dreams."

"And that beautiful young woman?"

"She was part of that dream. But she wishes she too had perished in that fire. She hides her scars from the world on an island off Gaul hoping one day to be whole again. That may never be, I fear. The blame awakens me nights. I miss her so, Chloe."

"Pray she is able to one day face what is, not what she once was."

"Is that your secret, Chloe? Is that how you get through each day?"

"Never mind me. Listen well, my son. Don't come back. There's nothing here. Your talent is better used elsewhere. Remember what I told you when you left the first time in that oversized elephant-wagon?"

"You told me nothing, Chloe. I remember precisely your words. You said, 'It's preordained that you . . .' And that was it. You hushed yourself, saying you had already told me too much. I always wondered what was preordained for me."

"The scales have been balanced, Lucius. No one durst ask for more before the gods become angry. The last evil in this valley was purged on the piazza the other night. There are other and far greater challenges for you now, greater things to restore than a villa, a library, or a valley floor full of broken dreams. The bishop's death was no accident, Lucius. Someone used the devil's hand to do the Lord's work."

"How can you possibly know that?"

"And that someone is—well now, I durst not say. Was it not you who brought this messenger of death here, eh? Were not your parents' deaths avenged along with the hundreds who perished in that mudslide through by the hand of that man in the desert headdress? Yes, call it fate, the Hand of God, or whatever visceral force you accept, but know that I've laid bare the truth, Lucius. If you accept anything of what I say this day, then accept this: by bringing him back to Umbria, your work here is done. You can accomplish nothing more by staying. So reclaim your messenger of death and go. He awaits you at the inn."

In the bowels of Rome, the blind beggar and his associates, Vesuvius, Peg-Leg, and Medusa, were enjoying their midday meal of soup of chicken, winter spinach, and cut potatoes that had been stored in a cold room since fall. Each took a turn reporting on the morning's activities. When it came round to Vesuvius, he spoke offhandedly—for it did not seem important—of two outsiders making inquiries about a young chap that, from the description, sounded an awful lot like Lucius.

"What did these men look like?" asked the blind beggar called Alfadur.

"Hooligans. One had a Germanic accent, and he only spoke a few words. He had one distinctive feature, though—an iron tooth. The other was from the East, had a ring in his ear and a shaved head."

"Why call them hooligans rather than foreigners? What did they do to earn that appellation?" asked the blind beggar.

"One had a knife in his boot; the other had one strapped to his arm. And they were not used to peel or whittle—they were daggers.

Carried by big, strong men with scars and tattoos, men you would not care to meet in the night."

"Excuse me for interrupting," said Medusa, "but a shopkeeper on my plaza spoke of similar inquiries from such men."

"Possibly our friend Lucius has trouble. Let's find out. Put the word out that I might have information they seek. Let's see if a blind man can see into their intentions."

The next day two men approached the blind beggar at his customary place against the wall of the Salarian Gate. One hung back while the other approached. He had an Eastern accent that the beggar placed somewhere around the Black Sea, maybe the Bosporus region from the way he pronounced his *E*s and *K*s. When the man squatted to talk, thinking as most did that blind people were also hard of hearing, the beggar smelled coriander on his breath. Chewing coriander was a common practice on the steppes—the vast plains north of the Caspian Sea. *The man is well traveled,* the beggar thought. *But is he a thief after the gems or, worse, a paid assassin?*

They spoke. The beggar's questions were answered shrewdly, the stranger giving up little, or so he thought. It did not take long for the beggar to conclude that it was indeed Lucius for whom they searched. The stranger departed with his companion, both satisfied that they were close to their quarry. They left the city and went south on the road to Campania.

Three days later the stranger that smelled of coriander returned to the Salarian Gate with his companion. Without a word, and in broad daylight, they lifted the blind beggar off his feet, threw him against the wall, beat him senseless, and then stole his money belt. Something had gone terribly wrong. Somehow they had discovered that Lucius went north to Ravenna fifteen days ago, not south. After giving the blind beggar a sound beating, the two headed north on the Via Flaminia.

On the road north, a comment Irontooth and Tauriac overheard at the posting station in Narnia seemed absurd. Then the stable master at Hostia repeated the same ridiculous comment. Lucius and his companion, the stable master said, were members of the Black Hand. A lethal society based in Sicily that controlled much of the contraband in and around Rome and elsewhere. Lucius, Tauriac knew, had no such connection; but the revelation, heard in two places, made him wonder who Lucius's traveling companion might be. That night, they stole two fresh horses from the posting station and sped north to Umbria. Tauriac guessed that Lucius could not resist visiting the valley where he grew up. Where, hopefully, he would linger visiting friends. That would give him and Irontooth the chance they needed to catch up.

Somewhere along the road north, Tauriac recalled the stable master giving him the news that Lucius was a member of The Black Hand, a secret society of criminals. "Ha!" he laughed in the face of the stable master and said, "This Lucius fellow has more angles than a Judas tree." But then he remembered that it was under a Judas tree where Lucius managed to cut the arm off Cacca Reba—cut if off because the Hun had underestimated the imp.

Tauriac would not make the same mistake.

Oblivious to the danger that pursued them, Lucius and Mahaki continued on, the gig passing lazily by Nucera-Umbra leaving the valley behind. Lucius felt no emotion. Nothing there was real anymore. Crazy Chloe was correct. It was time to move on, both literally and emotionally.

"You can go faster," said Mahaki.

"Why? What's the rush?" Lucius had no idea that both their lives were in danger.

The Via Flaminia cut through the Apennines, the mountain range that formed the backbone of Italy. This was Lucius's second trip north on the Via Flaminia, the main highway of the West, and he marveled at the skill of the builders who had evened the undulations and straightened the twists of the mountain road through the brilliance of engineering and, of course, the superhuman effort of slave labor. None of the engineering feats then could be done today. It was like what Ponti had always said, "The genius of lore exists no more."

Lucius looked over at Mahaki pressed up against the side of the gig. He seemed more relaxed now that they had passed Nucera-Umbra. How he could sleep through the grinding and bouncing was miraculous. He wondered, though, was this little man the messenger of death as Crazy Chloe said? Where in the name of Thor had she come up with that? And what really happened that night at the piazza? Could a man like Mahaki, half the bishop's size, push him over the railing of the Overlook? Of course not. There had to be another answer. Lucius usually disregarded things that made no sense, but letting go of this was hard. He wondered, and not for the first time, if there was another side to Mahaki, a more sinister side.

Without incident, they stopped at the summit near the Temple of Jupiter that first night. The second night was different. The innkeeper was away, and the stable master would not honor the cursus publicus authorization to exchange horses. Then, when Lucius persisted, it got ugly.

"The inn is full!" the stable master screamed with finality and stomped off. Rather than wait for Lucius to go through the ceremony Cybelina had insisted on a second time, Mahaki grabbed the ring from Lucius, caught up with the stable master, and thrust the ring in his face. The man stopped in his tracks, became nervous, and then suddenly every room in the inn was available. "I'll move people into the stables if necessary," he said wringing his hands.

The next day they descended the eastern slope of the Apennines to Cales and then turned north along the gorges of the Burano River. They spent the night at Forum Sempronii, where Mahaki announced he would go south to Ancona when they reached Fanum the next day.

Go south when I'm going north?! How can he do that to me!

Lucius would have none of it and said so. But Mahaki insisted. He had responsibilities that beckoned. Up until now Lucius had said little of his true mission, but the time had come to reveal it all.

"What lies ahead," he began, trying to be heard above the noise of the iron wheels, "is a challenge greater and far more rewarding than anyone alive has attempted." It was a bit much, he thought, but a good start. "Far greater than selling corn from the fields around Ancona, I might add."

"First of all, I do more than sell corn. Secondly, my young friend, I'm getting too old to take on any challenge greater than anyone alive has undertaken. I've had my share of challenges, thank you."

Lucius said nothing for a time, trying to come up with something different, anything that would have an irresistible impact on his friend. "I assure you," he began after a pause, "any past trials will pale in comparison to this one. Listen closely, for I will say this only once." And Lucius explained everything that had happened since he departed Umbria that first time: from the creation of the kingdom of Burgundia through the death of Gunther to Galla Placidia's ransom, pregnancy, and possible rise to the throne of the Western Empire. Alluding to the Statue of Fortune, there was no need to exaggerate its immense value. He told the truth.

When Lucius was finished, Mahaki leaned back in the gig, wiped his face with both hands, and looked up to the sky. "If half of what you say is true, you need more than this old man," he scoffed. "You need ten legions and Alexander the Macedonian to lead them."

"Does that mean you'll do it? You'll stay? I can't do all this alone you know."

Mahaki nodded. "How could I not. But let me say this: I won't enjoy seeing your head on a pike—nor mine."

"Good." And he snapped the reins. Lucius wanted to get beyond Fanum as fast as he could before Mahaki changed his mind. He said not another word until they did.

When they were several hours beyond Fanum, Lucius felt it safe enough to begin explaining a few more things. "Our first challenge is to accomplish what Alaric and his huge Gothic army could not."

Mahaki grimaced. "What?"

"Breaking into Ravenna. I'm told no one passes through the gates without authorization. No vendors, no visitors, no bureaucrats. Ravenna is a thickly walled stronghold with a singular mission: keep the emperor alive."

"Are you crazy, lad? Let me out right here."

Lucius snapped the reins over and over, laughing. "You'll have to jump."

The next day they reached the outskirts of Ravenna, which lay on the Adriatic Sea, two hundred and fifty-five miles northeast of Rome. They had gone through eight sets of horses—thanks to the posting stations and the cursus publicus—and two sets of wheels since departing Rome. The grand via of the empire was a mostly neglected roadway.

"You don't plan to ride up to the main gate and talk your way through, do you?" asked Mahaki.

"That's one way, yes."

"Have you noticed those small encampments we've been passing?"

Lucius had.

"Those are merchant camps. People from inside those big walls come out by day and make purchases of things they cannot buy inside, which suggests that the camps are full of smuggled goods from Dalmatia, contraband, stolen property, and those seeking pleasures of the flesh. I see this at other walled compounds when traveling south of Ancona."

"You mean like Forum Flaminii in Umbria," said Lucius.

"Exactly," said Mahaki. "Now, what I suggest is we spend a night at one of these encampments and see what happens. I suspect these folks have lifelong experiences in working the walls."

"What do you mean 'working the walls'?" asked Lucius.

"Be patient and you'll learn something."

That night, while Lucius stayed with the horses, Mahaki visited the various fires of the encampment he'd selected. When Lucius woke the next morning, they had a new friend at the fire, a shepherd—or at least a man dressed like one. He had two dogs, a staff, the oversized cape he lived in, and a red beard. Everything a dedicated, hardworking shepherd needed, except for one thing. He had no sheep.

That night, after negotiating a generous fee for his efforts, the shepherd led them through the marshes that surrounded Ravenna to the water's edge. The back side of Ravenna abutted an inlet to the Adriatic Sea. With all their belongings, the three got into a small, flat-bottomed boat and poled their way through the darkest part of the marsh, slipping under the low branches and overhead vines, and twice pulling the boat over sandbar ridges until they were up against the southeast wall of Ravenna. Here they left the boat and quietly negotiated a narrow strip of land to a small opening in the wall hidden by vines. It was a postern gate, a small opening to allow field workers in and out. Clearly the fields were purposely flooded long ago to better protect the walls, the tiny gate amid the vines forgotten soon after the flooding.

The shepherd knocked on the small door once, paused, and then knocked three more times. They waited. He repeated the sequence. Soon the small door opened, and the shepherd stuck his head in. "It's Rufus," he whispered. "These men are my friends. They bring nothing but their belongings. The carriers will not be needed." And he handed the invisible person what Lucius assumed to be a coin.

In a whisper, Lucius thanked the shepherd and said, "The horses and gig are yours. Treat them well." With that, he followed Mahaki through the opening and into a narrow tunnel connected to the house of a well-fed woman. All this reminded Lucius of the secret tunnel he had dug in Worms under the north wall.

Now, at last, he was inside Ravenna and set to face the next obstacle of this odyssey: make contact with Master-General Constantius, who he hoped would willingly help ransom Galla Placidia from the Goths. He could hardly believe he was at last inside the same walls behind which the emperor resided, or better said, hid. It renewed the fire in his belly.

The weather had turned. An early touch of spring was in the air.

Freya-Gund shuffled her way to the main square. Though only three streets away from the gate, it took her awhile. After all, a stooped cripple had to move painfully slow to be convincing. She was getting tired of this gawd-awful disguise. Not just because it hurt her back, the ruse produced nothing tangible. She blended into the crowd that lined the perimeter. In the center of the square, the officers of the Gothic vanguard stood. The main body waited outside the walls. They were about to depart for Barcelona. Since coming to Narbo, the Gothic irregulars had organized into Romanesque military units complete with uniforms, formations, standards, and rank. The hierarchy was now based on ability rather than sheer physical strength. No longer were they an unruly rabble but a well-ordered field army—or so they thought.

King Athaulf stood in the doorway of the curia, which served as his palace. At his side was Galla Placidia: radiant, bored, and very pregnant. They descended the steps and paraded in front of the officers, Galla two steps behind, the king speaking quietly to a few of his favorites.

The fire in Freya-Gund's eyes danced as she watched this charade. Who were they kidding? These apple-knockers were no more than a group of illiterate thugs glorifying themselves in Spartan-like ritual. This was no conquering field army. They were more akin to a mob who, after taking the walled city of Tolosa, fancied themselves conquerors. Bursting with misplaced pride because they pushed over walls ready to collapse from fatigue, they were now planning to bang on the gates of Barcelona—but Barcelona was not Tolosa and Athaulf was not King Leonidas of Sparta. Freya-Gund watched the leader step forward and bring his right hand to his chest for a well-rehearsed salute. Athaulf stood there motionless. An aide whispered to him, and he snapped to attention, banged his fist to his chest, and returned to the steps, Galla trailing behind him. The officers of this vainglorious vanguard marched off full of themselves and their duty. Thankfully, the pathetically awkward ceremony was over.

Freya-Gund overheard the talk coursing through the crowd: the vanguard would test the waters, the main body to follow in three days—*with Galla. Fuck!* That meant she had three days to decide whether to travel with them under a different disguise or stay here with the garrison. She could only guess about the gems. Would Galla take them to Barcelona or hide them here? Just three days—three short days before deciding. Since Sara's death, Freya-Gund had been unable to find anyone to feed her information. So many times she regretted her impatience. Only Ahriman knew how hard she worked, how many risks she took, to uncover the gems' whereabouts. This turn of events forced her hand. She needed a new scheme, and quickly.

That night she changed into a gauze chemise, painted her face like a Subura whore, scented her body with oils, and waited in the shadows of the building next to the curia. She concealed her charms beneath a beggar's cloak and hood. When the candle was blown out on the second-floor flat, she slithered into the entrance and mounted the steps. Tapping lightly on the last door to the right, she waited. It opened. She pushed her way in, closed the door with her foot, and dropped her cloak.

Unable to see much, Singerich saw enough to know it was a beautiful woman standing before him. He also understood why she was there. After all, was he not sought after by *every* wench in search of a better life? His large ego overrode his common sense and he was about to pay the price.

When the false dawn woke the roosters of Narbo, Singerich lay tightly bound to the bed that had hosted an extraordinary night of rapture. He thought it but one more of her sensual delights when the first rope went on. With the second, he was far too preoccupied with what she was doing to him to care. When the third loop snapped tight around his ankle, it was too late.

"Utter one cry and . . ." She did not need to finish. The cold touch of her blade finished the sentence for her. Although not a small man, he surely realized by their night of thrashing about that she was stronger. Freya-Gund slipped on her chemise, poured water into the ewer, and wiped away the face paint. She walked to the window and pushed open the shutters before turning to face him. In her natural voice, she asked, "Do you now know who I am?"

"Freya-Gund?" he said puzzled. "Great Zeus, woman, you're a strange . . . What are you . . . Wait, let me align my thinking. I thought you were—"

"Going after Lucius. Ha! That's what you wanted, wasn't it? What I'm after is not sewn into that *mentula's* cloak but somewhere here in Narbo. As for your two assassins, I wish them well. But don't be surprised if their heads are returned in a box, not his."

Singerich pulled at his bonds and then gave up.

"Calm down and listen," she said. "I know your dark side, Singerich. And it's more sinister than anyone here in Narbo suspects. For example, you *are* a scoundrel, an intelligent, ambitious one, yes, but an absolute, unrepentant predator. I know Galla hates you, for what I've yet to uncover. You're a slave to selfishness, there's evil in your heart, and when you speak, it's usually to lie. For that, and more," she said, softening her tone, "I admire who you are and wish for us to become *consors*."

"Is this how you put forth your wishes?" he asked, straining to move.

"I found out all I needed to by sleeping with those around you, including Sara. To trap a rodent, one must use cheese; a narcissist, a mirror; but a predator . . . Ahhh," she sighed, walking her fingers up his chest. "With a predator like you, one must use guile, for you, my love, are a wise man."

"What do you *want* of me, Freya-Gund?" he demanded. "Your prurient needs have been sated by my associates. I'm surprised you can still walk."

"We are two of a kind, you and I," she said, walking back toward the window. "How you think is not foreign to me, Singerich. You've been around power most of your life. Now you want it for yourself. Am I correct? Don't answer. I see it in your eyes. You want to be king, but Athaulf stands in your way, doesn't he. You thought he would be dead by now from his wounds at Massilia. But he lives on to fight and conquer. Next it's Barcelona. If he wins there, he may silence his detractors and you lose your chance for absolute power."

"Ridiculous!" he said, tugging on the ropes. "His detractors will never be still."

"For me, I want what's in the belly of that statue. We can help each other."

"I doubt that!"

"I may not be able to make you king, but I can clear the throne of its present occupant. It is far easier to kill a body than change a mind. The latter is up to you."

"Ha! Clear the throne. What, murder Athaulf?"

"Yes. And the bitch. How do you think my husband, Gundahar, became king of Burgundia? By his wit? His savagery? The man ran away at Faesulae. No, no, Singerich, never doubt me for a moment. I want the gems that were inside the Statue of Fortune—the statue I stole from Tibur, then chased halfway around the world before carrying it off to Worms. The question is: will what I seek remain here in Narbo, or will it soon be on its way to Barcelona?"

Their first night in Ravenna, Lucius and Mahaki slept in a storage shed near the marketplace. Luckily, the weather was agreeable. To their disappointment, inns were not permitted inside the walls, nor were there any private rooms available. The next day they visited a barbershop to get a better feel for the state of affairs within the walls. What they found gave them pause. The barber was Dalmatian, unfriendly to strangers, not conversant with current events, and did not have a room in the back to let—or so he said—like most barber shops throughout Italy.

After two frustrating days, they found living inside these walls akin to living in a prison. The people were remote, few made eye contact, and, if they spoke, it was to complain. The paranoia flowed from the palace. But a slit finally appeared in this veil of detachment. A woman selling imported produce from her relatives on the isle of Corfu broke a leg and needed help. Lucius and Mahaki agreed to assist her by bringing the shipments from the port to the market in exchange for a room. For food, they would transport these crates to and from her storage shed each day. Plus, for she was a daunting negotiator, they agreed to work her stall on Monday mornings, the busiest day of the week. Not only was the room they were given tiny, its south wall was adjacent to the community water fountain, the noisiest spot in Ravenna—so it seemed. Nonetheless, it was a room and a meal.

Each day Lucius would go to the palace and demand to see Master-General Constantius. And every day he was turned away. He tried everything: a personal note, important names, even a bribe, but nothing worked. For a week and a half this went on.

Then one day, while at the port picking up a shipment of figs from the isle of Corfu, he watched as an official-looking ship dropped anchor in the middle of the bay. A dock worker said it had arrived from Salona on the Dalmatian coast. Two military officers disembarked and were rowed to the dock. One wore the uniform of a high-ranking tribune, the other, a short red cape similar to those worn by the infamous scholares.

This was his chance. Watching them carefully, Lucius pulled the ring off his finger, grabbed the stylus from the crewmate making count, tore a piece of paper off his sheet, and wrote a hasty note. When the two officers climbed onto the dock, he approached the one in the red cape. "Please, sir, a moment," he said, thrusting the ring and note under the man's nose. "Give these to Constantius. Tell him I have enough means to ransom the princess. He'll understand."

"Be off, wharf rat. I have no time for such—"

"Make time!" shouted Lucius. "If you refuse, you may be in chains wearing that fancy red cape as a diaper. Do you understand me now?"

"Of all the—"

"I said, do you understand, sir?" Lucius spit the words with such conviction that the well-weathered officer actually blinked.

"He will, I assure you," interjected the tribune stepping between them. "He leads the garrison in Salona, been away for five years, and is not fully aware of what you just gave him," said the tribune. "I apologize for his failure."

"What!" shouted the officer, clearly infuriated.

The tribune turned fully to the infuriated officer. "The ring, Flavius, its the emblem of the Black Hand," said the tribune. "A *societas* from Sicily. It now controls much of the slave trade, contraband, and prostitution to the south. Their influence has grown since the invasion."

For the first time, Lucius fully appreciated this ring with the black hand design.

"Ravenna looks the other way in exchange for their keeping certain elements, shall we say, under control," said the tribune. "You have been away, Flavius Abinnaeus. Things change." Turning back to Lucius, he asked, "Now, sir, where can we find you?"

"It's in the note," he answered. "I expect to hear something before day's end."

"What if—"

"No what ifs! By day's end! I come here by way of Rome," he said, neglecting to admit the trip there failed. "Galla Placidia and I speak with one voice."

"I've sent the ring to the palace connoisseur. He has not yet reported back," Constantius said to Lucius as he was being led in to see him. "Like most things these days," he went on, "the ring is probably a fake. You have this much of my time." And he turned over a tiny glass atop his desk. "Very little sand remains in your favor."

How childish, thought Lucius. "Yet you chose to see me," Lucius said, sitting without being invited and doing what he could to not appear intimidated. Two guards positioned themselves at each end of the large table behind which the Master General sat. Taken aback by how the general looked, Lucius wondered if Galla realized what she was proposing. Certainly she knew the man was unsightly.

"Your note, there was something in its directness. No matter. Half your sand remains. Go on, convince me. Most want to see me on one point and then press another."

"Like an assassin," said Lucius matter-of-factly.

The general laughed. "Precisely, therefore these guards," he said, nodding toward the scholares that flanked him.

"If too vigilant, one might miss an opportunity, General."

Constantius smiled. "Ah yes, true. Opportunity. One must never ignore opportunity. However, you have nearly lost yours. The sands are nearly gone, my friend. I'm a man of action, not chatter."

"Does the name Freya-Gund mean anything to you, General?" asked Lucius, holding tight to his chair in case the guards tried to eject him.

"No," said Constantius.

"How 'bout Gunther and the Burgundians?"

"What of the Burgundians?" he asked, leaning back. "Didn't they lead the charge through the Salarian Gate?"

"And more."

"What more," asked Constantius, bridging his fingers under his nose. Lucius could see his words were making an impression.

"The Burgundians, particularly the sorceress called Freya-Gund, got away with something of great value that the emperor wants back."

"And why do you say that?"

"Because he sent one of his agents to retrieve it. The agent never fulfilled the quest, though. Lost an arm in the endeavor, but never did uncover the secret. His name is—"

Constantius cut him off and turned to the lead guard. "Marcus," he commanded, "you both may leave. We have a friend here."

Marcus banged a salute and both retreated, leaving Lucius and the general alone.

"Now, sir," said Constantius, "from this point on, choose carefully what you say and in front of whom you say it. Assume the four walls, ceiling, and floor have ears. Come, let's walk in the garden. The weather is not so bad this time of day."

When seated comfortably at a stone table in the garden, Constantius reopened the conversation. "What is or was this imperial agent's name?"

"Cacca Reba," said Lucius. The general did not flinch but Lucius could see his one neck vein swell. *So, Cacca Reba reported to him, not the emperor.*

"Go on," said Constantius.

"Freya-Gund is a Phrygian that Alaric assigned to the Burgundians long before they crossed the Po for the first time. She somehow identified, located, and stole the Statue of Fortune from a villa in Tibur by using—or better said, misusing—my uncle and his associates. Even the Burgundians did not know what she was really up to. I eventually uncovered the truth and located this statue in a cemetery outside Worms. Although guarded by a beast, I eventually made off with it and delivered it to Galla Placidia."

"How did you 'make off' with it if guarded by a beast?" he asked mockingly.

"By slaying the beast, of course."

Constantius laughed.

"Don't. The curse of Fafnir protected that treasure. I destroyed the dragon beast with a rock. When I took its head off, the curse was lifted."

"Quite convincing, young man. Up to that point."

Lucius smiled. "Dragons are a myth, of course. But not stone ones. Fafnir was a mere effigy atop the crypt where the statue was hidden—the curse was carved in marble above the effigy."

"Think me a fool?"

Lucius lifted his tunic. "Maybe this will allay your doubts."

He unlaced the vest the seamstress had handcrafted in Rome for him and laid it on the stone table between them. Next, he opened one of the pockets, pulled out the carefully folded tubular packet, and poured its contents onto the table. "This one gem," he said, rolling it toward the general, "is part of the Ptolemaic collection; it's beryl and quite, quite rare. We have six. This one gem can make the average Roman a wealthy man."

Constantius held it to the sunlight. "Hmm. Interesting."

"This," he said, pushing the vest across the table, "holds seven more such packets, each with about fifteen stones."

"Seven more you say."

"Yes, seven more, totaling over a hundred gems. There are more than a thousand gems of even greater historical significance at Narbo. Galla has them hidden away."

"Galla. You call her Galla, not Your Highness, Augusta, or princess?"

"She and I are very close—and you know very well she has never been ordained Augusta. Now, back to the gems. According to Galla, the statue holds the richest treasure lode in the world. Collected by Eutropius the eunuch, they were hidden inside the statue and found their way to Rome in the belly of a consul's ship." Lucius watched the general's every expression and could see he knew the history. *Good,* he thought.

Continuing, he said, "After the man died—I refer to the one who brought them to Rome—they somehow, no one knows exactly how, ended up in a villa in Tibur and were, let's say, rescued by the sorceress during the siege. How I got them to Narbo is—"

Constantius abruptly sat up, hushed Lucius, and pushed the gems and vest back toward him, whispering, "Say no more, lad. My aide approaches. He would never interrupt when I am out here except—" Constantius rose and met his aide at the foot of the steps. They spoke briefly. When he returned to the stone table, the blood had drained from his face. "We must continue another time. The Goths have taken Barcelona."

"Sure, he was here," said the innkeeper of the Icarus Horse Inn to the two assassins, "left some time ago. Do you two travelers want the beds or not?"

"We'll take 'um. Feed and water for the horses, too. Damn near killed the critters getting here. Rode straight through hoping to catch up with our friend," said Tauriac. "What's all the commotion about?"

"Funeral. They be entombing Bishop Lazarus tomorrow. Damn near every presbyter and bishop in the province will be in attendance. Held off the blessed event until the papal legate arrived, they did. That's why the only beds left are out back above the stable. Lazarus was a good man, he was. Sure will miss that sainted soul. How long you be stayin'?"

"A few days. Need to rest the horses," said Tauriac.

"Your choice," said the innkeeper. "Just make sure you bring no trouble. We've had our share."

The drums caused Tauriac to sit up. Looking out the cantilevered window, he could see an interment procession in the distance wending its way through the main gate and up Este Major. He knew the city well, having been here four years ago. Rousing Irontooth, they dressed quickly and climbed down from the loft. Then they took the shortcut over the corral fence and headed toward the main gate.

"Hurry," Tauriac shouted to Irontooth, who was still trying to lace up his trousers. "If we're gonna pick off a purse or two, we need to do it before they leave the main square."

They caught the tail end of the marchers as they left the square and started up Mt. Este on the switchback trail heading to the cemetery. Halfway there, Irontooth puffed, "I . . . I give up . . . This is too much . . . for nothing. Ain't nobody got a darn thing on 'um any*v*ay. . . damn you," and he turned back down the hill grousing, "Never did like funerals anyhow."

Tauriac shrugged and gave up as well. After retreating through the city gates, they came upon the big rock outside the city walls. Sitting quietly atop that rock was a hunched-over old woman selling food. They stopped to purchase whatever she sold, which turned out to be freshly baked honey biscuits.

"God bless you both," she said. "Come t' watch them bury that son-of-a-bitch, did ye?"

"No, just passing through," said Tauriac. He looked at Irontooth standing beside him silently eating his biscuit. After waiting for his companion to say something sarcastic, Tauriac took up the conversation again. "Understand your holy man had an accident."

"Maybe. And maybe not. How he ended up at the bottom of the Overlook is still a mystery." Wringing her hands like a ravenous waif, she added, "His death did do some good. It brung them other bishops to our fine municipality. A rich and wily bunch, too. They be staying on a bit longer to straighten out a curvy carrot."

"Oh," said Tauriac, not really interested but already wanting another one of those delicious honey biscuits. He pulled out two more coppers and handed them up. She tossed down a second biscuit and held up another, silently asking if Irontooth wanted it. He shook his head no.

"Yup. I hear that man Charisius, he's the metropolitan of this episcopate ye know, held up the burial so all them important folk had time to get here. Put Lazarus on ice at the butcher's vault so he wouldn't stink up the place—not that I'd mind. After they drop that one in the ground, they're gonna put the bishop from Gubbio on ice for a few days and turn this memorial into a synod. Word has it that the metropolitan's been changing the sacred rituals to suit himself. Gonna be some loud hootin' and hollerin' over that, I tell ye."

Mouth full of biscuit, Tauriac could only grunt. The only reason he listened to her babble was because he wanted a third biscuit. He looked at Irontooth again and couldn't believe that the man only wanted one.

"Yup," she prattled on. "All these high holy men staying around should fatten my purse. They could use some fattenin', you know. Sold more biscuits this week than all year, I have. These holy folk sure know how to spend," she said and laughed. Then she added, "Other people's money, that is."

"Oh," said Tauriac, suddenly interested. "Where're they all from?"

"Perugia, Cortona, Clusium, Iguvium, and places out west," she said pointing. "Nuceria, Toso, Mevania, and, of course, Spoletium from back thataway." She pointed again.

"Vhy do you say 'of course'?" Irontooth asked, speaking for the first time. Tauriac nodded, interested in her answer too.

"The metropolitan is from Spoletium—and by far the richest man in these parts since Ponti Lepius Filipi died in that mudslide.

Comes from a family ennobled by their land, he does, a noble family of landowners. Not one bit generous, mind you, but rotten rich."

"And how would you know he is, as you say, 'rotten rich'?" asked Tauriac, more and more interested in what the old hag had to say.

"When he opened his purse to pay, I looked down and saw what he had in it. Plus, I know every bit of gossip in this here valley. Want to know more?"

More? She'd said enough, thought Tauriac. He thanked her and headed back to the Icarus Horse Inn with Irontooth.

"Do you think that fancy carriage out back belongs to this metropolitan fellow?" asked Irontooth.

"Let's find out," Tauriac said in that wheezily nasal tone which usually foreshadowed mischief.

They found the stable master and he confirmed that the coach with the fancy crest on the door belonged to the metropolitan. Thus a plot was born. Later that night, Tauriac crawled under the metropolitan's coach and began working on the pin that connected the hitch to the front axle. The hitch was the extended wooden shaft that the horses would be harnessed to later. Using animal fat from the kitchen, he made certain the thick metal pin could be easily pulled free. The pull ring was missing, so he took one off a nearby coach and affixed it to the end of the pin. It took time. But he was patient. Tauriac wanted no slipups.

Three days later, Tauriac and Irontooth lay in ambush along the road to Spoletium. The funeral and synod completed, the four-carriage convoy split up near Forum Flaminii. Two went north toward Nucera-Umbra, another took the old Flaminia road south to Mevania, and the fourth, the metropolitan's carriage, took the newer roadway south, the one that never flooded.

Because the roadway was busy in the morning, their attack would have to be quick. They picked a spot with adequate cover, tied a rope to a fallen branch, propped it against a tree, and hid in the nearby bushes. Luck was with them. When the metropolitan's carriage approached, no traffic was coming from either direction. At the right moment, Tauriac pulled the rope and the branch fell, blocking the roadway. They heard the cursing as the two unsuspecting drivers pulled up.

"What is the difficulty," Tauriac heard a voice ask from inside the carriage.

"Just a fallen limb," shouted the older driver. "Be on our way in a moment, Your Excellency."

Irontooth, crouched next to Tauriac, nudged him and then tapped his wrist. Tauriac nodded. He'd seen it too. The older driver had the reins wrapped around his wrists. That would make this much easier. Up went their hoods and out came their knives; the road bandits were ready to strike.

Listlessly, the younger of the two drivers dropped from the driver's box and ambled by them without a care in the world. When he succeeded in pulling the limb to one side, Tauriac jumped out from the bushes, rolled under the carriage, and pulled the pin from the hitch, releasing the two horses.

The surprised driver reacted instantly. He released the brake, snapped the reins, and roared at the top of his lungs, "He-ya! He-ya!"

The horses did as trained and bolted forward. But instead of the carriage moving out of harm's way, the driver was ejected from his seat, the reins still wrapped tightly around his wrists. He hit the paving stones like a sack of potatoes; his hat flew in one direction, his boot in another.

"Stay put!" ordered Irontooth to the younger driver, pointing a knife in his direction. The young man just stood there with his mouth open, his eyes wide, and both hands still holding the tree limb, watching as the horses drug his companion down the roadway.

Tauriac walked to the door of the carriage, swung it open, and politely asked the metropolitan and his aide to step out. "We're not going to harm you, Your Excellency," he said graciously, "just relieve you of some of your burden."

The aide jumped out. Turning around, he retrieved a step-box from inside the coach and placed it on the ground beneath the carriage door. Then, along with Tauriac, he helped the metropolitan to the ground. Large, round faced, and sporting a full head of graying hair, the metropolitan was clad in a waterfall of cascading robes. Cutting the belt holding the purse around the obese metropolitan's waist,

Tauriac patted him down for a money belt. Finding none, he moved quickly to the aide. On him, he found a pouch filled with coins. After searching the inside of the carriage for anything of value, Tauriac thanked them both for their donations and bowed deeply. Then he and Irontooth disappeared.

Ravenna was a hundred and sixty miles away.

CHAPTER 5

The sun had not yet risen when there was a knock. Lucius rolled out of bed, scratched himself, and lazily shuffled to the door.

"Lucius Domitilla?" asked a voice in the shadows.

"Yes, I'm Lucius. What's this about—and why so early?"

"I am the patrician's *adiutor*, his personal messenger," handing Lucius a note along with the ring he gave the tribune at the docks. "He requests your presence at once, sir."

"The who?" groused Lucius, annoyed by the early intrusion.

"The patrician—the *magister militum.*"

"I'm sorry. It's the middle of the night, I'm half asleep. Who's this patrician?"

"Master-General Constantius, he awaits you at the encampment, horses are waiting. You should dress for travel. I assume you can ride, sir."

Lucius made a face; it was not pretty.

By the time the sun peaked over the walls and through the trees behind them, Lucius and the messenger traveled the thin corridor of dry land that ran from Ravenna to the hardened roadway. Once there, they turned north.

Two hours later, the military encampment of the III Theodosius legion came into view. Located on the Po River, it was cosseted by earthen mounds, topped by a palisade walkway, and surrounded by a wide ditch. Two corrals bordered the double-door entrance, the pens full of identically bred roans—the horse of choice for the cavalry.

They dismounted, gave their reins to the stable hand, and passed through the well-guarded entrance into a sea of white tents. Following the messenger and moving quickly toward a tight grouping of larger tents by the river, Lucius could not help but notice the clutter. It was so unlike the bivouacs on the edge of his valley where the legions camped when moving between Rome and Ravenna. He saw one legionary toss a dirty bowl into his tent. When he returned to sleep, Lucius thought, his bed would be crawling with ants. How uncharacteristically careless.

"Wait here," said the messenger, going ahead. Upon returning, he led Lucius to a nondescript tent in front of which stood a standard topped by an iron eagle. As he waited, three officers came out of the tent and rudely pushed past him. Two were tribunes, probably staff officers from their lack of upper-body development. Lucius had learned that distinction by hanging around the camp at Thor Pass. The third was a hardened warrior holding his plumed helmet in the crook of his arm, giving the impression he held a rooster. From the plume, Lucius surmised that he was the *primus pilus*—the senior centurion of the legion. And he detected one more thing: the warrior was not very happy.

Inside the tent Constantius was sitting on the edge of his cot rubbing the back of his neck. His face was washed of color and his hair was grayer than Lucius remembered. He looked haggard. *Could this be the man on whom Galla had pinned her hopes?*

An attendant busied himself with the folding chairs. Whatever the discussion had been, it was apparently no more to the general's liking than it was to the primus pilus's. He greeted Lucius with a nod, cleared his throat, which sounded very much like a croaking bullfrog, and spoke without looking up. "The days of good soldiering are gone, lad," motioning for the attendant to hurry with the chairs. "I'm up to here with amateurs," he said, touching his nose. Finished, the attendant rushed out. The general seemed to frighten everyone but Lucius.

"When I was young like you," the general began, "I willingly— and when I say willingly—I mean I trudged through it all, enduring whatever it was I had to endure: the summer's sun, the winter's snow, the rain, the mud, the incessant noise of the baggage wagons, and the sickening smell from the horses' asses. Sure, the camaraderie was good, as was the wine and local camp bitches. But we never lost sight that the turf was our bed, the boughs our blankets, and the swamps our fountains. Work was our mistress, lad, the weather our trial, and the fires of hell our future. Combat paled to the march. Look out there." He pointed through the tent flap. "Half those men are unseasoned, untrained, and incapable of the shortest march. The winter made women of them all. I came out here to inspect an army and found a bunch of milkmaids. Not one can throw a dart, thrust a sword, or wield an axe much less put fear in the enemy. A brick maker can fight better. They are the most unshaven, rumpled, and undisciplined bunch I've ever commanded."

He rose from his cot and began to pace. "I have appointed Flavius Abinnaeus to correct this situation at once or he goes back to Salona."

"The officer I encountered at the port?" asked Lucius.

"The same. A magnificent bastard he is too—a general's dream, a recruit's nightmare. He whipped that garrison in Dalmatia back into shape in six months. He'll do better here or else. Time is a luxury we do not have. The man can be a nitpicking son-of-a-bitch in times of peace, but he's brilliant in battle. With the loss of Barcelona to the Goths, our situation has changed. I need men like him in a hurry, so thank the gods he was here."

"Yes sir. Thank the gods," echoed Lucius.

"You know, a hundred years ago we had sixty-seven battle-hardened legions East and West. Constantine, that self-centric bastard, whittled that down to thirty. And years later Theodosius was hard-pressed to muster eight to face that usurper Eugenius and his general, Arbogast, at the Frigidus. Then poor Stilicho, a splendid general on many levels, rode all the way to Mainz to steal, literally pinch, conscripts from the frontier to face Radagaisus. His regulars, auxiliaries, and foederati totaled but thirty thousand against two hundred thousand raging madmen from beyond the Danube. Now look at us. I can't march even that many into battle if, God please pity us all, it comes to that."

"Why do you share this with me?" asked Lucius.

"Because you accomplished what my best agents could not. That tells me there is more to you than meets the eye. I had four different teams out there looking for that thing."

"You refer to the statue, I presume."

"Precisely," he said. Then he cleared his throat, adjusted himself, and began to pace. "Furthermore, somewhere along the way you met with that fucking conspirator, did you not?"

"By 'fucking conspirator,' sir, I assume you refer to Jovinus."

Getting no response from the general, Lucius went on. "If you do mean Jovinus, yes, we met at Mainz. He wanted the Burgundians to join in against you. And the former king of the Burgundians, a left-hander with wicked ways, was a willing conspirator before Gunther killed him. Then Gunther, a different sort with a clearer vision, became king and saw no future fighting with the likes of you, sir. Burgundia was his kingdom, peace his goal."

Constantius stopped pacing, grasped Lucius by the shoulders, and shook him. "You, my lad, you are my eyes and ears."

"Me, sir? Your eyes and ears? I don't understand."

"Yes, of course you don't. Let me explain. You possess intimate knowledge of our enemy. You know specifics on Narbo and its environs, the Goths' defenses, their inner workings, and, most importantly, their thinking. You have more insight into those we go up against than all my agents combined."

"Since you put it that way, yes I do. And in some cases, I've more knowledge than I'll admit to." And Lucius issued one of his coy little smiles that worked well on powerful men like the general. Not this time, however; Constantius was too intense.

"Answer me this," the general said, relaxing his grip on Lucius. "It's been a mystery so far. Because the Huns are a mishmash of mischief makers that will need to be dealt with sooner or later, I need to know what happened to my spy. Cacca Reba was the best window we had into the Huns' mysterious world."

"Ah yes, Cacca Reba. I expected we might get to him. Well now . . . hmm." And he paused to gather his thoughts. "Where do you want me to start?"

"Anywhere you like."

"I understand. Okay. Well, after his attempt to assassinate Gunther during his coronation—the boldest act I've ever witnessed—Gunther decided to get rid of him once and for all. We lured the Hun into a trap using me as the bait. He lost an arm to my sword, he did—a lucky blow, I assure you. Then after his recovery, the rascal ran off to his people on the Danube. At least that's what everyone concluded, and it made sense. In the end, what good is a one-armed warrior?"

"Indeed."

Lucius wondered anew why the general was being so open with him. Was he searching for a way to uproot the Goths before there was war, or was it something else?

"Sorry I brought it up," the general said. "Forget the Hun. He's done with. Back to my problem here. I've stripped the Verona, Aquileia, and Patavium garrisons to fill the holes here. Others like Milan, Cremona, and Dertona will send what men they can to a camp at Placentia for retraining."

"That's good, right?" asked Lucius, trying to boost the general's downward spiral.

"No," he snapped. "They're all wall-walkers who don't know a *testudo* from a church procession."

"A testudo?" asked Lucius. "What the devil is a testudo?"

"A formation we stole from the Greeks."

"Ah, a turtle. I'm familiar with that. I watched Gunther form his Burgundians into that phalanx. He quickly discovered what most do eventually—it doesn't work with round shields. They stole rectangular ones from Rome, you know."

Worried about more pressing problems, the general quickly lost interest in discussing formations. He said, "I'm desperate for veterans to train those neophytes out there. If I don't surround the new with those who've tasted blood, they'll run at the first sight of those damnable heathens. And the Germani put on a show with the paint, the horns, and all that screaming. Panic is the bane of every general—it's infectious."

"Well, have you considered winning without fighting? Maybe it's time to resume our conversation from the garden four days ago?" Lucius picked a chair off the stack and set it next to the cot.

"That's why I invited you here, lad," the general said. "Great Jupiter, has it been four days?" Slapping his forehead, Constantius flopped onto the cot once again.

"Can I speak openly here, sir?" asked Lucius, scooting closer. He remembered how paranoid the general was at having their words be overheard at their first encounter.

"Of course. These men care little of palace intrigue. They live in a different world." Just the same, the general called to an aide to keep everyone away from the tent.

Lucius pulled out the letter from Galla Placidia, handed it over, and watched silently as Constantius read it. The general remained stone-faced as he read. Then he held the seal to the light to authenticate it, got up, and moved to a lantern in the corner. "A man can face an uncertain future if caught with something like this," he whispered and burned the letter.

Lucius swallowed hard.

"Okay. Now what?" asked the general.

"I do possess a particularly unique set of skills, as you've already mentioned, and I am willing to use them to achieve what Galla, and hopefully you, want."

"Such as?"

"Such as the taming of the Goths. Or, said differently, the castration of the entire Narbonensis province over which the Goths have a stranglehold."

Constantius pursed his lips. "You amaze me, son. You truly do. But go on, show me how you castrate the most unpredictable wild boar in the West."

Lucius had waited a long time for this moment. He dropped his eyes, took a deep breath, looked up, and began: "I have two proposals." He paused a painfully long time to let the suspense build. With him, building anticipation was more a natural inclination than an act.

"First, some background," he said at last. "The Goths are near starvation, correct?"

The general did not answer.

"They have planted little and confiscated less."

Still no response. Lucius was discovering that the general was not an easy man.

"I saw firsthand where the inhabitants of Aniane and Gellon burned their fields before they fled. I have also been told that the hill people come down from the Pyrenees, nip at Athaulf's heels, and then disappear back into the mountains. King Athaulf failed to break into Massilia, is blocked by the Rhone River to the east, and is now looking south."

"They did take Tolosa," said Constantius at last.

"And how long can Tolosa's storehouses sustain that many Goths, General? A month, maybe two?"

Constantius looked down at his hands.

"Now, to another point," continued Lucius. "The aristocracy of Rome was bled clean by the invasion. I have personally run my hands through the mountains of gold coins that were taken from their villas, estates, and Rome's treasury. What gold the aristocracy has left, they keep hidden. Ravenna needs that gold to pay its legions, as meager as they are. You saw the gems I brought. I offer them to you to do what needs to be done."

"They can't eat jewels, lad."

"Of course not. But my gems, converted to gold bars, will buy enough grain to feed these people for a year."

"For the moment, let's say that's true. Where will you get the grain? There's barely enough in Ravenna this time of year and less in Rome."

"The man I travel with is an estate agent. He will contact those provincial landowners who hoard small amounts of grain in their storehouses and who are willing to release it if we pay substantially above the market price. He will arrange to have it delivered directly to Narbo or Barcelona, or to the Baleares Isles for the Goths to retrieve if they do not want Roman ships in their harbor."

"I see you've thought this through, haven't you." It was not a question. "What do you propose the Goths give up in return? Narbo? Barcelona? All of Narbonensis?"

"First they give up the emperor's sister. We get Galla Placidia back."

"Hmm. Interesting. What if the palace does not want her back?"

"We'll get to that. To prevent a war that you cannot afford to wage, Galla instructed me to suggest a way around this obstacle. Are you willing to listen to a woman's suggestion?"

The general shook his head in disbelief. "First a lad, now a woman. Go on."

"Don't attempt to reclaim the territory by force or by treaty. Instead, pit the Goths against the Vandals and the Suebi, who have occupied central Spain for the past seven years. But, now listen carefully, instead of *divide et impera*—divide and conquer—Galla suggests you invoke a fresh approach of *divide et complecti*."

"*Divide et complecti*? What is that?"

"Divide and embrace. Forsake tradition. Make the Goths more than foederati. Welcome them officially into the world to which they want to belong. Make them citizens of Rome. Give them Spain to govern. By doing this, you legitimize their occupation. Then, take one additional step by removing the pebble in their sandal. Have the bishop of Rome—"

"You mean the pope," interrupted Constantius.

"Yes, the pope. Have *the pope* overlook their differences. Have him refrain from calling the Goths' most cherished beliefs a rupture—"

"You mean a schism."

"Okay, a schism. A gulf between their beliefs and his. After all, Arianism is but a subtlety—a minor infraction—a petty dogmatic disagreement. The pope should practice what he prays and turn the other cheek."

"The other cheek, you say? Ha. Have you met Pope Innocent by chance? You can only say these things because you are not a Christian—no cock in the ring, as they say." And the general smiled. "Ambition will never trump virtue, lad. Forget the pope."

"I disagree. Did you know," Lucius began, "that the pope permitted a Tuscan soothsayer to perform the magic arts while the city was under siege by the Goths? When under pressure, he, like everyone, becomes a realist."

"Just a rumor, lad."

"A rumor? I say not. The Christian hierarchy is duplicitous. I know what a bishop does. With one hand on his heart, he slips the other into your purse."

"The same can be said of all systematic beliefs, lad. Isis, Odin, Zeus, and all his Mount Olympus offspring, can stir the soul while reigning havoc on their believers. Your approach is unrealistic. Make up your mind. Are you out to save the world"—and he laughed at that—"or Galla Placidia?"

It was the first time Lucius heard the general laugh.

"The world? No sir," he replied. "I'm just after saving the empire; I am a citizen by birth and instilled with Roman pride. To save Rome for Romans is the torch I bear. How many usurpers can we suffer? This generation has had more than any other: Eugenius, Attalus, Maximus, Constantine III, Jovinus, and before them—"

"Okay, okay, I'm familiar with the list," broke in Constantius, "and more shall rise to challenge the throne."

"Why? Why more? Why so fatalistic? It's weakness that gives traitors the opportunity. Honorius is no ruler; he is but a—"

"Hold on," said the general, grabbing Lucius's knee. He got up, walked to the flap, quickly looked outside, and then returned to the cot. "Okay, go on."

"I thought you said I could speak openly."

"On politics, yes, but not treason."

"Fine, then call me a traitor. Honorius is but a puppet. Strengthen the throne, I say. Galla is the answer, the only answer. Her pedigree is unequalled." Lucius leaned close in preparation for his next words: the *reussir son coup* of this entire effort. "She proffers a union with you, sir, a permanent partnership." There, he said it.

"A union," Constantius repeated rather easily, either not understanding or pretending not to.

Lucius leaned even closer. "A union with you, sir. The two of you as one."

Constantius rose. "Is this another of your—" He stopped short of stating the obvious. "She's married."

"That marriage will end one way or the other."

The general raised an eyebrow, said nothing. But Lucius knew he had him hooked. "It was not a Christian marriage, sir." Then he quickly added, "And it was performed under duress. The woman's a hostage. Never forget that."

The general was having a difficult time with this. Clearing his throat, he said, "That argument will not succeed in Ravenna or Rome. There's no evidence she was forced. What is your other path? You said 'one way or the *other.*'"

"Yes, the *other.* The other is more onerous, I'm afraid." He lowered his eyes and then looked up. "It rests on Athaulf's demise."

"Demise?" repeated the general, clearly surprised. "What does that mean?"

"He was wounded at Massilia and never fully recovered. The man rides like this." Lucius slumped over holding his side. "As long as the carrions circle, his assassination—"

"—is a real possibility," said Constantius finishing Lucius's sentence. "My, my, young man, you really are more than you appear."

Tauriac and Irontooth finally arrived before the walls of Ravenna. Both were weary, Irontooth was angry. They had been stopped twice by patrols, had had their weapons confiscated, and were now being rudely turned away by the guards at the main gate. Like all the others who'd tried, they soon discovered that there was no way to get through without credentials, credentials that were impossible to obtain. Milling around the gate for the second day in a row, they experienced an unexpected turn that reversed their dour moods. Lucius himself was riding their way.

"They return from the Po River camp," said a guard enjoying his lunch under the tree where Tauriac and Irontooth sat. "The third trip."

Tauriac scooted around the back of the tree, pulling his companion with him. "Don't let him see us," said Tauriac. "This is good josh."

"Vhat's so good? The little shit is surrounded by seven legionaries."

Holding his hand over his mouth, Tauriac whispered, "Wearing a cloak, isn't he? It's warm, yet he wears a cloak. Wake up, you dull-witted cretin. What's that tell ye, hmm? He still carries the gems on his person. If we can't get him, we get the cloak. To hell with Singerich."

Hidden by the tree trunk as they were, Lucius did not notice them when he passed. Reinvigorated by what they'd deduced about Lucius's cloak, they renewed their efforts to get past the walls. And, if that failed, they set their minds to figuring out a scheme to lure Lucius to them so they could at least get the cloak, if not his head. Over the next days nothing worked. Nor did anyone know where Lucius slept, much less who he was. So they set up a watch to see who came and went through the main gate, hoping something, anything, would fall into their laps.

After a week of continuous boredom, they were once again struck with good fortune. A wayfarer who happened to take a rest under their shade tree suggested they try the port. At first they scoffed at the idea, thinking the only way in was through the main gate. Then again, anything was better than sitting there day after day. So that night they "borrowed" a small boat and explored the port, just to check it out. The mouth was well-guarded—that they had expected. What they hadn't expected, and Tauriac noticed it first, was that the fishermen, particularly those who returned before sunrise, were generally ignored when they came in with their catches.

For the next three nights they commandeered the same boat and sat off the port pretending to fish. A pattern developed. Although all the other fishing boats returned directly, one came near the shore and passed close to a spit of land south of the inlet's mouth dragging a net. The fisherman was trolling for bait. And he worked alone.

The next night they lay in wait on that spit of land. But because of the weather, none of the boats went out. The following night was different. The weather cleared and they could see the boats and the fishermen working the nets. When the hour was right, Tauriac and Irontooth waded out into the chest-deep water off the spit of land and waited. The wind died, forcing the fishermen to row. That was even better.

Noses just out of the water, they crouched and waited. When the lone fisherman passed twenty feet offshore as he always did, Irontooth grabbed an oar while Tauriac pulled the unsuspecting fisherman out of the boat and under the water. The man flailed a little, but he was no match for Tauriac. He went limp. The guards were at least three hundred yards away and heard nothing. Irontooth climbed into the craft and started to pull the fisherman in.

"Wait," Tauriac whispered. He pushed the fisherman's head under one more time just to be sure. Then they eased him up over the transom and into the boat. Irontooth covered himself and the body with the netting, while Tauriac donned the man's outer garment and covered his forehead with the rag the fisherman wore, knotting it at the back of his head. Having seen the others with the same color head rag, they had decided it was a standard form of identification for the guards.

Tauriac rowed into the port without incident and tied up at a quiet part of the dock. Irontooth slipped out from under the netting and silently disappeared into the nearest shadows. Making certain that no one could see him, Tauriac then took off the fisherman's clothes, put them as best he could back on the body, and slipped it silently into the water. Grabbing the fisherman by the hair before his body drifted away, Tauriac took the butt of his knife and struck him hard. Then he climbed onto the dock, untied the boat, and pushed it off, its lines trailing. When daylight came, the dockworkers would assume the fisherman got careless and fell into the water, striking his head on the side of the boat as he fell—a highly unusual accident, yes, but nonetheless, a tragic mishap by an old-timer who got careless.

Using the shadows, Tauriac and Irontooth stole into the city with one thing in mind: Lucius Domitilla's cloak. And if Irontooth had his way, Lucius's head.

Two days after Tauriac and Irontooth slipped into the city, Lucius woke feeling exceptionally upbeat. Despite the bureaucratic entanglements, there was promise in the air. At last he would meet Emperor Honorius. Not one person in Umbria, except for his mentor, had ever had an audience with anyone this renowned. Lucius even acquired a new tunic for the occasion.

Admittedly, his dealings with the bureaucracy this past week had nearly driven him over the edge. It was that maddening. Yesterday he had encountered Araxius and Propius, the two men Galla suggested he see. The experience left him empty. Without knowing or caring about the emperor's position on the subject, these two supposed friends of Galla had obstructed Lucius's ideas wherever they could. Never once did either admit his project held promise. It made Lucius wonder if anyone, especially these two who Galla believed to be her faithful allies, really wanted the princess back. But that was not what bothered him the most. It was the petty squabbling between the two: who would be in charge of the ransom, if, indeed, there was one; who would take possession of the gems; who would count the gold after the transfer. Never once did either inquire how the gold would be turned into grain. Neither official held any interest in his "grain for a princess" idea; their interests were fully on the gems and gold.

Holding his tongue sapped every ounce of Lucius's energy. Their haughtiness was maddening. These men, who should have had no say in any of this, demanded the final word if by chance "this fool's affair" went forward, even though he, Lucius, held the means and Mahaki the grain.

"Arrogance follows power like a shadow," Mahaki said afterward. "Ignore them. Only succeeding matters, not how."

The bureaucratic pettiness notwithstanding, it was amazing how the doors of Ravenna flew open since Lucius's encounter with Constantius. He met with almost all the key advisors to the throne. Although imposing in terms of status, not one of them impressed him. In fact, the gatherings had not prepared him one smidgen for what he was about to face today—the day he would meet the emperor. Of course he'd been briefed on how to dress, where to stand, and how to act. But he still felt unprepared, and the strict protocols made him think that the emperor was a porcelain god that would break if a wrong word uttered or a wrong step taken in his presence.

Giving his appearance a once-over, Lucius rushed off to meet Mahaki who left earlier to assist the produce lady. The two had found some common interests, and Mahaki helped her at the stall far beyond what their agreement demanded. What Lucius did not know as he rushed to meet Mahaki was that two assassins lurked in the shadows of Ravenna searching for him.

Tearing Mahaki away from his acquiescent chores, they made their way through the city unsuspecting of the danger that prowled the alleyways and arrived at the gilded gates of the palace without incident. Waiting to receive them was the adiutor, the messenger who had guided Lucius to the encampment. He bowed, said a few words to the guards, and then escorted Lucius and Mahaki up the twelve marble steps to a large entrance room that, to Lucius's eye, resembled the *pronaos* of the abandoned temple on the main square of Assisi. There the guards checked them once more for weapons, offered each a silver bowl in which to wash their hands, and then led them to the base of twin staircases that swept down from the second level.

Another imperial servant took charge at the base of the stairs and preceded them up. The handrail was of pink travertine marble and the balusters were shaped like white owls. When Mahaki reached to use the handrail, the imperial servant politely instructed, "Please, sir, touch nothing."

Mahaki used it anyway.

At the top, they passed through two sets of doors before arriving at an oblong sitting room crowned by a spectacular vaulted ceiling. The gallery of half-columns that lined the room were in the Greek tradition: simple capitals with fluted shafts. Above the half-columns, the room was ringed by a continuous carved wood cornice beneath which, sitting in niches, were the busts of every emperor since Octavian. On the far wall above the main door was the figure of a reclining nymph flanked by colorful frescoes of pastoral scenes. The pastoral scenes evoked a kind of peacefulness, but the blatant nudity of the nymph was, even to Lucius's prurient delights, in poor taste. More to his liking was the mosaic floor, which boasted a giant-winged eagle surrounded by geometric designs of black and white tiles. And above, in the middle of the vaulted ceiling, an ingenious artist had recreated a stylistic depiction of the grape harvest in multicolored mosaic tiles, which, in its wondrous splendor, completed the room.

And there Lucius and Mahaki sat, surrounded by an opulence unequalled anywhere in the world, waiting patiently for their audience with the emperor.

Finally, the door at the end of the room opened and four identically dressed servants approached. It was time. Lucius took several deep breaths, kept his eyes down as instructed, and remained four steps behind the imperial lictor.

As they were about to pass through the open door to the throne room, Mahaki was pulled aside and ordered to remain behind.

Inside the throne room, Lucius halted twenty paces from the throne at a marked spot. When he gained the courage to look up, he focused on a spectacle he would soon not forget. A small, dark-haired man with boyish features sat stoically atop an ornate platform in an oversized cushioned chair. The back of the chair arched high above the man's head like a brilliant circlet that, to Lucius, resembled the half wheel of the Zodiac. It was supported by five thick legs, had two oversized arms, and was intricately adorned with carvings of what appeared to be animals. In front of the throne sat three square risers, or steps, one smaller than the next, each level adorned with a repetition of the astrological signs Gemini, Virgo, and Aquarius. His first thought: the Christian emperor sat encased in an array of pagan symbols. The contradiction would remain with him throughout this audience.

As for the emperor, he was dressed in a heavily embroidered robe of purple that was embossed with gold stitching. He was also wearing purple slippers, rings on each finger, and a thin strand of laurel around his head.

Emperor Honorius looked straight ahead, eyes fixed on a point behind Lucius, showing not one flicker of interest in who or what moved before him, consumed totally by the role he had been prepared to play since birth. Lucius pitied the man-boy; pitied him because he appeared inhuman, inborn, and unhappy. The childless emperor, although thirty, had had few real experiences. A man this empty truly deserved pity. Lucius knew the emperor spent his private hours obsessing over chickens and was the target of many of his subjects' criticisms, calling him such things as weak, foolish, indecisive, timid, lackluster, and, finally, retarded. Yet his ineptness, Lucius concluded, was what somehow kept him on the throne. For if he was more capable, he would be a danger and the privileged world of those around him would vanish.

Lucius knew the emperor's history. Born in Constantinople, pronounced "Most Noble" at two, a consul at three, and given the title of emperor at nine. When Theodosius, his father, died two years later, Honorius became the *de facto* emperor and had been reigning over the West since. Years later, in fear of the Gothic onslaught, he moved the throne to Ravenna from Milan and here remained a prisoner of his limitation; or, as some would say who knew the whole truth, a victim of those who controlled him.

Flanking the platform stood four guards. In the shadows were two men in dark togas. One carried a scepter, the other a book: symbols of power and knowledge. One was Araxius, provost of the Sacred Cubicle, with whom Lucius had met. The other was the chamberlain, with whom Lucius had not, nor would, meet. The latter was openly against the ransom of Galla Placidia and cool to anything short of total annihilation of the Goths.

The scene before Lucius was sterile. No one spoke, no one moved. It was eerie. Then the door behind Lucius opened and Constantius strolled in. He went straight to the platform, mounted the three steps, dropped to one knee, and kissed the emperor's ring. When he rose, they spoke briefly and then Constantius retreated to Lucius's side. The emperor and Constantius stared at each other as though communicating. Then the emperor nodded, rose, and, without showing his back, moved deeper into the shadows behind the throne and, along with the provost and the chamberlain, disappeared.

The general took Lucius's arm and led him out through a series of doors and down some steps, Mahaki trailing behind them.

"Well, lad," said the general, "you got what you wanted. He likes you. Said he felt an unusual energy when you entered the room. Honorius, you know, fancies himself an oracle of sorts. Believes he can look into a man's heart. His desire is for you to leave tomorrow for Barcelona. The III Theodosius will depart in ten days. Abinnaeus is doing a splendid job whipping those shiftless bastards into real soldiers. But ten days will not be enough I fear to—"

"Wait! Wait! I cannot leave yet!" insisted Lucius. "There is too much to do. Convert the gems into gold bars, purchase six hundred thousand measures of grain, and arrange for its shipment to who knows where. I need transportation, credentials, and a guide—there's far too much to do to leave so soon."

"When then?"

"A week, maybe two."

Constantius escorted them to the gate. "Tomorrow we shall discuss it. Come by my tablinum before the midday meal. And—oh, by the way, congratulations. Now that the emperor approves, most all the others will agree your plan is brilliant."

"Thank you."

"Tomorrow then. And know that all the manpower you need is at your disposal. From now on this is official imperial business: the grain, the ships, and the travel. Demand nothing less than full cooperation from all those involved. The power of the throne is behind you, lad. Never need you hear no from anyone—do you understand?"

Lucius did not answer. Something else was on his mind. "The emperor thinks me vulgar, doesn't he?"

Constantius did nothing more than smile. But that smile said it all.

Irontooth spotted Lucius and Mahaki earlier that day leaving the market. He and Tauriac had separated earlier in order to expand their search. Careful not to be noticed, Irontooth followed them to the palace and waited. When they did not reemerge right away, he hunted down Tauriac. He told him what he'd seen and that Lucius was not wearing the cloak. Together they rushed to the marketplace where Irontooth saw the little man with the headdress working. That particular stand was now closed for the noon meal; however, the woman selling cheese in the next stand told them where the produce lady lived. "Two vici that way, near the fountain," she said.

When the produce lady answered her door, Tauriac invented a story about a delivery from the palace for Lucius and his companion, while Irontooth stood to the side holding it. The produce lady led them to the shabby shed behind her house where Lucius and the strange little man were residing. They thanked her for her trouble, left the small package against the door, and left.

Minutes later they were behind the shed breaking in through a window.

Stopping by a vendor for something to eat, Lucius was excited. Not so Mahaki. The prospect of collecting six hundred thousand measures of grain and arranging for its shipment down the Adriatic coast to the Tyrrhenian Sea was too much to think about. He was overwhelmed.

"When this is over, Mahaki, you'll be rich," Lucius said, trying to excite his friend. "Never again will you need to work or want for anything. Think of it."

"With so much to do, I should be leaving this very day," he said. "Ancona is a hundred miles south, which will take me at least four days—"

"Wait. Wait. Wait. Slow down. First, we convert the gems to gold. Then we arrange for a military escort. You'll be able to use the IE."

"The what?"

"The Express, the Imperial Express—what we used when we came north. After that, I want you to be with me at Barcelona. I need you, my friend. None of this is easy. We'll meet with the general tomorrow and make demands. Didn't he say we should not take no for an answer? Well then, that's exactly what we'll do. After you return from Ancona, we'll travel with the legion to Arles."

"Don't you think the general is pushing all this too fast? What's the rush?"

"Let's go home," said Lucius without answering the question. Of course the general was pushing. That was what generals do.

"It's in your hands, my friend," Lucius heard Mahaki mumble, but he could tell the little man was not happy.

When they arrived home, the produce lady was leaving for the market. "Two gents came by," she announced in her recently acquired bubbly manner, sneaking Mahaki a wink. "They left a package. Said it's from the palace. Now aren't you two keeping high company?" she teased. "The palace, no less. Anyway, I directed them out back."

"What'd they look like?" asked Lucius. "The palace doesn't—" He paused. "How were they dressed?"

"Shabby, smelly, hadn't bathed in a while. One had an iron tooth."

"An iron tooth?" That got his attention. "How 'bout the other?" he asked.

"Bald, reeking of coriander, had a ring in his ear. Both strapping fellas with tattoos."

They thanked her and she went on.

"That doesn't sound right at all," said Lucius. "Let's go by way of the fountain and have a listen."

And so they did.

Quietly approaching the back of the shed, Lucius pressed against the outside wall. He heard nothing. They withdrew to the far side of the fountain to talk, aware the walls of the shed were as thin as papyrus.

"I'll knock, then run," said Mahaki. "You listen."

Lucius nodded. Mahaki tiptoed around to the front, rapped hard on the door, and then fled. Lucius had his ear seared to the wall this time. At first there was nothing. Then he heard the floor creak and a whisper. At least two men were in there.

He moved quickly to where Mahaki disappeared. They waited. Soon two shadowy figures crept out of the hut and disappeared around the side. One carried something balled up under his arm. Something that looked very much like Lucius's cloak.

Unable to see much because the intruders disappeared so quickly, Lucius saw enough. One of the men was indeed Irontooth, the Goth from Narbo. The one he'd encountered in the forest. *What was he doing here? Coincidence? Not on your life. And why steal my cloak, unless . . . hmm?*

The following night, Tauriac and Irontooth lay on the roof of an abandoned house that had a clear view of the back of the produce lady's residence. They could see two legionaries keeping watch at the door of the shed where Lucius and Mahaki slept. *Those two are in for a surprise before this night is over,* Tauriac thought.

Tauriac was angry. No, anger was too mild a description. Furious was more like it, furious to the point of being a danger to himself and their mission. It was not finding rocks instead of gems in the hem of Lucius's cloak that made him crazy; it was seeing that little man with the desert headdress. The elusive little one, the one who slithered like a snake, the one who had greeted him and his men on the docks of Ancona years ago when the Avar contingent first crossed the Adriatic and slipped onto the shores of Italy the summer of revenge—sweet payback on the people of Umbria. That one with the desert headdress was the mastermind of it all, the facilitator, and, in the end, a traitor.

Tauriac thought him a brilliant strategist until the church collapsed atop his six Alani guards. Six handpicked warriors whom he'd brought all the way from the Azov to perform a task for which he'd been handsomely paid—the assassination of the leader of their clandestine war party, Sassen the Avar; paid for by none other than Sassen's two brothers. Yes, that little son-of-a-bitch Mahaki killed his bodyguards as sure as if he'd stuck a knife in their backs. That was how the little bastard worked, all cooperative and charming, then *phfft*, a knife in the back or a pile of stones on the head. The last time he'd seen Mahaki was atop Assisi standing on the rubble of what was once a church. And in that moment he'd sworn that if he ever got the chance, he would pluck the little bastard's eyeballs out, rip his testicles off his body, and stuff them down his fucking throat. Yes! Yes! The great gods of Zorka, yes! Finally he would fulfill that pledge. A couple of palace guards were not going to stand between him and a vengeance he'd sworn a Tauri oath to take.

"It won't be long," he whispered to Irontooth lying quietly next to him. Then he turned his attention back to that cruddy little shed. *Yes, it won't be long now.* At every turn of the glass, the two guards, when they weren't dozing off, took a long walk to the front of the property, looked around, and then returned with only one thought in mind—fall back to sleep. Never had he seen two more useless sentries.

Tauriac poked Irontooth who nodded off. "Get ready. They're getting up."

Irontooth shook himself awake and got to one knee.

"There, there they go," he whispered, lifting the first torch. Irontooth fiddled around in his pouch for something. "Hurry up, damn you!" Tauriac whispered. "I told you to be ready!"

There, Irontooth found what he was looking for. He pulled out two flint stones and struck them together. One torch exploded into flames, then another, followed by a third.

"Now," said Tauriac. And they slung the torches through the air.

Two landed on the roof of the shed, the third atop the pile of dried grass that they'd heaped against the base earlier in the day while pretending to be sweepers. Constructed long ago, the shed was a dried-out tinderbox. Tauriac fidgeted watching the torches lay there smoldering and flickering. Then suddenly the roof went up in flames lighting the surrounding neighborhood followed by shouts and screams. People came running, carrying buckets and urns, all frantically trying to douse the flames with water from the public fountain. Not just to save the pathetic shed or whoever was in it—the shed and its occupants were surely beyond saving—but to keep the fire from spreading to their own houses. The shed was an inferno for only a short time and then collapsed into a pile of iridescent embers.

Tauriac lay next to Irontooth on the roof listening to the commotion below, daring not to peek for fear of giving their position away. To Tauriac, those sounds were like songbirds chirping in his ears. Yes, he had his revenge. But what of the gems? If not in the cloak, then Lucius probably carried them somewhere else on his person. If he had, they'd surely find some in the ashes later, if there were, indeed, any gems to begin with. More importantly, he had his revenge on Mahaki.

But now that it was over, Tauriac felt a twinge of regret for Lucius. He had liked the young rascal, had liked him ever since that time he purchased a honey biscuit from him and his red-haired friend atop that rock in Umbria. That was what, four, five summers ago? The two had come face-to-face once more on the river when the Amals were going to hang the troublemaker and again in the dungeon at Valance after he bought Lucius's sorry ass for six *solidi* from the Amals. The Amal chieftain had thought Lucius was on the verge of death from the beating his men had given him. But Tauriac knew differently. He also knew the Burgundians would pay a handsome price to get him back. That was before he realized that he once again backed the wrong man. The usurper Jovinus, into whose army he enlisted, had been defeated. After that, Tauriac had been forced to run off to Narbo to save himself. Now all he needed to do was lie here patiently, enjoy the pleasing aroma of disaster, wait for the embers to cool, and then dig around for the gems.

While Tauriac lay on the roof gloating, Singerich was back at Narbo wondering what his two assassins were up to. Had they caught up with Lucius in time? For some reason, he doubted they had. If only that troublesome woman had taken the bait and gone after Lucius, then he would not be worrying now, maybe he'd even get a good night's sleep. But then, he would not have her available to open the door that never should have been closed to him. He got up from the bed and went to the table where he poured himself a half measure of wine. He downed it like an overworked plow horse on a hot summer day. Returning to the bed, he sat on the edge and rubbed his eyes with the balls of his hands, cursing that woman for controlling his every move.

Of course he knew why he let her. Freya-Gund held the key to his pending kingship—a greatness that should have been his years ago after Alaric collapsed following the failed crossing of the Messina Straits following the sack of Rome. The throne belonged to him, not Athaulf. Was he, Singerich, not a Balthi of the ruling class? Was he not brother to Alaric's queen Stairnon? And as a youth, was he not chosen to attend the War Academy in Constantinople? Because of his unique gifts, was he not selected a member of, and then, finally, the head of the imperial guard in Constantinople while Alaric, the fool, chased around Greece knocking on the gates of walled cities and asking for tribute instead of taking it? Yes, he, Singerich, was the mastermind behind the sieges of Trieste and Aquileia but not Pollentia. Why not Pollentia? Because he knew Pollentia would fail—which it did. He should have received the hindquarter of the boar for that but, again, he was ignored by the council.

Did the Tribal Council give him credit for extracting four thousand pounds of gold and a like amount of pepper from the Roman Senate the year before the grand sacking of the city? No! Again, what he earned he never got. Why, with all his successes, was he continually overlooked?

Soon enough he would rectify the insults and claim his rightful place. And Freya-Gund was the means. All he needed to do was convince her that the hunk of bronze she called Fortune, which contained nothing more than a few pebbles, was no longer in Narbo but in Barcelona. Putting up with her was a small price in exchange for the big chair at the council table. Yes, she was the instrument he needed to empty that chair so he could fill it himself. And then one day he would go down in the annals along with the great Gothic kings Fritigern, Hermanaric, and Athanaric. For he, Singerich, would establish once and for all the great kingdom of Gothia.

As for the present, he belonged with the main force down in Barcelona instead of here in Narbo wasting the days away. Then there was the ever-present danger of being captured in a surprise assault by Honorius's legions. Narbo would collapse in a matter of days if attacked. Yes, he should be safely in Barcelona instead of supporting the greed of that bitch Freya-Gund.

Then he heard it. Boots on the steps—she was coming! What disguise had she donned this time? What mood was she in? A bead of sweat appeared on his forehead as he hurriedly tried to pull on his breeches. The door burst open; the wooden latch flew from the jamb. Freya-Gund swept into the room, slammed the door, and dropped her palla to the floor, leaving only a sheer gauze tunic covering her body. Pushing Singerich back on the bed, she murmured seductively, "You won't need those trousers right now, love. I have a nagging itch I want you to scratch."

Still lying face up on the roof watching the ashes float by and waiting for the smoke to clear, Tauriac began to grow impatient. *When in hell are these bastards going to be done with this fucking fire? It's all over and done with!*

Out of nowhere a familiar voice rose above the fuss and bustle of the fire brigade. And it kept repeating: "I know you're there. I know you can hear me. Come on down you two. Come on down." Then it finally added, "Let's not make this more difficult than we have to."

That voice! He knew that voice; it had an ominous ring. But how did anyone know where they hid? They were so careful. And they waited until the darkest hour when everyone was asleep. Was not the house beneath them abandoned, the alleyways empty, and all the shutters of the surrounding dwellings pulled? Not a soul could possibly have seen them climb up and conceal themselves behind this false façade--nor could anyone look down. What could have possibly gone wrong?

"Come on down you two," said the voice, "or we'll burn you out."

Tauriac slowly lifted his head. "I'll be an ass-smelling warthog," he mumbled. What he saw changed the sense of achievement into the misery of abject failure. The abandoned house they lay atop was surrounded by dozens of militiamen with weapons pointed—straight at them. In the middle of that gaggle stood the little man in a desert headdress. At that moment Tauriac realized they had fallen into an elaborate trap. An ingenious ploy that only one man could have pulled off, that clever little son-of-a-bitch Mahaki the Avar, Mahaki the instigator, Mahaki the embodiment of mayhem. For the second time in his raucous life, Tauriac was about to be taken down by the one who posed as an Angel of Light, but whose deeds were more akin to the Father of All Lies, *Diabolos* himself.

Lucius and Mahaki were finally meeting with Constantius—an engagement delayed by the fire. "We appreciate your postponing this until we dealt with those two," Lucius began. "May I say your scholares performed admirably, sir, particularly the sentries. Please make sure they are well rewarded." Constantius nodded and Lucius continued, "I have a confession, sir. I overstepped my charge when I suggested the *magister* perform a public execution. Not to make light of how I, and Mahaki, felt at the time, it was, you understand, said in the heat of the moment. If I may ask a favor. Will you hold them until I return? Then we can decide a fair punishment. Neither man is bad, just misguided."

"Fine. Now, I too have a confession," said Constantius. "Mahaki, can you withdraw for a moment while Lucius and I discuss a delicate matter?"

Mahaki obediently retired to the antechamber.

When the massive door closed, the general leaned across his desk. "I want you to know this before we go on. It's been on my mind for a while. I think you know Galla hinted at a union with me some years ago. Although gold is but a handful of sand when compared to her shining splendor, I think the princess may have duped you, possibly seduced you with her charms, into thinking this idea was yours. It was not. Though she's the most enlightened of females, she is a wily Spanish schemer beneath those elegant robes of hers. This suggestion of a union between us was put forth by an intermediary when she and the Goths were still at Frejus a year after her capture."

"How?" asked Lucius, remaining calm, wondering what game the general might be playing.

"She arranged for someone to sneak messages back to me from Frejus. Too preoccupied keeping track of the crossings at the Rhine border and the outposts under siege along the Danube, I dismissed the messages as forgeries by someone trying to cause her trouble here at the palace. Now I've changed my thinking, thanks to you. That said, I offer this counsel. Never mention anything about this possible union inside or outside these walls. If the emperor's advisors hear of it, well . . ." He fumbled around for words. "Let's just say the idea will die a fast death along with its propagators. It might also prevent her release forever. Be warned lest some threatened bureaucrat convinces the emperor it is a treasonable act. It's these kinds of whispers that cost Stilicho his head. For the moment, our objective is singular: free her. All else is mute. Do we understand each other?"

Lucius nodded.

"Good, now, bring back your estate friend."

Mahaki returned.

The general got right to the next point. "This delay gave me time to think. I am assigning three warships to your mission."

"Three?" gulped Lucius.

"Yes, three. Two Liburnians and a trireme called the *Isis*, the finest command ship at port. And they come with sixty legionaries, our best captains, and an experienced crew. These ships will take you both to Ancona and then will escort the grain flotilla to Massilia. There they will sit in port until Galla's release. The Goths can choose Barcelona or Narbo or anywhere else they want to receive the grain. However, the grain ships will remain at Massilia until she is free. Their agents can inspect it, touch it, and even taste it. But they cannot have it until we have her.

"Secondly, after she is released, and only afterward, we march right up to the walls of Narbo. Once surrounding that ancient place, we will send a vanguard into the Pyrenees where the talks of an alliance with the Goths will take place."

"Am I to assume this alliance is at the expense of the Vandals and Suebi?" asked Lucius.

"Yes, you may assume that," said Constantius. "The III Theodosius shall be backed by another legion already stationed at Arles and a third still finalizing its training at Placentia. If the Goths refuse our entreaties, then we are prepared to take Narbo and crush them in Barcelona. Remember, we have Galla at this point."

"Go on," Lucius said, sensing the general had more.

"I want you both to move onto the palace grounds while we ready the ships. The alleyways of Ravenna suddenly seem too risky for you both. Who knows how many other assassins have followed you here. You're both too valuable to let another attempt be made on your lives. You were lucky this time. Guards will trail along any time you leave the confines—if you find it necessary to leave. How you kept those gems safe all this time is beyond me."

Lucius opened his mouth to speak.

"By the way," the general added as an afterthought, "your credentials will read Euplutius, not Domitilla. I'll explain later."

"Are you finished, sir?" asked Lucius.

The general nodded.

"Good. To answer the question you never asked: I will *not* go to Ancona or Massilia by ship. Mahaki can handle that. Instead, I'll travel with the III Theodosius as far as Lerins. I have urgent business there. After the ships arrive with the grain at Massilia, I'll go to Narbo and then somewhere in the Pyrenees, Barcelona, or wherever you want me to be to herald the negotiations. I assure you Mahaki is quite capable of accompanying the grain barges to Massilia, but I need him with me after that if I am to be a part of the treaty negotiations with the Goths. He has an instinct for things others do not. And I trust him. As for Galla, my role is to free her. The moment she departs Gothic control she will do, I assume, as she pleases. Having said all that, sir, I again remind you that her marriage to Athaulf is invalid and will not present a barrier to anything."

Constantius threw up a hand. He did not want to discuss that any further. Getting up from behind the desk, he said, "Oh, by the way, Lucius. Last evening we received word that the princess had a baby boy."

Lucius blinked. "A baby?" Then he coughed, attempting to disguise his reaction. He had forgotten about Galla being pregnant.

"They named the baby Theodosius after her father."

"Oh."

"You sound disappointed," said the general, wringing his hands like he had something prickly to add. "The baby brings up an interesting point, does it not?"

"It does?" Lucius asked, fighting to regain himself.

"It does. If you do the calculation, which incidentally I have, Athaulf was recovering from the wounds he received before the walls of Massilia during a *certain period* in their personal relationship."

By his salacious emphasis on *certain period*, Lucius knew precisely what he meant.

"It makes one wonder, doesn't it," continued the general, "who might really be the boy's father." He looked at Lucius like he knew what no one but he and Galla could possibly know. "Were it to come to light that another less worthy planted his seed in that sacred vessel, it may well bring down the House of Theodosius."

Lucius gulped. "These scandalous suggestions most certainly come from none other than the emperor's chamberlain," said Lucius. "For whatever reason, that man wants to see the princess discredited. For a fact, because I was there in Narbo at the time, I know Athaulf and Galla spent personal time together *while* he recovered," which was a lie, of course. "For only a few after his wounding was the king unavailable as a husband, if you understand what I mean."

It would serve no purpose whatsoever to admit that he, Lucius, was actually the father of Galla's child. A scandal of that magnitude would not only ruin everything, but bring about the very thing he was trying to prevent. Then he remembered the note Galla slipped into the sinus of his cloak as he was about to board the ship that would take him out of Narbo's port. That piece of paper said she was pregnant and that he was the father. What had he done with it? Gad! What had Tauriac done with his cloak! If the note was found in his cloak, it would spell the end to all of this! He must, before doing all else, find that cloak.

With a sack over one shoulder and another under her arm, Freya-Gund walked out the front gate of Narbo. Not far from the gate waited three of her best warriors and a string of horses, four saddled and three racked. She had sent the rest, men and horses, north to Burgundia weeks ago—or what was left of them following their lengthy odyssey across Gaul chasing after Lucius and the Statue of Fortune. Freya-Gund handed each warrior a sack to be tied in with their other necessities. She had remained in Narbo nearly a month after the main Gothic force departed for Barcelona. If Galla left the jewels behind, she had done a masterful job at hiding them. With Singerich's help, Freya-Gund turned the city inside out in search of them. All for nothing.

Soon another group rode up. It was Singerich with seven men, fifteen spare horses, and six pack animals. Although untrusting of one another, they would all ride as a single train to Barcelona.

"Eager to be off?" shouted Singerich sarcastically.

"I'm not eager, you're late. Does the sun not shine on your side of Narbo, or is the fin on your sundial bent?"

He laughed. "I believe it was you who bent my fin, dear madam."

"Huh!" She spit, spurred her horse and off she galloped, the others rushing to catch up. Barcelona was a hundred and seventy-five miles south. Rather than travel the coastal route, they elected to take the old Roman road to Gerunda, which would take them up and over the well-trod Perthus Pass. Freya-Gund did not fancy the high mountain air of the Pyrenees, but the coastal road was prone to slides and other lethal treacheries.

The trip was not easy. It took four days of tedious climbing, and often walking the horses around dangerous washouts, to reach a never-ending succession of grueling passes before topping the highest point and beginning the long, gentler descent toward Gerunda. Having traveled above the tree line where still sat last winter's snow, Freya-Gund could now see beyond the barren, windswept mountains to the balmy pine forests of Spain. Breaching a ridge, she caught a glimpse of a still higher "hill hamlet" sitting in the clouds. She wondered how in the name of Thor people could live up there, struggling for the bare necessities, suffering the long winters, dying off when no one knew they even lived. She sat there on her horse for a time taking it all in: the craggy cliffs, blue sky, distant clouds, and thin air. Never before had she been at this altitude. Lower, and to her left, was a less-challenged village squeezed between a cold stream and a sheer rock wall. Of that village she approved. At the very least, life there appeared fit for human habitation.

Descending into the tree line, Freya-Gund's group gained some distance from the others. It was safer to stay close for a number of reasons, one of which they were about to experience. Before she could stand in her stirrups to shout "Hurry up!" to the others, a pack of wolves charged from the trees and hit the trailing packhorse. In an instant, the overburdened animal went down, the dominant male wolf tearing at the animal's hind leg tendon. Then, growling and snarling, the rest of the pack pounced on the helpless animal.

Freya-Gund pulled up, released the whip coiled around her left arm, shouted for her men to protect the other animals, and charged the pack. Snap! Snap! Spit her whip, catching one wolf on the ear and a second on the rump. Her horse stomped through the frenzied pack, kicking one gray through the air, his hooves coming down on the back of another, snapping its front leg.

Whirling around, she charged again. Snap! Snap! The whip cracked again and again, biting relentlessly into the flesh of the wild beasts. That did it. They had had enough. All but one ran off howling and screaming in pain. That one, the one with the injured leg, stood next to the downed packhorse, daring Freya-Gund to make her next move.

Smiling, she goaded the animal, "So you want more, do you?" She spurred her horse into a full gallop. The wolf lunged and they collided, but the speed and size of her horse was too much for the already injured animal and he was slammed backward on the ground. Dismounting, she grabbed the stunned beast by the two hind legs, whirled it around several times, and then smashed its head against a tree. It didn't have a chance, not with her. Not pausing, she pulled out her long knife, dispatched the packhorse, and turned to her men, who could not believe what they'd just witnessed.

"Don't just sit there gawking, move the rack and baggage to one of the spares," she ordered.

She remounted and rushed toward Singerich, screaming profanities at the top of her voice. "See what you and your bunch of layabouts caused!" she shrieked, blaming them for the loss of her packhorse. Before Singerich could say a word in defense, she ordered three of his men to attach ropes to the dead horse and wolf and drag them to the village below. "It'll fill their pots for a month. Not one of those timber wolves is to get close to my dead horse! If any takes but one more bite, I swear I'll feed all your sorry asses to those wild creatures, do you hear!"

All Singerich could do was nod his head. The woman was relentless.

On the sixth day, a deluge hit, unlike any Freya-Gund had witnessed. All day the rain and lightning overwhelmed them. Only eight wretched miles were made. After it stopped, the mud firmed and the air warmed. The next day they continued the descent in a tight file from the craggy headlands to the green pastures below. Stone fences, bougainvillea-covered huts, and groves of olive trees appeared.

Two days after that, the towers of Barcelona came into view. With the hardships behind them, the group's mood changed. The two parties became adversarial again, Freya-Gund ruder, if that were possible, and Singerich repressive. Despite mutual goals that might significantly alter their futures, Freya-Gund and Singerich still hated each other. He assumed the loathing was there because she could see the disdain in his heart. In truth, Freya-Gund hated him because she hated everything.

Approaching the city, the group saw the ring of campsites that the Goths set outside the walls of Barcelona. Felt tents, smokehouses, and latrines dotted the landscape. So hackneyed was the area, that firewood was nowhere to be found and, as a consequence, had to be hauled in from a great distance. Although the next winter was a ways off, some were already slaughtering their animals—never a good sign. The new arrivals soon discovered that the taking of Barcelona was not one of valiant conquest but one of faint-hearted capitulation. The Barcelonans feared the Vandals more than the Goths, not only for their past cruelties but because the Vandals had even less food. A successful harvest would make Barcelona a target. So after a brief skirmish with the Goths, the Barcelonans, wisely weighing all their options, came to their senses. They would work together, not only to survive the upcoming winter, but to present a joint front against the Vandals if it came to that. Among the semi-civilized, starvation made man reach beyond his grasp.

As for Freya-Gund, she refused to spend one more night in a tent. Informed that firewood was scarce, she ordered her men to follow the river to the sea and turn north to where the forest began. They were to camp there among the trees. She would come in a few days after locating a place inside the walls to quarter, possibly with a lonely old man with a comfortable house, maybe a widow with dual tendencies, or even a magistrate fearful of the occupation. With a city population of three or four thousand, a woman of her ilk had many options.

When passing through the walls, Freya-Gund was struck by the magnitude of their construction. They were high, maybe twenty feet, the thickness massive, and were interrupted by impregnable towers. Fascinated by their enormity and number, she inquired.

"Seventy-eight towers in all," said one of the guards at the entrance, "but if you can't man them effectively, what good are they?"

That spoke to the problem in Barcelona—a lack of genuine will, precisely what she and the other Burgundians had encountered back at Worms that first winter. In the center of Barcelona, a church and a temple competed for dominance of the skyline. Although the temple was muted by imperial order years ago, it remained secretly open to the many who did not subscribe to the religious edicts of a changing world. She learned that back in Umbria that first tumultuous summer.

Her first stop for information was the barbershop. She had learned that also back in Umbria—from Lucius. By sunset, Freya-Gund identified, contacted, and persuaded a retired legionary, once a conscript of the now disbanded XIV Constantine, to share his humble dwelling in exchange for "her selfless attention to his disabilities." He had settled in Barcelona twenty-nine years ago following the battle of Frigidus where he lost an arm and part of a leg. He could not work the land awarded to him for his service, so a son and, of late, a grandson worked it instead and brought food and milk once a week. The farm was quite prosperous and, more importantly, concealed in a remote valley. So far it had not been molested by raiders, either Goth or Vandal.

It was from this old soldier, a hero to these Barcelonans, that she first heard the news that stirred her soul—if a soul could be found inside her body that is. It was not that the queen of the Goths had given birth. That news was inevitable from the protrusion she'd worn like an adornment before departing Narbo. But that the baby was a boy. A son born to a king of the Goths whose queen was also a princess of Rome could present a problem of succession among the hapless Gothic settlers that now surrounded Barcelona. According to Roman tradition, not necessarily a Gothic convention yet, this male child could become heir to the Gothic throne. If anything happened to Athaulf, the child's existence could set off an untenable situation—*should anything happen to Athaulf or maybe even the newborn.*

Yes, a mishap. Hmm! She liked the thought—it was such a wonderful notion. A hint of saliva appeared in the corner of Freya-Gund's mouth as she pondered the idea. She needed to settle these cravings by stirring something up—anything would do. Except for the confrontation with the wolves, the trip across the Pyrennees was as boring as a castrated hound dog. Yes indeed, a mishap or two would stir things up.

CHAPTER 6

Riding with the baggage train of the III Theodosius, Lucius was at last on his way and, at last, free of worry. Only after regaining his cloak and finding no note hidden away in the sinus did he remember what actually happened that day aboard the ship—Scarface the goat had eaten it. Galla's being pregnant with his child remained their secret. What a relief.

The last ten days had been busy. During that time the Imperial Guard—the *scholares*—had fanned out across the Po Valley to trade Lucius's gems for gold. Old coins, torques, bracelets, temple reliquaries, and whatever else the people or the governing municipalities hoarded were bartered. To ensure against fraud, thirteen *consulti* accompanied the thirteen separate teams of scholares. At first it seemed like overkill to Lucius, but in the end, it wasn't. Within days, thousands of pounds of gold came pouring into the palace. It was charted and turned over to the imperial mint for smelting into 12-ounce bars. By the time the gems were exhausted, they'd amassed three and one-fourth tons of gold.

Lucius ordered fifty pounds minted into coins, gave part to Mahaki and hid the rest in his vest, boots, and the cloak he'd retrieved from the assassins, along with the few gems he'd retained. The question was, though, would two and a half tons of gold be enough to purchase six hundred thousand measures of grain? Mahaki promised it would, even with a hefty premium. The remainder of the gold would be used to pay for transport to Massilia. If a captain or ship owner balked at the requisitioning, the centurion in charge was to seize the vessel. An edict signed by the emperor made the threat of confiscation not only convincing but legal. After all, was it not in the best interest of Rome?

Bursting with excitement, Mahaki sailed from the port of Ravenna the day before Lucius departed. Now Lucius was headed in the opposite direction with the III Theodosius expeditionary force filled with optimism as well. The weather was perfect, and they made excellent time. If it held, they would reach the Aurelian Way, the main east-west route, in two days. Then they would have to cross the challenging Alpes Maritime, after which they would go straight to Arles—no more obstacles in their way. So far, all was going according to plan. That would soon change.

They reached Vinitmille without incident. The treacherous Mastiff at Monoecus was next. That leg—Vinitmille to Nicaea—measured only thirty-five miles as the crow flies. But those thirty-five miles would test man and beast to the limit.

Lucius got a bad feeling the day he first caught sight of the Mastiff. Even Hannibal would not take the challenge and went far to the north to avoid it. There was just something about those craggy cliffs that frightened would-be contestants. So instead of challenging that high road with its tall bridges, steep gorges, and dangers, Lucius decided to leave that to the legionaries. He would go on foot using the lower route. It was no more than a footpath, a goat path originally, that followed the sea coast, interrupted only by a small port at Monoecus and ending at Nicaea—impassable for wagons and pack animals. Lucius engaged a Ligurian guide, a descendant of the ancient mountain goat herders who had resided nearby since the dawn of time, to lead him on this little side adventure. His plan was to rejoin the main column at Nicaea. Whether this was a good idea or not mattered little to him. He just needed to be free of the incessant noise and the monotonous routine of the march.

That first night he and his guide camped on a point overlooking the sea. As he looked west toward Barcelona, Lucius wondered about Theodosius, the infant boy born to Galla Placidia—his child. For the first time, he felt a sense of pride well up inside him. What did the boy look like? What was he doing? And, more importantly, what did the future hold for the son he could never acknowledge: emperor of Rome or King of the Goths? Maybe one day the little fellow would achieve both. Ha! Who would have thought!

He sat staring out at the sea, thinking over the possibilities. Then he remembered Bruné-Hilda and his feeling of pride abruptly turned to one of abject betrayal. He picked up a rock and threw it as far as he could toward the sea. It wasn't enough. The stone bounced among the rocks and vanished. Lucius tried to force the shame out of his thoughts, but unlike the rock, it would not disappear.

The next two days, Lucius and the guide dallied for several romps in the sea and a flirtation with the daughter of a woman the guide knew in Turbie. As a result, they arrived at Nicaea later than planned. Lucius thought the legion had already passed. Then the guide learned that it had not yet arrived. Lucius thought little of it at first, but after days of waiting, he began to wonder. Then word came of a terrible accident. The bridge at the Massaliote Ravine had collapsed under foot with a horrific loss of life. The guide knew the ravine well. Because of its depth and width, he said, the legion would be forced higher—a lengthy and dangerous detour up into the Alps. Lucius decided not to wait, but to go on alone. The isle of Lerins was a day-and-a-half trek ahead. He paid the guide, gave him instructions on what to tell the legionaries, and departed along a trail that followed the shoreline.

After spending the night at Antipolis, a military stronghold on the sea, he took the supply barge from Point Croisus to the dependents' isle of Lerins. Having no idea what he might find, Lucius hesitantly stepped ashore. This quiet oasis in the sea, which he had thought so little of in the past months because of the challenges he had been facing, once again tugged at his soul. Though painful, this place drew him like a parched animal to water. It was just as his savior Patricius told him it would be: a place where a person can find his fundamental nature, where no one asks who you are or why you come.

Lucius found the little cottage he bought for his beloved Bruné-Hilda, took a deep breath, opened the gate, and walked slowly down the path to the front door. Taking another deep breath, he knocked.

There was no answer, nor did a dog bark or a goat bawl.

He inquired at a cottage at the end of the lane. "Yes," said the old man who resided there, "the young lady still lives in that cottage, although the poor thing has been keeping to herself lately—more than usual, I must add."

Lucius walked the island and soon found himself near the rain barrel where he first saw her so many months ago. How many months was it? He had lost track. It seemed a lifetime ago. Lost in his musings, he continued walking toward the rain barrel. When it was in sight, he looked at it—and there she was. Great Jupiter! Seeing her after all this time took his breath away. What had happened to her? Shocked, he instinctively stepped back. And like that first time, he hid behind a bush and watched her every move.

She stood there, her back to him, looking into the rain barrel. Just standing and staring. No water jug, no cup. Just standing and staring. Her hair was stringy and unkempt, she'd put on weight, and her clothes were torn and filthy. Her blonde hair had grown back, yes, but it was no longer beautiful as he remembered it being before the fire. Lucius wondered about the rest—but only for a moment. It was too painful to dwell on how damaged her once incredibly beautiful body was. Then it struck him. Struck him like a hammer. S*hould he be spying?* Would she not be embarrassed for him to see her like this? No, not just embarrassed, she would be pained, pained deeply, to have him see her disheveled and unclean. So he crept off the way he'd come. Returning to the cottage, he tried the door. It was open. Looking for something to write on, he failed to find anything, so he walked over to the old man's cottage again. The neighbor was turning the soil in his garden.

"Sir, if you please. Can you tell the lady—" He stopped mid-sentence. "You know, sir, never mind. I think I'll be a man about this and tell her myself."

The old man put down his hoe. "I would think about that, son. That may not be the wisest idea." It was as if the old man could read his thoughts.

"Oh?" said Lucius. "Do you know who I am?"

"Please," said the old man, "come inside. I have some hot broth brewing. Would you share a cup with me?"

"I'd like that," said Lucius.

When seated comfortably at the small table, the old man asked, "Who exactly is she? And, if I'm not too intrusive, please explain your intentions."

Lucius looked down for the longest time, and a tear fell into his cup. All his suppressed emotions came rushing back. When he finally looked up into the old man's face, for an instant, a fleeting moment, he thought he saw the face of his mentor Ponti Lepius sitting across the table. A quiver shot through his body, his hand trembled, and he almost threw up. Everything, all the bad that had happened this year replayed in his mind. He wanted to run. But running was not his way. Why did this old man, this total stranger, care? Lucius willed himself back under control.

"I'll tell you who she is, the long journey we've been on, and what we are to each other, if you give me just a moment more, please. I don't know what went through me just now. Your question opened a Pandora's Box of emotions."

After composing himself, and for the next turn of the glass, Lucius released a torrent of love, loss, and bitterness pent up for so long. All the turmoil he and Bruné-Hilda had been through since that first spring day four or five years ago—he lost track. He spoke of the near-suicide jump from the Overlook Piazza when he found out she was pregnant, their losses and triumphs, and about the deep love they shared. He spoke of her rape and the mudslide. The baby she bravely carried, kept, and lost. And then the sorceress and the fire. When he finished, it felt like the weight of the moon, sun, and a heaven full of stars had lifted off his sorry soul.

"Now's the time to get it all out," said the old man encouragingly. "When was the last time you saw her?"

"Months ago, maybe seven. I promised to return sooner, but everything got out of hand, nothing fell into place as quickly as I . . . as I promised her it would. Yes, I promised her!"

"You must understand, son, that there's emptiness in that girl. I stop by once a week to look in on the lass, her dog, and that goat. Maybe three months ago she lost interest in everything and began to imbibe."

"What do you mean 'imbibe'?"

"The devil's nectar, son. Wine. She drowns herself in drink. She drinks to forget. Every Saturday the boatman from the monastery brings two large jugs and takes two empties back. She used to water the wine. No more. Up to that point, the girl was improving. Her hair was back, the unsightly coloration of her scars improved, her broken leg mended. Along with her body, I could see her heart improving as well. Then somewhere along the way"—the old man shook his head sadly—"she lost it all, felt alone, or so she said. Thought you abandoned her or maybe were dead. Began neglecting the animals, herself, the garden, and the cottage. I suggested she board the animals. A friend of mine keeps them for now. She used to visit Bis and Scarface occasionally. No more."

Lucius began to cry.

"Now, now. Crying helps of course, but crying is not the answer."

"I should . . . should I go to her?" he asked, sobbing.

"That may feel good for the moment, but is it the best for her?"

Lucius looked up. This old man was surely more than a next-door neighbor.

"That girl has enough scars, son. Why on earth would you give her one more?"

"What does that mean?" he asked, wiping his tears on his tunic.

"She does not need for you to see her like this. Instead, you should give her what she does need right now, something to hold on to." The old man got up and walked to the cabinet in the corner of the room, retrieved a wooden box—a writing box—and set it on the table in front of Lucius.

"You're obviously educated, a student of the letters. Am I right?"

Lucius nodded.

"Then write her a message." He opened the box and retrieved a piece of fanius paper, a stylus, and a container of ink. "I know how to make it appear well traveled. Where do you reside? No, where does she think you reside?"

"Ravenna. She knows I went to Rome and then on to Ravenna. What do I say?"

"Tell her the one thing she wants to hear, the first thing you want to say. Give her hope, a communiqué to live for, a reason to claw her way out of the abyss, a letter she will think about every night and will reread every morning. For my part, I will say a messenger came from Ravenna while she was away. I'll be convincing, I assure you."

"Who are you really, old man?"

"That's not important. What is important, at this moment at least, is this." And he clasped his hands together as if in prayer, opened them again in supplication, then pressed them to his heart. "She needs nurturing, love, and most of all, understanding. Now, here's the stylus. Write. Write from here," he said, thumping his chest. "Never be ashamed of what you say when telling her you care, that you think of her, that soon you will be joined as one forever more. Give the young woman hope, give her expectation. What better gift can you give right now than faith in your devotion."

Lucius sat on the ferry barge watching the oarsmen row. He thought about Bruné-Hilda, the old man at the end of the lane, and the promising missive he had left behind. The old man had promised to change its appearance to make it look as if it had come from Ravenna by imperial messenger. Yes, one day he would rejoin his beloved, but the timing was obviously not yet suitable.

Two days later he rejoined the III Theodosius at Frejus. The leader's news was not good. They had lost thirty-seven men and twice that many horses at the Massaliote Bridge. All because one recruit tripped and a careless centurion allowed too many to cross at once. The injured, and there were hundreds, remained at Nicaea.

Arles was a hundred and thirty miles down the Aurelian Way.

Along the seashore two miles south of Barcelona sat a walled villa, complete with iron gate, stables, a private chapel, and a defensible tower. When the Goths attacked Barcelona, the wealthy owner sailed off to the Baleares Islands with his family and a retinue of servants. Athaulf commandeered the villa and gave it to his queen for her and the new baby's comfort. The well-guarded property included an entourage of eight servants, three gardeners, and two wet nurses. Athaulf was seldom there, preferring instead to be with his men roving the countryside in search of food. Although the villa had twenty-two rooms, Galla favored the second-level suite facing the sea. The constant breeze and the vista made living there pleasant, if not totally pleasing to one so far from home.

She sat in a large chair facing the balcony thinking, the cradle nearby. Except when one of the wet nurses had him, the baby was never far. She adored little Theo. He reminded her so much of Lucius with his full head of curly black hair and blue eyes. A handsome lad, he was, just like his father—and just as unpredictable. Yesterday he had actually smiled when she whispered the name of the one who sired him.

How long had it been since Lucius departed on that ship? She'd lost track. So much had happened of late: the week-long celebration over Tolosa, Sara's death and burial, the tedious trip across the Pyrenees that had almost caused her to lose the baby, and the stressful, but short-lived, taking of Barcelona. How she'd hated that dingy little tent where Theo was born. Now, at least, she was living like a patrician—a princess of Rome. She had servants, private religious services on Sunday mornings, a garden to walk in or the seashore to walk on. Only one thing was wrong: she was terribly lonely. If only Lucius were here, he could make her laugh, or sing to her, or play those silly games of his with her. Oh how she missed him. He made her feel like a child again, young and alive—there were no barriers. With him, everything came alive, all things were possible.

After the service last Sunday, she asked the presbyter if God had a plan for her. When he responded, "Why do you ask, my child?" she had no answer. Nor did he. She had simply wanted to talk with someone—anyone with a specter of intelligence.

Had Lucius failed? Why was there no word from Rome or Ravenna or Constantius? She shuddered when she thought about what the unpredictable Athaulf might do next. Attack the Vandals? Foolish. Cross to Africa? Maybe, at least that was the talk. After all, that was where the food was. Good gracious, Jupiter! If they did cross, no one would ever see her again. She would be swallowed by the sand or baked to a crisp crossing the deserts of that gawd-forsaken wilderness.

She rose from the chair and went out onto the balcony. Only two torches burned atop the towers of Barcelona. *Was it that late? Had she dozed off?* Her gaze went toward the stables inside the villa compound. A lantern gave off a yellow hue from one of the stalls. She was told a mare was ready to give birth. The stable master would sit all night with the creature. At least the poor thing had companionship, while she felt so empty, so deserted.

When she returned to the room, something moved. Startled, she froze and then stepped back into the shadows of the draperies.

Bent over the cradle, and cloaked in black with the hood pulled up, was someone touching the baby. "Get away from the baby," Galla demanded. "How dare you come in here."

Whoever it was drew back from her son, straightened, and turned. "Hello, Princess," a voice from inside the hood said, a female voice. "Don't panic, I didn't intend to alarm you." She pulled back the hood and there stood Freya-Gund.

"How did you get in here?" Galla demanded.

"You should know to never underestimate what I can do," Freya-Gund said matter-of-factly. "Now, *Princess*," she said. "We have an issue. You wanted me to believe that there were only rocks in Fortune's belly, didn't you? Rocks! Ha." And her thin lips warped into a sneer. "You're dealing with a goddess of Ahriman now, not some rustic or a left-handed bumble, you two-legged bitch!"

Galla stiffened at the suddenness of her verbal attack. "Believe what you will," she answered. "But rocks are all you'll get, you pig-faced sister of a sow."

"Okay. Enough with the name calling. Let's forget for the moment that we do not like each other." And she moved from the cradle to the center of the room. "You do have a beautiful baby. I understand it's a boy."

"Thank you," said Galla calming down. "Yes, a boy. Theodosius is his name."

"Of course it's Theodosius, just like your father's. How did you acquire all this?" she asked, sweeping her arm from side to side. "It's without question, the finest villa I've seen since Ponti Lepius Filipi's Capricorne. If I'm not mistaken, it was at Capricorne that you first met Lucius, am I right?"

Why did she bring up Lucius? Did she know something? Yet Galla could not help but smile at the mention of his name. "Capricorne is where I stayed," she said. "We met in that awful blacksmith's barn. I was disguised as a page, and he trying to play the role of provincial hero. He dragged me up one alleyway, down another, over walls, and through houses, nearly got me killed to save me from a threat that did not exist. I still have the scars."

"Umbria. Umbria. It's where all this began for the both of us, isn't it?"

Galla did not respond. *All what began?*

Freya-Gund continued, not needing a response. "It was there I found the door to my earthly Valhalla, the golden road, the trail that led me, alas, to the Statue of Fortune. Lucius's uncle held the key to that door for which I'd long searched," she droned on absently as though Galla was not there. "Yes, he was a drunk, clay in the hands of the wheel master. Sobered him up, I did, and then molded the fool into a shill."

"And then hung the sot from the walls of Rome, I understand," added Galla.

Freya-Gund pressed on, pretending that she'd not heard that accusation. "His precious Cybelina, the love of his life, still pines for what was and is no more."

"You used Lucius's uncle, and then you spit him out like a piece of spoiled meat. No wonder he hates you."

"Hates me? Lucius doesn't hate me. He fears me, and to some extent, I him. He's like a bird. You can't get close. And if you do, he flies off into the cornrows. No, Lucius does not hate my body or my essence; he fears my force."

"You know, Freya-Gund, you are the embodiment of Narcissus, motivated only by erotic interests—when you see your reflection, you see a lie, a woman consumed by herself, a black widow who devours all those who serve her."

The conversation was once more heating up.

"If getting what I want is narcissistic, then yes. But devour? Never. I chew my victims up and spit them out. Like one day I will to you, if you do not reveal the truth about the statue. But enough of that nonsense," she said, shifting back into her sweet, disarming demeanor. "You are now a mother. May I hold the baby?"

"I'd prefer you didn't. Theo is not well. The wet nurse should be along soon to take him."

"The wet nurse? You are not mothering your own child?"

"I'm having some problems I prefer not to discuss. To change the subject, how did you get here—to Barcelona, I mean? When did you arrive? I heard nothing."

"The point, Galla, is that I am here. And I plan to stay until I get what I came for."

"The gems."

"Yes, Fortune's gems, my gems. I know what was in that statue. I also know Lucius departed with a few sewn into his cloak. And that you replaced the rest with rocks to fool me and everyone else."

"You're guessing."

"No, Galla, Freya-Gund does not guess. The goddess of Ahriman does not *suppose* the truth. She has special powers of insight. Freya-Gund knows."

"Ha!" laughed Galla mocking her. "I am a learned woman and have read many things. My father insisted on it. So do not take me for a fool because I am a woman. Special powers, sorcery, the magic arts are mere rituals for the ignorant performed by a master manipulator. The Lord God Almighty is the only one who rules the netherworld. Your god, Freya-Gund, is dead. Lucius smashed his effigy into a thousand pieces. He told me so."

Freya-Gund's face turned red, she rolled her right hand into a fist, took a step toward Galla—then stopped. "Now hear this!" she shouted. "I, and only I, shall care for the children of Fortune! Yet unborn, I freed them and their mother from that dungeon in Tibur, gave Fortune new life, nurtured her, and carried her from one end of the empire to the other in search of a resting place where she could give birth. I will not rest until—"

"Freya-Gund, Freya-Gund. Fortune is not real, she is but a statue. The gems are not her children. This pursuit has driven you mad, can't you see?"

"Ah-ha!" shouted Freya-Gund. "Then you admit it! Her belly held gems, not rocks. Alas, your careless tongue has betrayed you! And you and Lucius have contrived to steal these little darlings from me."

"Fine. I admit it. Fortune's belly was full of the most precious gems the world has ever seen. But we stole nothing. If anyone is a thief, it is you. These valuable stones do not belong to you or anyone else. If anything, they belong to the people of Rome, to be used for the benefit of Romans everywhere."

"How magnanimous! The benefit of Romans everywhere." Freya-Gund's color returned, and she was once again under control. "What kind of nonsense is that? The benefit of . . . You know, Galla, you are such a—"

There was a loud rap on the door. "Are you all right, ma'am?"

"See what your shouting did?" scolded Galla. "Now the guards are here."

Freya-Gund grabbed Galla by the arm. Her lip curled. "That little one over there will never reign over the Goths or anyone else!" she seethed. "Never!" She pulled the black cape around herself, snapped up the hood, and ran out onto the balcony. Galla let in the guards, but Freya-Gund had vanished into thin air.

"Wake up, Galla. Come on, now. Please, please, wake up."

"Huh? What? What is it, Elpida?"

"The baby, ma'am. I came to take Theo to the wet nurse. I can't wake him."

"Must have dozed off," Galla said, rubbing her eyes. She tried to reconstruct the events of the night: Freya-Gund, the guards coming. She felt lightheaded.

"The baby, ma'am. Something's wrong! He's not moving. The guards turned me away earlier. They were searching for that lady. When I came back, I could not wake the baby, ma'am."

Galla slid out from under the blanket and pulled the cradle closer. "Go light a candle," she ordered, then reached in. The baby was cold and stiff. She picked him up and let out a scream that could be heard halfway to Barcelona. The villa stirred, candles lit, servants and guards scrambled down the hallway. All to no avail.

Baby Theodosius, a contender for two thrones, was dead.

Riding with the vanguard of the III Theodosius, Lucius got his first glimpse of Arles. When coming down the river last year, he and Scarface put ashore a few miles up the Rhone River and traveled a circuitous route to Narbo trying to stay well ahead of the pursuing Freya-Gund and her small army. He had not laid eyes on the city then, but he'd heard of its magnificence. From Arles, the praetorian prefect theoretically ruled over Gaul, Spain, and Britain. However, that kind of "governing" was tantamount to having a Greek satyr in charge, a charade of pompous hegemony. In truth, Gaul was now cut in half, Spain lost, and Britain abandoned. Maybe Lucius's efforts would restore a modicum of supremacy.

And like all the important municipalities, he knew the history of Arles's golden days. Even now, the city still had a circus, amphitheatre, and temple—a temple no longer in use. Constantine had so favored the place that he constructed a magnificent bath by the north wall. One of his sons was even born and baptized here. As a result, in part, the city emerged as a major Christian center during the prior century. Of late, several usurpers used Arles as their capital. Since the defeat of Jovinus, the VI Diocletian legion remained camped a few miles north of the city. For tactical purposes, the tribunes of the III Theodosius legion selected an encampment to the south where an embankment and moat remained from past engagements. It needed only new latrines dug. Lucius spent two nights in a tent with the legion before moving into Arles above a wine merchant's shop on the Vicus Circus Circus. The shop was called the Vinarius Supremus.

While Lucius attended to his personal needs, Constantius sent an *agentes en rebus* to Massilia's magistrate with instructions to notify him when the grain ships arrived. The *agentes en rebus*, or imperial agent, was then to go to Barcelona by ship and inform the Goths that the emperor's representative was ready to negotiate an agreement that would resolve all their food issues as well as their differences. Implicit in "their differences" was the ransom of Galla Placidia.

When Lucius heard of this, he rushed to confront the general. But the general was not where he expected him to be. It took awhile before Lucius found him fishing on the banks of the Rhone at a favorite spot below the drawbridge—the innovative structure that floated atop thirty-seven boats and tethered to twin stone towers, one on each bank.

Without preamble, Lucius got to the point. "Why, General? Why send an agent when you have me?" His words were direct, his tone haughty.

The general did not stir. Instead, he coolly baited a chicken bone hook with a worm, dropped the line into the river, and only then did he look over at Lucius. "Him, I can afford to lose. You, I cannot."

"Lose? I've moved among those people without consequence."

"Who knows what mood Athaulf or his captains or any of the Goths are in. When crazed by hunger, men can be unpredictable and irrational, even foolish. First we test the waters with an expendable—then we take the next step with you."

"As always, General, I talk before I think," said Lucius, pretending to grovel.

"Not always. Now, as long as you're here, ah—" He put down the pole and motioned for the guards to come. "Prepare this for the midday meal," he ordered, handing over a string of fish. Then he turned back to Lucius. "Where was I?"

"So long as I'm . . ."

"Oh, yes. So long as you're here, let's review all the possibilities."

"What possibilities, General? They agree with our terms or else. It's simple. While grain is a powerful inducement, though temporary, their becoming citizens of Rome is forever. How can they refuse such an offer?"

"There's a chafe, Lucius. The emperor did not take to the idea of citizenship. Didn't tell you before because—"

"—I'd back out, right?" Lucius said, finishing the general's thought. "Well, sir, I won't. While I believe citizenship is the right approach, I'm not a child. After Galla's release, what else do you suggest we offer to keep them quiet? The grain will not last. When it's gone, they will rise up again—maybe join the Vandals and Suebi against us. Is the emperor that shortsighted?"

"No, of course not. The compromise we offer is Spain. We give them Spain to administer as our foederati."

"Hmm. Spain." Lucius thought about that, rubbed his neck, and then nodded. "And foederati instead of citizenship. Hmm. You know, I've never seen Spain. Is it fertile? Warm? Wild? What?"

"All that and more. It's the size of Gaul, though not so fertile. The Northwest remains untamed. The people there are uncivilized and can at times be dangerous. But it is the Vandals and Suebi that present the real obstacles, not the locals. The two are dedicated enemies of Rome—and far less civilized. Therefore, for the Goths to receive Spain as a prize, they must tame the untamed."

"You mean make war against the Vandals and Suebi."

"We don't present it quite so frankly, you understand. But yes, that is the heart of the agreement."

"My, my, sounds strangely familiar, doesn't it?   Much like Galla's *divide et complecti.*"

The general smiled.

"What now, sir? Sit and wait for Euplutius's return?"

The general shook his head. "No, not sit and wait. Continue the training and keep the veterans from killing the recruits, that's what. One of those bumpkins started the chain reaction on the bridge that brought the damn thing down. Not only did we lose thirty-seven men, some the veterans I was counting on to whip these puppies into war dogs. There's always the possibility that we'll have to fight all three nations—the Vandals, the Suebi, and the Goths. In that event, a third legion, the one from Placentia, will be sorely needed."

"When does it arrive, sir?"

"Soon. Although not at full strength, they are by all accounts more hardened than the other two and spoiling for a good fight."

The days passed and no word came from Massilia regarding the grain ships or from Euplutius in Barcelona. While the general was preoccupied with the positioning of the Third Legion from Placentia, Lucius decided to travel to Massilia and wait for the flotilla. The road was excellent and the distance less than fifty miles. Off he went, planning to stay at the Golden Goat Inn along the way, a place renowned with wayfarers. The port at Massilia was even more famous. Ever since it was founded eight hundred years ago by Greek merchants, the municipality maintained a strong independence that some claimed bordered on anarchy.

The place was drenched in natural beauty, the vista from the hillsides breathtaking. The natural cove that served as the port was surrounded by promontories on three sides. The cliffs, cove mouth, and deep waters created a remarkably safe harbor for the bravest as well as the most timid challengers of the sea. Massilia was the oldest city of Gaul, and, since its founding, it was used as a forum where wine and oils from the East were bartered for furs and precious metals from the North. The imposing walls of the city were easily defended, which gave its citizens that eternal sense of autonomy.

After boarding the horses at the inn, Lucius began inquiring. Had any of the captains reported a giant, slow-moving flotilla out there? he asked the harbor master. Weighed down by tons of grain, a flotilla like that would surely be etched in a seaman's mind. Since no sightings were reported, Lucius spent his time touring the municipality and visiting the barbershop and *bibliotheca*, such as it was, always keeping one eye on the horizon.

Looking out across the waters in the direction of Barcelona reminded him, as it always did, of his new son. What was the baby doing? Was Galla taking care of him or were the servants? Did the little fellow have Galla's coloring or his? These thoughts of little Theodosius filled him with pride for only a short time before forcing them to the back of his mind. They brought to the surface other feelings—hurtful feelings—like his betrayal of Bruné-Hilda and his lack of will to say no to any spicy offerings. Women never understood man's ceaseless susceptibilities to temptations of the flesh. Was he actually beginning to have a sense of right and wrong, a touch of Christian principles? Probably not.

With nothing to do, Lucius fell into the clutches of the widow Corina, the niece of the merchant of wicks and lamps, the shop beneath the room he let. His intentions were innocent, hers were not.

She had moved in with the merchant and his wife several months prior, after her husband was lost at sea. Older than Lucius, she was raising a seven-year-old daughter. Also eager to break the monotony, and being more accustomed to the clamor of a fishing village than the tedium of a pent-up walled city, she looked for any excuse to get out. When not working in the shop, she would stroll through the main squares of Massilia selling onion biscuits from a basket on her arm. Because of the shortage of coinage, Corina was forced, like everyone else, to barter her biscuits for fruit, raw honey, wheat from a maid employed at a majestic villa on the North Ridge, or whatever else anyone had that struck her fancy. From time to time she did acquire a coin, which she hid in an urn in her room. Although this endeavor was to some extent profitable, her real objective was to get away from the shop.

On this day, after marketing her biscuits, she talked Lucius into climbing the hill above the city to enjoy a midday meal. He jumped at the chance. They found a wonderful spot with a view of the sea and a plot of soft grass beneath a shady elm. The weather was perfect.

A frisky sort, Corina was full of daring. She was also beautiful, with long dark hair, black eyes, and a button nose—and as dimwitted as a rock. That notwithstanding, Lucius found her interesting, even erotic. After eating, they lay looking out at the sea, talking and giggling about nothing important. Lucius was partway through an anecdote that always got a laugh, when she suddenly blurted, "I can climb this faster than you," pointing to the tree. Then she jumped up, pulled the back of her tunic between her legs, tucked it into the front of her girdle, and was off. Before Lucius could get to his feet, she reached up for the first branch and swung to a second, catching it in the crook of her bare legs, and, like one of those famed Phrygian acrobats, she kept going higher.

Lucius was still standing on the first limb trying to figure out his next move when she reached the top. "I give up," he shouted. "Next time, give me a fair warning."

"Okay, sure," she said, laughing. "Here's one. Climb down, stand over there by that root, take off your tunic, turn around, and close your eyes."

"What's wrong with my tunic?"

"Nothing's wrong. It's just burdensome. Now, come on, play along. This will be fun."

Lucius obeyed. This time he would best that silly wench no matter what the feat. He stripped down to his briefs, tied them snug at his hip, and closed his eyes as ordered, expecting an evenhanded challenge from this unpredictable urchin. But what he got was not what he expected. When he opened his eyes and turned around, she stood on the lowest limb, tunic and girdle in hand, totally and outrageously naked.

"Come catch me," she whispered.

Lucius moved closer. She jumped into his arms and they fell onto the soft grass, Corina on top. Ripping off his briefs, she tossed them in the air. They caught a branch on the way down and hung there like the extended wings on a legion standard. Over the next hour, they achieved every twisted contortion of rapturous delight known, and some he had thought unachievable. In the end, they found themselves, one against the other, draped over a low tree limb facing the sea. Finding this position as interesting as any, they were in the midst of another heightened moment when he spotted something moving on the horizon. A sail appeared. Then three. Then dozens.

"Thank the gods, they're here!" he yelled, pushing Corina away. "It's them. Look at that, Corina, look, the sea is full of ships—my ships."

"Yeah, well, those ships are a ways out and fighting the wind," she said, looking back at him and flopping to the ground. "Let's finish, then you can go play with your little ships."

"No, no, you don't understand. I've got to get down there and warn the dockmaster about what's comin' in. Wow! I never thought he'd pull it off. Look at that! The sea is full of those beautiful ships! My ships! I pulled it off!"

"Who pulled what off, Lucius?" she asked and then immediately intercepted her own question. "Who cares. Come on, forget those damnable ships. I've spent my entire life waiting for fishing boats to come in. Your business is right here with me, my love, not out there."

"I'm sorry, Corina, really."

She rolled onto her stomach and, for the first time, saw what he saw. "Great Bee-Jupiter, Lucius!" she yelled. "We're under attack!" She jumped up and ran to the edge of the hill.

Lucius ran after her before everyone in Massilia saw how naked she was. "Those are barges, not war ships," he said, yanking on her arm. "They're the reason I'm here. Now keep that cute butt of yours away from the edge before you're seen. What's the shortest way down to the port?"

"Slow up, my love," she said, pulling him toward the grassy love patch. "Those ships are hours out. Now finish what you started."

"I started? Ha! Well, I can't. Not now." He grabbed his briefs off the branch. "I promise I'll make it up to you, really I will."

"How?" she pouted.

"Come by my room tonight after everyone's asleep. We'll not only finish, I'll have enough grain to give to you and your daughter to last the year."

"Really?"

"Really. And what's more, there will be enough to make a thousand onion biscuits."

Lucius counted over fifty ships, all from a handful of gems. He could not believe it. He descended the hill, passed the walls, and went out to the farthest point on the port—the jetty as the locals called it. Oars working the water, the ships moved cautiously toward the shore, some reaching into the wind, others reefing their sails to cut their speeds, all headed toward a pre-selected mooring site outside the port. All in all, it was a splendid demonstration of seamanship. When the captains were satisfied with the positioning of the ships, they gave the order, one by one, to raise the oars and drop the bow anchor. The only ship that entered the mouth of the port was the largest of the three warships. And Lucius could see the dockmaster readying a position on the far docks for it.

Somehow Lucius mustered enough energy—most of which had been spent atop the hill—to rush to the ship's side. It was a long run around the outside of the port to the far-side landing docks. As he ran, he could see Mahaki on the sterncastle with the helmsman and the tribune, who, he knew from Constantius's orders, was the man in charge of the logistics of the expedition as well as the gold. Lucius got there in time and waited for the warship to approach. When the portside oars were lifted, a seaman tossed a line. Lucius snagged it out of the air, did a round turn on the mooring piling, followed that with two half hitches, and then snapped it tight. After the stern was tied, Mahaki disembarked first.

"Can't believe you're finally here," Lucius cried, rushing to hug his old friend. "Like a vision, you suddenly appeared on the horizon, and from halfway around the world. I was way up there"— he pointed to the North Ridge—"watching for you."

"Not quite halfway around, but it sure felt like it," said Mahaki, laughing. "If I ever, ever volunteer for sea duty again, kill me. Never been so sick, and I can't remember being so tired. Started to wonder if we'd *ever* see land again."

He gave a slight shudder and then continued, "After rounding Sicily, we brushed Sardinia, took on water at a beautiful place called Tharros, and then came straight across—the Tribune's idea, which the captains dreaded. Many of them had never been out of sight of land that long. But the son-of-a-bitch knew exactly what he was doing, could read the sky better than a winged unicorn. Schooled on the sea in Alexandria, he was. The man has to be the finest navigator in the empire."

"You're a full-blooded tar now, my friend—'an old salt' as they say," said Lucius, hugging Mahaki one more time, so happy to see him, particularly after beginning to doubt he would ever arrive.

"Yep," said Mahaki. "I can scratch my ass, pee downwind, and pull an oar to the beat of a tong."

Lucius laughed, slapping his back over and over.

"Ease up. I'm here. What now?" asked Mahaki, rubbing his shoulder.

"Sit and wait. That's all, just wait."

"What about the ships, the crews?"

"Guess we'll bring them in one at a time until we see what our agent in Barcelona comes up with. As we speak, he's there negotiating an agreement. When he returns—if he returns—we'll know."

Mahaki grunted. "Wait, you said 'if.'"

"I'll explain later." Seeing his friend's reaction, Lucius quickly changed the subject. "How much grain you got aboard?"

"Five hundred and seven tons."

"What!"

"You heard. Five hundred and seven tons of wheat, barley, and oats. Four hundred sacks a ship, give or take according to size. All there was. Bought up the last tit-sucking kernel from those marsh dwellers, I did. Ha! Should have seen it. At those prices, wagons came rushing down from the mountains, up from Racina and Faler, and as far away as those fertile valleys toward Fanum. Couldn't believe the reaction, they went crazy. We emptied every fucking storehouse and butt-hole fruit-cellar within fifty miles of Ancona."

"You've picked up some new words," chided Lucius with a smile.

"Yeah, so what. These dogs have their own lingo," he defended, smiling back. "Been at sea too long with those sweat-hogs, I reckon. My apologies if I offend you."

"Forget the cussing, we're short, Mahaki."

"I know. Don't fret, I'll fill it."

"With what?"

"Sawdust, of course; what'd you think? They'll get their six hundred thousand measures laced with sawdust, which makes a thick porridge by thunder, or bake it into a tasty loaf, a biscuit, or a fine sweet. The Goths will be too fat to fight when they get finished with what I brought 'um. Quit worrying. You look like I just killed your damn goat. Listen, you've been eating sawdust all your wrongheaded life."

"Whatever you say, my friend," said Lucius. "Freeing Galla is all I care about. Whatever that takes. But, you foulmouthed sweat-hog, if I see a fruit tree growing out of the king's ass, I'll make you pick the apples."

Mahaki frowned, then got the picture, and laughed. "Now there's an image worthy of keeping."

Wearing white robes and somber masks, four members of the Barcelona Funerary Guild hoisted the silver coffin to their shoulders. Soberly, they made their way slowly down the center isle past the mourners to the chapel's foyer and gently set the coffin on an ornate pedestal. After the lid was opened, the mourners filed by and either touched the infant's body or placed a remembrance inside the coffin. Then the lid was closed for the last time. The guild members, each of whom wore a mask representing one of the four emperors in the infant's lineage, lifted the coffin once again and began the final procession to the burial plot beside the chapel.

Galla followed immediately behind the casket, consoled by Elpida and the presbyter. Behind them came a large entourage that included Singerich, Wallia, the council, captains of the six Gothic military units, and twenty-four members of the curiaeles of Barcelona, among other notables and functionaries. Noticeably absent was King Athaulf. The rumors said many things: he was ill or angered or too full of sorrow to attend. For the moment, though, despite the distraction of the absent king, all attention now was on the burial. They gathered around the plot in order of rank, the presbyter spoke eloquently, and tears were shed by many, although few had actually set eyes on little Theodosius. When all was said that needed to be said, two ropes were slipped into place.

Just as the silver coffin was about to be lowered into its final resting place, a commotion halted the proceedings. Surrounded by six guards and slightly bent from the wound he received the prior year, Athaulf the king walked through the iron gate of the grounds. His hair was pulled back, tied, and greased. And he wore dark trousers with his favorite silk shirt he took during the raid on Rome; a wolf-skin vest covered his chest. Although a shadow of his former self, his presence still brought gasps to those who knew him.

A missing finger, facial scar, and painful tilt announced the man had been through a lot, yet he remained ruggedly handsome even though his temples showed signs of gray and the spring in his step now had a hitch. He limped slowly toward Galla, took her hand, and looked sympathetically into her moist eyes saying not a word. Moving to the casket, he dropped to one knee and bowed his head. His actions, though reticent, made those watching certain of his true heartfelt feelings: surely he loved the boy although unseemly late showing it.

After posing as an ardent mourner, the king rose and nodded to the bearers. They lowered the coffin into the pit. Scooping up a handful of soil, he sprinkled it over the top. Mumbling words of the old Norse gods, he straightened and turned to Galla, took her by the arm, and led her slowly to the main house. The mourners, not knowing what to really think of all this, dispersed.

That is, all but Singerich, who watched this performance with absolute disdain, his eyes following the king and his queen as they walked up the steps and disappeared through the main door of the villa. He moved to the grave where the masked Funerary Guild bearers were busily filling in the hole. Motioning for one to follow, he walked far enough away so no one could hear.

"We give him one week to mourn, maybe two, and then," he said, lowering his voice, "we strike."

The masked member of the guild nodded and started to return to the task of burying the infant, the infant who once held such promise, not only for the Gothic nation, but the entire Western Empire. Blocking the digger's retreat with his leg, Singerich added, "By the way, Freya-Gund, you are quite convincing as a man. Although you insist otherwise, I maintain you waste your time here. The gems are *not* hidden in that coffin."

They headed to Arles, Mahaki uncomfortable atop Lucius's spare horse. Upon arriving, they found the III Theodosius encampment unsettled. From what the sentries said, Euplutius had returned from Barcelona and the news he had brought was not promising.

"I'll let him tell you," said the general, shaking his head.

In came Euplutius. The agent was thin, stiff-necked, and jittery, those steely-gray eyes his only remarkable feature. The man was not someone you would immediately trust, much less respect, but he was one you would send on a mission from which he might never return. When Euplutius opened his mouth to begin, Lucius interrupted. "One moment, please."

"Let Euplutius speak," demanded the general.

But Lucius held his ground. "Just a short comment, General, before he gives his litany of bad news. Five hundred and seven tons of grain sits in the port of Massilia. The six hundred thousand measures you wanted will be met within a few weeks, Mahaki assures me. Also, I am happy to report that nine hundred pounds of gold is left over, even after the ships are paid."

"Well then, there we have it," said the general. "Fine work, the both of you. Now, Euplutius, if *His Majesty* here permits, tell these two exactly what you told me."

"Where do I begin?"

"At the beginning!" the general shouted, obviously not pleased.

"If I may," said the Imperial Agent, "from the beginning, then." And he cleared his throat. "Little baby Theodosius died."

"Died?" said Lucius. "You say died as in dead?"

"Yes, dead."

Lucius just stood there. Theodosius, his baby boy, dead. How could that be? With all the attention afforded royalty, how could the baby have died? He wanted to cry, strike out, accuse the agent of lying. But he did none of that, it would be foolish and would reveal too much, it could even give away his involvement with Galla. He fought to calm himself. "Okay. What else?" he said, pretending to dismiss it as just another piece of flotsam.

"Wait a gawd-blessed moment," interrupted the general. "You think no more of this than that, my impatient friend. Do you appreciate the implications of the tot's death?"

"Yes I do, General. More than you know. Now, can we continue?"

The general scratched his chin, gave Lucius a long look, and then turned to his agent, "Go on, Euplutius."

"Thank you, sir. It was quite the spectacle. They buried the tot in the yard of a villa south of Barcelona. I witnessed it from outside the gate. There's a chapel on the grounds. I believe Galla Placidia resides there in the main house."

"You *believe* she resides there," demanded Lucius. "Don't you know? And what of the king, did you meet with him?"

"Yes and no. I saw him, but we did not speak. The man would not talk to me or anyone. Claimed to be in mourning for his son."

His son! Lucius forced a cough. Then he asked rudely, "Then why, may I ask, are you here and not there waiting for his mood to change? Do you always give up this easily?" It was a justified scolding, not a question.

"The king's word-man met with me," Euplutius explained. "And, speaking for the king, he flatly said no largess on earth was enticing enough to free the princess. The king is obviously frustrated with life or angry at the world or maybe just everything that goes wrong with the Goths."

"Maybe all of that," said Lucius facetiously.

Then the agent went on about hunger and illness and about how a group of rebellious locals burned the fields at night and then ran off into the mountains. "Even the Vandals are fairing better than the Goths."

"I've heard enough," said Constantius. "All this plays into our hands, does it not? Makes Athaulf appear all the more vulnerable, eh? If no good comes from leading his people over those mountains, the king will surely be in trouble with his own people."

"Don't forget this," interjected Lucius, "if anything happens to Athaulf, we must start all over with a new king."

"True."

"Now what?" asked Lucius.

"We wait. The situation down there needs to ripen."

"All right," said Lucius. "Let it ripen if you wish. In the meantime, Mahaki and I have business to finish in Massilia. We are short ninety-seven tons. While we correct the shortfall, you shouldn't forget that those mountain passes close with the upcoming snows."

"It'll be months before that happens," said the general. "And those bellies are going to be empty long before that. You're spiking the grain with sawdust, I assume?"

Lucius nodded.

"How long might that take?"

Lucius looked to Mahaki.

Mahaki shrugged. "Ten days, two weeks. Maybe longer."

"Then get to work. We'll send word when the apples are ready for plucking." And he smiled like he knew more than he was letting on. "In any event, we'll expect you back here in two to three weeks. Euplutius left several 'watchers' inside the walls of Barcelona. They'll inform us of any changes. Enjoy the lacing. I did it at Pollentia. Believe me when I say you must mix in the sawdust really well to be convincing. The Goths are no fools."

Two freight wagons and four horses were all they needed. When close to Massilia, Mahaki began to inquire about old mills in the area. There were a few, but none offered what he looked for. Then an old man at a roadside vegetable stand spoke of an abandoned mill a mile or so off the road. "Hasn't been worked in years," he said, "but it was the biggest in these parts until it fell apart."

"Did it saw logs as well?" asked Mahaki.

"Actually, that's all it did. You gotta go east to find decent grain fields around here. This was good timber country before it got overworked."

"Perfect. Can we leave the wagons here while we walk in?" asked Mahaki.

"At your peril. There're bandits in these hills."

It was not much of a walk, nor was it much of a mill. The waterwheel had rotted away, all that was left of the sluices and gates were the supports, and the building had fallen in on itself. Mostly what remained was the nature: a hefty stream that had once brought the logs down from the hills when it flooded and an enormous mound grown over with bushes and vines.

"That's what I'm looking for," Mahaki said.

"What?"

"That mound you see there is not nature's work, my lad. Let me show you." He climbed halfway up the side, pulled out a bush by the roots, and dug into the hole with his hands, pulling out a handful of sawdust. "When we strip away years of nature's handiwork, we'll have all the sawdust we need," he said. "This hill is what's left of decades, maybe centuries, of sawing trees. This mill probably supplied the port with its pilings and the shipbuilders with planks. How far away are we from the port?"

"Four, maybe five miles. You'll see it when we cross the next rise," said Lucius.

"Good. Let's move on. We'll put those half-caste loafers that call themselves sailors and soldiers back to work."

Mahaki brought four hundred empty sacks from Ancona—all he could acquire. But they would need more. While Lucius went in to Massilia to find anyone able to make grain sacks, Mahaki traveled on to the port to begin the process of reclaiming the sawdust from the old mill, a huge task that would take every seaman and legionary they had.

By the next day, the operation was in full mode. Freight wagons took load after load of sawdust to the docks in sacks, and the tribune organized their distribution among the ships for the final step. While this was going on, Lucius not only found a hamlet nearby that specialized in sewing sackcloth, but he found an estate agent loitering at the barbershop who said the harvest was so good near Aquae Sextiae that he could obtain at least ten tons of whole millet if Lucius would pay the price plus ten.

He would.

"What do you think?" Lucius asked, watching the last of the Aquae Sextiae grain being dropped onto the dock. "Are we there yet?"

"Almost," said Mahaki. "Maybe five hundred and seventy tons, possibly five eighty. That'll be close enough for Goths who have trouble counting their toes."

"I'll head back then," said Lucius. "Keep an eye on things here. The tribune has had his fill of these captains, afraid a few might slip away and head home. I'm requesting an additional unit be sent down here from Arles. When the work's done, the men might get restless. When they drink too much, they begin to bother the women. Corina's been groped more than once."

"Yeah, my boy, and I've seen who's doin' the groping," Mahaki teased.

Guilt-ridden, Lucius snapped, "Maybe you should quit spying on me."

"Seriously, we've only sixty legionaries to control those worthless sea dogs."

"I'll get more, that I promise," said Lucius. "In the meantime, you should have the tribune lock off their oars so they can't sail off."

Lucius took his time going back. Six miles from Arles, the adiutor, Constantius's faithful messenger, came riding hard toward him.

"You're killing that horse," Lucius said pulling up.

"The patrician, sir . . ." He was puffing from the exertion. "He . . . sir . . ." And then the messenger got off his horse, held his stomach, and threw up. When done, he wiped his mouth, took several deep breaths, and went on. "He needs you at once, sir. Word just came"—he paused to belch—"that the Gothic king, sir . . . the Gothic king Athaulf has been murdered."

"Good gawd! And Galla? What of Galla? Was she . . . do you know?"

"We know nothing more, sir. We can only pray for the best."

Lucius pushed through the flaps of the general's tent.

"There you are. Good to have you back," said Constantius. "Did my adiutor—"

"Yes, he told me. What a shock."

"Yes, a shock. It's time for action. We were just speaking of you." He motioned to the man leaning against the center post. "Meet Captain Rusadir of the *Malaca Moon*. We are indeed fortunate, lad. This old friend here knows the coast better than any. He'll drop you near Barcelona on his way to Carthago Nova. His is the only ship heading that way. That's the good news."

"And the bad?" asked Lucius.

"Two hundred Irish hounds barking night and day, *cacca* everywhere. You'll smell like a barnyard for a month. That's his cargo—two hundred killer dogs bound for Carthago Nova."

"Why drop me *near* Barcelona? What's wrong with their port?" asked Lucius.

"The captain doesn't trust the situation. These Goths can be mighty unpredictable. With Athaulf's murder, they'll be even more so now. Our informant, the one who rushed up here with the news of the assassination, said there's anarchy in Barcelona. We need your eyes and ears down there, lad, and at once. Your connections are invaluable now."

"When do I leave?"

"Tomorrow."

"Tomorrow?" Lucius said with disbelief.

"We'll send word to Mahaki. Should we be worried about the grain?" asked the general.

"Yes. It's why I came. More soldiers are needed there at once. The situation falls more apart each day. Mahaki's worried the ships will slip away one by one."

"Why wet-nurse the bastards," said the general. "Unload all the grain now, pay the sons of bitches, and send them home. We'll find others when the time comes."

"Perfect," said Lucius. "Shoulda thought of it myself."

Captain Rusadir, seeing that he was no longer needed, told Lucius where to board his ship and left.

"Now, sir," said Lucius. "Tell me what actually happened in Barcelona. Is Galla safe? Who killed Athaulf? Their world's got to be upside down for sure. With Athaulf gone, blood will be spilled, the fighting—"

"Slow down, Lucius. That's why I'm sending you and not Euplutius. You survived those rascals for months without getting yourself killed. Few can say that. Euplutius hid out the entire time he was there. As a result, he learned pathetically little that we can use. So off you go. Do what your instincts tell you. You have no instructions beyond that. This is your moment, Lucius; your moment to be a *defensor*. Somehow, some way, you must rein in the Goths. The tongue is mightier than the sword—and a lot less costly."

"That cliché is a stale chestnut, General."

"Stale, maybe, but true."

The *Malaca Moon* released its moorings an hour past sunrise and picked up the current in the west fork of the Rhone River. Aided by a quarter foresail and twelve long oars, the ship headed toward the open sea. Once clear of the mouth of the river, and with nothing but open sea ahead, the mainsail went up, the foresail unfurled, and the oars lifted out of the water. They caught the morning breeze and headed southwest toward the coast of Spain. The trip was approximately one hundred and eighty miles to Barcelona as the crow flies. "Allowing for the seasonal drifts," Captain Rusadir began, "we should get you there a little before dawn the day after the morrow." Then he laughed, his smile sporting a gap of missing teeth, and said, "Unless the sea gods drop a curse upon me worthless head."

While the captain concerned himself with the affairs of the ship, Lucius, ignoring the superstitions of the seamen, spent the day riding the bowsprit like a horse, feeling the salt spray wash his soul. If there was a plan, he would be turning it over in his mind right now. But there was no plan. He hadn't even been given a hint about what to do when he got there, much less what dangers he might face. If Galla was dead, that would spell the end of his quest. With no orderly succession, anarchy would surely reign among the Goths. And if the place was in turmoil, what could he do? Among the Germanic peoples there was always chaos. No one foresaw the weak-kneed Gundahar succeeding Gunther to the Burgundia throne. The same with Athaulf after Alaric dropped dead. Was not Sarus the logical choice then? The new Gothic king could be anyone. And with that came a new course, like it was with Tiberius and Caligula, Marcus Aurelius and Commodus. History was a lesson taught but seldom heeded. So he rode the bowsprit with a clear mind, interested but unconcerned with what the next weeks and possibly months might bring. Since that wretched summer in Umbria, he was used to chaos.

Singerich paced back and forth in the garden of the villa. He was nervous. This is what he wanted, yes, but it was all happening too fast—first little Theo and now Athaulf. He heard a noise. Great hammer of Thor! He stopped pacing. And there she was, the death goddess herself, head up, eyes down, coming right toward him. He braced. When Freya-Gund was within hearing distance he muttered, "Now what."

She looked up sharply. He could see that his comment did not please her for the corner of her lip began to levitate. "Now what!" she shouted. "You dare say to me, now what?"

The sorceress was angrier than he had seen her in a while.

"Do you know what a disgusting, vulgar beast that ape Evervulf is? Well do you? I nearly puke when I think of what I did for you. I'd rather fuck a frog than that lump of dog meat. Now that I've kept my end of the agreement, you better keep yours. Find those gems, or else."

Singerich swallowed hard. "Evervulf was already angry with Athaulf, you know."

"Oh, was he," she whispered threateningly.

"Yes, he was. Because of what happened at the river Brutus, because of the slight to Sarus. That hate festered inside him all this time. You simply pushed him over the edge, that's all. How much effort could that take?" Singerich was bluffing, of course. He knew well the assassin of the king was all bluster and no balls.

"Evervulf is a coward at heart, Singerich. You failed to inform me of that. Angry at Athaulf, sure, but—and that is a mighty powerful *but*—I gave him the stomach. I created a warrior out of a rabbit by using these." She grabbed both her breasts. "And this," she said, patting her rear end. "All seemed . . . well . . . how can I put it. All seemed according to plan until, shall I remind you, a moment of frenzy overtook our assassin. He rushed from my chamber, confronted the king in the council chamber, and stabbed him right here," grabbing her crotch. "Hey! Hey! Smile if you want, but so unprofessional was he, he missed the mark. What kind of assassin did you send me? The bumpkin drove his dagger right into the king's manhood instead of his heart."

"It did him in, didn't it?"

"Yes, it did him in. After a slow, painful period it did him in. But the way it was done, his suffering, reversed the disdain so many held for your inept leader. So now he dies a martyr's death instead of a despised king; and the people are angry. For this very reason, assassinations are carried out swiftly, privately, ingloriously, and not in front of the entire council. If Julius Caesar had been stabbed in bed humping a whore, would he be. . ." She stopped, turned up her nose, and tossed the trailing edge of her tunica over her shoulder. "Now then, Singerich, now that the deed is done, where are my gems?"

"Well, not in Theo's coffin, you now know that; nor the villa. After "servicing" every one of Galla's servants, except old Elpida, I can assure you of that as well. What else do you expect of me?"

"Find the damn gems! That's what I expect!" She started to stomp off. Having one more thought, she stopped. "You keep your end of it or—"

"Or what?"

"It's not a hollow threat, Singerich. The boy is dead. The king is dead and the throne empty. I did what I promised; now its your turn. Freya-Gund never gets cheated, she gets even. Remember that. If you don't want to . . . you have ten days, then *puff.*"

"Be patient, damn you. I need the gods on my side now that the throne is empty. And I need you. Tomorrow we find out who it will be, Wallia or me. If me, I shall sing Odin's praises." He snickered. "And then I'll squeeze Galla Placidia's pretty little neck until she reveals where those gems are. As the new king of Gothia, that I promise on the hammer of Thor."

The next day, to the surprise of everyone, the Gothic elders chose Singerich to be their next king. From then on, like the fool that he was, he ignored Freya-Gund's entreaties. Instead, he gave orders to not let her near him and paid three of his faithful to dispatch the sorceress.

Nine days later they found Singerich, the proud new king of the Gothic nation, the proponent of the new kingdom of Gothia, dead.

Midway through the second day the winds died and with them the sea. "Strange," said Captain Rusadir, "this time of year it's the tempests you fear, not the doldrums."

They sat there, drifting with the current. Another ship appeared, its oars in the water, pulling hard north. "Ahoy, Captain!" shouted Rusadir when the ship rowed close enough. "Be you knowing the situation at Barcelona?"

"We do," came the reply. "The Goths have pulled up and moved on."

"Which way?"

"South," shouted the other captain, "last they were sighted at Dertosa. They have a new king, you know."

"No, we did not know," shouted Rusadir. "We heard only that Athaulf was dead."

"Are you watching that build-up over the Pyrenees?"

"Aye, Captain. Keeping a sharp eye on that we are. Afraid it might be a bad one for sure."

"Bad indeed. Good josh, Captain."

Lucius watched the other ship row on until it disappeared. Later, Captain Rusadir came to where he sat on the bowsprit. "The crew and I have made some decisions that will affect your journey, laddie. See those clouds." He pointed westward. "Not good. Don't often get that this time of year. When we do, it's wiser to give heed. We have two choices: pull in or run."

"What's that mean?" asked Lucius.

"Find a nearby port or row like hell the other way, which means going farther out to sea. That way we stay ahead of it if we can. If the Goths have moved south, Barcelona's no longer your destination, right?"

"Correct."

"And if that tempest is as big as it looks, we may get blown to a place we don't like to be and end up eating dog meat for a spell."

And that was what nearly happened. Four days later, Lucius sat in the port of a small fishing village on the west coast of the isle of Maior in the Baleares chain. A ship loaded with Saguntum refugees, who were avoiding the Gothic march, came into port on its way to Palma. The Goths were continuing south, they reported, on their way to the Pillars of Hercules. That could only mean one thing. The Goths were heading to Africa, the breadbasket of Rome.

With that news confirmed by another crew, Lucius decided to continue on with the *Malaca Moon* to Carthago Nova, which sat on the southeastern coast of Spain. His plan was to get ahead of the Gothic column. After pouring over a map the captain had, he concluded that from Carthago Nova he could intercept them to the north at Llici or to the west at Castulo depending on which route the Goths chose.

Two weeks later, he sat along the road outside Castulo watching the yoked oxen and two-wheeled carts of the Goths roll by. Strangely, their appearance was now more a nuisance than a threat—a shadow of the former Gothic army that conquered the city of Rome. He remembered them pulling into the Umbrian Valley that hot July day so many years ago. Back then, the legendary Alaric was king and at the height of his powers, feared by both East and West. Watching the king and his queen ride those matching black stallions, both looking tall and splendid in their saddles, was a day he would never forget. The people of Assisi stood atop the walls cheering them on, calling out their names. Behind them, high-stepping horses strutted into view pulling those famed oversized Gothic wagons, a teamster astride each left rear horse instead of in the box, a practice unique to the Goths. Their arrival in Umbria was a spectacle to behold. But that was long ago, a forgotten chapter in their glorious history. The toll from the migrations since the sack of Rome and the lack of nourishment was now obvious on the face of each man, woman and child. Having left garrisons at Tolosa, Narbo, and Barcelona, this fearsome horde had dwindled to a pathetic collection of starving vagabonds who presented a threat to no one but themselves.

Comfortable along that roadside outside Castulo, Lucius continued to observe this pathetic column. Fighting boredom, he began counting the wagons as they passed: one hundred, two hundred, three hundred. When he got to five hundred, he stopped. This too had become boring. Then one of the roaders pulled out of line to inspect a loose wheel. He cupped his hands and inquired. "Where is the princess, Galla Placidia? I've been waiting to get a glimpse of her all day."

"You mean Athaulf's queen?" the roader asked, amending Lucius's reference. "Galla is no longer a princess of Rome. She is now a Gothic queen."

"Yes, sorry, the queen, of course; is she riding a horse, a wagon, or being carried in a litter?"

"Are you an assassin?" he asked flatly.

Lucius wasn't sure if the man was being factitious or what, so he answered in kind, "Do I look like an assassin sitting here under this tree unarmed?"

The man stopped what he was doing and walked over to Lucius. "She rides in the house wagon pulled by four white horses. Probably two, four markers back. She normally spends the night in camp four."

"Four. You set four camps each night?"

"No. We set seven to ten depending on fodder, water, and wood."

The man finished what he was doing and went on. Lucius waited. With a few hours of light remaining, a house wagon pulled by four white horses came over the rise led by six outriders. Lucius jumped to his feet.

Walking alongside the slow-moving vehicle, he asked, "Is the queen inside?" And got a response he did not expect—a whip across the face from the lone teamster in the box and a boot in the chest from one of the outriders. Lucius did not hesitate. He swung up into the box, ripped the reins from the teamster's hand, pushed him over the side, set the brake, reached down, and pulled the iron ring from the thwart, releasing the horses—the outriders giving chase.

"Now," he said to the teamster lying beside the house wagon, "is the queen inside? This is a matter of life and death—hers; and quite possibly yours if she decides to report your rude actions to the elders!"

With that, the back door of the house wagon swung open and a familiar voice rang out, "What's going on now, dammit?" It was Galla.

Lucius jumped onto the roof of the house wagon, ran to the back, and looked down. Putting his hands on his hips he proclaimed: "It's your favorite nuisance from Umbria, Your Highness. I've come to free you from your tormentors."

"Of course it's you. Who else would come to the middle of nowhere, unarmed, leading an army of one, to try to save my sorry soul." And she laughed the laugh of that happy little girl she somehow always managed to revert to around him.

Quelling the curses of the guards, she declared that Lucius was not worth the effort to hang him. With that, she dragged him inside. After the outriders returned with the runaway team—not an easy task with horses glad to be free of their burden—and hitched them to the wagon, the journey continued toward camp four.

When settled in, Lucius took her hand and surrendered to the moment, tenderly expressing his sorrow for the loss of little Theo.

"Our loss, Lucius," she whispered. "It was *our* loss, yours and mine. Theo was such a beautiful baby, Lucius, with your eyes, your hair. He's buried at a villa outside Barcelona. One day we'll move him to Rome."

"Yes, one day," he whispered, tears forming in his eyes as looked at her.

After a time, she told him about Athaulf's murder. "A crime of rage by a servant named Evervulf," she explained. "He was a disciple of Sarus, Athaulf's rival since Moesia. Sarus believed he should have been chosen after Alaric's death. Eventually the two quarreled and Sarus was killed—or so the story goes. I was not there. So there you have it. One wrong begets another, one murder another. Jealousy and power can be a lethal concoction, Lucius. Then, heaven knows why, the elders selected that troublesome man, Singerich, to be king after Athaulf's death. Thank the Lord he did not last more than nine days on the throne, otherwise I would not be here or anywhere else on earth. The man treated me like a whore, made me walk barefoot, fed me scraps. I prayed for death. Dying in the land of my ancestors would have been a blessing heaven sent. That is what I prayed for Lucius—to die near Cauca where the greatest emperor to rule both the East and West drew his first breath."

"You refer to your father, Theodosius, of course. I forgot about your Spanish roots."

"It was Singerich who began this journey we are now on, until Wallia had him killed that is."

"Wallia? Wallia the *Tranquillus* was behind Singerich's assassination?"

"That's what I was told. No one tells me much, so I must rely on Elpida for news. It's gossip. Who *knows* what actually happened."

"And this Wallia fellow, who exactly is he?" asked Lucius. "The name is not a familiar one."

"Excellent question. Maybe you and that bold tongue of yours can disarm these self-absorbed malcontents and extract more than I, Elpida, or anyone else can. I must confess, however, that he does treat me well. I do feel like royalty again."

"Which, of course, you are."

"Thank you. He treats me suitably, yes, but stays his distance."

"Ah. Now what does that tell you?"

She shrugged.

"He lacks confidence, uncomfortable in his boots. Where is he leading you? Where does this train end?"

"Africa, Lucius, the hot deserts of Mauretania and Numidia. The homes of the Berbers, nomads, wild beasts, and crocodiles, places from which no one returns. Elpida told me that the plan is to cross near the Pillars of Hercules using who knows what. These Goths can't traverse the Rhone without a bridge. They failed miserably at Massina after the sack of Rome. I saw thousands drown with my own eyes. Gades will destroy them. Those straits are more treacherous than the open sea. I read that in the Annals of Tartesia as a youth. But then no one listens to a woman. Maybe they'll listen to you."

"Can you set an audience with this new king?" he asked. "Constantius awaits word at Arles with three legions. They're spoiling for a fight and ready to make war if my entreaties fail. I absolutely must see Wallia as soon as possible. Your brother the emperor has authorized a compromise if the Goths are willing. I have six hundred thousand measures of grain at Massilia to appease them and, of course, to gain your release."

"Six hundred thousand!? You did say six hundred thousand? How did you manage that much grain?"

"By using the gems, Galla. That golden Statue of Fortune, which traveled half the world, did so just to save your royal skin. As a Christian, you surely must declare Fortune a saint."

"Maybe what I've done to her and for her is even better. Now, back to the new king; he's a quiet man, but not easy. A proud warrior through and through, of course, yet, like all such men, he's mysteriously distant. I believe that to be but a shield, though. The elders think Africa is the answer to their sufferings and push him to cross. But, if my instincts are accurate, and I think they are, his heart is not in it. At the first sign of failure, he'll retreat, not out of cowardice, no, but because he believes the plan ill-advised. Have you seen how these people suffer? They eat bark, boil roots, and dig up grubs for nourishment. Most all the cattle are gone. The horses are next."

"Then he needs an alternative before the elders push all of you into an abyss from which no one returns. After all, I do have with me"—he pulled out the agreement with the emperor's seal affixed to it—"the answer to all this foolishness. I hold in my hands the makings of Gothia within the boundaries of the Western Empire."

"It is what they have always dreamed of, Lucius. That may well be the solution to their long odyssey as well as their suffering."

CHAPTER 7

Wallia was a brutish man, younger than the dead Athaulf, blond headed with a bushy beard and a half-moon mustache. His hands, though, were his most outstanding feature. They were enormous. In some ways he reminded Lucius of Gunther the Burgundian, only half a head shorter.

Through Galla's entreaties, Wallia agreed to meet with Lucius and their meeting was set at camp two, five markers west of Castulo. On this day, the columns rested not because they needed it, which admittedly they did, but because they bordered the most dangerous province in Spain, the land of the Siling Vandals. Lucius and Wallia sat outside the new king's tent bare to the waist, both enjoying the sun and talking.

"As a youth, I was stung by the 'sleep thorn'," Wallia freely admitted. "I awoke to the world around me at fifteen and soon became a favorite of Alaric's queen. You see, I once saved her from drowning when her horse threw her into a stream and she struck her head on a rock. Although not a Balthi like Alaric, Athaulf, Sarus, and the queen, I was invited to become her bodyguard. I became the king's too after awhile. Eventually I became the *Nagy Ferfi* of his personal guard—the 'Big Man.' So, Lucius my friend, you might say I owe all this to a horse that shied." He did not laugh or even smile when he said it.

Lucius did, and heartily. Then he said, "I once lost a foot race because an unbridled horse ran into my path near the finish line. My opponent's supporters squeezed its tenders at just the right moment."

Nor did Wallia smile at that. The new king went on, apparently eager to get something more off his chest. "I never actually sought authority, you know," he admitted. "Never wanted the responsibility.

Nevertheless, authority seems to find me in the darkest of places, just as you did out here at land's end, close to the very tip of the world some say." He rose, walked to a nearby bush, snapped a twig, and began to pick his teeth. "You know, Lucius, your proposition from the emperor, although fraught with arrogance, is quite intriguing. But it changes nothing. The elders are set in stone. While I see Africa as a possibility, they see it in a different way—more like their last hope."

"When we first met today," said Lucius intentionally letting the emperor's proposition percolate a bit more, "I got the strangest feeling that we'd met before. When you mentioned the king's guard, it struck me. Were you with Alaric and his wife, Stairnon, before the walls of Assisi? "

"Yes, I was at his side as always."

"And the man hanging by his neck from the wall, you helped cut him down, didn't you." It was not a question.

"You refer to that great warrior of the Vallone? Of course I helped cut him down. Who would deny that privilege. It was among my greatest honors. Furthermore, it was my shield we carried him off on."

"Ah, that was yours, eh? Incredible. I remember the day well. It was a remarkable honor for a Roman soldier to be treated so honorably by a foe. A tribute to my dearest friend that I shall long remember," said Lucius. "It was I who returned the tail of Ferox to your king that day. The tail the Butcher cut off the king's horse at the Vallone."

"I was too young for the Vallone," said Wallia. "I remained in Moesia under that sleep thorn's spell. I learned of it, as did every young warrior, listening as we did to the fops around the fire. My first battle was at Pollentia seven years later. One question, if I am not too bold," said Wallia, "How did you learn our tongue? I took you as one of our own this morning before I got a better look at you."

"I lived among the Burgundians for years, even played a role in Gunther becoming king. It was his daughter I ran off with—for whom I still pine, although . . ." He swallowed the rest; the telling played no role here.

"Yes, yes, of course. I saw you with her before we marched on Rome. If I remember the story, she and five other young maidens were dragged off and raped by the slave trader's men. And the Burgundians, incensed, destroyed their fortifications in retaliation, freeing thousands of slaves—many of Germani blood. Is that the way it was, or it is just another campfire yarn?"

Lucius nodded halfheartedly. Bruné-Hilda's rape was a memory he wanted to forget. "Yeah, it's true."

Wallia went on about that terrible summer. "Our camp was but a few miles south of your city. I witnessed what happened that stormy night, a night that nearly cost us our most important ally."

"You mean Gunther."

"Yes, the Burgundian chieftain. Indeed, I witnessed it all: the night of the bulls, the attack by the Avars, the church atop the hill under siege. At the darkest hour, the tempest rolled in as though ordered by the gods; it covered the valley like a shroud. Thor was angry, the lightning blinding, everyone forced to turn their heads. When it let up and the clouds cleared, I saw that nothing remained. The church, that magnificent villa high up on the hill, the entire right side of the city, was just gone. Then a deluge cascaded toward us with the roar of a lion, pounding the earth like stampeding elephants. A gigantic avalanche rumbled over the city walls right toward our encampment. I thought it would sweep us all into Hades, but it came to rest just short of the wagonburg. Sheer good fortune it was—for us anyway. Never saw anything like it before or since."

"You saw more than I," said Lucius, shivering from the chilling reminder. "Hiding in a vault beneath the church, I was fortunate to survive at all."

"I saw you wandering about days later. The word was to leave you be. That you were crazy with loss."

Lucius looked down. He had a difficult time recalling that part. "Let's forget that and talk about you," he said, changing the subject.

"I understand, lad. You lost everything all at once. I'll leave it for another time if you like." Wallia went silent for a few moments. "All right, back to me. After Rome, I captained a unit, a responsibility far above my rank. And it didn't stop there. It never does. After we stormed Tolosa, Athaulf reorganized us into units modeled after the legions. I became 'Master of the Horse'—whatever that is. And that led to my current good fortune."

"Your being at Tolosa explains why we never met," said Lucius.

"Before Tolosa I was at Massilia; was there when Athaulf got hit by that lucky dart. That wound finished him, though his end came much later. So tell me, Lucius, what first brought you to Narbo? The Rhine country is quite a ways north."

"I was chased there by a sorceress trying to reclaim a treasure that wasn't hers to reclaim—it belonged to Rome."

"Freya-Gund?"

"Yes, you know of her?"

Wallia nodded his head. "Of course I know of her. All Goths know of Freya-Gund."

"Is she in the column?" asked Lucius, having put that woman out of his mind.

"Don't know."

"But you know who she is?" asked Lucius not hiding his skepticism.

"I said yes! Though I was there when she threw open the gates at Rome, I only know *of* her. She's a 'Norn,' you see, a woman with supernatural powers, the one who killed Sassen the Avar and rolled his severed head down the center aisle of the warlords' summit. Right down the center she did and true as an arrow. What a woman. I won't soon forget that sight—nor will any of the warlords who witnessed it. Never saw so many stiff necks go weak. Not one would look her in the eye, nor dare touch one thread of her clothes. I'll give her plenty of room if I chance to encounter that woman."

"If she's here, I need to know—as does Galla." His tone was ominous. It caused the new king of the Goths to blink.

Lucius could see that the man did not want to talk about any of this, so he cleared his throat and changed the subject again. "Now, sir, can we return to the emperor's proposition. As I said earlier, Africa will cause you nothing but misery. The crossing, the desert, especially the heat, will use up what little energy your people have left. The proposal for a year's amount of grain and the governance of Spain gives you a guaranteed homeland and your people their lives back. Think on it for a night. I'll return before you resume this march to nowhere. And when you think on it, you should consider the hardships you'll be facing if you continue. Not to mention the dangers of crossing a hostile land and the hot desert where only scorpions survive. So consider the emperor's offer for the sake of the young. The elders want only to fulfill a dream. I wager half will die before they reach their promised land."

Early the next morning, confident that his points were well received, Lucius met with Wallia a second time.

"I have consulted the elders," said Wallia. "Although the emperor's offer is generous, maybe even wise, they feel Africa is the best course for our people." Lucius started to object, and Wallia hurriedly said, "Understand their thinking: Alaric's and Athaulf's pro-Roman attitude caused our people nothing but pain, earned us nothing but broken promises, hurled insults, and treachery behind every tree."

"That was yesterday, sir. We speak now of tomorrow."

"All the yesterdays affect the morrow. So, here is what we plan to do: The main column will be moved back to Castulo and remain there in twelve separate wagonburgs. While that is being done, three thousand of my strongest men will go with me across Baetica—Vandal territory—to the Pillars of Hercules. Once enough boats are assembled, some shall cross to Africa. The rest will remain on the coast to guard their backs in case anyone resorts to mischief. If the initial crossing is successful, we will call up the main column and all cross."

"Is that your final word?" asked Lucius.

"It is the council's final word, yes."

"Then I'm coming with you. You see, sir, if you do not take offense in my saying it, neither Galla or I think your heart is in this undertaking. We believe you understand how forbidding the straits can be at times."

"We all know that."

"Then I have your permission to come."

"At your peril, my friend, at your peril," warned Wallia. "By all accounts, Baetica can be a dangerous place, the Siling Vandals unpredictable. They are the obstacle, not the straits."

"I lived among a Siling clan at Scanborg-Andrazza. Their habits are not foreign to me. My knowledge might be helpful."

"How so?"

"They live in the past and are extremely superstitious, which, if manipulated, can be used as a weapon in our favor."

That statement was more prophetic than even Lucius knew.

The Pillars of Hercules lay six days southwest of Castulo. Well known for disasters, the provincials of Baetica believed that Bast, the Egyptian cat goddess, was seduced by Hercules and as a result of their union produced a two-headed child—the two Pillars of Hercules. The enmity between the two was said to be what destroyed all who challenged these waters. Whatever the truth, the straits proved disastrous for the unwise who challenged this myth.

Wallia called up his finest of horse and body for this risky expedition. Moving swiftly across Baetica, the terrain perfect for an ambush, the small force charged headlong through the domain of the Siling Vandals. An occasional arrow or a shouted insult was the best the Vandals could muster being spread out as they were over this vast area. That dispersion would coalesce when the Gothic presence became more widely known.

Lucius first learned of what to expect at Corduba. A villager warned that any attempt to cross the straits from the eastern end might prove disastrous. When asked why, the villager only shrugged and added nothing more, other than that he'd heard all his life that crossing at the pillars was the purview of the gods, not man. Lucius could not accept so foolish a notion. So, at every opportunity, he questioned the provincials until, finally, at Malaca he was told the real reason: the current. The current coming in from the ocean was constant and at times treacherous, especially this time of year. The only successful attempts were launched farther west from the Straits of Gades. While the strait was eight miles across at the pillars, it was four times that from Gades when allowing for the inflow from the ocean. It made sense that the incoming current had to be allowed for, so Lucius notified Wallia immediately after he heard.

Skeptical, Wallia and the two elders who were strong enough to come along on this arduous, fast moving adventure needed to hear the information directly from the source. They did, and also became convinced that the current had to be considered. The embarkation point, accordingly, was moved thirty miles west of the pillars to Gades.

When they reached the Straits of Gades, Wallia split the band into three groups: one was put to work constructing a fortified camp, another sent to gather what boats they could, and the third given the task of dragging logs down from the hills to be crafted into rafts and dugouts. In ten days they assembled, at least in Lucius's eyes, a flotilla of unseaworthy flotsam. So he suggested that they lash the dugouts together as he had done when floating down the Doubs and Soane rivers. He also knew they would need seaworthy oars. Poling, which the Goths were accustomed to doing when crossing rivers, would not work in the straits. He found a third-class shipwright farther down the coast at Baetis, where a meager river ran from the hills to the sea. With Wallia's permission, he traded six horses for a hundred and twenty eight-foot-long oars of rough hewn elder. These poorly made "tools of the sea" became the second faulty link in the chain. The third was the storm hiding far out to sea that no one noticed when the eleven hundred brave volunteers pushed off into the boiling Straits of Gades and headed toward Septa on the far coast. Hours later, the sun disappeared, the rains came, and the winds picked up.

The next day Lucius stood on the shore with Wallia waiting for at least one craft to return with word. The following day, a few men straggled back over land, never having reached the other shore. They landed, they said, farther down the coast of Spain near the pillars. In all, eight hundred and seventy-five men were unaccounted for. Those not upended by the storm were apparently carried off by the current. And so far as anyone knew, not one made it across to the shores of Mauretania.

That night Lucius tossed and turned in bed, the loss preyed on his mind. Was it the oars that failed? Had his sources misinformed him? Why couldn't he react like a barbarian and accept these disasters as a way of life? So many close to him had already passed on to the next life for no reason: Jovius Flaccus, the blacksmith; then Ignatius, the Butcher of the Vallone; his parents; Jingo; Ponti, in that horrific mudslide; Gunther; and his little Theo. Why didn't the gods to whom they prayed protect them? Where were Zeus, Odin, and the one called Jesus?

Depressed, walking aimlessly in the dark thinking about those he missed, Lucius noticed the fires for the first time, fires in the hills to the north, east, and west. If they were there other nights, why hadn't he noticed? *Good gawd, there must be hundreds of them*. Picking up the pace, he hurried to the embankment that protected the camp and approached the guards. One he knew well. "What do those fires mean?" he asked, pointing.

"Vandals," said Boorst. "Vandal campfires: We are suddenly surrounded by thousands of those swine. As if they knew before we did."

"Knew? Knew what?" asked Lucius, not making the connection.

"Knew that the crossing of the straits would fail. They knew how it would turn out."

In a panic Lucius rushed to Wallia's makeshift tent. It consisted of three wagons drawn up in a horseshoe with a center pole holding a canvas up over them. Six warriors sat in a ring listening to Wallia.

". . . or we fight to the—" He stopped when Lucius entered.

"Lucius, good, come in. Sit down here in front. We have a problem," he began.

"And I, a solution."

"Oh, you do now, do you."

"Yes. Before I offer it up, there's a price. Do we have an agreement?"

Wallia did not answer.

"Okay, so you want to drag this foolishness of crossing the straits out a bit longer. Fine, I can play along. However, let me say this: Are you now convinced that the straits cannot be crossed without large ships?"

Silence.

"There are wagons, animals, women, and children to consider if the entire nation attempts a crossing. You know that. And you saw what happened out there to that hapless flotilla."

"It was a storm!" said one of the others.

"What struck them was but a rain and a little wind, not a full-blown tempest. Is it your desire to put the entire nation at risk? And then, if everyone does cross, do you expect them to march east through an endless desert with no water, preyed on nightly by the hungry beasts of that wilderness, and ruthless nomads of Mauritania stalking the column night and day?"

Wallia still said nothing. He didn't need to. Lucius saw the answer in all their faces. The elders were fools to push for a crossing. And the encouragement they received from some of the locals was bogus. Whoever supported a crossing had to be in league with the Vandals. "Now, after witnessing our losses, the Vandals sit at their campfires waiting for the right moment to finish the rest of us off."

Not one word was spoken in defense of the expedition; all knew the truth.

Finally Wallia rose and said, "First, your solution to this mess, and then I'll give you my answer."

"I'm going back to bed," Lucius answered without a hint of malice. "When you come to your senses—every last one of you— wake me. I'll give you my solution then."

Lucius did not get far, nor did he expect to. Two guards lifted him off the ground and carried him bodily back into the makeshift tent.

"What possesses you at times?" asked Wallia. "What demon drives you to act as though you lead a legion of fire-breathing dragons?"

Lucius shrugged. He had heard all that before. "Because it always works—it's a gift I was born with. Now, what's your answer?"

Wallia nodded. The other six reluctantly acquiesced as well. Lucius had them by their tenders.

"We have an agreement then," he said flatly. It was definitely not a question.

"Agreement? No. What we have is an accord. Now, young wizard, stir this broth of chaos into a palatable soup for us. What, pray tell, is your solution to these campfires? You do understand that possibly ten thousand Vandals are out there waiting, right? Silings, Lucius. Siling Vandals, the worst of the worst."

"I told you once before that I lived among a rogue clan of the Silings at Scanborg-Andrazza. I know their dialect. It's not much different from yours. I learned the subtleness of their ways, how they think, what they believe in. But mostly I learned the essence of their dark moods. They are extremely superstitious. *Extremely!* And when I say that, I mean *exceedingly* superstitious."

"You've made the point. Go on."

"Now then, here is what must be done. Set a meeting, use any excuse, lie, or fable, just get me to their chieftain. I and I alone will go to him. After the Vandal chieftain hears what I have to say, he will let us walk away without one drop of blood being shed on either side, I promise. If I do this thing, if I save your sorry arses from your wrong-headed ways, on the hammer of Thor you pledge to do two things: free Galla Placidia into my care and join with us as foederati to the benefit of Rome and your people. In exchange, you will receive six hundred thousand measures of grain, which now sits in Massilia, plus a guaranteed homeland. Never again shall your jars be empty or your jugs run dry." When finished, Lucius took a long, deep breath and waited for the answer.

Not one of them said a word. They simply stared at him.

"Look not upon me as a mere messenger from Rome," he went on, "but as your savior for now and all times. Thank Odin with your every being that he sent me to you. For without me, this vanguard will be crushed under the Vandal boot and your people will disappear from the face of the earth."

Wallia looked down scratching the earth with his finger, then up, and then into the faces of every man in the tent. He could do little more than shake his head at the apparent audaciousness that flowed from the lips of the outrageous young man sitting across from him.

And so it came to pass. Wallia and his council succumbed the "audaciousness" of Lucius—the meeting was arranged. It was set in the surrounding hills north of the Straits of Gades. Lucius truly did know a great deal about the Siling Vandals. That they took part in the battle at Faesulae, crossed the Rhine River at Mainz eight or nine years ago to lay waste to northern Gaul, and, most importantly, he understood that they worshipped a particular god to the point of obsession. What he did not know was that the Siling Vandal chieftain's wife, Sigrun, was kin to Alcorn, the head of the Silings at Scanborg-Andrazza, and that the chieftain he was about to engage and the council who were there to listen, saw Alcorn as a traitor to the old ways. Why? Because Alcorn had become one of those self-righteous, postulating Christians. Lucius put himself in a bear pit with men of sordid pasts and blood on their hands. The meeting site was set out in the open air before a ring of hastily built shelters. It was night.

"I know your heart, Battaric," said Lucius, speaking directly to the Siling Vandal chieftain at the start of the conference.

"How does one know another's heart?" replied the stiff-necked chieftain.

"Battaric, members of the council," Lucius said, addressing them formally. "I was there at Faesulae," he boasted, "and saw you in your proud regalia, double-bitted swords, shields of wicker, helmets adorned with plumes of horse-hair, and *frightened to the core*. Yes, I said frightened, even though you and your allies outnumbered Stilicho's legions six to one."

"You were but a child then," spit the chieftain, obviously offended by what he perceived to be an out-and-out lie, not to mention the insult.

"I, sir, was there," replied Lucius with equal verve. "You play with fire to doubt me? Do you not worship the god Tyr?"

Battaric did not answer. The council members looked on, their expressions hidden from Lucius by the dancing shadows of the huge campfire.

"Tyr has many faces, a dozen eyes, and many sides to his persona. Is that not true?"

They all remained stone-faced silent.

"This god, the one you call Tyr, had two sons, did he not? And the eldest of the two murdered his brother so he could become eternally young. How do you, you, or you, know that I am not that surviving son, the eldest one, the eternal one, the all-knowing Batyr?"

Battaric laughed. "Throw him over the edge. Get him out of here. He makes a mockery of our gods and this council."

"Wait!" Lucius roared with such force that it caused those around the fire to freeze. "Did not the Burgundians war at Faesulae under your banner—two red diagonals on their shields? Stripes you no longer wear. Why? Because you were not only defeated at Faesulae but roundly disgraced. How would I know that if I was not there? Ah-ha! I see you begin to believe. Good. Let me go on. You were warned of the trap the Roman general Stilicho set during the night, were you not? Of course you were. I heard it all, for I was there. And did not the Burgundians break out to the south to avoid the Roman snare while the rest of you froze in place? You knew not what to do and were eventually routed, correct? Yes, you ran off broken and beaten. After that, every last one of you, every single warrior, removed those two red stripes to hide the cowardice of your actions. And did you not later assassinate Radagaisus, the bumbler who led you over the Alps? I was there on that battlefield, in the clouds, in the trees, and witnessed your every frailty, each weakness. Do you want me to name those spineless *wilters* who ran off? Well, do you?"

"No!" shouted one of the councilmen jumping to his feet.

Lucius lowered his tone. "Did I hear a no," he said calmly. "I suggest you sit back down and hear me out." The man obeyed. Lucius now knew he had them in the palm of his hand. Ironically, the hated Alcorn, kin to the chieftain's wife, had been the one who revealed this dirty little secret one night back at Scanborg-Andrazza about the Siling Vandal's cowardice at Faesulae.

Battaric picked up the knife lying before him and slid it into the sheath affixed to his wide leather belt. "Let's walk," he said to Lucius, motioning for two councilmen to follow. The four walked from the fire to the edge of the hill. Far below, Lucius could see in the moonlight the Gothic encampment, the Straits of Gades, and the distant torch lights of Tingis on the far banks of Mauretania.

"Now," Battaric said, "tell us how you know the Burgundians wore our stripes at Faesulae, the break-out, the horseshoe trap, and everything else. If Alcorn told you, I'll kill him."

"Enough of Faesulae, Battaric. Let's move on to discussing the Rhine River so that you understand my presence is, and has been, everywhere. You retreated north over the Bernard Pass to Mainz full of rage for everything that was Roman. How could you not hate them after suffering such a humiliating defeat? Once recovered—it took a year, didn't it?—you, along with your cousins the Asdings and others, including the Alani, Suebi, and Alemanni, took advantage of the ice that formed on the Rhine that year and crossed over. You destroyed and burned everything until you realized you were ruining the necessities you needed to survive in this foreign land. So you kept going south in search of food and fodder. But the provincials to the south scorched the vitals for which you searched. That was when Goar, the Alani king, became discouraged and returned North, taking the best of his warriors with him."

"As did Guntiarus, the Burgundian king," interjected Battaric without thinking.

"So you finally admit I speak the truth. Good. With Goar and Guntiarus gone, your people felt abandoned, alone, vulnerable. The Suebi and Alemanni were of little comfort. Then failure at Narbo, failure at Tolosa, failure at Barcelona, Tarraco, and Valentia—should I go on?" Lucius looked hard into Battaric's face. "I see from your expression that I should not—however, I must. Then you settled here in Baetica as a last resort. Tiring of the heat and living on a terrain that yielded little, you tried to cross the straits to Mauretania but got swamped. That's why you patiently waited for the Goths to make the same mistake before surrounding them."

The chieftain remained silent. But Lucius could see the man's fingers digging into his palms.

"You see, Battaric, I was sent here to save you from yourself. Why do I say that? I say that because just beyond the beyond are two hundred thousand Gothic warriors waiting for Wallia's return, which, if he does not return, could possibly mean the end of all of you. So listen to these words closely. I heard Wallia say them before this expedition departed: 'If I do not return from the pillars for any reason, then I want all of you to call down the ethos of the ages upon our enemies—the cataclysmic events of Ragnarok. Have the heavens fire; the stars vanish; the earth convulse; the mountains fall; and every man, woman, and child of the Siling Vandals victimized by the wolves of Odin. When all that is said is said, and when all that is done is done, let the gods of our ancestors make the winter of all winters encrust the earth, make the winds blow, make the sun vanish into the jaws of Fenrir, make the seas rise and the ships of the dead appear on the horizon. Let it be as written in the Book of Aesir that Ragnarok shall reign over our enemies forever.'"

Just then, as though Lucius willed it, a flash of light shot across
the sky followed by a clap of thunder. The faces of the councilmen
turned white. They could see a storm rolling in from far out at sea.
Not an unusual occurrence—*except for the timing!*

Lucius had them reeling.

"Stop!" shouted Battaric, throwing up his hands. He turned to
the others. "An inner tugging from the past says you should both
leave us. I sense that the son of Tyr has words for my ears only."

After they departed, he asked, "What are you doing to my people
with these words?"

"You go against your beliefs, Battaric. You contradict the
god to whom you have sacrificed to all your life. He is the god of
agreements, not discord. You have misused him. For that he is angry.
He wants order—not chaos. Pray for enlightenment, give sacrifice,
and then the answer will come. Now I must return to the coast. My
work here is done."

"Why not fly if you are truly the son of Tyr?"

"Because," Lucius said, moving closer to Battaric, "I do not have
wings. And," pausing for maximum effect—"because we both know
this is but a game I play for the benefit of your council. Tell me, have
I not given you enough reasons to let your avowed enemies march
off from here unmolested? You will not be dishonored, nor will you
be a fool. A massive Gothic army truly sits just beyond your reach.
Do you want it to attack? Your council certainly wants none of it
now, unable as they are to separate truth from fable. They're old and
fear the god of their ancestors more than they fear you. They will not
chance angering Tyr, providing, of course, that you keep my little
game our secret."

Battaric laughed out loud, obviously taken aback by Lucius's
wanton admission. Then he said, "You have made hearts of stone
tremble with this little game. Who are you?"

"Just a simple Umbrian, Battaric, who wants to save Rome
from the likes of you and them," Lucius said, pointing down to the
encampment on the straits.

And so it came to pass that Lucius's grandest bluff worked.
The council, if not the chieftain, fell prey, like so many before, to
his slippery tongue. Free passage, however, did not come easily.

Although the vanguard of the Goths, or what was left of them after the mishap on the straits, was allowed to leave, the road to Malaca was fraught with venom. Cursed and spit upon by the Vandals as they passed, the Gothic contingent nevertheless marched out of harm's way without incident. But this was not to be the end; the Gothic King Wallia vowed one day to avenge this insult.

It took some time, but Lucius finally found wagonburg four concealed among the birch trees two miles south of the Via Hercules and west of Castulo. It sat hidden not far from a stream. Although the leaves were gone, the thick grove gave sufficient protection against the cold north wind. Winter's wrath was nearing. He found Galla Placidia's house wagon, knocked on the small door, and waited. Impatient, he banged harder. A slot opened and an eye peered out.

"She's not here," said a small voice. It was Elpida, Galla's elderly servant lady. "You'll find her down by the stream washing her things."

"Washing her—"

"I know. I know," said Elpida. "She insists on doing it herself. What can I do?" Her tone gave the equivalent of a shrug.

When Galla saw him coming, she dropped everything and jumped into his arms. She mussed his hair and kissed him on the cheeks, forehead, chin, and, finally, the lips. It was more like a girl at play than a love kiss, though. "Well?" she said at last.

"Well what?"

"What happened? Did they cross? Was it hard? Did the Vandals—"

"Whoa, girl, slow down," he said, lowering her gently to the ground. "One question at a time."

She blinked coquettishly, her big dark eyes sparkling, and then she recaptured her poise, smoothed out the wash apron she was wearing, and shifted to a cheeky one-legged stance. "Speak for gawd's sake!"

"The vanguard made it across and now camps on the desert's edge deep inside Mauretania," he lied. "Pack up your things. You're off to the hot sands of Africa as soon as possible. Or, if you prefer, you can take the easy road out of this like the queen of the Nile. For that I brought a slithery asp. One bite on the wrist, and *puff*! No more Africa."

Her smile collapsed. She looked right at him, her expression blank. He could tell she was formulating a response. "At once, you say? We must depart for Africa at once."

"No. I said soon."

A fire quickly built in those dark eyes and then disappeared just as quickly. The corner of her lip cracked a bit, followed by a tiny smile.

"I'm free, aren't I?" she said flatly. "You did it. Say it, Lucius, damn you. You succeeded in setting me free, didn't you?" And she danced about, ran to her wet garments, picked up a handful and whirled them above her head before slinging every last one into the air. One landed on his head, the wet running over his cheeks. He slid it off, chuckled, and threw it into her basket.

"Well, aren't I?" she asked, this time with less conviction.

"Unless Nero's mother rises from the grave, you are as free as that bird in the tree over there," he said, pointing. "Wallia needs only for the elders to agree."

Letting out a whoop that sent a nearby squirrel scurrying, she ran toward the house wagon to share the news with her faithful Elpida. Lucius gathered up her things and followed. He prayed only that the Master General Constantius held to his part of the agreement.

The next afternoon, Lucius was guided to a barn where Wallia and the elders sat waiting on milking stools and piles of damp hay. Not the most distinguished venue but adequate. Several guards leaned disinterestedly against the supports. As Lucius entered, he heard a shout, "The hero of Gades arrives!" It was Wallia announcing Lucius's arrival in this uncustomary, congenial way. He was sitting cross-legged against the back wall. And despite the relaxed air in the barn, the stench—both human and animal—nearly knocked Lucius over.

Wallia continued in the same upbeat manner. "Our hero asks, no, he demands a *Non Sistere*—an Express—to depart at once for the encampment of those Romans who once wished us harm." His voice was more authoritative than Lucius remembered. And the tone caused the council to sit up straight. "This Express, our champion here demands, must carry a message that says we are now willing to settle our long-standing differences with Rome and begin talks of a lasting peace." With that, Wallia rose.

The elders stirred, apparently hearing of this for the first time. They began exchanging comments among themselves. Was this a surprise? The more heated the discussion, the more Lucius realized Wallia did not prepare them at all. At last Bittar, the eldest and wisest of the council, got up. "Not so fast," he said in such an odious manner, it had the immediate effect of silencing the chatter. Lucius knew that this man, more than any, treated Wallia like an adolescent. "There are other ways than giving in to this one's demands that would serve our people better. Capitulation, after all we have been through, would not only be dishonorable but unwise. We are a nation of free men, not slaves of Rome."

Some did not agree. Two began to push, one threw an elbow, another a fist, until the disagreements spread to all corners of the barn. The failure at the straits exposed a deep fissure within the council. And Wallia was ready to handle it. He nodded to the guards who brutishly reestablished order. When calm returned, Wallia walked to the front of the group. This was a different Wallia than the one Lucius first met.

"Members of our venerated council of elders, you have seen more since we crossed the big river into Moesia than any of our people. And for that, you have earned the respect of the younger. Parts of these migrations have been worth the hardship, most have not. It's understandable that this is difficult for your old ears to hear, your stomachs to swallow, and your hearts to comprehend. But it's time you do; time to admit our errant ways; time to move into the future by shedding the baggage of the past. How many were there when Fritigern's warriors slew Valens's legions at Adrianople, the victory that put fear in Rome and confidence in our arms?"

Three hands went up.

"That triumph, thirty-seven years ago, made Goths everywhere feel invincible. Then the massacre at the Vallone happened, a disaster that shook us to the core. To soothe our wounded pride, we said it was treachery, but most know different. How many of you were there?"

Four more hands went up.

"My first engagement was Pollentia," Wallia went on. "All of you were there when we made fools of ourselves, just as we did in Greece when our king knocked on gates that would not open. Then Stilicho chased us across the Straits of Corinth. Because of *his* golden tongue, we became his foederati and billeted our people throughout that hard, terrible land called Dalmatia that even Alaric came to realize was a fool's errand. Well, my comrades, we can afford no more Vallones, no more Dalmatias, and certainly no more Pollentias. Those days are over!"

He paused, glanced at each man briefly and then picked up the timbre. His voice gained a new unassailable quality. "You knew I was not Balthi when you chose me as your king. The Royal House of Balthi no longer rules our people; Alaric, Stairnon, Athaulf, Singerich, and Sarus are dead. Nor am I of their religion. My tribe, the Ediulf, has remained faithful to the old ways, unlike the Balthi. We consider a wooden shield a sacred symbol, not the cross. I was born in a house of wood, not cloth. Men worked the fields, our women the hearths. Campfires were for hunting trips, not daily living. We Ediulfs laid down the plow only to defend ourselves. When was the last time any of you harvested the crop you planted? The Balthi led us into one disaster after another because of their lofty dreams of Gothia. Only fate should determine fortune, not wild aspiration. We are a proud people. We take but one woman and treat her like a human, not cattle. And we care for our young—male and female— unlike the Romans who callously abandon their girl children at the crossroads.

"Yes, comrades, once we grew crops, bred horses, fired our own swords. Now we eat worms and steal. We lost our way, became criminals, shamed the One-Eyed One and abandoned the teachings of the Great Mother, Hertha. No comrades, I choose not to be a dreamer, but the purveyor of resurrection, the restorer of pride. For all these reasons and more, I am making peace with Rome, which includes releasing the princess."

He paused, waiting. There were no objections, so he went on. "In exchange, if our negotiations succeed, we gain for our people a permanent homeland and enough grain to sustain ourselves until the next harvest—our own harvest. Lordly member of this venerable council, I, your chosen king, have spoken."

Lucius was in shock. Never in a thousand years did he think that Wallia would stand up to the elders. Because he was not of the ruling class—the royal Balthi—Lucius had assumed the man was a puppet, a person unworthy of the crown. Well, if that was true once, the man was deserving of it now.

The next day a three-man Express rode out from the barn. They pulled spare horses and two pack mules. Their mission was to get over the Pyrenees before the snow closed the passes and then to make contact with Constantius's legions, wherever they may be. Hopefully they had remained at Arles these months and had not crossed over the mountains to Spain. If that was the case, Constantius might not be as agreeable to the original accord. The three men were ordered to ride day and night and told to stop only to rotate horses. As they left, Lucius handed the leader a packet with two messages. One dealt with the agreement, the other was a report on what had happened here, the strength of the Vandals in Baetica, and the failed crossing of the Straits of Gades. In the report, he warned Constantius not to make the mistake of knitting back together an already broken people by pushing too hard. Lucius insisted a single grain ship be rushed to Barcelona as a good-faith gesture while the treaty was being finalized.

After the Express departed, the main body of the Gothic nation packed up for the move back to Barcelona where they would await the outcome.

Fearful some might be displeased with her release, Lucius and Galla left on horseback shortly after the Express for the safety of Barcelona. With them, at Wallia's insistence, rode sixty handpicked warriors, plus Galla's faithful servants in three high-speed gigs. They reached the villa near Barcelona exhausted. During the absence of the Goths these many months, the Barcelonans had recovered somewhat and had a modest supply of food available to feed Galla's sixty *bucellarii* and servants. That first night they slaughtered two horses, set a bonfire on the beach, and the entire entourage enjoyed roasted meat for the first time in weeks. One of the servants even managed to get his hands on enough wine to heighten the glow.

Before the light was lost and feeling good from the wine, Lucius wandered to the chapel's graveyard where little Theo was buried. Maybe it was the wine, maybe just curiosity, but whatever inspired him to go there took courage. Neither he nor Galla spoke of the baby since his return from the Straits of Gades. The excitement created by her pending release overwhelmed everything else. Besides, Theo's death was a painful topic.

He moved slowly toward the monument that marked the infant's grave, a boy whose birth had held so much promise. The grave marker was square, angular, and a little higher than Lucius was tall—an impressive tribute. In the fading light, Lucius did not at first see what lay at the base of the monument as he walked around it reading the attestations chiseled into the stone phallic. The words proclaimed the boy's lineage in both Greek and Latin: his great-grandfather, Valentinian; grandfather, Theodosius the Great; Arcadius and Honorius, his uncles; and Theodosius II, his cousin, who still reigned over the East from Constantinople. Reminders of his son's glorious ancestry brought a tear to Lucius's eye. He had so much potential, so much promise.

"Hey, what's that?" he mumbled aloud. Ah yes, a ring of runic symbols. *Hmm.* No doubt put there by one of the Gothic sops. He tried to read the runes but their significance was lost on him. Along with so many others, Lucius did not understand the mysterious symbols of the North.

Only after circling the monument twice more did he see it for the first time. It lay there in the darkest shadow of the gravestone. Nor did he recognize what it was right away because of the light. Not wanting to disturb it, he bent down for a better look. He thought it might be a sacred commemoration from a grieving local. Strangers sometimes left mementos at the graves of prominent people. But since it lay in the shadows, his eyes had to adjust. Once they did, he let out a gasp.

"It can't be!" he muttered, grabbing it with both hands. Taking a deep breath, he juggled it, examined it more closely, and then cursed aloud. What he held was important, even crucial, and it could change everything. It was the packet he'd given to the Express riders to deliver to the Master General Constantius. He ripped it open, and there they were—two written messages—sealed, undisturbed, and obviously undelivered.

"Who would . . . ?" A metallic jingle interrupted his thoughts and was just that quickly muffled. He looked up. The light was gone, save for the half-moon. But he could see something behind the chapel; a human form lurked there in the moonlight. Slipping the packet inside his tunic, he moved quickly into the absolute darkness of the chapel wall where he skimmed cautiously along toward the prowler. When he reached the spot, he saw nothing. Maybe he was just seeing things. Squatting down, he pulled out the knife from his boot and listened. The only sound came from the beach. Slowly, he swept the area once, twice. Then a twig snapped somewhere beyond the fruit trees near the outside wall that rimmed the compound, followed by a scuffing sound, then silence. Whoever it was seemed to have vanished into thin air. He then heard the fading sound of hooves beating north toward Barcelona. Who was it? Did the person only want to make sure someone found the packet? If so, that person was surely the one who had put it there.

Lucius moved toward the part of the wall from where the scuffing sound had come and attempted to climb up to peer over, maybe get a look at the rider. But there were no hand or foot holes, nothing to grab on to. Whoever climbed it must have used something. It was much too high to scale without the help of a rope or ladder.

The moon, and just when he needed it most, went behind a cloud, stealing what little light he had. Unable to see, he felt his way along the wall in search of whatever the intruder might have used to climb up. Not far along, he felt something wet, definitely not water. Rubbing his fingers together, it felt unusually slippery. He put his fingers to his nose. It had a strange yet familiar odor and tasted salty.

His search for a ladder or rope proved fruitless, so he started to work his way back from where he started. Then the moon abruptly reappeared. He could see just enough to tell what was on his hands. Agh! Gawd! He spit. It was blood! How in the love of Zeus did blood get on the wall? Unless, and he relished this next thought, unless the trespasser hurt himself climbing over the wall. *Good!*

Deserved him right! But then . . . there was far too much blood for that. The man would be incapacitated losing that much.

More curious now, Lucius started to look around. Blood was on the ground, on the bushes, everywhere. "What in the world . . . ," he mumbled. Something moved, causing him to look up. It was a large bird landing atop the wall, followed by another and another. Bald-headed birds. Carrions! *My gawd! What are they doing here?* Then he saw. Beneath their claws, and somewhat hidden by the branches from a tree growing on the other side of the wall, hung three human heads.

"Great Jupiter!" he shrieked, scaring off the vultures. When the last one fluttered away, it dropped something that hit him in the face and then bounced off his shoulder and onto the ground—it was an eyeball, a human eyeball. He jumped, now seeing the scene more clearly. The heads were suspended by their hair: the side of one's face mangled, an eye missing; the other two had their mouths agape as though crying out in horror. And as grotesque as they were, there was no mistaking their identities. The heads belonged to the three Express messengers.

Lucius rushed back to the beach. "We've a problem," he whispered to Galla, who was thoroughly enjoying herself. "Come." And he pulled her away, into the villa, and up to her suite of rooms. Not until they were sitting on the bed did he hand her the packet.

"What's this?" she asked.

"The agreement for your release, the grain, and everything else. I'm not sure how or why, but the Express never made it beyond Barcelona."

"Where in the name of Satan . . . ?" She grabbed Lucius and shook him. "How could you possibly know that?"

"I know! More than that, I found this atop Theo's grave," he said, thrusting the packet into her chest. "It was put there for one of us to find."

She examined the contents of the packet carefully, furrowed her brow, and then jumped up and swore, "This is fucking, fucking serious, Lucius."

"Yes, I know its serious."

"Who, Lucius? Who dammit! Tell me, who would do such a thing?"

"I thought you'd know. One of the council members, maybe a captain not in favor of the agreement, an angry Goth? Do you know of anyone who hates me or you, or feels so threatened by what we're doing that he would resort to this?"

"The elders are called that for a reason, Lucius. They're old, and they wouldn't have the stomachs, nor could any of them outrun the Express."

"They could launch their own Express to overtake Wallia's. How difficult would that be?"

"Not impossible, but unlikely," said Galla. "The elders don't hate me, Lucius. I can tell that. They all embraced me before we departed. But the act of placing this packet on Theo's grave has an odor with a familiar smell."

Lucius rubbed his chin. "An odor with a . . . I got just a glimpse of someone watching me. Whoever it was ran off after I picked up the packet and scaled that outside wall like he had wings. Quite a feat for any normal person, wouldn't you say?"

"Freya-Gund," said Galla ominously. "She slipped onto these grounds once before. I thought I saw the last of her when we moved south. Maybe she's still around here waiting for another chance to get at the gems or me. It could be her."

"What is it to her if the Goths reach a peace with Rome?"

"Maybe nothing, maybe everything. The woman obsesses. She had a hand in Athaulf's death, you know. I'm certain of it."

"There's more," added Lucius. And he told her of the three heads hanging from the wall. "This cannot be the work of one person."

"Gawd, Lucius, of course it can," she shrieked. "She's evil, has powers beyond the norm! The bitch is capable of anything!"

"All right, okay," he said soothingly. "Remain calm. Forget her. Let's focus on freeing you from this hellish life. The packet must get through to Constantius before he brings the full force of Rome down on the Goths. If that happens, the Vandals will take over Spain and maybe Gaul. Do you know how many barbarians, all less civilized than the Goths, camp on the other side of the Rhine hungry for land? Out and out war could entice every last barbarian to cross over and come down here. Can you imagine the bedlam?"

"Then it is up to you, my love, to rush across the mountains and deliver that packet personally to Constantius. Take my bucellarii and leave at once. Stop for nothing or no one."

"How could I possibly do that, Galla? Those bucellarii are your only protection."

Thanks to an anxious leader, he and six of his bucellarii rode out with Lucius long before the first cock crowed. They reached Gerunda by nightfall without incident and continued on early the next morning, traveling as fast as their string of horses could carry them up into the Pyrenees. The snow at the summit was deep but passable. Two days of hard travel later, they passed through the mist hovering over the pass as they descended and began the final leg of their arduous journey to the lowlands.

In the distance—roughly ten miles off—Lucius saw a fast-moving column coming their way. The bucellarii thought it was a contingent from the Gothic garrison at Narbo on their way to Barcelona. But Lucius disagreed.

"See those standards," he yelled above the beat of hooves. The noise from the horses plus the whistling from a following storm made hearing nearly impossible. "Only legionaries carry standards and pennants. It's the Roman army and they're on the march! I fear we arrive too late!"

For two hours Lucius and the seven bucellarii descended the pass before encountering the forerunners of the column. As the Roman soldiers neared, the bucellarii left the road in favor of a more defensible position among the trees. Lucius boldly sat atop his horse to await the Roman leader.

Burdened by heavy packs and wearing identical *sagums*—the heavily greased wool military capes that they traveled and slept in— the footmen passed at a quickened pace paying Lucius no attention. He watched them pass on both sides, sitting motionless atop his horse in the middle of the via. Carrying only a short sword each, the footmen's heavier weapons were surely being transported by a baggage train somewhere beyond the two columns of cavalry that approached.

The one Lucius was patiently waiting for finally came into view riding a white horse sporting a silver bridle, metallic nosepiece, and propped tail. Helmed, plumed, and wearing a short red cape, the leader rode alone at the head of the cavalry. Cuirass of oiled leather, greaves plated in metal, the man was resplendent in a thousand years of traditional pomp. And he was snorting with anger. Lucius, protected only by a cloth cloak and a flimsy shield of words, came face-to-face with a tried and true warrior—an antagonist of the first order, a man he unfortunately recognized. Atop that easy-gaited palfrey sat Flavius Abinnaeus, the primus pilus of the III Theodosius, the man Lucius encountered at the docks of Ravenna, the one to whom he'd given the Black Hand ring, and the officer Constantius selected to whip the raw recruits into hardened warriors.

"Hail, Flavius!" Lucius yelled, saluting the officer.

"Hail, your ass!" Flavius snapped. "Get out of the way or I'll have the column run you over."

"What brings you this far south?" Lucius asked, looking beyond Flavius to the dual lines of cavalry with their brownish-red uniforms, greaves gleaming in the sun, boots uniformly cross-laced, and swords shining. Most unusual, at least to Lucius's eye, were the standards bearing the legions' insignias that the two *aquilifers* carried. Who were they trying to impress? This wasn't a parade! Other than Lucius and his seven bucellarii, there were no other eyes for miles.

"Our mission, thankfully, is no longer of your concern. We now make glorious war—a war we should have made months ago, no thanks to you," Flavius sneered.

"War? By my count you are but five hundred. What kind of war can five hundred make?"

"We are eight hundred afoot, one hundred and forty-seven mounted. This is the vanguard for the III Theodosius and the VI Diocletian. The auxiliaries from Milan, Dertona, Cremona, and Placentia are in reserve and spoiling for a fight."

Lucius took a deep breath. "Has Constantius and his generals approved this?"

"Of course," groused the officer. "Only you would think a loyal officer of Rome marches without orders. We are bestowed with the honor of testing the enemy. The main force follows on the morrow."

"Where is Constantius billeted?" asked Lucius anxiously.

"At the *castra* of the III Theodosius, of course. The encampment is south of Narbo, half a day's ride from here. Now, move aside."

"This glorious war of yours, this spilling of unnecessary blood," Lucius said, holding fast to his blocking position on the via, "will do little more than slay the future."

"I've never liked you or your views," Flavius sneered.

"I am a garnered fermentation," Lucius said with a smile, disarming this bullheaded officer. Although the man was respected by Constantius and his peers, Lucius knew he was a hot-head that could do more harm than good at times like these.

"Where are you from, Flavius? Where bred this fiery demeanor you wear like a crest?"

"Emona, east of Aquileia," he said.

"Then, sir, I suggest you reverse course, unless plowing the back five outside Emona is your most fervent wish. A major storm brews up in those mountains."

With that, Lucius slapped his horse, signaled to the bucellarii to follow, and hurried off toward the III Theodosius encampment a half day's ride away.

And Flavius Abinnaeus, the loyal primus pilus, the senior centurion from Emona, resumed his headlong march toward one of nature's unexpected disasters.

As the sun set on the III Theodosius encampment, Master-General Constantius wiped his brow. He had just finished a brisk walk, which normally worked to clear his emotions. Not this time. He felt frustrated. Yes, he had retaken Tolosa and Narbo this past month. And of course, his legions captured thousands of Goths. But he had run out of reasons to dawdle. Tomorrow he would have to give the order to march on Barcelona. And he dreaded it. The *speculatores* were even now up there checking out the Col de Perthus, the pass they would use. Although his army would only be in the high country for two and a half days, he did not want to, as he put it when he gave the order, "lose a single warrior to the elements." A weak excuse he knew, but it had worked yesterday and the day before that. His officers, though, had pushed for an alternate route, the lower pass near Veneris. But Constantius had scoffed at that and said, "The mud, the uncertainty."

Word from Lucius was what he actually waited for. And as he had told his impatient officers, "Better to pass the time here and be sure, than rush off and be sorry." The vitriolic *legatus* of the VI Diocletian, more than the others, had been persistent though. The man wanted to dash across the mountains to crush the Goths at Barcelona or Dertosa or Valencia or wherever they were, ignoring the dangers. Of course, the younger *legati* always put valor ahead of consequence. Like what happened at the Massaliote Bridge. Constantius lost too many there and didn't want a repeat. Mithras be damned, if only he could live his life without consequences, without those ass lickers at Ravenna scrutinizing his every action. So he waited and ignored his generals, hoping each day was the day that word would come that would allow him to avoid war against the Goths and whoever else dared to stand up against Rome. But no word came. Where had Lucius disappeared to? And the Goths, they seemed everywhere yet nowhere.

Suddenly the tent flaps opened and in came his adiutor. "He comes, Excellency," he said in a calming voice. "Out there in the evening din, the Lord of Chaos has been spotted riding like a wounded bird, like the entire world is in disarray."

"So," said the general, getting up and straightening his tunic. He brushed his hair with his fingers saying, "Lucius Domitilla has finally returned from the hell-fires of Spain."

"I'll send the bucellarii back," Lucius said, exiting the headquarters tent. The cold hit him in the face overwhelming his elation. Oh, how he hated to leave the warmth of the general's felt tent. The weather turned nasty the last twelve hours.

"How long will it take those two ships?" he asked of the Master-General who followed him out of the tent. "More die each day. Eight hundred sacks of grain will save many lives."

"Not long," said Constantius. "Be patient. I ordered a few shiploads up the Rhone in anticipation of this. Believe me when I say it will not take long. Two will sail for Barcelona just as soon as my orders reach Arles."

"Sure hope it's swifter than what we went through in there," Lucius said, referring to the meeting that had just broken up. An agreement was reached, sure, but it took all night. Two subordinate generals wanted nothing to do with a treaty of any sort. Trained for conflict, they wanted war now while the Goths remained weak with hunger. And one of the tribunes had actually shouted, "To hell with the princess! This sitting is taking a toll on my men's morale."

Constantius, as was his custom, listened but offered little. Sure, the reasoning was sincere, the exchange frank, but most used the meeting to vent. Still, war was not the solution. Lucius, having the advantage of seeing Spain from one end to the other and meeting with the Vandals and some other provincials, had made the most convincing case.

Being rooted in western Spain for seven years, he argued, the Vandals, Suebi, and Alani, a rugged bunch of individuals, would be even more of a challenge if the Goths were eliminated. "These barbarians from beyond the Rhine are like rats," he said. "Destroy one and a dozen more come."

The only path, he assured them, was to reach an accord with Wallia. Strengthen *his* people with grain and then let them resolve their own issues with the Vandals, their longtime sworn enemies. Furthermore, he continued, "Wallia is not of the Balthi Clan like the last three kings, nor does he carry past transgressions like festering wounds. He will be loyal to Rome now that he holds sway over his elders. It is us, after all, who broke the promises over the years, not them."

Lucius might as well have smacked the two generals across their faces with the palm of his hand with those words. But Constantius had stood by him. "The past has been rife with broken pledges by the Senate," he said. "And for that reason, and only that," he added, "did they sack Rome." And so the meeting went into the night, back and forth, up and down, in and out, until a resolution was reached. In the end, it would be peace, not war—providing the vanguard led by the primus pilus had not already ignited a conflict.

Three separate six-men *Non Sistere*, a Roman adaptation of the Express, were sent to head off Flavius Abinnaeus and his men. Lucius prayed only that they reached them in time. One *Non Sistere* followed the vanguard's route, another used the lower, eastern pass at Veneris—the one that was always mucked up—and the third was sent by way of the higher, more westerly pass that Lucius thought to be a fool's errand because of the snow. Strangely, contact was never made with the vanguard, nor was it ever heard from again. Could the mountain storm, the one Lucius had forewarned them of, have swept them away? Had an avalanche pushed them into a ravine, or buried them? Or had mountain tribes overwhelmed them? None of these arguments seemed feasible; for surely there would be some survivors. Yet the eight hundred afoot and the one hundred and forty-seven mounted, plus their baggage train, were nowhere to be found.

Ten days later, two ships loaded with grain arrived at the port of Barcelona along with a short message from Master-General Constantius. A few days after that, Wallia met with a large Roman delegation headed by Euplutius and two tribunes at the low pass near Veneris; the discussions moved quickly. Galla was to be given her freedom *only* after the remainder of the grain arrived in Barcelona. On that point, Wallia remained steadfast. The Goths agreed to become foederati and to fight anyone who threatened "Rome's hegemony over Spain." The Goths interpreted that portion of the agreement as the emperor's outright approval to war with impunity against whomever they chose once they recovered their strength. Finally, the Goths were to receive those prisoners the Roman's captured at Tolosa and Narbo. That number, Lucius came to learn, might be as high as eleven thousand Gothic warriors. And it was understood the first opponent in any war waged by the Goths would, of course, be the Siling Vandals at Baetica. Wallia would avenge the unpardonable act of being spit on when his contingent departed the straits.

Lucius stood outside the circle of negotiators watching the agreement being signed. It all seemed so surreal—ink to paper and it was done. But it was not a fantasy, was it? All the trials leading to this moment flashed before his eyes as he watched Wallia reach for the stylus: fleeing from Freya-Gund, transforming Galla Placidia into a symbol of patriotism, opening the Statue of Fortune for the first time, the despair of Bruné-Hilda, the death of baby Theo, the harrowing sea voyage to Rome, stealing into Ravenna, the trip across Spain, the failed crossing at Gades, and the escape from the Vandal trap. Yes, all that and more had led to this moment—a barbarian's willingness to put his mark on a piece of fanius paper that he could not read. Yes, in Lucius's final analysis, it was all too bizarre.

For the Goths, though none around that table would put it to words, the agreement was tantamount to finding a life-saving log in the middle of a turbulent sea. Without this agreement, as a people, they were done for. But for the Romans, the signing was an admission that they no longer had the wherewithal to mount a long, bloody campaign against anyone. The glory days of Caesar, Marcus Aurelius, and Theodosius were over. Their only remaining strategy now was to slow the retraction of the Western Empire. The idea of saving the glory of days of yesteryear was dead.

Or was it?

After the signing, Lucius rushed back to Barcelona to tell Galla the news: after five and a half years of captivity, she was to be freed.

He knew she had come to love her captors, a people removed from her own in so many ways. Although the initial eight hundred sacks of grain satisfied the immediate needs of only half the Goths, the agreement allowed the struggling columns to slaughter some of the draft animals once they arrived back in Barcelona. After all, their survival was now no longer dependent on migration. At winter's end, crops would be planted and a more settled existence would spring forth. Daily life for these wanderers would, after so long a time, be less of a struggle. Watching the columns break off and reestablish themselves in and around Barcelona caused Lucius to recall his favorite psalm that Ponti Lepius Filipi had read to him when he was a little boy: "All flocks and herds and beasts of the field will regenerate—such is the cycle of life." For the first time, he understood the true meaning of that ancient wisdom.

Now the events shifted to the movement of the great store-houses of grain from Massilia to Barcelona. One evening, three ships pulled in to the port of Barcelona, unloaded, and then headed back out to sea. Every few days more arrived, unloaded, and left. Each ship would make at least three trips. When the count reached twelve thousand sacks of grain, Wallia gave Galla Placidia permission to ready her train for departure. Her entourage would include sixty bucellarii, ten servants, and Lucius. They would depart only when the count reached fifteen thousand. For an entire week, not one ship arrived. The tension built. Where was the last of the grain shipments? Had something gone terribly wrong?

Since the murder of the three Express messengers, Galla Placidia had been guarded night and day by her bucellarii. After all, did she not personify the Gothic nation's survival as well as Rome's questionable future? But this night of the half-moon was different. With everyone's attention focused on the horizon and all eyes searching for the arrival of the missing grain ships, the security around Galla's villa eased for the first time since the three heads were found hanging from the wall. And that was precisely what the purveyor of mischief was waiting for.

Although disguised as a lowly fishmonger at the open market these many weeks, she was attuned to all that had happened. Her tentacles were everywhere. On this night of the half-moon, Freya-Gund worked her way along the beach from Barcelona to the villa. Once there, she squeezed through a varmint tunnel under the wall, a well hidden opening she had widened months ago, and then made her way through the garden toward the rear of the villa. There, secluded, she waited and listened. Like a cat on the hunt, she could be very still for long periods. She could hear the men in the stables organizing the necessities for the long trip to Ravenna after the last of the ships arrived. Others were off to the camps biding farewell to friends and family. She understood that the final grain shipments might arrive any day. This was her chance to do what she had been salivating over for such a long time.

Although Freya-Gund had a keen insight into everything happening in and around Barcelona and the villa, there was always a risk. She understood that she needed to be very clever and very, very careful. A few hours after dark, a faint light flickered through the shutters of Galla's second-level bedroom. The doors to her balcony were closed, shuttered, and barred, but they presented no obstacle to Freya-Gund. The month before, while the Goths were away from Barcelona attempting to cross the straits, she prowled the villa grounds freely, preparing for this very moment. Freya-Gund knew the straits would be a disaster and that the Goths would return to Barcelona in due course.

Now she would strike like a cat at its prey. Giving "the precious princess" all the time she needed to pretty herself for bed, Freya-Gund patiently waited for the right moment. When the candle was at last extinguished and all was quiet except for the activity at the stables, she smiled wickedly and began to climb. The vines Freya-Gund used to scale the building in the past had been removed. In their stead, she used six small openings in the façade, openings she herself had created by scraping away the mortar between the blocks. She'd done this awhile back anticipating that the vines would be cut away. Freya-Gund was always one step ahead of the cretins who tried to outfox her kind.

Once on the second-level balcony, she removed three anchors from the building loosened the month before. Removing the anchors gave her an opening through the hinged side of the door that was farthest from Galla's bed. She wedged herself through the opening without a sound. Once inside the chamber, she stayed hidden behind the heavy draperies that covered the four doors to the balcony. The thick drapes had muffled any sound that she or the door made when unhinged.

Standing there, Freya-Gund held her breath for as long as she could to connect with the sounds in the bedroom. Two were sleeping. Yes two, she could tell that by the breathing. Was the second person a guard, one of the servants, maybe Elpida? Just in case it was *not* the old woman, Freya-Gund pulled out a knife and steeled her nerves. Who might it be? Whoever it was, they would die this night.

She dropped to the floor and slid under the thick drape that she was hiding behind. Lying flat, she listened. All the breathing came from the direction of the bed. Whoever was here was in the bed with Galla. That was a twist, someone in bed with the precious princess. Hmm . . . A drop of saliva rolled from the corner of her mouth and dripped onto the mosaic floor.

So then, she mused*, the princess decided to have her puffy plugged one last time before departing—departing this earth, that is.* A different urge swept through her body. An urge that was foreign to what she was about to do. Quickly she willed it away. This was no time for prurient thoughts.

Slithering to the door that led to the inside hallway of the manse, she put her knife in her mouth, rose slowly, and felt for the bar. Carefully, silently, she slid it in place, sealing the room from interruptions. Then she turned to face the bed. Freya-Gund stood there waiting for the thumping in her chest to return to normal. When it did, she crept to the side of the bed where the crib once sat, the side where Galla always slept.

Standing over the bed looking down, she saw little more than an outline of two forms under the blanket, one bigger than the other. Freya-Gund pulled out a rag, rolled it into a ball, and put it in her right hand, ready to stuff it into the sleeping princess's mouth to muffle any scream. With her other hand, she took the knife from between her teeth and placed the sharp point next to Galla's neck.

Before she could strike, Freya-Gund was violently lifted off her feet and thrown bodily across the room. Crashing into the wall, her knife flew one way, the balled-up rag another. Suddenly, the room came alive with people—big people—and light, lots of light. She had been thrown against the wall and pinned there by two bucellarii. She seethed, struggling to get loose, as Lucius sat up in bed, smiled disingenuously, swung his feet onto the floor, and walked leisurely to the door and threw it open. In came more people, some with swords drawn. Lucius returned to the bed, threw back the covers, and revealed a straw dummy where Galla supposedly slept. At that moment, Freya-Gund realized that she had been lured into an elaborate trap, a trap only one person as devious as she could have possibly devised. And that scheming son of a jackal was Lucius Domitilla!

She sneered and struggled and cursed, but it was to no avail. The wild animal of Phrygia had been finally snared.

Lucius pushed through the bustle on the loading docks. The long awaited ships from Massilia had finally come this morning. One of them was actually the ship that had taken him to Rome. He watched as the endless line of *geruli* lifted the fifty-five-pound sacks out of the ships' holds and onto their shoulders and then walked them down the narrow plank to the wagons that were a long hundred and fifty paces away. Not complicated but very inefficient. The wagons could be rolled closer and double planks could be put to the ships. It would speed up the whole process. He looked for someone in charge, then thought better of it. He had more important things to do than make order out of chaos.

The ship he was looking for was at the far end of the dock. As he approached, he could see the captain putting his mark on each sack as it left the ship. Apparently Mahaki had devised a system to avoid theft. "Captain," he yelled, before being knocked down by a carrier that stumbled off the narrow ramp. Brushing himself off, he tried again. "Captain Papylas. Hey! Look down here! It's Lucius, Captain, the passenger you took to Rome. The one with the goat."

The captain walked to the railing and searched for the source of the voice amid all the hubbub before locating it. "Yes, Lucius. Yes of course it's you. How could I forget? And what a nasty goat he was. Hey! Come aboard. Thought you'd be at the other end of the world, laddie."

Lucius climbed up the gangplank and boarded. "Was . . . was there as you know. You took me," he said, short of breath from the climb, "and Ravenna, the Pillars of Hercules, and everywhere in between." That plank was so precarious he wondered how the carriers managed it at all.

"We be unusually busy right now, Lucius, as you can see. Now, lad, move out of the way, you're blocking the workers."

Lucius moved behind the captain.

"Good, that's better," said the captain, who seemed to have no interest in why Lucius was there. "We sail as soon as the carriers unload. Don't want the other vessels getting back to Massilia before me."

"How soon might that be, Captain?" Lucius asked, watching him mark each sack with a number.

"We've unloaded a hundred and thirty-five by my count. We've another two hundred and seventy to go. Maybe sunset, providin' that bloody dockmaster don't have a problem with me total. He held us up last trip he did, which makes me be all the more careful this time."

"There're three important passengers that need reachin' Rome," Lucius said artfully imitating the sea jargon as well as the accent. "Can ye help me out?"

"Sorry, no. If the sea nymphs smile on me kindly, lad, I kin get another load out of Massilia."

Lucius dangled a small pouch of coins under the captain's nose. "Sea nymphs be damned, Captain Papylas, this here be gold, not lead nor copper."

Papylas threw an arm in front of the next carrier and turned to face Lucius. "Important passengers, ye say?" And he felt the pouch to gauge the weight. "Hmm. Interesting, very interesting."

"Very, indeed," said Lucius, seeing the man's eyes light up.

The captain let the carrier pass, handed the marker and count sheet to a crewman, and then dragged Lucius across the deck to the far side of the ship. "For half that, I'll take 'em as far as Massilia, my friend. For the other half, I'll see to it personally that they get on another merchant ship headed for Rome."

Lucius thought about that for a time. "Fair enough," he agreed. "Ye can't depart until dark. That's gotta be part of the agreement, understand," he said. "We don't want anyone seein' these passengers boarding if possible."

"Oh?" said the captain. "Some mischief I should know about?"

"Ye see captain, well, it's very unusual circumstances. One of the passengers will be in chains."

"No problem. We'll lash the bastard to the mast if ye like."

"You may have to. Oh yes, another rub. This prisoner, the one ye referred to as a 'bastard,' is actually a female, a dangerous and cunning woman with the bite of a scorpion and the strength of a man."

"Ha! A *woebat*. Now, what be you up to these days, Lucius?" nudging him in the ribs.

"The queen of the Goths is about to become the princess of Rome again. She's the one who paid for my passage to Rome and will see to it that ye are rewarded with more passages if ye do but one additional favor."

"And what might that be, laddie?"

"Not ask questions. Two of the queen's bucellarii will accompany this 'woebat' all the way to Rome, or, with Massilia now in the picture, the magistrate there may want to send his own guards on the final leg to Rome. This be imperial business, ye see. I'll give ye a letter from the princess to that effect if you like."

When Papylas stuck out his hand, Lucius dropped the pouch of gold coins into it. This done, they clasped each other by the forearms in the barbarian style to seal the agreement. Then Lucius started down the gangplank. He had much to do and so little time. At the bottom, he turned and asked, "One last question, Captain, why the rush to depart?"

Said the captain: "This little fellow who oversees this operation is strict, but generous. He pays handsomely for a quick turnaround."

Lucius laughed. "I'll say he's generous. That little *wilter* is spending my gold, he is. I know him well," said Lucius innocently, thinking he did know him well. "Tell Mahaki you spoke to me and that he is to meet me in Arles after all the grain is shipped. I leave with the princess by land on the morrow. My work here in Barcelona is done."

CHAPTER 8

An unusual calm descended upon the port of Barcelona. A light wind rippled the waters ever so slightly. With the unloading complete, only one ship remained at the dock. A Gothic warrior appeared from the deeper shadows and moved from stanchion to stanchion snuffing out the torch lights until the port was thrown into complete darkness. Only then was a bound figure dragged out from behind a row of grain sacks and carried bodily to the lone ship at the far end of the loading docks, put aboard, and then lowered into the hold. The lines were set free and the ship slipped quietly out to sea. Freya-Gund was on her way to Rome to pay for crimes against the State.

The sun rose on a bright new day in Barcelona, Spain. A crowd gathered outside the villa to catch one final glimpse of their queen—a woman they had grown to admire and love. Since her capture five and a half years ago, Galla Placidia had not only wormed her way into their hearts but also their souls. She would be sorely missed, for she was a part of them now and would be forevermore. And for those Goths who had converted to Christianity, they found a common cause with their queen. Yes, in so many ways she had become one of them, and they in turn had accepted her. Now she was leaving them with this one last gift: salvation from certain starvation. They wondered if she had been sent by the Almighty, the one to whom they now prayed. Mixing the old with the new, Galla Placidia became an alien blend of Valkyrie and living saint?

Fifty-eight bucellarii sat atop their mounts waiting. Eight servants, along with all the necessary supplies for the trip, also sat waiting in a line of wagons. The doors of the main house flew open and the crowd cheered—Galla Placidia, their queen, appeared. She was dressed inappropriately in long trousers, a short tunic, and a half cape with a hood. The hood, to be put to good use later on this long journey north, hung down her back.

She could be seen taking a deep breadth and then skip down the steps like a little girl at play to the house wagon waiting below. Giving those waiting a brief wave, she caught the hub of the front wheel of the house wagon with her left foot, the top with her right, and pulled herself up into the driver's box. When settled, she looked back at the main entrance expectantly. In her other life, no one would have dared to keep her waiting. But it was different here. That was why she felt such kinship with these people and they to her.

Soon enough, Lucius came out dragging a sack of belongings, bounced it down the steps in a devil-may-care manner, threw it atop the house wagon, and then climbed up to secure it for the trip. He then dropped into the driver's box next to Galla and gave a signal. The gates swung open and the amorphous procession began amid cheers and tears. The small convoy passed slowly between the throngs of faces and waving hands, some happy for the chance to see Galla up close, others sad for the reality of her departure. After all, they were not only losing a queen but a good, dear friend. Galla did little more than nod, unaccustomed as she was to adulation from a people to whom she had come to know as her equals, not her subjects. The crowd, sometimes four and five deep, stretched all the way to the walls of Barcelona. But eventually it thinned and finally dissolved into a curious few. Soon that too died and Galla and her escorts were wholly alone and on their way to Narbo. They expected little trouble. Still, the house wagon remained in the center of the train, the bucellarii armed and ready for whatever might come.

The journey was not difficult. They used the pass closest to the sea. The road, normally rife with slides and erosion, had been well tended to the last few months because of all the comings and goings of the negotiation parties. By the time Galla and her escort reached Narbo, Constantius, two legions, and their auxiliaries were already on their way to Arles.

In Narbo, Galla rested her entourage. Her old accommodations at the Curia building were put at her disposal. She and Lucius took separate rooms, a measure of decorum acknowledged. Although correctness mattered little to Galla after all she had been through of late, these years of captivity softened the stoic sensibilities that had once been set in stone by the well-honed aristocratic protocol in Constantinople and Rome.

After the morning meal that first full day in Narbo, Galla suggested Lucius accompany her for a walk. She had something to show him. Wrapped tightly against the morning chill and speaking not a word of where they were going or why, she led him through the vici of Narbo to the south side. When they came to the Church of the Nazarene, she tried the front and side doors. They were locked.

"Dammit to hell," she mumbled, and began thumping on a nearby door. The presbyter, asleep in his quarters, awakened and answered the door.

"Do you remember who I am?" she asked.

He did.

She then demanded that he unlock the doors to the church, and then leave them alone. He did as ordered. When they were alone, Galla took Lucius by the arm and led him through the slivers of light coming from the high narrow windows to the front left corner of the church where a figure of the Blessed Mother stood on a tall pedestal. The corner was dark, the stone walls damp, and the atmosphere colder than normal without the multitude of warm ceremonial candles burning brightly.

Only Freya-Gund would be comfortable in such an environment, Lucius thought.

In Mother Mary's arms was the baby Jesus. *Maybe Galla wanted to say a prayer for baby Theo.* Thinking he was supposed to do something, Lucius dropped to both knees and blessed himself as he had seen other Christians do over the years.

Meanwhile, Galla struck a flint. On the third attempt, the candle caught fire. She raised it above her head. The light washed across the statue. Although Lucius had not been here before, the illumination revealed an effigy that was strangely familiar. From the folds in her garment to the hand supporting the babe to Mary's eyes—yes, her eyes. He tried to touch the statue but it sat too high. Higher than its companion in the far corner. Why higher? The other churches he had been in usually had a pleasing balance to their statuary. Asymmetry made the faithful uncomfortable; all things were supposed to be in harmony inside a church. Bishop Lazarus had certainly taken great pains to achieve that when he built Holy Trinity atop Mount Este. And the church in Rome atop the cavern dwellers was in balance from the aisles and pews to the windows and statuary. Why this unevenness?

"Quite something isn't it," Galla said, interrupting his thoughts. She was gazing approvingly at the statue. Apparently she was not expecting an answer.

Lucius focused on Galla's expression. What was she up to? "Why have you brought me here, woman? Do you try to convert me to Christianity after all this time?" His voice echoed off the bare stone walls. The place was a cave without people to give it warmth or meaning.

"No, I am not trying to convert you."

"Has it something to do with baby Theo?" he asked.

"Not really," she answered, "but he was about that size when he . . ." She choked back the rest of the words.

"That was thoughtless of me," he said, moving closer, touching her tenderly. "I'm sorry. You need not be reminded."

She put her hand up.

"Okay," said Lucius. "I'll be quiet. What?"

Galla took a deep breath. "A wise sage once told me," she began, "that the best place to hide something was in clear view. Well, I promised you back in Castulo that I would one day reveal where I hid the gems. So, I'm keeping that promise. You stand beneath Fortune's feet," she said looking up with a sense of unbridled admiration. "I had her remade."

Lucius followed her gaze to the statue's face and studied it for a time. Of course! Now he saw it—the nose, the mouth, the strong chin. Those spectacular jewels on her forehead had been covered by a plaster mantle, the seashell removed and replaced with the babe, and the swollen stomach covered by the swaddling. But the most ingenious part was placing the statue beyond the reach of the faithful. If they could touch it, they would know that it was metal, not the more ordinary stone or molded clay. Too often metal statues were stolen to put their substances to a more practical use, the artistry and significance ignored. He turned to Galla.

"Are they . . . ?" he asked, referring to the gems.

"Yes, over a thousand, Lucius, all concealed beneath a thick layer of pebbles just in case."

"Certainly, of course, just in case," he said absently. And then he smiled that familiar sly grin. "You are very, very clever, Princess, possibly too clever. Have you checked to see if someone—a devious jackal like Freya-Gund perhaps—was even cleverer?"

"No."

"Don't you think we should have a"—moving a nearby bench closer—"look."

"No. No I don't," insisted Galla, stopping him.

"Why?"

"Leave her be. If someone did outsmart us—"

"You, Galla, outsmart you," he interjected sarcastically. "Remember, I was in Rome."

"Yes, of course, outsmart me. Then that person did and the deed is done. There's nothing we can do."

"True, but—"

"No buts. If the gems are still in her belly, as I believe they are, then we'll take them when we go. But we leave Fortune here. She would not like to return to Rome or anywhere else. Fortune's odyssey is finished, Lucius. It's quiet in this far corner of the world. She has her child, her eternal beauty. Fortune's content."

Lucius searched Galla's face once more, looked deep into those dark eyes. Something new was there, something he had never before seen. Maybe it was a pining for an experience she would never recapture. Five years of captivity had changed her. Was she identifying with this statue, envious of Fortune's solitude while her old life of stoic behavior was about to be reborn? A rebirth she viewed as a bottomless abyss. The hollow adoration awarded the granddaughter, daughter, and sister of emperors that would once again devour her soul. These years of captivity would make her even more of a living icon. Lucius understood that the drain of being pampered was no longer a penchant she cared for. She would miss slipping off to drink from a cool rill or bathing in a warm lake, washing her own things, stretching out on the beach, roasting her own meat, and making love simply for the pleasure instead of becoming nauseated beneath a man who disgusted her. That was what Lucius read in her eyes as they stood there with Fortune looking down. Was he wrong? Or did he know her future better than she knew her own?

Lucius took the candle from Galla and lifted it overhead for one last look at the statue. A shadow swept across Fortune's face. As it did, the right side of her mouth appeared to crease into a smile. Lucius smiled back and then blew out the candle. He and Fortune had traveled a long way together. Yes indeed, a long, long way.

Suddenly, a vision of Bruné-Hilda struck him. The image was not new, but it had never been so vivid. The vision had her standing in the shadows of that hut displaying her naked body, the scars that had transformed her so completely visible. Tears welled in his eyes like they had before on that day. He looked up to Fortune for reassurance. *Is this okay, Fortune? Is it okay to leave you here in the darkness of Narbo like I left Bruné-Hilda back on the isle of Lerins?*

Fortune did not answer.

The mighty Rhone River lay ahead. Beyond it sat Arles, the municipality that Constantine the Great had rewarded with the last of the grand baths in the empire. The twin drawbridges across the wide river were lowered and the city gates thrown open. And the princess of Rome approached those gates to the sound of a single trumpet.

At the gates, the bucellarii dismounted and the others climbed from their wagons. A sedan chair sat waiting to transport her into the city. But she would have none of that. The rituals of yesteryears were gone. Her arrival harkened a new day. Galla shook her head no to the sedan chair and then snapped her fingers. One of the bucellarii brought to her, her favorite white horse and lifted her gently into the saddle. With the others on foot, they entered the Second City of the West to the bravos of the citizenry. The grand madam of Rome, the only one who had stood strong when the City of Light was nearly darkened, had returned from the dead. And to this end, Galla took her first step toward conquering the conquerors.

Bridle in hand, Lucius led Galla's white horse along the Vicus Constantine toward the main square. The route was lined with people; others were hanging from windows and rooftops, all hailing the renowned member of the House of Theodosius. The last person of her pedigree to pass through those gates was Constantine himself, and that was nearly a hundred years ago. No one paid attention to the one leading the magnificent white stallion. Why should they? Nonetheless, Lucius puffed out his chest with prideful thoughts of his family and Umbrian friends racing through his mind. If by chance anyone gave him a casual glance, that person would never have believed the role that this nobody from nowhere played in this drama. Who would suspect a young man with his background could be involved in so laudable an endeavor. Of this, myths were made and words written. And celebrated legends played out more believably with the aristocracy than with the *vulgaris*. These exaggerated ideas, thoughts found only in his heart, made him gush all the more as he led the procession down the main way.

The vicus led straight to the square where three municipal buildings, a church, and a theatre made a pleasing if not symmetrical grouping. One of the municipal buildings was the curia where the praetorian prefect held sway over Gaul, Spain, and Britain. The governance of this vast region was once the most sought after seat of authority in the West. But that was before the Vandals broke out of the North nine years ago and the Goths came five years after that, interspersed throughout those years were several usurper uprisings. With the dissidents defeated, the princess now in their midst, and the treaty with the Goths signed, one of the most turbulent decades in the history of the empire had stabilized.

Riding atop that magnificent white horse, the petite, dark-eyed princess could not possibly grasp the sheer depth of what her presence signaled. Not so with Lucius. His more humble beginnings had taught him many things: to be aware, to interpret the tears, and to read the expressions. They said that her arrival in Arles meant more than just a temporary refuge before continuing on to Ravenna and her old life. Her appearance within these walls meant the present was once again connected to a more glorious past following a rough patch of time. Though she might not grasp it entirely, she was surely cognizant of the extraordinary impact her presence was creating.

Lucius looked up at Galla and saw how tightly she held to the saddle horn and how uncharacteristically blank her eyes looked. Yes, the farewell at Barcelona, although inspiring, was unreal. The Goths loved her because she was a novelty, a symbol of a privileged world that came down to their level. But the citizens of the Second City of the West had a different take. She embodied a thousand years of glorious history. A thousand years of tradition. Nine hundred and eighty years of prosperity. When all seemed lost, here she was, young and vibrant—the embodiment of hope. Her release from captivity meant all was not lost. There was a future for Arles and the entire Western Empire. Although Emperor Honorius was childless, the House of Theodosius could continue through Galla. She would rekindle those dying embers. That was what the people saw; that was what they felt. That was what Lucius grasped.

The procession arrived before the steps of the curia. At the top waited the members of the curiaeles who governed Arles, the praetorian prefect who ruled Gaul, Spain, and Britain on Rome's behest, and Bishop Patroclus who oversaw this ecclesiastical region of such importance to the church. All were resplendent in official garments pulled from storage for this rare occasion, the odor of mold permeating the air. Unlike the citizenry, the officials lacked spontaneity and were unsure of their roles, where to stand, and what to say.

Galla remained astride her horse waiting. Nothing had been rehearsed, everything impromptu, the officials had been given no guidance; therefore an awkward moment fell across the square. Galla looked down at Lucius.

He shrugged and then mouthed, "Patience."

She slumped in the saddle and waited. This was going to get interesting. From somewhere inside the curia a door clicked and then slammed shut. Disturbed by the noise, a flock of pigeons fluttered off. From that same "somewhere," Constantius strolled, or better said, limped out. He was followed by three legates and several tribunes all dressed in their finest military uniforms. Constantius wore a dark leather cuirass over an off-white tunic, a red-fluted cape reached to his knees, and metal-covered greaves adorned his legs above the chewed leather boots. He was slightly bent, and his gait was unsteady. He looked wounded. Those at the top of the steps parted just enough for Constantius to assume the center position. His face was expressionless, his demeanor uninspiring. Another uncomfortable moment passed. He removed his plumed helmet and secured it in the customary place—the crook of his left arm.

Galla gasped.

She motioned to the bucellarii for help dismounting and assumed a place next to Lucius who was steadying her horse. She reached under her cape and pinched Lucius on the ass. "What was I thinking!" she said without moving her lips.

"Well, Princess," Lucius whispered out of the side of his mouth. "There stands your future, the man with whom you'll spend the rest of your days, or his."

Galla looked at the man at the top of the steps again. Then she looked down at her feet. Guarding her lips with her hand, she muttered, "What in the name of Jupiter, Zeus, and Jesus happened to him? He's gray, stooped, and bandy-legged. This hero of the West has turned into an ugly old man these past five years."

"So what? So he walks like a goat, wheezes, and reeks of coriander."

"Funny, Lucius, real funny. Athaulf was many things, my friend—crude, cruel, and insensitive. But the man became more attractive with age. He was an Adonis. What happened to this one?"

Pretending to steady the horse, Lucius turned his back to the steps. "An old back injury has taken its toll of late. Though stooped and bandy-legged, Galla, he remains the most powerful man in the West, which, I remind you, includes your brother Honorius and the regent Eudoxia of the East. Overlook his appearance, damn you. It's what he heralds that's important."

Galla's expression froze. Her eyes moved from Lucius to the bucellarii and then to the powerful men at the top of the steps. All awaited her next move. She leaned toward Lucius and whispered, "I can't go through with this! Why didn't you tell me he got old and ugly? It's you I love, not him. I suddenly find bending to the will of expectancy distasteful."

"Relax. You're overreacting."

"No, I am not. I've actually come to my senses. We must fly away to Barcelona before I get consumed by all this pomp. That's where happiness lies, not here. It's where our little Theo is buried; where I can be a woman, not a symbol; where we can ride freely, the wind in our hair, the stars overhead. Look at him. He's a cripple. Is this what you want for me, Lucius? Well, is it?"

"Listen, Galla," he said between clenched teeth, wanting to shake her. "Julius Caesar was forty when he began his conquest of Gaul and fifty-something when he conquered Cleopatra."

"Ha! That man's no Caesar, nor I the Harlot of the Nile, damn you!" she countered, her voice carrying too far.

"Hush," he ordered. "To those watching your every move"—he motioned to the throngs that pushed into the square—"you are a savior, a restorer, a symbol of hope. The life you are destined to have is no longer your choice. Duty does not always call you to where you want to go. You know that. You've known it all your life. A thousand years of history awaits the next chapter—and that chapter is in your hands."

"History! This is all about history?"

"If you want to change it, then be willing to live it. That's why we did all this."

Her face drained of color and she stiffened. Occasionally she glanced up at the man to whom she, in a weakened moment of angst, suggested a union. The people waited. The officials at the top of the steps shifted back and forth nervously. Was the powerful master-general going to make the first move to avoid a stalemate? Or was the princess of long lineage about to walk up the steps in supplication to, admittedly, the most dominant male in the West? The square was bursting with anticipation.

For a time neither blinked. Then Galla's years of training set in. Galla took one step forward, looked hard toward Constantius, and then extended the back of her left hand. Taken by surprise, the general did not respond at first. Finally, he reluctantly handed his helmet to a tribune, adjusted his cuirass, and slowly walked down the steps. Reaching the bottom, he paused to collect himself. Then he limped toward Galla, dropped to one knee, grabbed her extended hand and touched it to his forehead in supplication. She smiled weakly, Lucius smiled broadly, and the onlookers broke into spontaneous applause.

Saying not a word, Constantius rose, took three steps back, bowed, and began an uneasy retreat to his commanding position at the top of the steps.

"Remind me, Lucius," she whispered without turning her head. "You and I, we were going to save the empire for these *fucking imbeciles*?"

Lucius tried not to laugh but he couldn't help himself. He remembered her saying those words that first day when he arrived in Narbo toting the Statue of Fortune on the back of an ass. He now realized, more than ever, that he had his work cut out for him before they reached Ravenna. The amalgamation of these two powerful people was already beginning to unravel before it even got started. Could the princess really be struggling with the notion of saving an empire that she could one day become heir to simply because her vehicle to the throne was gray, stooped, and bandy-legged?

The harbor master rushed into the office of the magistrate of Massilia, the city on the coast of Gaul from which the grain ships were dispatched. "Our prize merchant has met disaster!" he shouted, waving a tattered piece of parchment. "The *Memphis Gold* towed her into the port of Frejus. Half the crew's missing, the others dead, some slit from here to here," he said, running a finger across his throat. "And the captain, sir, your good friend Nero, was found half naked, his manhood sliced clean off and stuck in his—"

"Enough. I got it. Good Lord," the magistrate said. And then he let go a loud belch. He had eaten his noon meal alone for the third straight day. "Remind me, where was the *Seafarer* bound?"

"Rome, sir. Picked up a load from the—"

"Why! Why! Of all the people, why my poor, dear friend Nero."

"Something more, sir, if I may. Fixed to the bulkhead by this knife—Captain Nero's knife—was this." He handed the magistrate an official order cylinder. The magistrate rudely yanked it from the dockmaster's hand, opened the cylinder, and pulled out the missive.

He did not need one more problem right now. It was an official *imperare* to deliver a prisoner to the chief advocate of the state in Rome.

"All right, this is a routine directive. So?"

"I suggest you read the rest, sir," said the dockmaster.

He did. It was a list of the prisoner's crimes against Rome. And the document was not signed by some insignificant bureaucrat; it was signed by the emperor's sister herself. The magistrate's hand began to tremble. He remembered something about a prisoner transfer from one of the grain ships to the *Seafarer*, but not much more than that. Other than he remembered signing a corresponding order, but he had failed to look at the details. Running this municipality smoothly was bordering on madness. Had he known the gravity of the situation, he would not have sent Hulk, the biggest, dumbest jackal in his militia, to guard her. Instead, he would have ordered two of his best.

"Good Lord!" he moaned, realizing the magnitude of his error. He was in enough difficulty with the patrician after Boniface's report to Ravenna after the barbarians' assault. And it was all because he was about to surrender the city when Boniface's lucky dart wounded the Gothic king. *About* to surrender, not *surrendered*, which, he thought, was not enough to warrant his dismissal. If not for the bishop's intervention though, he'd be picking blueberries outside Aix.

"What of the prisoner?" he asked.

"No one knows, sir. The report said the shore boat was missing, and they have yet to find it. We can only assume the prisoner made it to land and is now running free somewhere beyond Frejus."

"Good Lord, man! Are they searching?"

"The report does not say, sir."

"Then we must send our own people. Remind me, how far is Frejus?" the magistrate asked.

"By sea, a hundred and twenty miles if you remain safely off the coastal rocks; three days with a fair wind and six with only oars in the water. A land Express can reach Frejus in a day and a half."

The magistrate stroked his chin. "Not a word of this, understand? Not one single word. Now, send in my adiutor. He's taking his meal in the garden. We're going to find that escapee if it takes our entire militia."

"You do know we are dealing with a woman here, right?" asked the dockmaster.

The magistrate's mouth dropped open. "A woman, you say? A woman! How could a woman be party to all that shipboard mayhem?"

"Maybe she had help, sir, possibly the Hulk."

Before word reached Massilia regarding the disaster aboard the *Seafarer*, Freya-Gund lay on the rocks east of Frejus battered and bloody. Her clothing had been stripped through her ordeal and all the items she needed to survive—food, bedding, and weaponry—had been lost when the skiff capsized a quarter mile off shore. She was in trouble. Having lost consciousness, she awoke to a gentle hand stroking the back of her neck, and then she blacked out once more.

Time passed. How much, she had no idea. There was no sound. She was chilly, but not cold. Running her hand down her body she felt nothing but skin. Then it came back to her: the boiling surf, the reef, the skiff flipping, the rocky shore, and then darkness. She tried to open her eyes twice before realizing they were already open. Wherever she was, it was ink-black dark. By feeling around, she could tell that she lay on a wood platform a foot or so off the ground and up against an irregular rock wall. A musty smell filled her nostrils. *She was in a prison!* Sitting up abruptly, she slammed her head against a rock overhang and fell unconscious once more.

A narrow shaft of light struck the wall and inched down. When it touched her left eye she awoke with a start. Somewhere a small opening let in a ray of the morning sun. She shook herself but lay very still, letting her eyes adjust. This wasn't a prison. Nor was she aboard a ship. She remembered little of what happened before it all came back. The captain raping her the first night out, how she had surprised the crew when they were attempting to save the one who had accidentally fallen overboard, the gullible guard she had bewitched, the broken railing and the throats she had cut. Yes, moment by moment it was all coming back. All but one thing. What had happened to that oversized idiot who helped her? They had left the ship together in a small boat.

She rolled off the shelf being careful not to hit her head this time. Sitting on a nearby rock was a wooden cup containing water. She drank deeply then looked around. Her wooden bed was tucked into a cutout in the wall of what appeared to be a natural cave. The shaft of light came from a small, crease-like opening facing the morning sun. Already the ray was slowly disappearing as the sun rose, but it left enough light for her to see that this cave had been fashioned into a dwelling place. There were three other sleeping recesses cut into the other walls. Whoever rescued her must only reside here on occasion. A permanent habitat would have more than a single water cup.

Freya-Gund squeezed through the slit and out into the light. The vista dazzled her senses. A beautiful sea of vivid indigo blue stretched out to the horizon. The terrain surrounding the cave was a formidable collection of sharp pinnacles, crevices, and jagged outcroppings awash in exotic shades of reddish hues. Never had she seen nature so beautiful. Stepping beyond the cave opening, she saw more shoreline down below. Then she gasped. The rust-colored mountains around her dove into the sea creating an uneven line of tiny inlets and rock walls that were sculpted into every imaginable configuration by the surf. Beyond the shore, the sea was dotted with islets, protruding rocks, and underwater reefs—deadly reefs. Of all the places to attempt to land at night, this had to be the worst.

Chilled by the breeze, Freya-Gund searched for some kind of makeshift clothing. The landscape, though spotted with heather, thorny brooms, and umbrella pines, produced nothing of use. She needed vines and leafy palms to fashion into a cape and footwear. Moving to the edge of the outcrop, she saw the body for the first time. It was lying face down in a small inlet below. From the size, she knew it was the guard from Massilia, the one the crewmen had called Hulk, the one she had seduced with lies and tempting promises. The giant who had pushed four crewmen overboard in one bull rush when the railing gave way.

Climbing down took time in her weakened condition. When she returned to the cave, she had the Hulk's clothing, boots, knife, and a wax-sealed container of olives that had floated ashore with the other flotsam from the skiff. By midday she had refashioned the clothing to fit and had cut the boots so they could be useful. After consuming her fill of olives, she squeezed the juice out of a handful of them and spread it over the raw scratches on her hip, legs, and arms. It soothed the burning.

Now she faced the challenge of freeing herself from this impromptu rock prison. The problem was that she had no idea where she was. Only that she was somewhere on the southern shore of Gaul. She remembered that they had arrived too late at some no-name port last night. Or was it last night? It didn't matter. The chain had already been thrown across for the night at the port and the captain had decided to lay off rather than go on. Then a clumsy seaman keeping the night watch fell overboard. When the crew responded to his screams for help, her awestruck guard set her free and together they flew into action. When, by good fortune, the railing gave way, she freed the anchor line, allowing the ship to drift out of reach of those in the water. And before the others knew what happened, she cut two throats and caught the captain putting on his pants. For certain, her demon-god Ahriman protected her from harm that night.

A voice from outside the cave broke through her reverie. "Hello! Are you alive in there? I'm comin' in!" Freya-Gund crawled into the recess and waited; her knife ready. Through the crease squeezed a little man covered in rags with a long, scraggly beard. He was holding a sack like a newborn lamb. "Got some food here," he said, putting the sack down. "Deitzer is outside. Don't expect you want his sort in here. He did help me bring you up the cliff, though. Didn't let him touch nothin' but your feet. So don't be worryin'."

The little man opened the sack and withdrew a bowl that he filled with a dried apple, part of a loaf, and some boiled fish. "That's all you'll get today," he said, as he set it on the floor and withdrew.

"Wait," said Freya-Gund. "Where am I?"

"You're in hell, lady. The world sits out there toward the setting sun. There's a tiny village maybe two hours west; Boulouris it's called. Beyond that lies Frejus. The other direction is blocked by mountains and ravines. Yep, mountains and ravines, mountains and ravines. That's all you get around these parts. They call this place, the Esterels."

"Where's the good road? The one the Romans built."

"Can't be reached directly. A goat trail's five hundred paces thata way," he said, pointing up the mountain. "It'll take you to that fishing village, which connects to a dirt road that'll take you to the Aurelian Way. Beware of that fishing village, though, and the Aurelian Way. Our supply boatmen said they're lookin' for survivors from the *Seafarer*."

"How can they be looking for survivors already? I've just—" She flinched. She had said too much.

"Lady, you've been unconscious for several days. Been keepin' you goin' with water and mush. Fed you like a baby, I did. Don't know why, but somethin' tells me that you and that big one lying down there in the surf are not survivors of that ship but part of the problem. So be careful." Then he and his companion left.

Freya-Gund jumped up and ran as fast as she could after them. "What is this place!" she yelled.

"You've landed in hell, I told ya. It's a commune. Colony of the Cursed is what the damned call it, where the wretched of the earth come to die. Beware of the other caves. If leprosy's not in your future, the Black Death might be. Those caves hold the forlorn, the hopeless, and the desperate. Those unwanted until they pass on. Then we burn 'em and their belongings. When you're strong enough, you need to go. Heed every word I say until then. Touch none of the piles of firewood, nary a stick."

"Why?"

"Each pile belongs to one of those wretched souls. They're obsessed with being cremated when they die."

"A cult?"

"When you watch what the sea birds do to an unburied corpse, you'll understand."

She nodded. Needing to know no more, she returned to the cave. Once there, she gulped down the last of the olives and drank the brine. After throwing away the other food that she suspected was contaminated by disease, she tied the cup and bowl in a piece of the cloth from Hulk's clothing and lashed it around her waist. Departing the cave, she climbed to the goat path and headed west toward the fishing village. Even for the likes of Freya-Gund, a journey through hell was a numbing experience. Each breath she took could very well bring with it the whisper of a life-threatening disease.

"I've been chasing you all over this place for two days," complained the messenger. "No one in this gawd-forsaken hellhole of a municipality seemed to know your whereabouts. Here! It's from that little *shit* master Mahaki."

"You mean ship master," corrected Lucius.

"No, you heard me right the first time," the messenger said, thrusting a tube of river cane into Lucius's stomach. Inside was a message.

"Hey! Watch it," scolded Lucius. "Why so rude? I was hoping he'd be here personally, you understand. What happened?"

"Obviously he's not coming," the messenger replied sarcastically. "He paid me to deliver this, but the son of a snit didn't even think to give me a single copper for lodging. Slept with the street beggars for two nights, I did. I need a bed, got one?"

"No. But I do have this!" And Lucius grabbed him by the back of the neck and shoved him through the doorway. "Now be on your way, you lowlife!"

Lucius retreated up the stairs to his room. It was a dingy little place, nothing like what he had grown accustomed to in Barcelona. After plopping down on his cot, he slipped the message out of the tube. It was definitely in Mahaki's hand. It read:

"By now you realize I am not waiting for you at Arles. My job is done, and my soul at rest—yes, Lucius, my soul. You did not think I had one, did you? By the time you receive this, I will be halfway to Ancona. Thank you for the stipend. The gold bars that were not needed to pay for this elaborate project will allow me to live out my days in comfort. *Grates et tribuere!*

"The captains kept me abreast of the news. You succeeded where most dare not try. Much unpleasantness was averted (the war, I mean), a princess ransomed, and a good many bellies filled thanks to you. Hail Lucius! The Roman hierarchy should be indebted to you, instead they will probably find a way to proclaim themselves the heroes and, I am sure, discredit you.

"Though you thrust this endeavor on me, the part I played did, however, lift a heavy burden from my heart—a heart deadened for too long. Thank you. For so many years I bore an unbearable hatred. Life held no meaning. Understand, my good friend, the Mahaki you came to know is actually the Mahaki I once was. I was changed by events that were so dastardly, so catastrophic, that my very essence became lost in a cauldron of hot bitterness. Contempt ate at me to the point where I lost all measure of right from wrong and could not distinguish insult from praise or death from precious life. The taste it left was bitter. And the actions I took, well, some might say they were justified, others might argue that I deserve to be hanged.

"Be that as it may, I am now once again sane. Redemption, although not sought, did wash clean my soul. I will tell you no more except for this: some of what I did exceeded my intent. Remember that! Thank you and farewell. Your friend, Mahaki."

His mind working, Lucius put down the strange missive, which said much while saying nothing. What sins? What could he have possibly done? Take more gold than he should have? Falsify the grain count? Huh. Did the bishop's demise weigh on his soul? Lucius tried to recall what Mahaki had said after that debacle with Bishop Lazarus, but whatever it was had faded in the clutter of so many other events. Whatever he had done, one point came through—the man had had a fit of conscience.,

Before he could give it more thought there was a knock. *Did that stupid messenger come back?* He threw open the door, ready to give the idiot a good boot in the pants. Instead, meekly standing there was Galla's elderly servant-lady Elpida.

"We depart for Ravenna in the morning. The lady wants to know if you can be ready?" she asked.

"Of course I'll be ready," Lucius answered eager to be out of this rat hole. With Galla residing at the praetorian prefect's sumptuous residence outside the walls, he took this room in order to maintain a respectable distance. The noise and the smells here were overwhelming though. "Where do we meet?"

"At the east gate—the Aurelian," she answered. "The lady suggests dawn. It's just a suggestion, of course. She'll be late as usual."

"As will I," he said. Laughing, he closed the door. He slipped Mahaki's message back into the tube and tossed it onto the bed, giving it no further thought. But he should have. There were clues in that missive about the life-changing tragedies Lucius had gone through these past six years that had remained unanswered.

The III Theodosius departed three days earlier along with Master-General Constantius and his staff. Galla had not spoken to the general since their exchange on the steps of the curia. As Lucius packed his few things, he thought about the new challenge that lay ahead. He must change Galla's attitude toward the general, even if it took the entire five-hundred-mile trip to Ravenna. That was his priority now. Solving Mahaki's puzzling missive could wait.

Six days later, Galla's entourage camped outside a small walled city that sat on the seashore halfway between Frejus and Monoeci. They planned to rest the horses and replenish their supplies.

The following morning the weather warmed and a beautiful sunrise beckoned. So Lucius and Galla walked beyond the walls of Antipolis to a public area overlooking the sea to gain a better view of nature's handiwork. And it was stunning. The fluffy clouds, the array of colors, the coastline, and the blue hue of the sea were spectacular.

As they sat watching the ever-changing panorama of the sunrise, Galla asked, "Do you think Freya-Gund is in Rome by now?"

"Depends."

"On what?"

"The captain. Some captains pull in for the night, some push on. The most daring take a direct heading and pass through the narrows between Corsica and Sardinia, others pass north of the Thumb of Corsica. Wind, weather, or something as small as a strange sighting in the sea, is unsettling when no land's in sight. I've seen it firsthand. Why do you ask?"

"Just wondering, that's all. Is she out of our lives for good, or . . ." She let the sentence hang.

"With her," Lucius said, trying not to be pigheaded, "one never knows." He certainly did not want to think about that woman any more. "Just as one never knows about you."

"What on earth does that mean?" she asked, knowing very well what he referred to. They had not spoken of the *issue* with the general since leaving Arles, so she remained elusive. "That woman's the most craven bitch on earth."

"You refer to Freya-Gund, of course."

"Are you putting me on her level?"

"Of course not. I refer simply to this notion that you glimpse but never grasp."

"And that is?" she asked playfully, continuing the game of verbal hide-and-seek.

"Saving your own people by first taking your rightful place in the aristocracy, you very well know what I refer to."

"Not that again, please." And she gave him a good shove.

"You're going to give *that* up, eh?" nodding across the water in the direction of Rome, "for that," pointing to a young couple wiping the runny nose of a crying child.

"Lucius, Lucius, Lucius," she said mockingly. "We're wealthy, young, and full of life. We'd have servants to do those things."

"Galla, please," he said, getting irritated. "Close those beautiful black eyes of yours and concentrate. Think of what life would be like with me, like not doing what delights you every second of every day, like being unable to avoid each unpleasantness, like not having everything done just the way you like it. My humbler life would be your life. Why ruin one for the other, dammit. What every person dreams of is in your grasp. So why make a fool of me, of use, by suggesting something that cannot be? I risked everything, including my life, to resurrect your future. For *you*, Galla, I did it for *you*, not me, and not *us*. I brought you back to the threshold of greatness, a threshold you now refuse to cross because of some childish dream of love."

"To love, to want a normal life, is that what you call *childish*? Do you really think that!" she shouted.

Lucius looked around to see if the young couple was listening. "Keep your voice down," he whispered.

"No. No, Lucius, no I won't. Why do you want me to marry that old man, a man who has spent his entire life leading, giving orders, knowing very well that I will become his prisoner now instead of

Wallia's? Do I not have a choice in this? Do I not deserve to live in the real world?"

"Foolish questions are not worthy of answers. You know, Galla," he said, putting his mouth closer to her ear and lowering his tone, "sometimes you can be a spoiled little bitch."

That did it. She jumped on the bench they were sitting on, put her hands on her hips, and wailed like a child at the top of her lungs.

But Lucius refused to bend. Pulling her back down, he continued in a low voice, "I want for you what you *should* want for yourself."

Curling her upper lip, she hissed, "And what is that, my reluctant lover, father of my deceased child? Please, tell me."

"To marry a powerful man, have a son, attain the status of Augusta, and then reign as regent until he comes of age. Your childless brother will not live forever. In fact, when I saw him sitting there on the throne that strange, peculiar day, he appeared half dead already."

"Probably. He dies slowly from inactivity," she offered flatly.

"More likely from being useless. Didn't your other brother Arcadius pass away young? Nor was your father's lifeline that long. So there you have it. You must think with this," he said, tapping his heart. "Instead of with this," thumping his lower stomach.

"Bull!" she shouted, not caring if the young couple heard. "You are forgetting that—*oh*!" She rushed to the railing, leaned over like she was going to throw up, and then spun around, her face contorted. "Constantius is too old to do what a husband must to father a child. And don't look at me so coyly, you understand exactly what I mean."

"You don't know that. But if inadequacy does become a problem, I'll sneak back to Ravenna and . . . well, you know."

"An artless attempt at naiveté, Lucius, if you think something like that might work. Hiding out until night, sneaking in and out, thinking no one will ever know. You are a fool, Lucius Domitilla, an ignorant, shameless, brazen fool." Then she trudged off in a huff.

When they returned to the encampment outside Antipolis, a contingent of legionaries from the III Theodosius were setting up their tents next to the bucellarii encampment.

Lucius rushed ahead to confront one of the bucellarii guards. "What's this all about? What are they doing here?"

"Not sure, sir. You might want to ask one of them. They just arrived having spent the last few days up in the hills."

It appeared to Lucius to be two full centuries—a hundred men each. "Where's your centurion?" Lucius inquired approaching one of the soldiers whose setup was complete.

"Da *princeps*? Over by da prison wagon," he answered in a painfully grating accent that made Lucius want to scratch himself. "Gat us a wild one during the night, we did. 'E'll tell ya about it."

Lucius approached the princeps, the ranking centurion who was giving orders to what appeared to be one of the many young *retentus* conscripted at Arles. The centurion was a thick, grizzled warrior of about thirty. He was scarred on both arms and moved with a hitch in his gait as he paced while giving orders. Lucius had no problem interrupting him. "May I inquire why you are lagging three days behind the main column, sir?" he asked.

Not looking up, the centurion growled, "I know who you are. Ask anything but that. My answer may not sit well with the *praefectus*."

"Unhappy with your assignment, eh," Lucius said with a chuckle. "What you say will remain right here, I assure you. So I would like an answer. Why do you lag behind the main column?"

"The patrician—"

"Constantius, I assume."

"That's correct, Master-General Constantius. For some reason he agreed to this asinine request that cuts against not only my grain but everyone in my command. In all my years—" The centurion stopped abruptly, probably remembering how close Lucius was to the general. "Excuse my impertinence," he said.

Lucius nodded. "My lips, I promise, are sealed. Trust me, I know frustration. Go on. Why do you lag behind?"

"When we passed the port of Frejus, the columns were making good time, the weather was good, and everyone was happy to be heading home. Then we came upon this massive search in progress. Since it was none of our concern, we ignored it. A prisoner had escaped, an important criminal it was said. The militias of both Frejus and Massilia were combing the countryside like it was Octar the Hun they hunted. They requested our help. When the main column marched on, Constantius ordered my century and one other to stay back and join in. Our bad luck."

"Huh. We saw nothing like that when we passed through Frejus," offered Lucius, suspicious this might be a cover story for something else. Could all these men be deserters?

"You saw nothing because you trailed us by a few days," the centurion explained. "The hunt led us up into the foothills. That's probably why you saw none of it back at Frejus. And, let me tell you, that's some wild country up there; a thousand places to hide and as dry as a bone. We got lucky, however, caught up to her in a small village way back up in those hills."

"Her?" This tale was sounding even more ridiculous. "All that manpower devoted to a *her*. In the name of Jupiter, man, what *dastardly deed* did this woman do?"

"You laugh, but in addition to a registry of crimes long as my *mentula*, they say she was the one who threw open the gates to the Visigoths."

A chill ran through Lucius's body. He stammered, "The . . . the Salarian gates . . . to Rome?"

"You heard me. Difficult to believe, isn't it? After I saw her, it was even more unbelievable."

Lucius fought to regain his composure. "I sure hope you chained that adulterated daughter of Wicca good and tight. She's a squirrelly Mother of Satan if there ever was one and not to be underestimated. Where is she?"

"Over there," the centurion said, pointing to an enclosed wagon. "The magistrate from Massilia calls that wanton bitch a man-eater. What she did to the sea captain shouldn't happen to a dog. But I tell you, I don't see it in her, and I've seen a lot. Have a look."

"I, sir, have a long history with that woman. If she is who you say, I'll take more than a look."

Before the centurion unlatched the door to the prison wagon, Lucius made sure that there were enough soldiers in position and with swords at the ready. The centurion grabbed his arm. "She has the strength of two men, they say—though I don't put much faith in such claims. Just the same, be careful."

Lucius entered the enclosure. It smelled. He found a ventilation slot and pushed it open, which also let in some light. A defeated figure lay curled up in the corner.

"So," he said with as much hostility as he could muster, "they finally broke you. Never thought I'd see the day."

No answer.

"How pathetic you look wrapped up like an infant. Where're your fangs now, Freya-Gund?"

The huddled form stirred and the blanket slid off. She sat up. "I'm not who you think," she said meekly. "I told them a thousand times that the sorceress they believe me to be, I ain't." Her voice was weak and strained, and not the voice he expected to hear.

Lucius took a second look, backed out of the wagon and down the step before turning to the centurion, "You brought me to the wrong prisoner. This is not the one who threw open the gates to Rome."

"It's the only prisoner we got. What's the problem?"

"She's not the one, I tell you! This woman is neither a sorceress, nor the one who threw open the gates!"

"You're sure."

"Do you want me to bring the princess over here to convince you? You have been tricked. You're certain this is the one they searched for—the one on the run?"

The centurion nodded his head. "If the magistrate of Massilia traveled a hundred miles with seventy of his militiamen to help Frejus conduct the search, I'm convinced he's in a position to know for whom he searches."

Lucius thought about that for a time. "Unlock that door again," he demanded. "I want another chat with the woman."

Bringing a cup of water with him, Lucius stepped inside and left the door open to permit more light and a welcome exchange of air. Offering her the water he asked, "Who are you really, madam? You are not who they think. I can vouch for that."

The woman stiffened, drained the cup, and arched her back, a new expression washing across her face. "I am Binah," she said in a squeaky little voice, one that could pierce the sensibilities, "a Great Mother of the Kabbalah. I, and others like me, hold the keys to the universe. It nurtures us all."

"Is that a fact, Great Mother?"

The woman appeared to be consumed by some far-off ethereal haze. Probably accustomed to a dismissive response, she went on. "My soul has been passed from person to person to person since time began and capable of making the commonplace quite extraordinary."

"How is that, Great Mother?"

"I possess the gift of second sight, you understand. Yes, you smile, but you heard me correctly—second sight." After saying that, the woman who called herself Binah looked hard into Lucius's eyes for a far deeper reaction. Finding none, at least not one that seemed to please her, she again pushed ahead. "You do not believe me authentic, do you?" she said matter-of-factly. "I see it in your expression, your stance, the way you look back at me. Don't let doubt interfere with your earthly inadequacies—few actually believe at first."

Not knowing what to say, Lucius could do little more than gawk.

"I am the keeper of the ten spheres of the Sephiroth—the doctrine of the astral body. In the mysterious world beyond, the world of the Kabbalah, it is I who has been assigned to ignite the guideposts along the path."

"The guideposts," he repeated blandly. "You light the guideposts along the path. And what guideposts might those be, madam?"

"The guideposts through the valley of the unholy, of course. Are you not aware that spirits can materialize out of the ether when the posts are not lighted? The villagers of Bagnois en Foret call me freak, a madwoman, a crone who wants to snuff out *their* lights. Ha! They are envious, maybe resentful, of my powers and how I raise toads, nurture snakes, and pray to a greater force, a higher power that puts fear in their sorry souls. They hated me so much, they told the authorities, 'She is her. That one there is the criminal for whom you search, the one on the run.'"

Heaving a sigh, she fell back into the corner. She rubbed her eyes with the backs of her hands before going on. "They say to the magistrate of Massilia, 'She is the diabolic one who murdered your crewmen, the one who pays homage to Ahriman, the demon behind every diabolical transgression aboard that ship, the witch who tramples goodness into the dirt.' That is what they said of me, that is what they shouted while watching my wretched body being dragged from my cottage and thrown before the feet of the magistrate. My bad fortune was returning the day before after a journey to the Place of Dread. So the authorities made assumptions from the lies heaped one upon the other. Lies that convinced them that I was the one for whom they searched."

Lucius stopped her. "Enough, madam, enough! From what you say, I presume the people of—how do you say it, Bagnude en Fotet?"

"Bagnois en Foret, sir."

"Yes, of course, Bagnois en Foret. The only sense I can make of this terrible ordeal is that they, your neighbors, wanted to be rid of you, your snakes, and your frogs so used this episode, shall we say, as a suitable means."

"May the spirits watch over you for believing in me, kind sir. Now, can you convince my jailers? I wish only to return to my cottage in the forest. My pets beg for my safe return. They need me." The poor woman slumped back and began to sob.

Extending his hand, Lucius said, "Of course, madam. For certain, I shall help you out of this quandary for which I share the blame. It was I who sent the woman you were confused with on this long journey to Rome. But you may find it more convenient to one day in the future find a new home, you poor soul. It appears you have worn thin your stay by postulating the mysteries of Kabbalah to the unbelieving—not to mention your penchant for raising frogs and snakes in their midst. Let me relate a brief tale of my own. An astral shaman who once resided in my municipality disappeared from the face of the earth under unsolved circumstances, or so I was told. It happened in my community of Assisi years before I was born, you understand, but her story was whispered from ear to ear for years. Some say she was consumed by her own beliefs and evaporated into the 'ether' as you call it; others say she was cruelly murdered and thrown into a hole by well-meaning Christians. Whatever happened to that poor woman, it was the way she lived that caused her to die. For your own good, dear lady, let this experience be a lesson before you meet a similar end. And doubtful as it may sound, good people can turn when confronted by alien superstitions."

CHAPTER 9

The bucellarii stood by their horses, reins in hand. A ways down the Aurelian Way, two centuries of legionaries waited impatiently. The entire party was eager to depart Antipolis. The men, delayed long enough, wanted to get home. Lucius pulled Galla to the far side of the wagon to say good-bye in private.

"For the last time," she said, lifting her head from his chest, tears welling in her eyes, "why are you being so bullheaded?"

Seeing those tears, a burst of compassion swept through him. "I am who I am," he whispered, holding her even tighter. "I must finish it once and for all." He kissed her on the top of the head. "Our only choice is to end it here and now, or we'll be looking over our shoulders forever," he said, tenderly wiping her cheek with the back of his hand.

She took that hand and held it. "Are they secured?" she asked.

"Yes, quit worrying. Everything will be all right, I promise," he reassured her. "We went through this over and over last night. The two hundred and fourteen gems are well concealed," he said as he pounded his chest. "I have food, spare horses, and four bucellarii—four of the best—to watch over me. After taking that old woman home, I'll go wherever I must go to end it. I swear, Galla, as strange as that woman appears to be she sees what we do not. It's in her eyes, her attitude, in the air that surrounds her. I can feel it. What will it take to convince you that I know what I am doing?"

"I know you do. You always do. But it sounds so risky."

"Freya-Gund touched things when in her village. Those things scream out a message to that strange woman over there. Old Crazy Chloe was like that back in Umbria. These kinds of women see the world in ways the rest of us do not."

"Even more than all those searchers could see?"

"The sorceress hid out in one of her snake pits, she says, stole some of her clothes and then slipped away after the militia passed. Quit worrying about how the net is woven. As long as it catches the fish, everything will be fine."

"Net, fish. What are you, a fisherman now?" she asked with a smile. "Be careful is all I'm saying," letting his hand drop. "Is that asking too much? We both know this is unnecessary."

Lucius reached beneath the wagon's tongue to retrieve the reins and slowly tied them to the brake handle. What he actually wanted to make sure of was that the bucellarii and her servants remained out of earshot.

"It is you who are ignoring the real issue, you know," she whispered.

"No, Galla, it's still you, it will always be you," he said while getting up off his knees. "Listen and listen carefully." He put his mouth near her ear and said, "I want you to promise that the moment you reach Ravenna you will seek out Constantius and give him every chance to, you know . . . court you. Do you understand?"

She nodded and then gently pushed him away.

"And I'll repeat this for the hundredth time: *give the man a chance*."

She rolled her eyes, saying nothing.

"Next," he said, ignoring her response, "if for some reason I do not make it through this, I want you to see to the release of Irontooth and his comrade Tauriac. You have the influence, so use it, please, for me. Their misadventure was no more than the result of Singerich overreaching. They are but victims of a power struggle not of their making."

"As was my deceased husband, Athaulf," she interjected a bit too loudly.

"Stay quiet. I do not need these men to hear us. Yes, poor, star-crossed Athaulf. But Irontooth and Tauriac are not star-crossed, just misused." She did not react, so he pressed ahead. "They are prisoners of war, so to speak, a war we no longer fight. The only crime these two committed, understand, was against me. And for that I hold no animus, nor do I want them languishing in some dungeon for the rest of their sorry lives simply for foolishly trying to set me and my friend Mahaki on fire."

She did not so much as crack a smile at that. He shrugged. *Had Galla lost her sense of humor?* "You remember who Irontooth is?" he asked. "Let me remind you, just in case. He was the one who guided me through the forests to Narbo back when we were first reunited."

Finally a smile. That comment she found to her liking.

"You know, Galla, had Irontooth and his men followed their first impulses, being the marauders that they are, none of what followed would have happened. I would still be walking in circles in the forest—or dead—and they would have the statue with the gems. Think hard on that. For whatever the motives, we all survived the experience. And for that, Irontooth deserves something better than a life of stale bread and swamp water. As for Tauriac, the man saved my life back on the Rhine River when the Amals tried to hang me. I owe him for that as well. Now then, do I have your promise?"

From the look—pursed lips and narrowed eyes—she was clearly getting impatient. Unfortunately, he had more to say. "Now, for some final advice. You need to do more than ride through the gates to reestablish yourself in Ravenna. Ignoring the *city* could be a mistake fatal to your cause."

"By the city you mean . . ."

"Yes, Rome. If nothing else, my time there taught me that the aristocracy remains extremely powerful despite what they lost during the sack. Their estates continue to generate enormous wealth. My friend Mahaki, although an agent for lesser landowners, reinforced this idea through his own experiences. They rely on men like him to market their crops and to collect their rents. A mean business though it may be, it remains a profitable one. These estate owners can go a long way toward supporting any move you make for the throne. You are following this, aren't you?"

She blinked absently.

"You've not heard a word I said, have you?"

"Yes I have, but," she said, searching for the right words. "Can . . . you . . . please," she stated slowly, stretching out the words to make her point, "finish this lecture before I doze off?"

He gave her a playful nudge. "Oh yes, one last point, and it is not to be made light of. Don't overlook the church when you make your move. Its influence has increased tremendously since your capture. You've been away from it a long, long time."

"When did you become an expert on matters of the church, for gawd's sake?" she said exasperatedly.

"Never mind when. Taking note of the social order does not require an expert, you know. The church's influence is evident in every municipality. I've met more bishops in my travels than kings, generals, and princesses combined," he said, giving her another nudge. "Now listen. Not only does the church control the hearts of men, its clerics are educated and therefore immune to the old influences. But beware. When one hand goes to the heart, you can be certain the other reaches for your purse. Not only are these clergymen wealthy in their own rights, their abilities to create new wealth increases with each passing year. No one opposes them, except my friend Mahaki. But that's another tale. Upward thinking plebeian families use their sons as weapons to burrow their way to patrician status through the church. I not only suggest you take heed but that you take advantage."

"Take heed? Heed? Is that the best you got? Heed! Do you actually think I would prefer the church over an empty future? *Do you?* Lucius my love, Athaulf's eulogy was more uplifting than this sermon. You torment me with drivel. If you see the rest of the world so clearly, why not ours? Your advice sounds more like a death knell than hope. Tell me, honestly, why do I feel that this is to be the last I will ever see of you?"

He blinked.

"Well?"

"However you interpret it, what I must do now is imperative to your future and to that of Rome. Why is that so hard to see? You, Galla, whether you like it or not, represent every Roman's last hope. For you to be safe now and forevermore, I must put an end to Freya-Gund. Otherwise, she will haunt us forever. If it is necessary to give her the gems I carry, I will. If that doesn't do it, I'll use other means. We—and by *we*, I mean you, me, and what's left of the Western Empire—are out of choices, Galla. That woman is lethal. Look at the hurt that lies in her wake. She somehow single-handedly took over the Kingdom of Burgundia, our lives, and a ship."

"You plan to kill her, don't you." It was not a question.

"I would prefer that she accept the gems as a treaty of sorts and return north to govern her own kingdom—such as it is. However, with her, one never knows. As you said last night, it should have ended in Barcelona. What fools we were to send her to Rome."

"Not *we*, Lucius. *You.* I wanted her dead."

"Yes you did. I was wrong, I admit it. Now the outcome will be in the hands of the Fates. I or that woman will become their instrument."

"Like I said," she murmured, starting to tear up again, "your . . . your words sound more like a eulogy than a temporary farewell—like this is the last we shall see of each other. And if this be God's will, I'll never forget what we had together."

"Nor will I, my dearest. Nor will I forget you."

"On the other hand, Lucius, if this is your way of abandoning me, you no-count, lowborn, son-of-a-sea captain, I will never, ever, forgive you. No matter what the future holds, without you, I will forever curse the darkness. It is you, Lucius, who makes me whole, not the prospect of a throne, the garlands of adoration, or the remainder of the gems I have hidden in my baggage."

So focused on what he was about to do, Lucius had completely forgotten that the bulk of Fortune's gems lay hidden beneath her packed clothing for the trip to Ravenna. Thank the gods she was protected by so many armed soldiers.

"Ah, yes, I forgot that you carry the bulk of them. Fortune's gems shall initiate a comfortable life for you with or without me in it." He gave her a long embrace, helped her into the wagon, and then walked away without looking back. Although his loyalty to Galla was above reproach, Lucius realized that he could not split his love between two women. If he survived the chase, he would have to make a choice between Galla Placidia and Bruné-Hilda.

A six-spoke, two-wheeled, broken-down old cart rolled into Bagnois en Foret. In it sat Lucius and the astral shaman. Although it was instantly apparent that the villagers were not happy to see their

new arrivals, the shaman was glad to be home. The village did not
sit in a valley or atop a windswept hill but was cut into the side of a
slope. The houses were of stone, the approach bad, the road followed
the line of least resistance, and there was not a fence in sight. Crops
grew in terraced gardens nourished by redirected offshoots of a
small mountain stream, and the villagers were refreshed by a single
central well. It was a lonely oasis amid a mixture of lush trees and
naked boulders.

Straggling behind the cart were the four weary bucellarii.
Although the astral shaman had pointed out a way that cut the trip
by half, the roughness wore the men and horses to the core. Then, to
no one's surprise because remote villages were all the same, it was
made clearly evident that strangers were not welcome. Exhausted
and ill-tempered, they rode on through the village to the shaman's
cottage and collapsed. Lucius was invited to rest inside the cottage
while the men set up camp as far from the snake pits as they could.

Revitalized after a night's sleep, Lucius turned his attention to
his main objective: tracking Freya-Gund. After feeding the bucellarii
a hot bowl of meal, Binah and Lucius relaxed in the main room
enjoying a special blend of herbs in hot broth. "It will open your
senses as we connect with the beyond," she said.

He watched her as she moved to the hot kettle to refill his bowl with
her tasty brew. Reflecting on their journey up to the village, he found
the woman's insights more original than barmy. To confuse genius
with madness can be so easy at times. In fact, and to his surprise,
Lucius found that she not only had a higher level of intelligence than
the average person but that she had a greater degree of insight into
the nuances of the beyond than he thought possible. Only when he
probed into her secrets did she react strangely. And though ignorant
of grammar, letters, and numbers, the woman was truly wise about
the world and how it worked. But then, many women of his own
valley never afforded a formal education were astute. Brunda, Crazy
Chloe, and his own mother came to mind.

Sipping the hot brew she handed him, he became lost once
more in the melancholy that washed over him during their earlier
conversation about Bruné-Hilda. He was shocked back to the present
when she barked, "I said, Lucius, do you have anything of hers?"

"Huh. What. Anything of whose?" he asked absently. He had poured his heart and soul into telling her the tale of Bruné-Hilda's woes. "You mean my scarred and injured beloved?"

"No, the other. The one you despise with the heat of a thousand suns, the one who torched your beloved."

"Ah, Freya-Gund." Just saying her name snapped him out of his malaise.

"Of course, Freya-Gund. Why would I want something belonging to that young thing you left suffering alone on some desolate island sanctuary? Now wake up and listen. If I am to connect with the Bride of Mayhem, I need a belonging, an item, anything close to her."

Lucius sat up straight struggling to clear his thoughts.

"Well?" she asked impatiently.

She now had his attention. "Yes, of course, something of hers." He jumped up, went into the curtained enclosure where he slept the night before, and retrieved something very special to Freya-Gund. As he was about to return, he stopped, not sure if what he was doing was right. *You dulcet dolt, when did you become so cautious!* Emboldened by his own rebuke, he returned to the table and set an opaque green gem in front of the shaman. "It belonged to Cleopatra. Like Freya-Gund, emeralds were the queen of the Nile's favorite gem."

"Has the woman handled this gem? Held it in her hand, carried it on her person?" she asked, examining it closely and then juggling it. She then slipped it into her mouth and sucked.

"Hmm. I get nothing." She tossed it back like a worthless pebble.

Lucius snatched it out of the air, wiped it off, and slid it back to her side of the table. "This stone could make life easier for you, madam. If you were to own it."

"Forget the emerald, young man," she said, pushing it back. "Pull yourself together and think. Do you have anything else especially dear to this woman? A pair of sandals, a cloth that she blew her nose in, an undergarment?"

Then it struck him. *Why didn't I think of it before?* He exited the cottage and made his way to the rickety old cart they had come in to retrieve a sack of items. Returning, he pulled out the sorceress's most prized possession and laid it in front of his hostess.

"You're jesting of course," the shaman said. "A whip?"

"No, not just a whip. It was part of her. Wrapped it up her arm, she did, and carried the haft in her palm like a weapon. As intimate as any garment she wore, I assure you. She used the knob like a prod, poking anyone who got in her way. And when angered, damn, was she accurate with that tip. It was her signature *provocateur* and it left its mark on anyone who dared oppose her."

The astral shaman grabbed the whip, examined in closely, and then slowly, cautiously put its butt against her forehead. The effect was instantaneous. Her eyes rolled, her mouth opened, and she began to gag. "Vision. I have this vision," she mumbled, then started to wobble.

Lucius tore the whip from her hand and threw it to the far side of the room. Then he caught her before her head hit the floor. For an instant he believed her dead. She was stone white. Then she coughed, started to breathe normally, and slowly regained her color. After a time, she sat up and casually inquired, "Why is everyone looking at me?"

"But we're alone, madam," Lucius said. "There is no one else here. You must be having some kind of a spell."

She shook herself and looked around. Then she rubbed her eyes and said in a raspy voice, "Of course, a spell. I do have them when the other side converses with me. It will pass quickly." She got to her feet, steadying herself with the table. She walked to her chair slowly and sat. Then she continued talking as though this was a normal occurrence. "That is what happens when you connect, you see. My thoughts"—her voice was gaining strength—"jump about like lightning in a thunderstorm when stirred by the other side. The vision, however, was quite clear. And I should warn you, it was rather fearsome. I saw her green eyes glaring at me from beside a pile of stones. This fiend for whom you search is not just a sorceress, young man, she is a *shem*."

"A shem, you say. What is a shem?"

"A wizard of evil, the watcher of the gate. And she hides near the Source."

"The source? The source of what?"

"The Source, young man, the Source, the font of life. It sits at the top of the duct. The sacred duct that nourishes the multitudes below, gives life to the groves, replenishes the ships."

"Madam, your vision, though vivid to you, befuddles me. Not illiterate on these matters of the beyond, I know nothing of what you speak. The source? The duct? The groves? To what do you refer?"

"Yes. Yes. Of course. I'm sorry. How could you possibly know? You are a stranger to these mountains. The Source is a spring that feeds the people of Frejus, their fields, and the other creations of the Great Mother along the way. The duct carries the blessed waters."

"Ah. The aqueduct."

"Yes, the duct. This person for whom you search has followed it into the high hills and lives off its blessings and the wild game it attracts. She has intimate knowledge of its workings and uses it to save herself from what she believes to be an entire army of searchers pursuing her. Even with her powers, she remains unaware that I was captured in her stead."

"What else did you see in this vision?"

"It is not so much what the vision reveals, as it is how you react to these revelations. Open your mind to what I now have to say. To catch a jackal, use stealth; to reap, sow. These proverbs are lessons taught by ones with insight far mightier than mine. They are useful lessons that are taught, but seldom learned. So listen closely: What is deemed heavy is often not. Some take, others cultivate. The cultivators reap the rewards. This is life's lesson, this is time's journey."

"Lesson? Journey? What?" he said impatiently. "I see no lesson here."

"Then you are too thick. You must strip away that protective armor of morality. My mentor taught me that trickery, treachery, and slyness are tools of the victorious. If you permit events to run their course, the outcome will never be in your favor."

"Trickery, treachery, and slyness," he mumbled. "Trickery, treachery, and—I have a rhetorician's degree in deception, madam, yet I do not understand these lessons you teach."

Motioning for Lucius to sit, she took his hand and said, "Let me explain until comprehension is attained. Why is a mountain not a valley? Why is a grape not an olive?"

"I have no idea."

"It's in how it's perceived. A mountain is a mountain because you see it as such. Is that clearer?"

"No!"

"This is going to be a long, long day," she said resigned. "I can see that now."

Surrounded by a small flock of sheep and trailed by a hound, Lucius moved in an easterly direction. The afternoon going was slow and the dog, Tungus, was of little use. He kept wandering off. Frustrated with the entire setup, Lucius thought of turning back. He left the bucellarii with the shaman, as she insisted, and was moving alone into the higher country pretending to shepherd this borrowed flock. Well, not borrowed exactly. He had paid handsomely for their use. As for the dog, the shaman promised more out of the animal than he was getting.

By sundown he reached the aqueduct and set down for the night. At this point of the ascent, the stone pipe, about two by two feet on the outside, lay atop the ground and was guarded by a path on each side. From its discharge point at Frejus, the pipe ran twenty-five miles up into the hills before reaching the spring, which the shaman called the Source. The spring itself lay ten miles farther up from where he rested, providing the astral shaman was correct, of course. Since there were no aqueducts in Umbria, Lucius was unfamiliar with how they were built, worked, or maintained. He knew only that the water was constant and pure and that the actual opening inside the stone enclosure varied between eight and ten inches.

When he awoke the next morning, he counted sixteen sheep. Three were missing. Since he had no visceral attachment to the animals, he decided to move on with those he still had; a real shepherd would find the others. The unfriendly Tungus not only kept his distance from Lucius, but he was also not much of a sheep dog. The next night another sheep wandered off and he still had miles to go. While the shaman had admitted that taking Tungus would necessitate keeping closer track of the sheep himself, she had also sworn that the dog would eventually be of use, for he could stalk a scent and see in the dark. So far he was only a nuisance.

That day the gentle slope transformed from plush vegetation to hilly scrublands where more lavender grew than trees and bushes. Soon Lucius found himself in the arid Alpine wilderness strewn with fallen rocks. Ravines, defiles, and embankments became nature's staircase into the clouds and presented fewer options to travel, while the hillsides burst with a plethora of colorations and blends.

As he moved the sheep to higher and higher ground, he revisited the shaman's vision. Freya-Gund's location was clear, she told him. The sorceress was perched atop a high hill a short distance beyond the Source. From there, predicted the shaman, she could spot a search party a day before it arrived. She insisted that Lucius's only chance to get close to this devious adversary was to become part of the everyday landscape by becoming a duct inspector working the line, a lone hunter after wild boar, or a simple shepherd taking his flock into the high country to fatten them on the fresh spring grasses. The shaman reminded Lucius more than once that "the runner," as she referred to Freya-Gund, as crafty as she was, still believed she was being hunted by a thousand militiamen. She had no idea someone else was arrested in her place.

As Lucius slowly made his way up the foothills of the Alps following the aqueduct surrounded by baaing sheep and an undependable dog, the stone pipe suddenly disappeared under the earth. He panicked. Without it how could he find the spring! He ran aimlessly back and forth searching before focusing on a cut through a distant hill he had been stubbornly ignoring. As he at last deduced, the cut was manmade and the pipe resurfaced beyond it.

He continued on until, at another point, the duct's path exceeded all imaginable feats of engineering skill. It became attached to the side of a canyon wall and ran that way for at least a thousand paces before once again finding flat terrain.

Lucius was forced to do what the pigheaded Roman engineers had refused to: detour off line for a half mile. The early Roman builders had let nothing get in the way of dead reckoning. How they managed such an achievement three hundred and fifty years ago, he announced to the droopy-eyed Tungus, was impossible to comprehend. The expense of putting thousands of workers to the task, the brilliance of the engineers, and the loss of life building such a miraculous structure had to be staggering. He wondered if the people it served over the centuries appreciated the sacrifices that had been made to bring fresh water to their municipality for drinking, bathing, and floral gardening.

With those thoughts ringing inside him, he at last reached the source of the water. From the droppings around it, his flock was not the first to visit it. He also knew that if Freya-Gund was in the area—as the shaman had foretold—she was watching his every move. With that as a possibility, he kept his hood up, moved about with a different gait, and remained beneath the occasional tree so as not to unintentionally surrender the fiction of a lazy shepherd absently tending to his flock.

The Source, as the astral shaman called it, was a generous spring fed from underneath and captured in four descending manmade pools, one pouring its waters into the next. The first pool was about ten feet square and fed the main duct that descended, Lucius estimated, two to three thousand feet during its twenty-five mile journey to Frejus. And there were at least a dozen drop pits along the way that helped control the run.

The other three manmade pools had iron-ringed gates and wooden sluices to handle the excess water. The sluices fell away in different directions before releasing their flows, probably to avoid erosion and to nourish gardens no longer there. Above the spring rose a shear rock wall to a height of possibly two hundred feet. He could just make out a few old structures on the plateau atop the wall. Could she be up there? It was "beyond the Source and high up" as the shaman foresaw.

After the sheep watered, he cautiously made his way around to the top while remaining concealed beneath his cape and hood. The top was flat, had once been sowed, and the few remaining structures were rendered useless by the elements. It was evident that no one had used them of late. And it came as no surprise to him that the vantage point from this high up offered a spectacular view of the distant sea. Farther on, maybe a half mile to the north, the foothills abruptly transformed into mountains rising in irregular tiers to breathtaking heights. The voice in the shaman's vision said Freya-Gund was perched high on a hill beyond the Source. Could that first mountain tier be it?

Trying to act like a shepherd in search of a suitable meadow, Lucius kicked over a few rocks, felt the grass, and pretended to be preoccupied with anything other than the mountain ridge. Appearing satisfied, he returned to the spring and brought up the animals. Once settling them on a grassy patch, he selected a shady spot under a tree. Lazily he dropped to the ground and leaned against the trunk. Pulling his hood low, he folded his arms to give the impression that he was taking a nap. Instead, however, his eyes flowed back and forth across that ridge searching for the fiend who haunted his life. From up there someone could see halfway to Frejus. And with the variety of irregular contours that nature had built into that high ridge, there were hundreds of hiding places. Lucius could see cuts, caves, and deep ravines everywhere. The sorceress, if she had enough food, could conceal herself in any one of them for weeks.

By nightfall he had familiarized himself with every inch of that high mountain ridge. After building a fire, he hobbled the dominant ram to prevent him and, hopefully, the other sheep from straying. Then he tied Tungus to a tree. When he was done, he stepped into the shadows behind the fire to remove the gems from his vest and to divide them into two leather sacks. Once he had the gems secure, he pretended to bed down just outside the halo of firelight. Confident that he could not be seen from the ridge, if indeed anyone was up there watching, Lucius pulled the bullwhip from one of the sacks and hooked it to his belt. Then he tightened the keep on his boot knife and slipped quietly into the deeper darkness leaving everything else behind.

After performing two tasks that required him to climb two trees, he circled west using the darkness as a shield for about half a mile before encountering the lowest point of the ridgeline. Carefully calculating his next moves while sitting under the tree pretending to nap, he silently mounted the slope and began making his way up, slithering over small rocks and between large boulders. If there was a demarcation between the foothills and the Alps, this had to be it. Soil was absent, the vegetation primarily mountain moss growing out of cracks, and trees were scarce.

When he reached a comfortable elevation, one not too close to the top, he halted. He quickly looked around and then curled up in a ball and fell asleep. He awoke when the false dawn touched the horizon. Yawning to get the air circulating throughout his body, he stretched once and then continued up the mountain.

Crawling on his belly, he stopped every ten yards or so to listen and then repeated the process until the steep ascent began to level. About to resume the climb, a small rock came bouncing past him. Had he rousted an animal? Holding his breath, he lay flat and very still.

Something moved beyond the boulder he lay behind. Animal or human, he could not tell. Scooting to the right side of the boulder, he listened for movement. Paying little attention to his immediate surroundings, he moved one more scoot—too far. Without warning the whole mountain seemed to fall away. With the presence of mind not to cry out, he tried to grab on to something, but there was nothing to hold on to; everything was slipping away with him.

Swallowed by an opening in the hillside, he went down and down, scratching and clawing, trying to slow his descent as the world around him appeared to spin out of control. All of a sudden—*umph!* He hit bottom, feet first. Stunned, he lay there. How long he did not know. His eyes became blurry and his head started whirling, and then suddenly he was back home in Assisi. His father was at the table arguing with the slaver Calla Lanilla. And he saw himself being chased around and around the room by Lanilla's ruffians. He watched himself leap off the balcony into the spinach patch and land hard, turning an ankle. The pain of that landing was sharp. *The pain! The pain! Good gawd the pain!*

He rolled over and over before finally sitting up. And just that quickly Lucius was back on the ridge sitting up and holding his ankle. The pain was terrible; he had actually twisted it in the mountain slide, the same ankle he turned in the spinach patch. Steeling himself and cursing the futility, he stood. Yes, good, he could stand—but just barely. Feeling stupid and clumsy, he shook himself, wiped the blood off his forehead, and started up, praying that he had not given himself away. Digging his fingers into a hole here, a crack there, he inched upward. But the crest was a long way off and he was not sure he had the strength.

When he was about to give up, a head appeared at the top of the abyss. He froze. A rope dropped and a voice said, "Grab it!"

Minutes later he was staring into a pair of greenish-gray cat eyes. They belonged to Freya-Gund. The suddenness of the encounter, the disadvantage of it all, caused the bottom to drop from his world. Then he heard that fiendish laugh and the bitter taste of bile rose into his throat.

"Look what the spirits of hell have regurgitated," she squealed. "The Lord of Chaos comes to me unannounced. Well, well, well, Loki always rewards the faithful—it's a fantasy come true. Hee! Hee! And look what he brought me." She ripped the bullwhip from his belt. "Another gift. Only the gods know how naked I felt without it," she spit. Then she began dragging and pulling him along the rocky ground until she reached a dome hovel that, at first glimpse, looked like a pile of stones. Once inside, she threw him on the bed. As he lay there weakened, helpless, and hurting, the astral shaman's words came back to him: "She hides beyond the Source and stands beside a pile of stones." *The astral shaman was indeed blessed with the gift of sight. All she had foretold was true.*

The hovel Freya-Gund dragged him into was a strange structure and appeared to defy gravity. Kept upright by one rock leaning upon another, it formed a circle of arches with no interior support. Inside this large stone tent was the single bed he lay on. It was made of thick logs elevated by four stout legs. Over against the back wall was a cache of food, a water skin, two rough-hewn spears, and a makeshift table with three balls of dough leavening in the air. She was making bread? But where was the oven? Or was she baking bread using the sun on a spit, as the soldiers did?

"I see you are mesmerized by this place," she said with a sneer. "I was too at first. These rocks appear to depend on one another for support. Hee! Hee! Before I lowered the rope to retrieve your sorry ass, I made sure you were likewise not dependent on others as you were in that godforsaken villa outside Barcelona. You tricked me then but you will never, ever, do it again!" she said vehemently, her face reddening. "Never! Never!"

Lucius started to sit up but she pushed him back down.

"Yes, Lucius, I watched your every move from this perch until I was certain you brought no one up here but those sheep. How foolish you looked trying to shepherd those critters. Even a fool could see you had no talent for the task." She laughed scornfully—

then stopped abruptly. "Since you came alone, the question is why. Why would you make such an ill-advised journey alone? I'm curious, Lucius. In fact, I'm *dying* of curiosity," she said, lifting him by the lacing of his tunic. "Hee! Hee! Just *dying* to know." She dropped him on the floor, the dust flying in all directions. "I like that word, don't you, Lucius? Hee! Hee! Dying is so final."

She circled around as he lay there daring not to move. "Yes, I am dying to know what made you think you could challenge a conjurer like me on her terrain—especially since I hate you so. And now look at you, alone, without hope, and suddenly a cripple. What a shame. Not that I care, but isn't that the same ankle you injured in the spinach patch? Yes, of course it is. Ha! Satisfy my curiosity, Lucius. What were you thinking coming here?"

"This!" he said, not cowered in the least by her bluster. He had heard it all before. Sitting up, he exposed the vest with the small pockets on the front and back. "This holds all that remains of the Statue of Fortune, the riches you've chased after these past two years. See, I've brought them all to you in person."

"Two years? Ha, a thousand years, not two." Her tone was hostile, her earthy stance provocative.

"Only two years, Freya-Gund, just two. A lifetime it must seem, but only two. I followed you up here for a reason, so listen to my words and listen to them carefully. Your future and mine depends on what I now tell you. From our past encounters, you must know that there's always been a purpose behind my, shall we say, craziness. Even after all you did to me and mine, not even your Lord of Misrule, that evil god Loki, would sanction the course upon which I now embark."

"Bah! Course! Embark! The words you use. Get on with it, Lucius. Why are you here? What lies do you tell this time? My only interest is in the jewels. Every last one of them—you know that. Are you going to give them up voluntarily or must I cut them off your dead carcass."

"What, you think me a fool? I hid them in a place you'll never find," he said, pointing out the arched door to the vastness beyond the ridge. "They could be anywhere out there. They could be yours— but only if you say the words I came to hear."

"Ha! Words! What words, Lucius Domitilla? Nothing hides from this," she said triumphantly, wiggling her nose. "I smelled you miles off. I saw you water the sheep and examine the old buildings and feign a midday nap. You got up the hill in the dark, yes, but then the gods gave warning and again filled my nostrils with your unpleasant odor. Before I could pounce, though, your clumsiness intervened and down you went. Now, tell me," she said, rubbing her hands together. "I'm dying of curiosity. *Dying*. How in the world did a bumbler like you find me when no one else could?"

"Never mind that. The time for name calling has past, Freya-Gund. I am not here to trade insults but to reach a truce."

"A truce, you say? Ha, ha, ha. A truce!" She mocked him in that insidious way she had that pierced him like splinters under the quick. But Lucius remained calm. This war must end now.

"Yes, Freya-Gund, a respite, a pact, a truce, whatever you choose."

"Tell me, Lucius, why would I, or anyone, believe your lying lips, eh?"

"Do or don't, it matters little. My proposal stands: you get what's left of Fortune's gems after you swear on the specter of Ahriman, on your father's grave, and on the cross of the crucified Christ that you will take what's left and return to Worms. Is it not time, Freya-Gund, to fulfill *phantasma*, to use this moment as a touchstone for the future? Your Highness, your kingdom mourns your absence," he said, pointing north. "The queen has been away far too long in search of her Golden Fleece. All Burgundia will fall at your feet when they see the wealth you bring home. And with the power this wealth brings, you can rule the vast lands of the North. Think of all you can be woman. The goddess of Ahriman, the queen of Burgundia, the possessor of the greatest treasure the world has ever seen! Why do you trade insults with a scoundrel like me when all this is yours for the taking?"

Physically stirred, Freya-Gund's chest began to heave. His words were obviously intoxicating. And she had probably not expected him to drop the treasure she obsessed over these many years at her feet in exchange for a mere promise. Furthermore, Lucius noticed that when he said, "Your Highness," her eyes widened. He measured her every reaction to make sure he ignited a spark. Although risky, even foolish, he understood that if he misjudged this woman's reactions it could mean the end of him. Surely somewhere inside her black essence rested a speck of dignity—he hoped. A drop of spittle appeared at the edge of her mouth, a bead of perspiration on her forehead. Something was oozing up from inside. As dark as her core was, could it be that a fleck of respectability was surfacing? His words were having an effect.

"You're serious," she said rubbing her chin, her voice softening. "Of course you are. It makes sense. Why else would you risk everything by coming up here alone?"

He could see that icy demeanor melting. Lucius, having rehearsed over and over what he was about to say next was now ready for the final *credula postero.*

"I've had enough running," he said, "and you have as well." It was not intended to be a meaningless comment but a flat-out statement from the heart. "Using the genius the gods awarded you at birth, you pillaged the greatest treasure hoard the world has ever seen, amassed by generals and warlords over the centuries from conquered kings, satraps, and dynasties stretching from Parthia to Egypt and all the city-states in between. The emerald favored by Cleopatra is among those that I brought. Galla identified it."

"Ah, the emerald of the Nile." She rubbed her fingers together as though she was massaging the fated stone. Her shoulders slumped and the dying fire in her eyes disappeared completely. "So you know the history of this wonderful gem and all the others, do you?" Everything about her softened. "But do you know that this celebrated plunder, the greatest treasure the world has known, was hidden away by the most brilliant thief to walk the face of the earth?" She wiped away some of the saliva on her chin and spit the rest on the floor. "A resourceful man he was too. His name was Eutropius, you know, a eunuch in the service of the emperor at the palace in Constantinople. Did you know that as well, Lucius?"

Lucius shook his head.

"His is a fascinating story. Can you believe one man so capable of all that? A superb scoundrel he was, too. Yes, truly magnificent. At first his accomplishment was only a rumor whispered from village to hamlet to cave. But for me, when I first heard the tale, it became more than idle gossip among wrinkly old women and used-up old men who never strayed ten markers from their doors. It became my measure of grain, my way out of the isolation my mother had enslaved me in. Yes, Lucius, this treasure of treasures inflamed the center of my being. Think of it, a treasure so vast . . ." She became lost in the ecstasy of that long ago epiphany that had elevated her out of a life of abject poverty and boredom.

Watching this transformation maturate, he remained silent.

Regaining herself after a momentary reflection, she continued, "Eutropius's treasure became my panacea, the remedy for all the foulness of my youth. And I saw it as my opportunity to rise above the squalor of Phrygia. Born into a twisted enigma of the Fates, I was determined to use that treasure to transform myself into a handmaiden of Odin and thereby lift myself to the greatness that I believed I deserved. Some would say I was reaching too far. Ha! Only the gods knew how ready I was to sell my body, my self respect, and, yes, dear Lucius, *even my eternal soul.*"

Suddenly, her mood swung wildly the other way; something inside was working its way out. Her cheeks reddened, her jaw set, and the small finger of her left hand began to twitch. Were the old demons of the dark side back? Lucius threw up a hand to halt the regression by saying, "But the entire hoard of gems disappeared, did it not? Stolen by a member of the aristocracy, wasn't it?" Not waiting for an answer, he went on. "Yes, I know the history, Freya-Gund, the entire sordid affair. It was taken to Rome in the belly of a consul's ship only to disappear again. At first you thought that was the end of your dream, but it wasn't, was it? *It was your chance!*"

As before, his words held a strange power over her. Again, she struggled to compose herself. The redness in her cheeks remained, but the twitching stopped. Wiping repeatedly at her mouth, she said,

"Yes, a chance, Lucius, my last chance. Admittedly it was small, but at least a possibility remained. But my knowledge of Rome was naught. Yet I was compelled, some would say driven, to start the search all over."

She shook herself like a dog before continuing. "This nose was my guide, this body the instrument; I followed every rumor, seduced anyone—male or female—threw open every door for no other reason than to get a speck of information. Nothing mattered. Whoever had the treasure did not know what they had. Of that I was certain. And finally, after years of searching, your broken-down, nutless uncle and his former lover Cybelina, with their intimate knowledge of Rome and how it worked, miraculously fell from the sky into my lap. More importantly, they were full of loathing for everything Roman."

"And that hatred put them under your spell," interjected Lucius.

"Yes, under my spell. What a stroke of luck. All those disgusting trysts and blind alleyways finally bore fruit after so many frustrating years. After the three of us along with Cybelina's army of servants threw open the gates to Rome, your uncle led me to Tibur while the Germani tribesmen were sacking the city. And there it sat on the second level of a grand villa, innocently displayed in a hidden sanctuary overlooking a vast garden of hedges—hawthorns, hemlocks, and box-hollies. Do you find it odd that I can remember that much detail? Well, it was a moment of clarity. A moment I shall never forget."

"Yes, I find it odd."

"Well, it was a special time in my life. I had at last found the mother of all hoards—the Statue of Fortune. Then, you, you loquacious mole, stole it from under my nose. And during the crowning glory of my life."

"Your coronation, of course, and what a—ouch." Lucius winced, not from the remembrance but the throbbing. A pain shot up his leg to his back. It took his breath away. "Damn . . . it," he panted, grasping his ankle. The sudden sting made him nauseated; then the pain subsided. But the mood was broken. It did not matter. All that needed saying was said. Whatever was percolating inside her would boil over or subside.

The flush on Freya-Gund's cheeks quickly drained, taking all her energy with it. She sighed. "You really mean to end it here, don't you?"

"Yes," he said, massaging his ankle.

She slowly got to her feet and walked to the doorway. For the longest time she absently stared out. "Then I say this to that: yes we shall. Yes, indeed, we shall. I'm tired of being strong, tired of being a sparrow in the rain. I want this to end as well as you—no, I want it to end more than you do. You have my word."

"On the grave of your father? On the cross of Christ? On the—"

"On the grave of my father," she replied with a sincerity he had never before heard from her. "Yes, yes, *cum grano mensura*—'with a full measure of grain'—I swear on my father's grave. As you should be aware by now, though, I am not one of them. Therefore swearing an oath on the cross of Christ would be as meaningless to the Christian God as it would be to me."

"Well, well, a touch of morality," he said and then smiled, which always offset the nip of reproach. The last thing he wanted now was to offend her. Yet he could not help but doubt. She was, after all, a sorceress. Despite his doubts, he had no choice but to take the gamble if he wanted to end this war. "You are a genuine mystery to me, woman," he said affably.

"We all must sacrifice who we are for that which we choose to become," she said, giggling like a little girl.

Did that hide a deeper meaning? If it did, Lucius did not care. Blinded by the circumstance he found himself in, he was determined to bring this entire odyssey, once and for all, to a sorely needed end.

Lucius sat on the heavy log-framed bed watching Freya-Gund wrap the bullwhip around her left arm. When done, she let the pointed handle protrude from her hand just enough to poke anyone who might get in the way. That whip and handle had left their marks from one end of the empire to the other, and everywhere in between. Noticing he was watching, she said, "I felt naked, Lucius, absolutely naked without my snake. You should never have taken it." The way she said it was strange—her tone, almost childlike, was void of her customary sharpness. "Few others would challenge my whip's magic. Like that goat of yours, this weapon has been my constant companion. It has served me well. By the way, where is that hoary thing?"

He shrugged, pretending not to know. But of course he knew. Scarface was on the isle with Bruné-Hilda protecting her—hopefully. To say that might open a door he wanted to remain closed. As far as Freya-Gund knew, Bruné-Hilda was dead, burned to death inside that hamlet on the Doubs.

"You're a strange one," she said. "Although comrades, you keep things from me. Is that killer goat out there hiding in the shadows in case you need him?"

Lucius smiled, reading nothing more into that than a casual aside from a recently transformed scoundrel. This was a new Freya-Gund—a not-at-war-with-the-world Freya-Gund, a woman who wore a different attitude. And she wore it well as far as he was concerned—at least that was what he so desperately needed to believe if this moment of comradeship was to become the reality.

"Did you, in your wildest, ever see us as foederati?" she asked, pressing a finger into his chest, a finger with a long, pointed nail.

Trying not to flinch, he responded, "No, but I always hoped," pushing her pointed nail aside. Lucius took a step back, crossed his arms, and cleared his throat. "Now listen closely," he said firmly but not rudely. "I tied the gems in a tree. That tree is marked thusly—"

"Thusly? Where in Hades did you come up with *thusly*?"

"Okay. Okay. They're tied in a tree marked like this." He drew a familiar Christian symbol on the dusty floor. "A dog is nearby, but don't worry, he's tethered. But keep your distance, he's unpredictable. You need only understand that every tree for which you search has a different marking and may be difficult to see. The marking is on the south side of the trunk—the sea side."

"I know south from north, Lucius. In the name of the god of a thousand aliases, when did you mark those trees? I watched your every move down on that plateau, so no tricks."

"No, no tricks. You just thought you saw me; I wouldn't have gotten so far up this ridge if you had. In any event, the trees were already marked, probably by some transient cultist group trying to get away from the world until they tried to grow food. Some paradise that plateau is; it has the poorest soil I have ever seen. I simply chose the tree marked with the fish because it retained its leaves."

"Those are not leaves, Lucius. They are needles."

"Okay, needles. Now please hear me out. The gems are high up in that tree secured in a leather pouch concealed in a cluster of green foliage. Do you think you—"

"Don't insult me, Lucius. When saddled by a dream, it rides me like a steed. You, of all people, should know that. Now, you clumsy oaf, stay off that ankle and relax. I'll do the rest." And with that, she left.

For a few seconds he again wondered if he could trust her. He knew her history all too well, a mystic who preyed on the gullible from Phrygia to Spain. Then he quickly dismissed the idea. After all, since that day in the dungeon of Capricorne when he lost his innocence to her *corruptela*, he had held this unexplainable power over her. She thought him the reincarnated Attis, the son of Cybele who was castrated, died of his wounds, and then resurrected. For the sake of Galla and everything Roman, he prayed that that spell over her held forth one last time.

Very soon he was bored. Lucius fixated on the arched roof of this dome-like structure and wondered how it defied the physical laws of the universe. Everything that went up fell eventually. Why didn't it? Since there were no center posts, what kept it from collapsing? It couldn't be the shape of the stones because every stone was different—sphere, cube, rectangle. His friend Patricius, the one who nursed him back to health in the prison of Valance, had spoken of such a structure on the isle of Eire. There, he remembered him saying, this strange-shaped hovel was common, and each one built entirely out of fieldstones with no vertical supports. At the time, Lucius laughed at the absurdity. But his friend swore that the only object holding such hovels together was a center piece much like the keystone in an arch. And then he'd told Lucius that a fellow shepherd had once knocked the piece out to vent the place of smoke and had been crushed to death as a result. "It all fell in on the poor bastard," were Patricius's exact words—and "bastard" was the only foul word Lucius had ever heard him use.

Lucius hobbled outside and retrieved a sturdy pole—actually a crudely shaved tree limb—from a pile of similarly fashioned limbs that were no doubt used to support the walls during the dome's assembly. Dragging it inside, he began poking at the ceiling to see if any of the stones were loose. He did not wish to end up like that hapless shepherd.

From time to time he stopped to look beyond the edge to the plateau below. Seeing no sign of Freya-Gund, he went back to poking the ceiling. At last he came across what he thought might be the keystone. It was different from the other rocks, worked into a pentagon shape by a skilled hand and fitted perfectly to the five irregular rocks around it. Why it took so long to find, he did not understand until he realized that it was off-center.

With the keystone well intact and no stones loose, he lay back down on the floor and continued to study the genius of how the fieldstones were pointed one after the other toward that single keystone. But why was it off center? There had to be a reason.

Forgetting for the moment his search for loose stones, he carefully raised the pole to the keystone and tapped it lightly. It made a different sound, a reverberation more solid than the others. He lay back once more and began to wonder what would happen if he rammed the pole into the keystone. Would it pop out like it did for that shepherd, or would it simply growl like a bear during a winter nap and ignore the jab? He began to speculate beyond the normal: Did that stone know it was vital, even critical, like the queen bee to the hive or a sea captain to his ship? Or did the stone, like an emperor, take for granted that the role it played was ordained by the gods? Although he had now bitten into the apple of the absurd and knew it, he continued speculating. Did the keystone have a soul, ears to hear, and eyes to see? Was the duty it now served to the other stones its hell or a reward for a good life? With such inane notions whirling in his head, his thoughts began to cloud and he fell asleep in the middle of this strange structure that was held up by a single keystone.

Freya-Gund was not having so peaceful a time down on the plateau. When she saw Tungus up close for the first time, she froze. *A wolfhound!* Instinctively she grabbed the stub of her ear, the ear that had been half bitten off in a ferocious fight with a savage beast that had nearly done her in. And that beast was a wolfhound. Oh how she detested that breed! And for reasons only the minions of the netherworld could explain, wolfhounds instinctively despised her too.

Catching Freya-Gund's scent, Tungus's hair stiffened and he began to pace back and forth. Then he started to growl, a growl that slowly built into a baleful howl. There was something about this stranger that made him boil. Baring his teeth, he tugged at the tether that bound him to the tree.

On this lonely plateau that was far from everything, the tension between these two built until a battle between the progeny of a vicious breed and the goddess of Ahriman was inevitable. Freya-Gund drew up a knife from her boot and slipped it into her girdle. She knew the animal was watching her every move as it pulled and scratched, trying everything to break free. Glaring into the wolfhound's fierce red eyes, she slowly uncoiled her whip and let it drag behind her while cautiously, tauntingly circling just out of his range. The whip she so cherished, so much a part of her since she left Phrygia, was no ordinary instrument of pain. Crafted by an Anatolian artisan, it sported a tooled weighted handle, a square keeper with a twelve-plaited thong that was tapered to a thin point, and was eight feet long. The fall, of chewed lambskin, still retained bloodstains from two prior human obstacles. This magnificent weapon was not only fashioned to inflict maximum pain, it was in the hand of an expert who took pleasure in its every bite.

Watching Freya-Gund closely, Tungus snarled and continued to pull at his tether, desperately trying to free himself. But the leather was too new and its measure too thick. When the fall of the whip cracked above his head for the first time, he did not budge. The report bounced off the rocky wall of the ridge and echoed down the hillside. The birds, frightened by the sound, scattered in every direction. Although the sound did not faze the wolfhound, he tensed, waiting for what came next.

This time Freya-Gund took careful aim. Snap! Crack! Tungus yelped as the blow struck him on the hindquarter. Snap! Crack! Blood spurted from his head. Letting the whip trail behind her like a snake, she continued to circle. The next blow caught his shoulder.

Sensing his disadvantage, Tungus retreated, putting the tree trunk between him and his assailant. But when he did, the tether shortened.

"Hee! Hee! No matter where you go, there I be," she gloated.

Smelling blood, Freya-Gund walked around the trunk until she got another clear shot. Snap! Crack! Snap! Crack! More blood. Again he moved, again she circled. Snap! Crack! Tungus let out another yelp. This time the whip had torn a nail off his front paw. He shifted to the right but to no avail. The tether was wrapped so tightly around the trunk that he could no longer maneuver. With escape impossible and avoidance useless, he did the inevitable and gave up. Letting his ears droop, he dropped to his haunches and began to whimper. Freya-Gund had managed to make one more living creature cower.

She smiled and then let forth a fiendish howl. Three squirrels scurried down a nearby tree and took off down the mountain.

Feeling the rush of victory, she pointed the finger with the sharpened nail at the cringing animal. It was a warning for the hound to stay put or else. Only then did she resume her real mission and began searching for the tree with the fish symbol that faced the south.

Though remaining still as ordered, Tungus licked his injured paw and began plotting his revenge.

Freya-Gund returned to the mountain dome swinging a leather sack by the string. The whip was once again wrapped around her arm and she appeared calm, almost serene. "I had a small problem," she announced upon entering.

"Oh," he said, sitting up from where he lay. Still half asleep, he wiped his eyes and then crawled over to the bed and rolled up onto it. "What problem could a resourceful person like you possibly have?" he asked, massaging his ankle. The swelling had increased while he slept.

"You did not bother to warn me about the dog."

"The dog? I told you—"

"*Not that he was a wolfhound!* You know how I despise that breed." She tossed the leather sack containing the jewels under the bed like it was a worthless collection of rocks.

"Wolfhound? Why would I warn you he was a wolfhound?"

"Forget it! It's over with!" She paced back and forth several times. "There's more," she growled. "I counted every gem twice. There are only a hundred and fourteen in that sack. Where are the others, Lucius? Fortune's belly surely held five to ten times that amount."

"That's it. That's all there is, Freya-Gund. I swear. It's what's left. We used the rest to purchase the eight hundred thousand measures of grain as part of the agreement with the Goths." He was lying about the grain, and for no reason. Lying was so much a part of Lucius that he did it unconsciously. And he was oh so very good at it. "We freed the princess and prevented a war by filling their bellies."

"Hmm. That just does not sound right. I saw the grain ships, but eight hundred thousand measures? How in the name of Jupiter, my young friend, did you gather so much at this time of year?" Freya-Gund was aware, as was everyone, of the food shortages at the end of winter.

"I had an associate, a land agent for estates on the far coast of Italy. He's the best at what he does; a little man with a wonderful talent for bartering."

"I still can't believe you—"

"Of course we paid dearly for every measure, you understand. Each landowner holds back a certain amount of grain from his harvest in case of an emergency. My associate understood that. To encourage them to release what they hoarded, we paid a hefty premium over the market price, and, well, how should I put this, the emperor's men twisted a few arms and kicked a few knees when necessary."

"Paid with what? Few will take a gem in payment. Why? Because they have no knowledge of its value."

"You're right. And we knew that. So we converted the gems I carried to Ravenna into gold. The emperor's personal guards, the scholares, went into the municipalities near and far with an edict signed by the emperor. Again, we were forced to barter the gems below their actual values. The process, admittedly hasty and at times harsh, collected a mountain of jewelry, old coins, and religious artifacts that had been removed from the temples when—"

"I know, I know, go on with your story."

"Yes, you do know everything," Lucius said with just a hint of sarcasm. Then he said, "The *aerarium* melted it all into gold bars."

"Melted it? Why?"

"Now you're playing games. Be serious. Anyway, everything that was needed was put at my associate's disposal: an adequate militia, gold bars, and a second edict from the emperor. With these, he amassed the grain and a flotilla to transport it all. My man not only has a knack for the impossible, he has a magical tongue."

"What became of this brilliant envoy of yours, this genius with a magical tongue? Sounds like a valuable man," she said. "We could use a man of his ilk in Burgundia."

"He abandoned me the hour the task was finished. Went back to Ancona."

"Ancona, you say, the Greek city on the Adriatic? The beehive of the Avars? Your friend resides there?"

"So he claims."

"Tell me more of this little man, this land agent with the slippery tongue and magical touch."

"Why?" he asked.

"Just curious. What's his name?"

"Mahaki," Lucius answered, thinking nothing of it. "The man calls himself by one name only, simply Mahaki."

Freya-Gund stiffened. "What did this Mahaki look like? No, wait, let me tell you. Short, of course, you already said that. Mostly bald, graying—maybe totally gray by now—wears a triangular *kufeya* headpiece held in place by a braided crown of camel wool, and has a tendency to cover his face with the trailing cloth. His eyes lie far apart and he has full lips."

"Then you know of him," said Lucius.

"Know *of* him? Ha! You fool. I know him well. More importantly, I am familiar with his underhanded methods, which you call 'a knack for the impossible,' his untrustworthiness, which you call 'clever,' and everything else about the man. I have seen his handiwork."

"Underhanded? Untrustworthy? How can that possibly be, Freya-Gund? I spent months with the man, slept in the same room and ate at the same table. I relied on him at every turn and have not one regret to show for my trust."

"Have patience, and I will tell you. Where did you first meet this Mahaki fellow?"

"In Rome, he was sitting under a tree. Wait. No. That's wrong. I actually first met him in Umbria after, well, you know. After you and Gunther left with that horde to do what you did to Rome, Bruné and I left the valley and traveled north in a house wagon. The rig was so big that it was difficult to handle at first."

"I do not care about the rig. Go on, please."

"When leaving the valley, I knocked this wayfarer into a ditch at the One Hundred Mile Bridge. There's not much else to the tale. Bruné bandaged him up and we dropped the poor fellow where the road splits at Nucera-Umbra. We were going north, he to Ancona. Never saw him again until I came across him sitting under that tree at the port of Rome."

"Hmm."

"What?"

"And you never once put together who this little man was. All that time you spent trading gems for grain, you never once had a suspicion? Never once did he reveal his true self? Never once did you even inquire?" She sounded dumbfounded.

Puzzled, Lucius could do little back than stare at her.

"How can that be? You're so clever, at times too much for your own good. And you never suspected anything. A land agent, huh? That's what he calls himself now, a simple, unassuming, hardworking land agent. The biggest surprise is that he did not run off with your gold bars or kill you for the gems."

"What in Hades are you talking about, woman? Run off with the gold, kill me for the gems? Hey! Tell me, what do you know that I don't? Why do you hold such ill will for an unassuming, hardworking land agent?"

"That man is no land agent. He's the instigator of everything that went wrong for your people that long, hot summer in Umbria. Mahaki is an Avar."

"Impossible," he laughed, not believing a word of it. "He looks nothing like those people. Besides, he's old, he's small. How can he—"

"Old? Small? What does old and small have to do with anything? He is not your everyday, foul-smelling, sheep-fucking illiterate like most Avars. And I can tell you this with certainty: he is the one who schemed until he achieved his revenge on those self-righteous valley people you call *friends*. He's the one who sent pieces of marble back to Gamzat for every male Avar to wear as an *aide memoire;* a remembrance stone of the destruction of their precious Lucic, that Avar village done in by your valley's religious zealots simply for its marble. Do know the story of Lucic, do you not?"

Lucius nodded, getting a sinking feeling in his stomach.

Freya-Gund continued, "Those amulets were chipped from the church for one purpose only—to keep the hatred alive. He needed to keep it alive until a leader arose to take the vengeance that he himself could not take, a vengeance that consumed half his lifetime. That leader finally arose. Sassen the Invincible, born, coincidentally, the year Lucic was destroyed. The white-haired devil traveled all the way from the Black Sea with a force large enough to destroy your people. Thanks to the Burgundians—Gunther actually—Mahaki destroyed only part of what he set out to. Unfortunately, that was the part dearest to you." She said smiling broadly.

His eyes widened and he took in an involuntary breath.

"Yes, Lucius, it was Mahaki who brought down the church atop that hill. He spent years studying its construction. Knew every pillar, arch, and keystone from bedrock to tower, understood its strengths and how to probe its weaknesses. Once it collapsed, his work was not yet done. No, Lucius, it was not done at all. He goaded Sassen into dragging those giant marble blocks that the bishop pillaged from Lucic to the edge and then pushed them down the hill. You know the rest. Down, down they came. Crashing into the grand villa of Capricorne—Ponti Lepius Filipi's villa—destroying it and creating a giant mudslide that took everything else with it. You do see it all now, don't you? It was Mahaki who killed your family and friends. It was Mahaki who destroyed your world."

Dumbfounded, Lucius fell back. None of it made sense. How could one little man accomplish all that? He lay there on the bed looking up at the ceiling. Then he forgot about the ceiling and the stones and flew off into the ether of all the yesterdays where the past hid waiting to be recalled. Everything that had happened that painful summer flashed before him. The forbidden festival, the jugglers who could not juggle, the acrobats who could not perform, the rampage of the wild bull in the main square, and all the other deceptions that had led to the destruction of the church atop the hill.

After the longest time, he finally spoke. "What of the sheep?" he asked.

"The sheep? What sheep? We're speaking about the man who destroyed your life and wasted a treasure on last year's grain, and you inquire about sheep?"

"Forget Mahaki. The pain is too deep. I want to know about the sheep down there on the plateau. What of them, Freya-Gund? They're my responsibility."

"You want to forget Mahaki? The pain is too deep? This is the man who contrived against your people. You *really are* deranged, Lucius."

"What of the sheep?" Lucius asked stubbornly.

"All gone, except for the ram. He was lonely, poor critter, so I cut him loose. Now someone else can tend to his needs. In the end, dear Lucius, you were a horrid shepherd."

"Did you cut the dog loose as well?"

Turning red, she said, "Forget the fuc—" then stopped. Softening, she asked, "How's the foot? I found these in your baggage." She held out a wad of cloth. "Why in the name of Jupiter do you wear wraps instead of trousers? They're such a bother. Didn't living among the Burgundians teach you anything?"

Lucius shrugged. Keeping all the yesterdays out of his thoughts required every bit of his willpower.

"Here," she said sweetly. "Let's bind that ankle so you can walk." Moving closer, she tripped over the pole. "Damn! What's this?"

"Oh, that. I was poking around checking for loose stones in the ceiling. How this place stays up is a mystery." Then it hit him. The thought of that beautiful church collapsing atop him surfaced in a flash of muted agony. Fighting to keep that memory at a bearable distance, he cursed aloud.

"What, your ankle?" she asked.

"No, not the ankle," he answered, "the nightmare of that church coming down on me flashed by. I was beneath it all hiding in the bishop's treasure vault beneath the altar when it happened, you know."

"Yes, of course. You were buried alive, weren't you? What a slow, painful, horrible way to die, dear boy, just horrible. Tell me about it."

He had more immediate issues than the telling of that experience. He had to concentrate on the now or lose everything he had worked toward. "A marvel of engineering, the ceiling above us, eh?" he mumbled insincerely, desperately trying to clear his thoughts of the past. This surprise revelation about Mahaki was shocking.

"Yeah, a miracle of miracles," she said sarcastically. "Now, get down on the floor and put your foot up." She knocked his good leg off the bed and unrolled the wad of cloth that most Romans used in the cold months to keep their legs warm. "Real men wear trousers, you know."

"I know," he said with a sigh. He stretched out on the floor before her, his legs pointing toward the bed. "I've worn trousers. Hard to get used to. They pinch."

"Pinch. Blah. You are far too *sissified* at times, my young friend. It is time for you to become a real man."

She sat on the bed and raised Lucius's left leg to her lap. After removing his boot, she tossed it under the bed and began wrapping his swollen ankle with the strips of wool cloth. He relaxed, forbidding the revelations about Mahaki to haunt him for one more instant by focusing his thoughts on the ceiling. The light coming through the doorway reflected off the far wall and cast shadows on the dome ceiling painting an eerie effect. The stones seemed to move. And if one did fall, it would surely kill him. As snug as the stones fit, there were cracks that permitted an occasional glimmer of light to sneak through. Cracks meant leaks, leaks meant deterioration, and deterioration meant loose stones. Those cracks were the reason this odd creation was in fact so ridiculous. The riddle was solved. *Now what do I think about!* He focused his attention on the doorway for a while, then the heavy-legged bed, anything to distract himself from that long ago summer and the knowledge that Mahaki was the cause of so much chaos.

He felt a twinge.

"How big you gonna wrap that thing?" he asked, raising his head off the floor.

"Almost finished. You want to walk on it or spend the rest of your days up here on this mountain? Now lay back and shut up."

He did as told, remembering how she had taken good care of Gunther when struck by that arrow during his coronation. Huh. That was a long time ago also. Bruné-Hilda was still so beautiful then, their little house inside the walls warm and safe. He smiled. The future held promise then. Much had happened since those wondrous days inside the protective walls of Worms. And but for a turn here, a curl there, everything might have been different, so very different. If that Hun, the infamous Cacca Reba, had not stumbled across them . . . What a rude twist of fate. Then Mahaki's letter, the one that had been delivered by the rude messenger at Arles, quickly shot into his mind. His letter! *So that's what—*

He felt a tug followed by a stabbing pain. "Hey!" he yelped, forgetting the letter. "That's the sore one, damn you!"

"Not as sore as it's gonna be," she spit.

He knew that tone. And the sound of it was not comforting. "What are you talking about?" he roared, shooting up to a sitting position.

And that quickly the entire situation inside the stone chamber erupted. A loop snared his right wrist and her boot slammed into his chest knocking him back, the air exploding from his lungs. Stunned, he lay there motionless for just an instant, but that instant was all Freya-Gund needed. She leaped to the other side, wrenching the rope tighter around his wrist, keeping him flat on his back. He tried to wiggle free. *Why could he not move?* Then he realized what she'd been doing while he lay there studying the ceiling, trying not to think of Mahaki or the church. His bad ankle, though bandaged, was lashed tightly to the bedpost by the leg wrappings.

Working quickly, she secured his arm to a stake protruding from the floor—a stake he had tripped over twice during her absence but had thought nothing of. He should have. All that she was doing now had obviously been planned out ahead of time. Again and again he tugged at his bindings but to no avail. In a moment of clarity, Lucius understood it all. He had been cleverly and utterly duped by the master of deception.

The rascal of Umbria was now a helpless captive.

Watching him flail about with his free arm caused her to spew forth one of those insidious, high-pitch snickers. No amount of thrashing and no amount of swearing did Lucius any good. The bed he was tied to was as immovable as the stake.

"Lucius, Lucius, you're so gullible," she said, shaking her head. "I not only have the gems in my possession, and let Ahriman be praised for that, I also have you. Some wait a lifetime for a single moment like this. You stole what I had, and I have it back. Hee! Hee! What could you have possibly been thinking coming up here to confront me—me, Freya-Gund, the goddess of Ahriman, the mistress of mayhem, the destroyer of Rome."

Angered by her audacity, he began to violently pound at the bed with his free foot.

"Now settle down before you break that good leg," she chided, shaking a finger at him—the finger with the pointed nail. "Here, let me protect you from yourself." Using the whip, she lassoed his free leg and secured it to the other bedpost leaving him spread out like a fork in the road. In no hurry now, she retrieved a stake from somewhere outside and, using a rock, pounded it into a crack in the floor a few paces above his head. It took three tries, but she finally managed to grab his other arm and tie it to the stake. He was now completely at the mercy of the most unrelenting and cruelest woman anywhere on Mother Earth.

To emphasize her control, she put one final blow to the stake, straightened, and, with casual aplomb, threw the rock out the door.

"Now, let's see what we have here," she said, running her tongue seductively over her lips. Moving closer, she hiked her tunic above her knees and stepped over the top of him, just like she'd done that first day long ago in Gunther's tent. Refusing to play along, he turned his head away, unlike that first day. He knew what she wanted. Oh yes, he knew too well this woman's depravity. Freya-Gund was totally naked under that tunic and she wanted him to see, wanted to tempt him. Once, he had been young and curious. Not now. He had seen the best of her, and the worst, and wanted none of it. More worldly now, he understood that these seductive maneuvers were not only a sick game, but a sport that gave this depraved person a kind of decadent sexual pleasure.

"Get that bare ass out of my face, bitch. I've already seen more than I care to." And he aimed an endless stream of invectives toward her.

"Quiet down, straw boy," she said, laughing. "I thought that little display might bring back memories of our first encounter, an encounter with a real woman, not one of those Umbrian pigs." She lowered her tunic and moved to the side. "Yelling won't do any good, you know. No one can hear your pleadings this far up."

"I plead for nothing, woman!" he said vehemently.

"Oh no? Well, you soon will. Now then, let's return to our first encounter. What was it? Four, five years ago when we entered your putrid valley, a place where men run around in women's attire and not trousers? Yes, five years I believe it was. How could one ever forget all those confused, frightened faces?" Changing her throaty delivery to a tantalizing silky whisper, she dropped to one knee and drew enticingly closer. He could taste her hot breath, feel her breasts moving in and out, her stomach pressing against his.

"Remember what I did then?" she asked, her mood growing ever darker. "Sure you do, love."

His eyes widened.

"You were an innocent then, but I changed that, didn't I?"

He blinked.

"No, not that. I refer to the sticks, the osier sticks. The sticks condemned you once, didn't they? But Gunther stopped me from doing what I should have. Well, he won't be stopping anyone now, will he? Hee! Hee! Because he's dead! I saw to that, didn't I?" Freya-Gund had relapsed back to the deadly witch Lucius had always known her to be. What a fool he'd been to think he could change her.

Rising to her full overpowering height, she pulled a small sack from her waist synch, opened it, and spilled the contents into her hand. It was her notorious osier sticks.

"They let me keep them, you know. Everyone fears taking these magic sticks from a sorceress. Now," she said sucking him into the vortex of her stare, "as you recall, Lucius my dear, when I drop these on the ground, if a black, any black, covers—well, let's not spoil the suspense. Let's wait and see. Hee! Hee!" With that, she tossed the sticks into the air and followed them down with those cat-like eyes.

"Ah-ha! Look there! See! Oh, I'm sorry, you can't see can you. Let me look for you. You do remember, don't you? That which speaks loudest has no voice. Ah, too bad, Lucius. I am so, so sorry, truly I am. Three whites covered by a single black. You lose."

"Lose what, you bitch!" Lucius roared, not intimidated by her antics.

Unfazed by his bravado, she went on, "Let me tell you more of Eutropius. May I speak of Eutropius, Lucius?" Her voice shifted once more into that mesmerizing whisper. "Remember Eutropius, that minister I told you about who resided in Constantinople, the one who first amassed the gems through a long registry of sordid connivances, then hid them away in the belly of a statue—a statue we came to know as Fortune? Hmm, remember? Well, let me remind you of, shall we say, his shortcomings. The man was a eunuch, a sterile man, a man without every man's prized possession—his manliness. Nod your head, dear, or simply say yes. Remember?"

Grudgingly, Lucius nodded once.

"Very good. Now then, let me continue: your drunken uncle Barnabas walked, or should I say stumbled, into my world. Some might see that as a mere coincidence, maybe even destiny, since your uncle was, what? Come on, say it. What was he, Lucius?"

He kept his lips clenched tight.

"Aw, you're not talking because you know where this is headed. How very disappointed you must be. Let me relight the past. As a student at the academy, and afterward I believe, your highly intelligent and ungodly handsome uncle had a history of seducing the young wives of Tibur, Campania, and Rome, did he not. Those indiscretions, alas"—she clasped her hands under her chin and sighed loudly—"earned him the scorn of the husbands within the aristocracy. And in a rage of vengeance, your uncle was arrested, convicted of a bogus crime, and condemned to the slave ship *Isis*. Ah, but the best was yet to come, wasn't it, Lucius?"

He glared at her.

She ignored him and continued, "Paid handsomely by a betrayed husband for the service he was about to perform, Captain Bajmak, on the first day at sea, had your uncle spread over the ship's anvil and . . ." She rushed to his side and knelt next to his ear. "And with a skuzzy galley knife, he unceremoniously emasculated him. What does emasculate mean, Lucius?" she asked innocently, sitting back on her heels. "Oh, you're still not talking? It means he had his nuts cut off! Poor dear. Your insensitive uncle, the wife fornicator and master whoremonger, the man who spilled his seed throughout the *cubiculi* of Rome, was now a useless hulk unwanted by women everywhere."

Slapping her hands against her thighs, she stood and said, "Well, sir, killing you right now would be such a pleasure. But eliminating your manhood? That would balance the scales for the time I lost chasing after you, would it not? Good, you agree. I find consistency so satisfying, don't you? So much better than splinters under the quick, forcing salted pork down your throat, crushing your bony ass under a pile of boulders, or my favorite—you do remember my favorite, don't you, Lucius? Hee! Hee! Remember what I did to the hound that bit off my ear? Of course you do. I fed the son-of-a-bitch to the hogs!" With that, Freya-Gund pulled out her knife and positioned herself over Lucius's outstretched body.

"Wait! Wait!" he shouted, finally surrendering to the moment and abandoning his false bravado. "Why are you doing this? You swore on your father's—"

"Ha! Ha! Ha! What a fool you are, Lucius. Father! Father! Father! I have no father, you worthless hunk of pulp. My mother was raped by a squadron of the worst dregs on the face of the earth. Aw, Lucius, Lucius, why must I always explain. So you tell *me*, straw boy, with so many dregs having their way with my mother, who was the one who sired me? Eh? Point him out so I can go piss on his grave. You don't know, do you? How sad. Well, neither do I, nor does my mother or any of those who had her that day. So much for that pledge, eh?"

With the knife at the ready, she dropped to the ground and raised his tunic. For some reason she hesitated. Her eyes glazed over and she slid the flat of the knife down the length of her nose and across her lips. When she did, the corners of her lips curled, spittle appearing at one of them. For a brief moment she was somewhere else. Where? Or was she listening to a noise? Maybe sensing some danger? Then she shook herself, forcibly warding off the distraction.

"Now, Lucius Domitilla, let's turn this brash, bony-assed, straw boy that I say you are, into a nutless wonder like your uncle Barnabas. Even those who think you wise would now call you fool, wouldn't they? If they only knew how you walked into my little trap. And they would have no sympathy at all for you if they could see you splayed beneath my knife instead of running off my jewels. Hee! Hee! Look how it flashes, Lucius. You were duped, my gullible twerp. Before we finish, I promise death will be your fervent wish, just like it was for your uncle before I hung him from the walls of Rome. A great favor it was I granted him, you know."

As Lucius tensed, waiting for the knife to reduce him to quivering pulp, out of the corner of his eye he saw a hairy blur fly through the air. It landed on the sorceress's back and dug its teeth into her shoulder. She let out a wail and spun. In a mad fury, she threw off her attacker. The knife went flying from her hand into the air, bounced off the ceiling, and dropped straight down between Lucius's outstretched legs, nearly performing the gruesome deed on its own.

Then, and for the first time, Lucius got a better look at the assailant. Raging mad, eyes of fire, it was Tungus the wolfhound. The screeching and gnashing of the combatants could be heard for miles if there were ears to hear and reverberated off the craggy cliffs to the valley below. In a death struggle, Tungus and Freya-Gund battled back and forth across the dirt floor of the dome in a ferocious, grinding frenzy that Lucius never imagined possible much less survivable. Lashed to the floor and struggling to release himself, he watched Freya-Gund regain her balance and stumble back to the far side of the dome. Blood was oozing from her shoulder and arm. Despite her wounds, she fought back with the rage of a cornered beast. But Tungus was her equal: charging, scratching and biting, going for her legs, her arms and her head, doing everything, it seemed, to keep her from the doorway. If nothing else, Tungus knew how to fight.

Lucius had already released his right hand from the rope when the two, wrestling back and forth across the dirt floor, rolled over the top of him, Freya-Gund holding on to the dog's ears, Tungus's fangs inches from her neck. When they rolled by a second time, they pulled one of the stakes free, the one just driven into the ground. Lucius sat up, retrieved the knife, and quickly cut himself free. His first inclination—run! But what if she won the battle? How far could he get on that ankle? His hand brushed the pole lying nearby. Instinctively he grabbed it. Getting to his feet, he raised the pole to the ceiling, found the keystone, and drove the pole into it with all his strength.

Nothing.

Again he struck, still nothing. An inward rush of energy washed over him and suddenly he felt stronger. Mustering that strength, he gave it all he had. Hitting the keystone dead center, it cracked. A small piece fell to the ground. Encouraged, he gripped the pole at the end and jammed it into the opening. Using it as a lever, he widened the hole. More pieces came down, and then, surprisingly, the entire keystone fell to the floor. When it did, the north wall groaned. He struck the ceiling again and again. Then the north wall shifted just a little and an entire row of stones crashed to the floor, followed seconds later by another row.

No sooner had he decided that it was time to leave, than his left ankle gave way. He fell to the floor. When he did, several stones came down and pinned him to the ground. A new feeling set in. This time it was panic. Lucius was in trouble. Freeing himself from the stones, he rolled over and over, thinking he would never get there. But he did. And with a final burst of energy, he cleared the doorway just in time.

As he did, the entire north wall, the side Freya-Gund was pushed up against, collapsed on top of her. The east side of the dome, the side where the bed sat, rose above the resulting dust cloud like a monument. It swayed back and forth before surrendering, falling atop the heap of rubble that was once the north wall. The resulting dust obscured everything. Lucius could do no more than sit there—frozen, helpless, bewildered. Then the breeze carried the dust away and he got a clear look at the aftermath. Only a large pile of rocks remained where the dome once stood. Dazed, Lucius sat there staring at the heap. Slowly, his milky awareness cleared. Indeed, the entire structure was gone. No one could have possibly survived the collapse. Freya-Gund was at the bottom of the pile.

He'd won. Yes, he'd won!

He'd won the war. The sorceress was dead! Freya-Gund would never bother him, Galla, or Bruné again.

Then his thoughts solidified even further. Did a mysterious omen enshroud him? As vain as the thought was, he couldn't stop there: Were the gods of a greater wisdom protecting him for something bigger? To be tied fast in a lair with a determined killer ready to strike and come away not only in one piece, but victorious, was more than merely good fortune. Indeed, it had to have been preordained. "How do I survive these things?" he shouted for everyone to hear, but there was no one there to hear his words—no sheep, no dog, no one. He was now alone next to a pile of rocks and far away from everything.

While he was rewarding the gods for his good fortune, he heard a sound from the pile—a familiar sound. Was that a whimper? Struggling to locate the source, Lucius hobbled about until the sound led him to the side of the pile where the bed once sat. The stones there were not high since that part fell forward instead of straight down like the other side. Throwing off the stones one by one, it did not take him long to uncover the bed. Its sturdy structure had kept it in one piece. A tail popped out from underneath it. Unbelievably, Tungus had saved himself by crawling under the bed. Once free, the wolfhound limped about. Shaking off the dust, he came over to Lucius and, for the first time in their short acquaintance, licked his face.

"Good boy, good boy," he said while petting the animal. Then he remembered. "The gems!"

Feverishly, he began throwing off more stones until he found the leather pouch sitting exactly where Freya-Gund had tossed it when she first returned from the plateau. His left boot and her knife, slightly bent but usable, were also under the bed. His own knife, which she had taken from him earlier, was probably buried somewhere in that pile of stones along with her.

He sat very still. Every so often he would hold his breath, listening for any sounds of life from the other pile. But he only heard the wind whistling up from the plateau. While listening, he came to the realization that Freya-Gund had met an end unbefitting the queen of Burgundia and that her body now resided in a most unflattering sarcophagus of ordinary fieldstone atop a commonplace prominence. No one would ever find her body, and if someone did, that person could never possibly imagine what happened here. Even a Greek playwright could not conceive so bizarre an end to such an extraordinary human.

Lucius hobbled beyond the pile of stones to the stack of tree limbs used in the construction of the dome. He selected one and fashioned it into a crutch. Undoing the wrapping Freya-Gund had put on his injured ankle, he slipped his swollen foot into his newly found boot and rewrapped his foot over the top of it. Tying the sack of gems to his waist, he moved to the edge of the ridge to study the easiest way down. The breeze helped clear his head. Once deciding on which way to go, he turned to Tungus.

"Come on, boy," he said. "Let's go find some food and water. And—" He started laughing and laughing at how close he had come to losing the battle and everything else. When he regained control of himself, he added, "And let's go recover the rest of the jewels from the other tree. The one you were tied to."

The night before, in a fit of last-minute selfishness, he climbed that tree and secured half the gems in a sack.

When he bent down now to give Tungus a big hug, he noticed the bloody lash marks and the injured front paw for the first time. Wounds obviously caused by a whip. "So that's it," he said, patting the dog. "For no reason, she attacked you, didn't she."

Infuriated by the beating, Tungus obviously chewed through the tether and followed her scent up the hill to extract his own measure of revenge.

"Well, well, well," he crooned, scratching Tungus behind the ear. "Done in by her own hand, you might say—an irony of ironies, a twist worthy of Aeschylus."

CHAPTER 10

S cooting on his rear, using the crutch only on level terrain, Lucius made it down to where Tungus had been tied. By the time he reached the bottom, he was sore and exhausted. But it was a small price to get off that hellish ridge. Ha! He would recover; Freya-Gund would not. Despite a painful ankle, he climbed the tree Tungus had guarded to retrieve the second sack of jewels he deviously hid. With the ram running free and no sheep to tend, he continued down the mountain to the spring that the astral shaman referred to as the Source. He now understood why it was called that. The cool waters not only refreshed, but they would save him from a slow, miserable death. He could travel no farther on his ankle. Coming down had convinced him of that.

Once renewed, he surveyed the gates and connecting mechanisms of the aqueduct. Quickly deciphering how the sluices worked, he went about cutting off the flow—a mild inconvenience for the people of Frejus in exchange for an enormous service to himself. And why not? Was he not Lucius Domitilla, the great dragon slayer of Umbria? Surely they would soon know that he accomplished what a thousand militiamen could not. And just as surely, someone, some able bodied workman, maintained the aqueduct year round. When the nearest attendant realized that the flow had stopped, he would follow the duct up the mountain until he located the problem. So simple. So reasonable. And there Lucius would be waiting. How long it might take, he did not know. A matter of hours, maybe a day. But no more than a day, of that he was certain. The duct keeper would carry every tool needed and all the caulking necessary to repair the problem. That meant a pack animal. The citizens of Frejus could not be without water for long. Yes, it made perfect sense. The duct keeper would rescue him.

In the distance, too far away to be noticed by Lucius, a modest storm rolled in off the sea. It was nothing to worry the locals about. Storms often came in from the south this time of year. So the fishermen went about their business, cleaning the catch and mending the nets after a rewarding morning at sea.

But this storm was different. When it brushed ashore east of Frejus, it mixed with the air over the sun-drenched rocks of the Esterels and strengthened. Instead of sweeping gently upward as it usually would, the clouds slammed the earth and began to boil, lightning shooting in every direction—a phenomenon seldom seen on this southern coast of Gaul. The higher the storm rolled up the escarpment toward the high Alps, the more intense it got. By the time it reached Lucius, it was a raging tempest that blocked the sun and bent the trees. The rain froze into balls of hailstones.

Blinded by the debris and ice pellets, Lucius and Tungus frantically searched for a recess in the sheer rock wall that guarded the spring in which to take cover. Before they could find cover, though, the two were drenched and Lucius's head was bleeding. A gust of wind knocked him against the rock wall. Never had a storm come up so fast. Finally, he found a protective fissure in the wall. He hunkered down next to Tungus and attempted to stop the bleeding with the bottom edge of his tunic. At least they were safe from the storm.

The high ridge came under assault next. And it wore the storm like a garment. He thanked the gods that he was not up there helpless against the torrents and fearsome bolts of lightning shooting up and down and sideways. Why were the gods so angry? One of the bolts exploded near the edge of the ridge, followed instantly by a clap of thunder. Its echo knocked the wind from his chest; Tungus began to howl. "That was a near miss, wasn't it, boy!" he yelled above the wrath of Thor, pulling the frightened dog to his chest.

That last strike was powerful, but not as close as Lucius thought. It actually struck a ways off, a direct hit on the pile of rocks near the edge of the ridge—the very pile that Freya-Gund lay beneath. The bolt hit with such force that the energy exploded the rocks, and fragments flew in every direction, one flying halfway down to the Source. When the worst of the storm had passed and the surge of rainwater washed some of the mud free from under the pile, it happened. A rock near the edge of the stack, the side that took the brunt of the strike, teetered a few times. Then it lost its balance and rolled away. A second and then a third rock followed. Had the lightning caused the pile to shift, or was it a delayed reaction from the wash? Then, incredibly, something rose from the opening created by the three missing rocks. It was abnormal and hideous. What was it?

A leg. A leg that was cruelly bent, bare, and bloody.

More rocks rolled away. Unthinkably, another body part appeared, also bloody. It looked deformed, like a human hand reaching to the sky begging for mercy, but with only three fingers and a thumb. Could a mere tempest revive the dead? If so, the way the thing moved, it was barely alive. Could lightning rekindle genesis? Or, as so many in these superstitious times feared, was the final judgment near? The Apocalypse, had it begun? Were the dead coming alive?

When the sky cleared, the hand and leg vanished and the world atop the ridge returned to normal.

Or did it?

Oblivious to what occurred on the ridge, Lucius began the tedious process of removing each gem from the sack and inspecting it. Before now he had actually shown little interest in the gems, except for the famed emerald of the Nile. As he finished inspecting each gem, he placed it into a small group by color. Because he had no paper, he wrapped the small clusters in leaves and slipped each one ever so carefully into one of his vest pockets—the same vest he had worn since Rome. Engrossed by this tedium, he worked until dark, stopping only to admire the exquisite beauty of certain stones. With only a sliver of moon to guide him, he completed the final three groupings by feel and then dozed off.

It was still dark when he woke. He felt for Tungus, but the dog was gone. Probably scrounging for food, he thought, and shifted to a more comfortable position. His ankle still throbbed and the hard ground was nearly unbearable. Then he heard it, a clank followed by a metallic scraping. Was someone honing a knife against a rock? He held his breath and listened. Yes, that was the sound of a knife being sharpened. What else could it be? He pushed the vest deeper into the recess and reached for his crutch. Getting to his feet, he shuffled toward the opening. The noise stopped, but he saw nothing. *Damn the moon!*

Then movement. A shadow flickered across the pool. *What?* Ah, only a night flyer. Probably an owl, maybe a bat. He relaxed. A whimper broke the quiet, followed by a whine. Was Tungus hurt? *Did that damn dog do something stupid?* Lucius hobbled closer to the upper pool.

Without warning, a dark form jumped out from behind a tree brandishing a weapon. The moonlight reflected off it enough to let Lucius know from the glint that it was a piece of metal. Whoosh! Down it came. Though injured, Lucius was still quick. He blocked the assailant's arm with his crutch. The weapon broke in two, one end falling to the ground between them. Pushing his assailant away with the end of his crutch, Lucius swept up the broken piece. He was about to throw it out of harm's way when he realized from the feel of it that it was not a knife, but the forged shank and blade of an ordinary garden hoe.

"What are you doing?" Lucius shouted. "You think me a stalk of grain!"

"What am *I* doing?" the assailant roared back, stumbling to his feet and trying to catch his balance. His tone was one of fear, not aggression. "What did you do to my spring?"

"Your spring?" Lucius asked skeptically.

"Thought you be an animal, I did," said his assailant.

"Animal!" Lucius roared back, still unnerved, unable to see more than the outline of the man. "A thief in the night gets treated better."

"Yeah, well, you be treated worse by the magistrate if it be you who opened the spill gate," he scolded. Then he added, "Somebody ruined my supper and half my night, not to mention the thousands down line who went to bed with only a drop of water and will wake up with less. And now you made me soil my drawers."

"Simply close the damn gate, why don't you."

"Bah! I cannot. The pin fell into the pool. Been fetchin' for it with me hoe. Don't stand there gawking, help me find the wretched thing. I be in no condition to get in there now. The water's a spillin' while you be alookin'."

The upper pool was only a few feet deep. Remorseful for the trouble he caused, a feeling foreign to Lucius, he scooted over to the edge, slipped in, and felt around. Soon enough, he found the foot-long metal piece that secured the main water gate.

"That be it. Now, hold this closed while I secure the blessed thing."

Wading over, Lucius did as instructed. When the spill was cut off, the duct pipe filled and fresh spring water once again flowed toward Frejus.

"Now," said the duct keeper, "let's light a fire, have a look at each—"

Lucius stopped him there. "You sorta smell. I suggest you clean up first."

"Fine idea. What be ya name?"

As the man disappeared into the shadows, Lucius told him, adding, "I am a friend of Binah, the astral shaman, down at Bagnois en Foret. Injured myself up on the high ridge, then lost my supplies. Would have died a sorry death had you not come along."

"Bah! Dyin' isn't that easy, lad. Young'un like you would last a long time without food. Those sheep yours I saw wanderin' 'bout down below?"

"Yep. All eighteen."

"Don't fret, lad," said the man returning from the shadows. "Others 'ill gather them up for ya. No thieves up in these hills. You and that dog I saw sniffin' about not much on herdin', are ya?" It was a question that needed no answer. Then the man asked, "What now?"

"Any way you can get us off this mountain? This ankle ain't much for walking."

"Got me two donkeys tied up down there. You can ride one to my service hut. The suppliers will be comin'. Their pack animals be empty by the time they get to me, so they be able to take you down. The magistrate sends supplies up the line every ten days or so. Mine's the last. Can ride, can't ya?"

"Yep, I surely can. So then," he said, feeling more comfortable and a bit hungry. He asked, "They bring fresh food and all, do they? That's fuggin' nice."

"Fuggin' nice? Ya say fuggin' nice, do ye. Hey, lad, we keep those folks down below alive. If it be ye down there, wouldn't ya be sharing your favors for a daily dose of fresh, life-giving spring water? Now then, let's make a fire and get dried off."

It all happened as he hoped. Lucius rode down the hill on one of the donkeys used to carry tools. When they reached the caretaker's hut, two suppliers were already there waiting with a variety of food choices and items used to maintain the aqueduct: a sack of grounded limestone and sand they called "beetle rock," used to reinforce the outer shell, and a supply of lead needed to seal the inside leaks. Four other huts were also stationed along the miles of pipe. Each housed a repairman whose sole purpose was to keep the water flowing, not only for the people of Frejus, but for the parade of trade ships that docked there daily. Yes, as the astral shaman had oft repeated, the Source *was* the fountain of life for these parts.

With the events atop the ridge behind him, Lucius rested comfortably at the astral shaman's cottage. He and Tungus had collected ten of the lost sheep along the way, which he then donated to her. The reclusive woman, victimized by intolerance, though grateful for his generosity, was now herself being narrow-minded. At least that was how Lucius viewed it. His abbreviated version of events up the hill did not satisfy her at all.

"There's more, isn't there," she said while moving about her kitchen preparing a meal.

And there was, although Lucius was not yet aware of how much more. When the astral shaman gave Tungus a piece of biscuit, he licked her hand. Recoiling, she turned white, the same reaction she had when Lucius first gave her Freya-Gund's whip. The shaman clutched her throat and reached to grab on to something.

"What is it?" jumping up to grab her.

"Danger, Lucius, a darkness lurks. I feel it." Flopping onto a chair gasping, she took three deep breaths, wiped the hand that touched Tungus's tongue on her apron, and then untied it and threw it in the corner. Feeling better, she looked back at Lucius who stood there gaping. "What really happened on that ridge, Lucius? There's more—spit it out, everything."

Thinking about how to respond, Lucius moved behind her and began massaging her shoulders. After some time, he mumbled, "Yes, there's more," pausing to choose his words carefully. "I wanted to spare you, that's all, knowing you did not want to be party to a . . . a murder of one so potent as Freya-Gund."

"Potent? You see her as simply potent? That woman's the embodiment of the devil. Speak, boy, speak!"

Slowly he spilled the truth of the entire sordid episode. When finished he said, "My work is done now, Binah. She's dead, killed by Tungus and myself, and will never bother anyone again. The woman lies beneath a pile of rocks higher than I am tall," holding his hand above his head.

"No, Lucius, you're wrong. She fooled you. Her spirit lives on Tungus's tongue. The dead do not ignite sparks in the undead."

No sooner had the word *undead* flown from her lips than Tungus began to convulse. He rolled over once, spun in a circle, regurgitated, spun, and then regurgitated again. This time at Lucius's feet. Lying in the puddle of vile-smelling vomit was a finger—a human finger sporting a pointed nail. Pointed in the manner Freya-Gund had fashioned the first finger of her left hand, the hand that held the handle when the whip was wound up her arm; the same finger she used to target her victims.

"Good gawd, Binah," he said horrified. "It belongs to . . ." But he could not say it.

"Who?" she asked, lifting it from the vileness. "Who does this finger belong to?"

"You know," he whispered. "Tungus must have bitten it off. I told you it was a struggle to the death . . . until the walls fell."

"Walls do not just fall, Lucius. A greater power is required. I've seen things you cannot imagine, lad. And sorceresses like her don't die, they morph."

"Morph?"

"Metamorphic regeneration. It means they change their appearances, sometimes their physical forms."

"Can they bring themselves back from the dead?" he asked.

"Of course not. A superior force is essential for that, one greater than themselves."

"Hmm." He rubbed his chin, thinking. "You mean a god."

"Yes."

"Possibly a god like Ahriman?" he asked.

"I never heard the name before those legionaries arrested me. And I know of many gods."

"Well, I have, and she believed passionately in him, even professed to be his disciple. I smashed his effigy with an axe after the mudslide. At the time, I blamed them both for everything that happened to my valley. My mentor's ancestors built a shrine to honor the god Charon—but Freya-Gund swore the statue was of Ahriman."

"I have heard of Charon, Lucius. Beware, for he is very influential, particularly among the rabidly superstitious."

"Like the people of Bagnois, eh? Well then," said Lucius, "you've found the culprit if there is one, haven't you? But rest assured, madam, Freya-Gund is dead. I saw her demise with these eyes—eyes that do not lie. This finger proffers a false reading. She is gone forever. I know it. Once a dog bit off part of her ear, you know, and she fed the poor critter to the hogs."

"Agh! You fool!" she screamed. "Why would you say such a thing? Don't you know the gods have ears? You have brought chaos to my house with those words, you insensitive troublemaker." She began to pace rapidly to calm herself. When she did, she apologized profusely for the outburst.

Lucius raised a hand in acceptance.

"You must take Tungus away," she said. "Yes, away, far away." And the poor woman swept the large dog up in her arms like he was a puppy. "Please, please," beginning to sob. "Take him as far from these cursed hills as you can. Swear you will let no harm come to my faithful Tungus."

Lucius bid farewell to the woman who raised frogs and snakes. Hobbling to the waiting cart with Tungus at his side, he rode off with three bucellarii; the fourth had taken up with a widow in Bagnois en Foret. By the time they reached the Aurelian Way, Lucius made up his mind. He ordered the bucellarii to ride as hard as they could to rejoin Galla Placidia's party before they reached Ravenna. They would carry with them a special message, a message for her eyes only. He, in turn, would go to Canois—a small village on the sea— having convinced himself on the long ride down from the Alpine foothills that he had done all he could to put Galla on the throne of Rome. And that was what the message to her said. But, in truth, had he? Of that, he was not certain. Was her marrying Constantius the sole solution, or should the emperor Honorius be put out of the way in favor of Galla? If that was required, Lucius was no assassin. Yet, for some reason, he pondered that course long and hard on the ride down. Did the result actually justify action? Or should a resourceful person like himself find another path? That made him think of Tauriac and Irontooth languishing in Ravenna's prison.

Then he dismissed that idea as well. Maybe he should simply let the Fates take over. Let things happen of their own accord. That question reared its head again and again while en route to the Aurelian Way. Should he do more, put himself at risk, maybe sacrifice everything? Silly as it sounded, the question remained.

And what about Galla? Was leading Rome really her destiny? With all her pedigree, was she really fortune's fate? Yes, she stood up to Freya-Gund, and she did manhandle the most powerful man in the West, not to mention how she survived captivity by winning over the Gothic king and his people. But was it her destiny to rule Rome? Whether it was or not, he had done all he could. Now what remained rested with her, literally and metaphorically. She was by every assessment, and in the end, truthfully a resourceful woman. Yes, it was time to leave managing the empire to the gods and tend to the charred life of his true love. His mind was made up.

As he left the red hills of the Esterels, the wide bay of Canois came into view. The sloping escarpment surrounding it was blanketed with vineyards and fruit trees that, he knew, supplied more than the cluster of homes housing the field workers, fishermen, and boatmen of Canois. Those plush hillsides also fed the island people of Lerins. The approaching buildings of Canois lay beneath a promontory that served as a signal tower to the islands, which sat out there a few miles off shore.

Once he reached the village, he rented a room at a wayside inn and did little more than sit on the beach each day, Tungus at his side, staring out at that distant spit of land waiting for his ankle to heal—at least that was his excuse for dawdling. After putting all of what happened behind him, he was now consumed by what lay ahead. What would it be like returning to a simpler life? Could he really just walk away from the shadows of power? Would caregiving satisfy his restless spirit? Were the two hundred and twelve precious gems—minus the two he'd given to Binah—hidden in his vest enough to get what he wanted out of life? And so what that he sinned against his beloved; when a man falls into a barrel of apples, should he not take a bite? Of course he should! But that shouldn't keep him from returning to Umbria with his broken beloved, have a family, and rebuild the big villa on the hill? Or become a sedate estate owner and morph—he liked that word morph—into the next Ponti Lepius Filipi, the great elder statesman of Umbria? Would that be enough after all he had seen and done? Not long ago the answer would have been obvious, but now it was a question. Then he sat straight up, slapped his forehead a few times, and promised to quit gnawing away at himself with such stupid shit. How could he possibly compare himself to Ponti Lepius, the man who, many said, should have been emperor? That dose of reality—and the slap in the face—brought him to his senses.

Looking out across the wide channel, he wondered what Bruné-Hilda was doing right now. Was she alive? Still brooding down by the rain barrel? How did she look? Was Bis still with her? And Scarface? Had the goat stayed clear of trouble or did his keeper, whoever he was, tire of his antics and have him for dinner?

Over the next few days these same thoughts kept creeping back into his head with chronic repetition. Then one day, when the supply skiff arrived as it did every day, rather than watch it come and go from a distance as was his daily habit, Lucius gathered Tungus, hobbled aboard, and paid the fee. Soon they were headed across. He had no plan, only an obsession, an overwhelming desire to touch Bruné-Hilda's face, to hold her, to tell her how much he loved her. And what of her neighbor, the insightful one—the old sage who advised him to leave the island sanctuary and "permit the girl to mend"—had he watched over her this past year as he promised?

Lucius looked up at the four men rowing the skiff. He caught one staring at him, probably wondering who he was. Lucius long ago had given up questioning why people stared at him. Maybe it was the way he dressed or his curly black hair or his oft-mocked cocky air. Whatever it was, he no longer cared. He was what he was and could do little about it. So he leaned back against the strut and stared back, which usually resulted in the person looking away. Not so this time.

"Aren't you that clever one?" the rower asked, "the one who meddled in the dealings of Burgundia?"

Lucius's mouth dropped. *How in the world . . . !* He sat up and took a longer look at the man. He had a thin hawk nose, piercing dark eyes and a shock of hair not quite covering a scar on his forehead. "You have me mistaken for someone else, sir. I am a simple wayfarer with a bad ankle who comes only to reclaim the past."

The man quit rowing. "Aha! Your voice exposes you. It's the way you slur the *S*'s. You are Lucius of Umbria, I'm sure of it. You drove Cacca Reba mad and helped elevate that giant of a man, Gunther, to king. We chased you to Scanborg, where I caught you stealing that ancestral sword the Burgundians Dagunda—aha! your eyes say what your lips deny—and then we followed you to Worms where Cacca Reba lost a limb and later his life. All because of you. Had his throat slit clean through by a boy, he did. Couldn't defend himself against a nine-year-old after you did what you did to the sorry sot."

"Why, sir, are you given to such eccentric postulations? Why lay such outrageous babble at my step? I know not who you are or of what you speak. A person who could defeat a Hun must be a Goliath, not a studious one such as I. Look at me. Do I appear strong enough to cut off an arm?"

"See! You show yourself! Not always so quick-witted, are you? Did I say he was a Hun or that he lost an arm? Well, did I?"

"Look here at this face, sir," Lucius said indignantly, sticking out his chin. "Look closely. Do you observe lines of wisdom that could elevate a wild barbarian to the throne of his nation? Or any throne of any nation for that matter? Eh? And these hands. See!" thrusting them under the man's nose. "Do they belong to a magician like Warlock the Wretched? Or do you, by chance, mistake me for Alexander, Jason, or Achilles?"

"Ha! You dissuade me not with this bluster. No. You *are* that bold one. By the goddess of certainty you stand accused. Your history is known to many, *friend*, not just this sorry soul Who rows instead of rides. Listen to my words: I accompanied Sassen to that valley of yours, although not myself an Avar; was forced to deal with those scum and watched while they avenged a hate planted long ago on the banks of the Black Sea. That seed nearly got me killed, it did, when that church collapsed atop us all."

"Take a breath, sir, before you explode," chided Lucius, seeing the redness sweep across the man's face.

"Explode, ha! That imp Mahaki—" He stopped short, his face puckered and he swallowed some deeply rooted angst.

What is it with Mahaki? How many enemies did this man make?

The man regained himself. "After Sassen the Avar lost his head to that bitch of a woman, I rode south with a man named Tauriac to get my share of what was promised but came away from Rome with nothing but a sore ass."

"Was I to blame for that as well, sir?"

"No. Be patient, listen. I'll get back to you. Everything that happens always seems to come back to you, doesn't it. After the Goths cast us off following the sack, we joined that crazy Hun Cacca Reba. That bastard dragged us across half the world chasing after some treasure stolen from Rome and hid away at Worms. I was there at the Judas tree when the Hun lost his arm and there too at Valance when the legions squished that usurper Jovinus because someone dissuaded the Amals and Alani to stop fighting against the Romans. That someone was you, wasn't it? Whenever a setback arose, you were always in the middle of it. My star never rose because of you, *friend*. Tell me, do you have a pact with the devil, or are you just his instigator of chaos?"

"Sir, I cannot redirect the stars, alter the tides or cause pigs to lay eggs. If your station in life is to row a barge, I say row. You cheat your mates by speaking about devils and Huns instead of putting a back to that oar. Furthermore, my good man, you challenge my kindly nature with nonsense. Maybe I should complain to the abbot of the monastery and have you relieved of these humble duties. You seem convinced lightning strikes whenever I'm near. So row, my good fellow, row me to that island and save yourself any mayhem my attendance may cause your person."

The man took up his oar and resumed his task, saying nothing further. When the craft reached the island of the dependents, Lucius grabbed Tungus's rope and nimbly eased into the surf and never looked back. So focused on what he must do, he overlooked the fact that the oarsman might present an obstacle, even a threat, to his activity here.

Lucius made his way across the island, Tungus trailing behind. No more than a mile- and-a-half long and half as wide, the island was large enough to serve its single purpose—to house the dependents of the monks who lived a life of seclusion on the outer island. Lucius had been here twice now: the first time out of curiosity; the second to see his beloved on the way to Arles. Only he was urged away by her kindly old neighbor who told him she suffered from a deep darkness, a darkness that his presence would only drive her further into. So he'd left without speaking to her, leaving a letter for her instead with the old man. Now he feared what he might find.

Not sure why, Lucius was drawn first to the rain barrel. He had this morose connection to it, this object he'd seen Bruné by on both visits. But the rain barrel was gone. Huh! That was not a good sign. Where did she get fresh water? Preparing for the worst, he walked slowly to her cottage. He found a rope in front and haltingly tied Tungus to the fence, delaying the inevitable—afraid of what he might find inside. Hesitantly, he knocked on the door and waited. He was nervous. No, more than nervous, he was scared. A bead of sweat appeared on his forehead. Lucius braced for what was to come. Then there was a growl. Could that be Bis? Yes, Bis—Brug had been killed at the hamlet on the Doubs River.

The tiny peephole door cracked open and then quickly slammed shut. There was another growl, followed by shuffling feet. He waited—then knocked again. Someone released the crossbar and the door slowly creaked open. The shadows half concealed her as she stood there barefooted, hair covering the right side of her face. She wore a long-sleeved, loose-fitting stola that just touched the ground and gathered tight beneath her breasts by a scarlet sash. Eyes alert, she looked nothing like the out-of-sorts person he spied on at the rain barrel a year ago. Taking all of her in with one sweep, the sight of her rendered him breathless. And what he could see stunned him. She was beautiful again.

"Lucius," she whispered flatly. "You've come home."

A feeling swept over him unlike any other. "Yes, my sweet, I have come home. Where you are *is* home to me. That is even clearer now that I see you. As for why it took me this long there is no answer."

Not moving, they stood there staring at each other. So much happened, yet nothing had changed between them—at least that was how he felt. Being home felt wonderful. And home *was indeed* where she was. Why had it taken him so long to understand that?

Lucius shifted back and forth awkwardly. Then he said, "I have brought a new friend to join our family." He nodded toward the gate. "His name is Tungus. Dimwitted but faithful. If not for him, I would not be here. Saved my life, he did."

"Leave him tied for now," she ordered in that familiar way that so pleased him. "Bis has become protective lately." With that, she stepped aside so he could enter.

"And Scarface?" he asked, walking into the darkened room.

"Lives with the monks. Thinks he's king over the she-goats— you know, grumpy, arrogant, and primps like . . ." The full impact of his sudden arrival hit her all at once. She turned away and began to sob.

Not knowing what to do, Lucius crossed and uncrossed his arms, scratched and adjusted himself before stepping forward and pressing against her back. He whispered tenderly, "I'm sorry, my sweet. Sorry for you, sorry for us, for being away, sorry for your hurt and loneliness. Can you ever forgive—"

"No!" she interrupted, pulling away. "It is I who needs forgiveness, Lucius. It was I who sinned, not you. Me, Lucius, it is your beloved Bruné who has forsaken you." She clapped her hands. Through the curtain shielding the rear room came a man—not a particularly young or handsome one either.

"This is Dado," she said. "He is my husband. Often he brought me grain for my body and consoling for my soul. He chased the darkness from my life, Lucius. Now we are to have a child."

"Grain," he mumbled, blocking out the rest. He heard similar words from her on the Overlook in Assisi and did not want to hear them again. "I have been forsaken for a cup of grain? How ironic." He began to pace back and forth, back and forth across the room. "I saved Rome for fifty shiploads and now lose you for one measure." He opened and closed his fist. "One stinking, lousy measure of grain!" He stopped, letting his eyes work back and forth between her and the other man. "He, this one here, is your *husband*—is that what I heard? And baby, did I hear you say you are to have his baby?" They were accusations, not questions.

She nodded.

He saw the pain that rushed up into her face, thought he saw a tear. With nothing more to add, his face turning red, he left, slamming the door behind him.

As he and Tungus made their way to where the ferry was docked, his thoughts flying back to that terrible summer when, in the midst of all the turmoil, their love began. It was all so bitter-sweet then. And so magnificent was she: golden hair, fair skin, the vestal image of innocence. Always so much in a hurry, her feet barely touched the ground. Yet his love for her that began that horrifically hot summer in Umbria, a feeling he had never before felt, now suddenly turned sour. The pleasure he'd felt sitting on the hillside above their secret place watching her swimming nude with the other Burgundian maidens now sickened him. Of course, those moments were seared into his memory—how could they not be. But would his new feelings toward her wash them all away?

When the young maidens were attacked by Lanilla's ruffians and Bruné raped before his eyes, he remained in love with her. Then months later, after her father took his revenge on Lanilla's compound, she laid her secret at his feet—she was pregnant. Already overwhelmed by the mudslide that destroyed his family and friends, her news made his life not worth living. If not for the tempest, they both would have jumped from the Overlook Piazza. Now, older and wiser, his love suddenly soured, he simply felt like running, getting as far away from here as he could. But to where? There was no place to run. Ha! It took six hundred thousand measures to save Galla

Placidia but only a single measure to lose the one thing he actually wanted—a life with Bruné-Hilda. Was his life becoming a Greek drama or was this just an isolated turn?

Lucius sat staring at the promontory on the distant coast. His cart sat beneath it, his horse stabled at the inn nearby. Maybe he should swim across, hitch up and drive off. Bruné-Hilda, his anchor, had cut him loose. Once again he was afloat on a sea of grief. He slumped into the crook of his arms and cried like he had never cried before. Tungus, at first confused, nestled close.

How long they sat he did not know—nor did the tears stem the pain. Time did not matter. She did. He desperately needed her. Others he'd lost flashed before his eyes: Ponti Lepius Filipi crushed beneath the massive stones of Lucic, his parents and Jingo buried in the mudslide, his uncle and the Butcher both hung, and Gunther, who entrusted his daughter to his care, poisoned. And so many other faceless friends, like Flaccus the metal smith, Old Gustus and Brunda, all taken to the next life. Now his soul-mate Bruné-Hilda— ravaged by rape, mutilated by that inferno—casts him aside like a bag of garbage. Would there be no end to this circle of madness?

The only other person left in his life was now, at his insistence, charting her own course to become the first Augusta of the West. Should he follow that path like a loyal puppy? Forsake his dreams by becoming a slave to the aristocracy? Was that where all this was leading him? Maybe these setbacks were no more than the underpinning for a higher calling. So many doors unopened, so many gods to follow—although he had not yet chosen any one of them to worship. What to do? Where to go?

He sat lost in thought, mesmerized by the view and the sound of the gentle surf lapping the shoreline. Then in his dream world, a hand reached out and brushed the back of his head, followed by a gentle touch on his cheek. He was hallucinating. Of course—he often felt a touch that was never there. Then the apparition pressed against his back.

"I love you, Lucius," the apparition said, her breath sweet.

He turned his head only slightly, fearful the apparition might vanish. Then he caught a familiar scent and knew this was no phantom..

"Look at me, Lucius," she whispered with that gentle but commanding presence he was so fond of. "Look at me carefully."

He did. She stood there illuminated by the light of the sun, her blonde hair hanging long and silky like the first day they met. She pushed it off her face. "See," she said unabashedly, turning her head to one side. "See the scarring. Can you tolerate looking at this the rest of your life?"

How to answer?

"And this," lifting her tunic to reveal her thigh. "Would this revolt you? And this," uncovering her right hand. "Yes, it has healed, and the claw has straightened a bit. I appear almost normal, don't I? But I'm not. And though the soreness comes and goes, it is the pain I will see in your eyes each morning that will hurt the most."

Lucius did not understand. *Why was she here? And those words, what did they mean?*

Reading his thoughts, she said softly, "Dado is not my husband, Lucius—he is my lover. I am no longer with child. We lost the baby halfway through. I lied about everything. I wanted to hurt you for abandoning me back at the hamlet on the Doubs, for running off while I lay half dead beneath the ashes. So many times since then I prayed for sweet death. Yet the thought of you coming kept me from walking into the sea. But you never came."

"I did come, Bruné-Hilda, I did."

"You never came for me, Lucius."

"Your neighbor, that old man up the lane said you were out of sorts, distraught, could possibly hurt yourself." He paused, taking all of her in. "I spied on you at the rain barrel, you know. You looked troubled. 'Crazy in the head,' were the old man's words. 'Go away and let her mend,' he begged. The letter! What of it? I left it in his care, a missive swearing my undying love, promising to return soon."

"Letter? There was no letter, Lucius. No mention of you being here. Not one word. The old man passed away five months ago without so much as a mention of you. Dado is his son, you know."

"His son!?"

"Yes, Lucius, his son. Ah, you find that devious, don't you?" She stiffened, walked in a small circle and stopped. "Well, suddenly, so do I. The old man wanted me for his own, you understand, and then for his son when he knew he was about to die. There was not a word from you, not one. What was I to do, Lucius? What? You abandoned me at the Doubs River, then discovered me here. After one good look at me, you sailed away to Rome, never to return—until now. I was discarded like an old milk bucket to a world far from the one I knew. Far from—"

"Stop, Bruné! Stop!" he shouted and then calmed to a whisper. "I am here now." He reached out with both hands, but she backed away. "Those scars mean nothing to me. In my eyes you are the most beautiful girl I have ever known, and you always will be. Nothing has changed. Some say it takes a day to find, a week to know, and a month to fall in love with your eternal mate. I did all that the instant I first saw you; and from that moment on, the thought of you traveled with me wherever I went."

They stood there staring at each other, trying to make sense of all that was said, all that happened: his leaving her for dead on the Doubs, running away on the specious advice of a convincing old man, her taking up with another man, and a letter of love never delivered. Yes, so much happened, so much gone wrong.

"Here, take my hand," he said at last, "let's walk."

She did, but reluctantly. They walked along the shore for hours talking and crying, even at times quarrelling, but always renewing and, slowly, reconciling. Then she suddenly became lost in a fog. Sitting on a piece of wood, she drifted off.

"I'm here on this island," he said, after watching her for a time, "but not you. You're somewhere else. Where are you, Bruné?"

She folded her hands neatly in her lap and bit her lip. "At the hamlet on the Doubs River, Lucius. Back at that place you never inquire about."

"I thought the memory too painful, that's all."

"It is. But aren't you curious?"

"Of course."

"So am I, Lucius. So am I. I need to know the truth back there, the reason you left me. Understand, Lucius, more than the unexpected, the unexplained can sap everything from one's soul— love, life, goodness, and most of all, accountability. I was like a fallen acorn—ugly, alone, and unwanted except for the pigs. Now you suddenly appear and want me to return to the old Bruné, to be instantly reborn. Well, it does not work that way."

He swallowed hard, searching for the right words. But they never came.

She slid off the log and onto the sand. Leaning back, she propped herself up with both arms and began to collect her thoughts of that anguished morning two years ago. Her lips moved yet no words came. Then suddenly the memories of that terrible morning came rolling out like a thunderstorm—a flash, a pause, a clap followed by a boom. *Yes, they were never that far off, were they?* At last she began to release—it seemed—what had been pent up for so long.

She was in bed with her son, Brute, lying there in the Tonantius cottage unprepared for what was soon to come. Lucius slept that night in the nearby smithy shop along with Bis, Brug, Scarface, and the boatman who brought them there in those awkward yet efficient tied-together twin dugouts. She recounted how wonderful she felt lying there in those predawn hours free of the turmoil they left behind: her father's death, the marriage of her brother to that witch, their coronation, her incarceration in her own house, the stealing of the statue. How she thought they'd left Freya-Gund in their wake at Besancon after their ingenious escape. Yes, she truly thought they were free of that and everything else.

As she relaxed on that sandy shore of Lerins, for the first time she gave voice to the terror of that morning two years ago. How, in those moments when the predawn attack came, Tonantius had hurriedly hid her and her son along with his family in the fruit cellar below the cottage. They could hear the curses as the sorceress's men tore through every building of that little hamlet before eventually finding them. She and the others were drug up out of the cellar. When Tonantius and a few others resisted, a struggle ensued and the underbelly of the straw roof caught fire, and puff, up it went. There was disbelief at first, and then horror reigned inside the walls of that cottage, she said. Holding her son close, she broke free and ran to the window to get out, only to be pounded into the sill by those bigger and stronger. So many were on fire, so much mayhem. It became hard to breathe, the heat unbearable, and the inferno inescapable.

"The flames, Lucius, the flames were everywhere around me!"

Bruné-Hilda paused. But the vision of her being engulfed in flames made Lucius's own thoughts fly back to that day. From where he was hiding during it all, Lucius remembered seeing men diving out the windows of that cottage, breaking through walls, anything to get away. There is nothing on earth more frightening to man or beast than fire. Yes, he remembered it too well. Never could he forget slithering away between the equipment of the smithy shop when they first came under attack and then finding a safe haven first in the water troth and then inside a nearby drinking well. From there he watched in disbelief as the Tonantius cottage went up in flames and his beloved, or so he had thought, consumed in the conflagration. Now that he knew the truth, he felt shame.

Bruné, having caught her breath, continued the telling of that day: On fire, one warrior fell on top of her, she said, another stepped on her back, another her face. Tears welled in her eyes as she recounted the helplessness, the impending doom, and the sudden calm of approaching death. Then an arm reached up from the fruit cellar, she said, dragging her back down, the force tearing Brute from her grasp. The last thing she saw before the fruit cellar door blocked her view was the baby being tossed out the window. Then the roof collapsed, a beam slammed the cellar door atop her leg, and the frantic screams of those being incinerated filled her ears. With that scorching remembrance still burning, Bruné began to sob.

Lucius did not know what to say at first. He pulled her close and held her tight. Eventually, he insisted she get it out once and for all. After wiping away the tears, she went on.

Just when all seemed lost, the neighboring Vesonti clansmen came in force and drove away the attackers. After the hot ashes cooled, they joined the survivors in digging out the fruit cellar. Miraculously, she and the Tonantius family were alive in the fruit cellar. In addition to a broken leg, Bruné-Hilda suffered burns on her arm, hip, and leg, lost her hair and a chunk of scalp, had a cracked bone in her face, a broken shoulder, and, the most obvious, skin torn from her cheek.

By this time, she said, Freya-Gund had melted away along with her men. One who saw her retreat said the sorceress carried the baby off, another said she threw the boy in the river. Because Brute was in line for the Burgundian throne, Bruné feared the worst. After all, was the ambitious bitch not married to her brother, a brother who was now the king of Burgundia? Did she not make her own succession possible by poisoning the prior king, her father? In any event, Bruné long ago resigned herself to the knowledge that she would never see her son again. For certain, Freya-Gund would one day reign *alone* over all Burgundia. "To accomplish that," she blurted angrily, "the sorceress would surely kill whoever else got in her way now and in the future."

With those words ringing in Lucius's ear, Bruné fell silent, staring absently at the mainland. Only the water lapping at the shore could be heard. Then, with a deeper sadness, she added almost as an afterthought, "After months passed on this island, or maybe it was a year, out of nowhere a mood swept over me like phlegm from the ancient god Loki. At the darkest hour, I would sit up in bed and scream. For I dreamt my son was found hanging from a tree! With this image haunting me, Lucius, a melancholy the likes of which I had never before experienced consumed my soul. Then the thought of your desertion drove me deeper and deeper into despair. I was beyond hope, beyond every human emotion. The gods, Lucius, the gods of my ancestors offer no resolution for the absolute hatred I felt for the entire world, including you."

"What did you do to survive those times?" he asked calmly.

"I cursed the gods, you, and everyone that lived normally, that's what."

Lucius reached out and held her before breaking the uneasiness with, "I loved the boy too, you know. I would have raised him as my own. But now we must look forward, not back."

They walked on silently, consumed by their own thoughts of this experience. Toward the far end of the island sat a tall boulder similar to the one outside the walls of Assisi from which Lucius once sold honey biscuits and sweet water, the rock from which he and Jingo first spotted the smoke in the pass on that spring morning long ago; the morning that Bruné-Hilda's people arrived in the valley; the morning that changed his life forever. Although he did not realize it at the time, the coming of her clan to his valley foreshadowed

one of the most earthshaking events of the age—the sack of Rome
by an illiterate, ill-mannered, and ill-bred barbarian horde. And it
was on that same rock that Crazy Chloe predicted Lucius's rise to
prominence the day he and Bruné-Hilda abandoned the valley. Yes,
that rock was their talisman.

And the similar rock at the end of the isle of Lerins, which so
reminded him of the past, would now play a role in what was to
happen next. Climbing atop the rock, Lucius pulled Bruné-Hilda
up, putting his arm around her waist when she dropped down beside
him. From there, they had a commanding view of the mainland.

"Look!" he said excitedly, still panting from the exertion. "Look
there my sweet. It's all ours, yours and mine," pointing toward the
mainland. "See the shore, the cliff, the mountains, and the world
beyond, it all of it belongs to us. When sitting on the banks over
there waiting for my ankle to heal, I composed this elegy and sang it
to myself over and over."

"An elegy, you say."

"A ballad, an idyll—it rhymes. Listen, it goes like this: My heart
did break, my heart did cry. Longing and yearning, I wanted to die.
At the rain barrel it was, a lost love found, a life rekindled, it knows
no—"

"Stop, Lucius! Just stop!" she said and not too kindly. "What are
you telling me with stupid words that make no sense?"

"This." And he unlaced the top part of his tunic. "Look," he said,
tapping the vest. "In here are gems from around the world. Phrygia,
Egypt, and places you've never heard of."

He gently spun her around and away from that foreign world
that lay across the water, looked deep into those brilliant blue eyes,
and said, "Forget your scars; forget the yesterdays. Love's magic
erases everything. Let it wash away what's done. Know that I'd
worship your shadow if it was all that remained—never again need
you doubt my devotion. When you told me Dado was your husband,
my dreams drained out of me. I felt empty for the first time in my
life. Now suddenly I'm full of hope, full of love, full of you. You
complete me in ways I cannot. Never, ever, will I allow you to drain
my soul of your love again."

With those words, he dropped to one knee, looked up, and in a halting voice asked, "Will . . . will you . . . will you marry me? And not at some obscure future date as I suggested at Scanborg-Andrazza and then stupidly repeated on the road to Speyer, but now—here— on this island of solitude. Marry me today, now if possible. No more waiting, no more unfulfilled promises, and no more separations. I want you forever more, for better or worse."

She looked at him on one knee, stunned, obviously caught off guard. Fiddling with the leather thong around her throat, she said, "There is more I must tell you." Reluctantly, she pulled on the thong she fondled and up came a small wooden cross. "See this," thrusting it forward with a sort of reticent pride. "See, I have accepted Christianity. I am a follower of the One True Lord, Jesus Christ."

He looked up at the cross. *A heathen suddenly a Christian, how can that be?* "So?" he said aloud, which was about all he could think to say.

"Can you accept that into your godless world?"

"I asked for your hand, not your soul. If it restores you inside, then"—he searched for words worthy of the moment—"then let this God of yours heal you. I need only marry you, not your beliefs."

"Then I accept your proposal."

And so it was. The barbarian princess of Burgundia and a godless son of Umbria, two young people from totally different worlds thrown together by the changing times, hereto pledged themselves to each other and would together face the darkening times that lay ahead.

Abba-Father Honoratus of Lerins, having returned from his duties in Arles, and after receiving a generous donation of course, agreed to overlook an inconvenient church doctrine. Even though he refused to perform a ceremony between a Christian and a non-believer, or allow the ceremony inside the church, he did permit an old monk named Capasius—who had co-founded this sanctuary with him—to sanctify the union on the crusty south shoreline of Lerins. Witnessing the service were Bis, Scarface, and Tungus, faithful protectors all.

Although dangers known and unknown lurked on the mainland, these two young people—marked by their experiences—not only survived the travails of a changing world, but the journey made them strong enough to face whatever was to come—or so they thought.

But unbeknownst to them and the world beyond, one "travail," plotting trouble even inconceivable to Lucius, was seen limping down from the distant highlands dressed in rags and missing a finger on her left hand.

Freya-Gund, the goddess of Ahriman, lived.

Epilogue

The Lord of Chaos

So, dear reader, you're curious about Galla Placidia, aren't you. So was I. I'll be brief. After parting with Lucius at Antipolis, she needed the entire journey to Ravenna to convince herself that ascending the throne, as Lucius wanted her to do, was Rome's only hope. The emperor was childless, as we said, and the prospect for a male heir was not good. Furthermore, for the throne to be controlled by parasites was suddenly unacceptable to her.

When Galla saw the majestic walls of Ravenna come into view, the setting sun illuminating their majesty, it reinforced her sense of duty. Flush with obligation, her focal point narrowed: That sense of duty embedded since childhood bubbled to the top. Unfortunately, her enthusiasm waned when she got another good look at the man she must marry to make this happen. It was not easy to reconcile this hunched over and bow-legged old warrior with the man her brother totally relied on to keep the barbarians and the coteries of endless usurpers at bay.

From the moment those of "selective appointment" swept her away to the palace, she became lost in the hysteria of her deliverance. Then the euphoria passed and for four days Galla lay in her apartments on the second floor in the north corner of the palace full of disgust for everything that was Ravenna. The royal court was ugly, unrelenting, and self-absorbed. Galla doubted whether she had the stomach for all this pomp after experiencing what it was like in the outside world: the freedom, the romping with Lucius, the daily pleasures of living normally.

Filled with angst, she hurried off a note to Constantius requesting a few more weeks to get her thoughts in order. Calling upon the strength of spirit, she managed to overcome the boredom of confinement and the revulsion of a man who sweated constantly, smelled like a goat, and looked like an aged grandfather. All that notwithstanding, once again she recaptured her senses and on the second Saturday of January, after an uncomfortable courtship, Galla Placidia married Master-General Constantius. As a reward for her sacrifice, over the objections of his advisors, the emperor ordained her Augusta—the highest possible honor to bestow upon a woman. Galla was now not only a person of pedigree, but a person of rank. Remember, dear reader, she was not only the daughter of the great emperor Theodosius, she was also the maternal granddaughter of Valentinian I, a stripe neither her brother in Ravenna nor her kin in Constantinople wore.

"Beware," was her unsaid message. "Remember how my voice rose above the weak-kneed senators during the sack of Rome." Her inner strength was the only torch to shine then and would again. How could any one overlook the way she survived years of captivity by winning over her captors and marrying their king? Thanks to Lucius's faith in her, Galla's time had arrived.

But there is more to her story, dear reader. Those endless rumors: One had it she possessed a mysterious wealth that allowed her to buy influence in ways even her husband could not afford. And then there were her other "involvements" so alien to a woman of any ilk at that time. She invoked her will in the selection of a new pope, pushed Constantius to war against heretics in Africa, and encouraged him to turn Italy into a "bastion of safety" so it would not fall into the hands of the barbarians like Spain, Britain, and parts of Gaul. She even freed two criminals named Tauriac and Irontooth. And although widely unpopular, her greatest coup was seeing her husband's ascent to co-regent of the West.

Two years after her marriage to Constantius, Galla gave birth to a daughter, Honoria. A year and some months later, she bore a son and named him Flavius Placidus Valentinian. Could an old man like Constantius have fathered these children? Hmm! Over the years, her influence over the emperor grew. As a result, her husband, now the co-regent, was elevated to co-emperor. Not long after that her husband died. Was it over? Had the flame of her ascendancy burned out now that he was gone?

Bending to tradition, Galla Placidia withdrew into seclusion for a year focusing on her two children. Not long after she returned to an active life, the unexpected happened. Her brother the emperor died suddenly at the age of thirty-eight sending both the Western and Eastern empires into a spiral of unrest. The timing could not have been worse. A general named Castinus stepped into the vacuum in the West, and ignoring Galla completely, elevated a civil servant named John to the throne. Yes, dear friends of history, this was a game-changer. Galla was now in trouble.

Feeling afraid for her son, Galla threw herself on the mercy of the emperor of the East, Theodosius II, the son of her deceased half-brother Arcadius. She fled to Constantinople to save herself and her children but was received with mistrust. Using all her guile, Galla slowly "wormed her way" into the good graces of her niece, Pulcheria, sister to Theodosius II, and eventually his wife, Eudocia. Since the first years of the emperor's reign, which began at age seven, Pulcheria and Eudocia, at one time or another, had exercised enormous influence over him. Galla's patient manipulations worked. Theodosius II eventually warmed to Galla and her two children, particularly her son, and championed her cause which led to the overthrow of John the usurper on the throne of the West.

Subsequently, at the age of six, Galla's son, Valentinian III, became emperor of the West with Galla Placidia in charge as regent. Yes, Galla was now in charge of the entire western empire! She had now fulfilled the journey upon which Lucius had set her years before. She reigned over the West for twelve years until her son became of age. And on November 27, in the year 450 by the modern calendar, she died at the age of sixty-two. Her son ruled for nearly five years beyond her death until his assassination at the age of thirty-six.

Now then, you certainly must wonder, what role, if any, did Lucius Domitilla play in all this intrigue? Some say quite a lot, others just shrug. What actually happened is yet to be revealed. All we can do is listen to the whispers. One day that tale will come to light if Galla's missing diary, providing there *really* is one, is ever found. This is what we do know: from time to time a shadowy figure was seen slipping in and out of what was thought to be a secret entrance to the palace at Ravenna. Could that have been Lucius? Furthermore, Galla traveled often—too often, some say—between Ravenna and Rome making what appeared to be unnecessarily long stops at Forum Flaminii, a trading center on the edge of the Umbrian Valley where it is known that Lucius resided with his beloved Bruné-Hilda a few miles away in a hilltop villa.

Also, dear reader, you might wonder about the sudden deaths of those three notable figures: Constantius, the Emperor Honorius and John the usurper. Could it be that. . . No! That would be outrageous to even contemplate. On the other hand, there were reports of an unusual woman with three fingers and a thumb seen lurking about at the most inauspicious times. Could it be that . . . Nah! Isn't it strange how the imagination takes hold and runs wild?

Whatever the truth, not a word has been recorded or credible witnesses come forward to validate any of the rumors just mentioned. Accordingly, the readers of this accounting must *assume* all this is but more scandalous gossip so prevalent during these darkening times. Or should they? Hmm!

,

8513591R0

Made in the USA
Charleston, SC
17 June 2011